AM

Suspicion of
Madness

Also by Barabara Parker
in Large Print:

Suspicion of Betrayal
Suspicion of Innocence
Suspicion of Malice
Suspicion of Vengeance

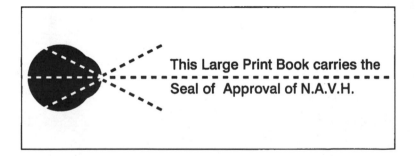

Suspicion of
Madness

BARBARA PARKER

Thorndike Press • Waterville, Maine

OBS
F
(lge. prt.)

Map designed by Laura Parker

This is a work of fiction. Names, characters, places, and incidents are either the product of the author's imagination or are used fictitiously, and any resemblance to actual persons, living or dead, business establishments, events, or locales is entirely coincidental.

Published in 2003 by arrangement with Dutton, a member of Penguin Group (USA) Inc.

Thorndike Press® Large Print Basic Series.

The tree indicium is a trademark of Thorndike Press.

The text of this Large Print edition is unabridged. Other aspects of the book may vary from the original edition.

Set in 16 pt. Plantin by Elena Picard.

Printed in the United States on permanent paper.

Library of Congress Cataloging-in-Publication Data

Parker, Barbara (Barbara J.)
    Suspicion of madness / Barbara Parker.
      p. cm.
    ISBN 0-7862-5422-X (lg. print : hc : alk. paper)
    1. Connor, Gail (Fictitious character) — Fiction.
2. Quintana, Anthony (Fictitious character) — Fiction.
3. Attorney and client — Fiction. 4. Florida Keys (Fla.) — Fiction. 5. Women lawyers — Fiction. 6. Large type books.
I. Title.
PS3566.A67475S873 2003b
  813'.54—dc21   2003047364

This one is for Richard Curtis.
My Agent; my umbrella.

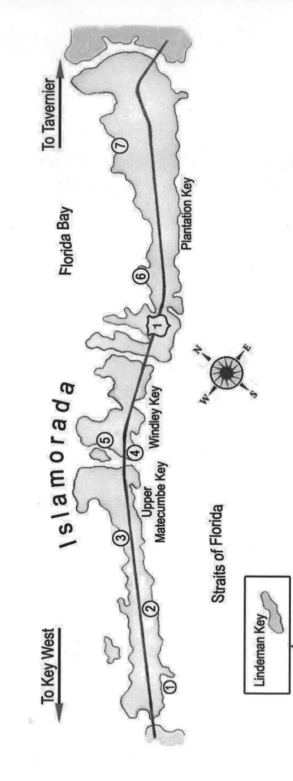

LINDEMAN KEY

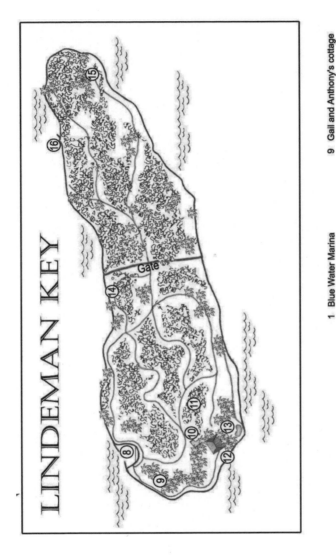

1 Blue Water Marina
2 Holtz and Lindeman, PA
3 Movie Max Video
4 Holiday Isle
5 The rock quarry
6 The Lindeman family graveyard
7 The Morgan house
8 Buttonwood Harbor

9 Gail and Anthony's cottage
10 Billy's apartment
11 Lois's cottage
12 The Buttonwood Inn
13 The Greenwalds' suite
14 The caretaker's cottage
15 Joan Sinclair's house
16 The old dock

1

Billy slid open the file drawer and lifted some papers. The gun was still there, a Smith & Wesson revolver. He'd come into the office a couple of months ago looking around for cash and had seen the gun. He put it in the waist of his jeans, pulled his T-shirt over it, and pushed the drawer shut with the toe of his sneaker.

The lobby was empty and the lights were off, except for a floor lamp that made his shadow dance across the wall. In the restaurant bar he used a key nobody knew he had to open the liquor cabinet for a bottle of Jack Daniel's. He heard voices from the kitchen: his mother and stepfather deciding how many stone crab claws for six people at dinner tonight. *Five,* Billy silently corrected.

He went out the side door to the veranda and down the steps. The sun had set, and he could see the evening star hanging over the horizon. The pale outline of a sport-fisher moved toward Lower Matecumbe Key.

He twisted off the bottle cap and threw it into a hedge. The hotel was closed for renovations, no guests wandering around. The carpenters had quit at five o'clock and headed back to Islamorada in their boats. Small landscaping lights illuminated the sandy path that wound through the resort. Billy tipped the bottle up and counted how many gulps of Jack he could take without spewing it. He coughed and wiped his mouth on his shoulder.

Where the path curved back toward shore, and the lights ended, Billy picked up the golf cart tracks that led toward the woods. He came to a chain-link fence marking the end of the property, pushed open the gate, and went through. The trail was barely visible in the tangled under-brush. In summer the mosquitos would be thick enough to breathe, but by now, mid-October, they were mostly gone. In a clearing near the water, mangrove shoots reached up through the soggy ground like long black fingers. There was enough moon to see the exposed rock, and Billy jumped from one to the next until the ground rose and dried out and turned to buttonwood and strangler fig. Shortly he found the path leading to the water and a dock pointing north.

PRIVATE PROPERTY, KEEP OFF. The sign was faded and cracked, but it didn't matter because no one used the dock; no one tied up here except to get high, and there were better places. The sea had chewed into the pilings. A few of the planks were missing. A pile of lobster traps, dumped years ago, had turned black with mold.

Billy reached the end and unfolded the metal chair he kept under the fish cleaning table. He took the revolver out of his waist and set it on the last plank, aligning the barrel with the edge. The dock was bathed in blue light.

Back on shore, leaves rustled. The dogs had followed him. He heard them panting, heard them moving around, deciding whether to come out on the dock or not. Billy didn't look around. He told himself they weren't real. Black dogs with square, heavy skulls and paws as big as his fists, tags jangling on their choke collars. Not real.

He lit a joint and sat there with the bottle on his thigh and watched the stars. The moon wobbled on the ocean.

There was a ripple and splash under his feet, and he leaned over to see what it was.

A mermaid with red hair. The moon rested in her extended hand like she was holding a white ball. She turned her head and smiled at him, and her hair floated around her.

It was hard to move his lips. "Sandra. Hey. I'm sorry. You know that, right? Sorry."

A boat hummed toward Tea Table Channel. Its running lights vanished behind an empty mangrove island and reappeared on the other side. Two miles away headlights moved along U.S. 1. A dim glow on the horizon marked Tavernier, and farther away, Key Largo. Miami was over the curve of the globe.

Billy, we've asked Mr. Quintana to come talk to you. He'll be here tonight.

Pinching the joint between his fingertips, Billy sucked in and flicked the last bit toward the water. The gun was still on the end of the dock. He looked at it and slowly released the smoke in his lungs.

A long, low growl came from the shadows behind him.

He stood up with the gun, fitted the end of the barrel in the hollow of his right temple, squeezed his eyes shut, and pulled the trigger.

Click.

12

His arm jerked involuntarily. "Shit." He took a breath and jammed the barrel under his jaw.

Click.

"Jesus!" He turned the gun to look into the chambers. They stared back at him, empty. *"Aaaa-a-a-a-aghhhh!"* The scream turned to a laugh. Billy staggered, colliding with a lobster trap, which tipped off the dock and made a green sparkle of phosphor as it hit the water. Weighted with concrete, it revolved slowly and went down.

Can't do a damn thing right, can you? What do you use for brains?

The dogs started barking.

"Shut up." Pivoting toward shore, Billy pulled the trigger. *Click-click-click.* He hurled the revolver toward the trees, heard a thud. Bracing his back against a leg of the fish table, he slid down. Splinters caught on his shirt.

The bottle had turned over. Billy shook it and finished what was left. His stomach heaved. He smashed the bottle on the rusty water pipe running up the side of the cleaning table. The light dimmed as a cloud drifted across the moon and caught there. He picked up a piece of glass and closed his fist around it. He watched drops of purplish liquid leak out and run down

13

his arm. It was warm. It didn't hurt.

In Key West last year a Tarot card reader on Mallory Square had told him he would die suddenly at an advanced age. Billy believed half of it, that he'd go fast, but not the other. The lady had been lying. She'd been trying to spare him the truth. But so what. Everyone lied.

Billy covered his head with crossed arms.

I told you to watch him! I told you! You let him drown, you little fuck! What have you done?

He wondered if the gun had fired. He felt the side of his head, and his fingers came back bloody. But where was the hole?

Lying on the deck he tried not to smell the muck and dead fish and decaying clumps of turtle grass. He raised his head and let it drop, again and again.

"What . . . is it?" The question was . . . the question was . . . Maybe the gun had gone off. Maybe it hadn't. It was hard to say. Maybe he was dead but he didn't feel it yet. What would that feel like, being dead? Like falling asleep. Sinking to the bottom.

The dogs stood on the shore. Their eyes glowed green, and their lips curled back over their teeth. A noise like faraway thunder came out of their chests.

14

When Billy flopped over on his back the shit-crusted fishing table swam into his vision. He frowned until the tall wooden frame beside it came into focus. Pull your fish out of the boat. Hang it up by the tail or a gaff hook in the gills and gut it.

He crawled over to the lobster traps and broke one apart. Wood rotted fast in the Keys. Nylon rope lasted longer. Billy watched his own hands tying lengths of rope together, making a slipknot.

It was admirable. *Damn good job, son. Pat on the back. Thanks, Dad.*

He dragged another of the lobster traps between the uprights of the horizontal beam. He threw the rope over the beam and held on to both ends until he felt steady enough to climb onto the box. The wooden slats creaked under his weight. He dropped the loop over his head, ran the free end of the rope through it, pulled tight, and knotted it.

The lights on the horizon raced away from him, then back. The moonlight was turning the sky silver. So bright. It made the stars fade out.

Billy spread his arms, balanced for a moment, then stepped off the dock.

2

The Florida Keys are a chain of low, ragged islands that serve as stepping stones for the road from Miami to Key West. Drinking water is piped in, Cuban refugees occasionally wade ashore, and with every hurricane warning, cars and boat trailers jam the highway trying to get out. The view of the ocean is stunning, but if you don't fish, there isn't much to do.

This was about the sum of Gail Connor's knowledge of the Middle and Upper Keys. She was more familiar with Key West, which had enough history, banyan-shaded streets, and white clapboard to make it worth a three-hour drive. The small communities along the way she never paid much attention to, except for the obligatory stop at Theater of the Sea so her daughter could feed the dolphins. Gail herself was usually watching the highway for the mile marker signs tediously counting down to zero. Not her idea of a romantic getaway. But just after lunch on Tuesday, Anthony Quintana called with an invitation.

Gail had politely refused: "Oh, honey, I can't *possibly* go, not in the middle of the week."

Then he told her where they'd be staying: The Buttonwood Inn. Clients of his, the Greenwalds, owned it. They wanted him to drive down to take care of a small matter involving Mrs. Greenwald's son, Billy.

Gail did know one other fact about the Keys. Among the clutter of RV parks, mom-and-pop motels, and poured-concrete condos, there were a few places so charming, so lush with landscaping and four-star cuisine, that only the wealthy could afford them. Gail couldn't. Anthony could, but he didn't have to. In exchange for his legal advice, the Greenwalds were giving him a room and three gourmet meals a day. Hammocks under the palm trees, a private beach, no alarm clock, no traffic to fight, no phone calls from clients —

"Stop, stop! I have a law practice to run."

"We'll have the island all to ourselves,"

17

he said. "They're doing renovations. No other guests. I'm going to ask for the cottage with the private hot tub."

"You've been there before," she said.

"Only once, about four years ago."

"Did you take someone with you?"

His low laugh caressed her ear. "No, I hadn't met you yet. Come with me. Please, *amorcito*, don't make me sleep alone."

"Anthony, I really can't —"

"You have a secretary, no? A cell phone? A laptop?"

"Karen's school is doing the Biscayne Bay clean-up on Saturday, and I promised to chaperone."

"A stick with a nail in it. *Qué divertido.*"

"All right. I'll go, but I have to be back on Friday night. We should take two cars."

"No, no, I'll come back with you." He sighed.

"*Te quiero.*" She made a kiss into the phone.

"I want a lot more of those, *mami*, for being so good to you."

It had taken Gail the rest of the afternoon to wrap things up at the office, beg Karen's permission to be gone for a few days, and pick out the right clothes. Her mother came in, closed the bedroom door,

18

and leaned on it with her arms crossed. She was a small woman of sixty with curly red hair and bright blue eyes.

On her knees in the closet, Gail pawed through her shoes. What to take? Sandals, flats, sneakers, black ankle-strap stiletto heels — "Karen is fine, Mother. She made a scene because it's in her contract as a twelve-year-old. She adores Anthony."

"I was thinking about *you*. Every time that man calls, you go running."

"That is not remotely true." She zipped the shoes into a bag.

"Darling, your grandmother Strickland had a saying: 'If a man can have the juice from your oranges, why should he buy his own tree?' "

"Can we please not discuss this right now?"

"I'm just making an observation," her mother said. "Nobody has mentioned marriage ever since he put that engagement ring back on your finger. Or am I wrong?"

"Yes, you are wrong." Gail shoved hangers across the rod. "We're thinking of next June." She turned around with a dress under her chin. "Do they wear black in the Keys?"

"A little short, isn't it?"

Gail laid it on the bed with the others.

It was nearly eight-thirty when Anthony turned off U.S. 1 at a floodlit sign with a leaping swordfish and the name BLUE WATER MARINA. Gail didn't know what key they were on, but the last mile marker she could recall was number eighty, which meant eighty miles to Key West. Boats on trailers filled one end of the fenced lot; at the other, loud music came from the open windows of a restaurant specializing in seafood, no surprise. Ahead were the docks with sportfishers, cabin cruisers, and sailboats snugged in for the night.

A sign for The Buttonwood Inn directed Anthony to a long green awning that would keep the rain and sun off the cars parked under it. Martin Greenwald had assured Anthony that his Cadillac would be safe for five days.

"Three," Gail reminded him. "I have to come back on Friday."

He leaned across the front seat and kissed her. "Don't be too sure of that."

They rolled their suitcases along the dock, Anthony with a garment bag over his shoulder, looking *muy guapo* in pleated slacks and an open-collar white shirt that showed off his tan. Guessing wildly at what to wear, Gail had put on a sleeveless dress

20

printed with tropical flowers. Her high backless sandals clicked on the concrete. She carried a big straw hat in one hand. There were three swimsuits and two pareos in her bag, along with her notebook computer, a printer, and a stack of files from her office.

A pelican flapped slowly away from one of the pilings and settled on the tin roof of a tiny house built cutesy Key West style with a wood porch, wicker chairs, and an abundance of potted palms. A gold-lettered sign said GUESTS ONLY. BUTTONWOOD INN. The lights were off, and the space at the dock was empty.

"Where's the boat?" Gail swatted at a mosquito on the back of her knee.

"It should be here." Anthony laid his garment bag over his suitcase and opened his cell phone. He had already called twenty minutes ago, as instructed, when they'd reached Tavernier.

A breeze came up, turning sailboat rigging into bells and bringing the aroma of fried fish wafting across the marina. They hadn't eaten on the way down. The Greenwalds were planning a late dinner on the veranda, a simple meal as the chef would not return until the grand opening next week. Gail had taken a look at the

Inn's Web site. The veranda would over-look the water. There would be ceiling fans, tiki torches in the yard, good china on the table, a wine list with hundreds of choices. After dinner, a walk along a moonlit beach to their cottage. A soak in the immense bathtub, then to bed. A four-poster, king-size bed.

She backed up: There would be, during dinner, some polite chatter with Mr. and Mrs. Greenwald. The son, Billy Fadden, age nineteen, would be there. So would Martin Greenwald's sister, Lois, who acted as general manager. Unless the Greenwalds mentioned it themselves, in no event would Anthony spoil the meal, or breach his code of ethics, by turning the conversation toward what had brought him there — the murder of a young woman employee of The Buttonwood Inn. Those discussions would wait until morning and be held in private.

Sandra McCoy had been single, twenty-two years old, a local girl. The newspaper had called her "a pretty redhead." She had rented a small apartment on Plantation Key, commuting by shuttle boat to The Buttonwood Inn, where she had worked in the office. A week and a half ago a hiker exploring an abandoned coral-rock quarry on Windley Key had found her body. Her throat had been cut. The last person known to have seen her alive was a clerk at a video store in Islamorada, where Sandra had rented a movie. The receipt had been time-stamped October 3 at 7:52 p.m. Her purse and the bag with the video had been found the next morning on the ground next to her car.

Without leads, Monroe County Sheriff's detectives were talking to everyone who had known Sandra McCoy. They had been out to The Buttonwood Inn twice, but by circumstances of timing, had spoken to everyone but Billy. They wanted him to come to the substation to answer some questions. Anthony would go along. He had been hired to do what he was so good at: standing between a client and the police. Except that Billy wasn't officially a suspect. He had been in Islamorada that night, but according to the Greenwalds, he'd been home by eight o'clock.

Gail had been curious to know about the family, but Anthony hadn't given her much. Billy an only child; his mother, Teresa, originally from Cuba; his father a fishing guide, an American. The parents divorced and Billy's mother married Martin Greenwald, who had retired early from a Wall Street bond trading firm after two serious heart attacks. Martin had bought the island and built a resort on it.

End of story. Anthony never said more about his clients or his cases than he had to. Gail might have admired this if she hadn't felt so shut out. She studied the diamond on her left hand, a flawless blue-white solitaire. She had seen other people — other women — looking at it enviously. But they must also have noticed that there was no wedding ring to go with it. Sometimes Gail wondered if they thought that she — a lawyer in her mid-thirties, a tall blond with bony knees and elbows but without the compensation of curves that most men prefer in girlfriends they give diamonds to — had bought the ring for herself.

Walking a little farther, she gazed toward the island. It would be two miles south, rising up from the shallows beyond which the bottom would dive into the darker blue waters of the Florida Straits. Her view was obstructed by a jog in the breakwater and the black silhouette of foliage. It would be safe out there. Sandra McCoy had been dragged from her car and murdered only a few miles from where Gail now stood.

Anthony dropped his cell phone back into his pants pocket. "The boat is on its way. It should be here any minute."

"Thank God. I'm starving." Gail looked longingly at the restaurant across the parking lot. "I wonder how fast they do take-out?"

"Be patient. We'll have a good dinner, go to bed early . . ." He nudged her hair aside with his nose and spoke into her ear. *"Vamos a hacer el amor hasta que me supliques 'papi, no más.'"*

The words slowly translated themselves in her mind. Make love until . . . you beg me to stop. "Mmm, that might take all night." She bumped against his hip. "Tell me something. Why does Billy need a lawyer? If he isn't a suspect, and the police only want to collect information about the victim, why do you have to come along to hold his hand?"

Anthony shrugged. "Well, Martin and Teri called for my advice, and I thought it would be better if I went with him."

"Yes, but why?"

"Because, sweetheart, I never assume that when the police ask a client to drop by for a visit, their motives are innocent. When the client is nineteen, I'm doubly careful. And if the police have heard, who knows how, that my client used to give the victim money to buy liquor for him, I

25

hear alarms go off."

"Oh, I see. Liquor. Is that all?"

"Maybe not. In the morning I'll talk to Billy and see if he has anything to add to the investigation that will not at the same time incriminate him in something else. If this is the case, as I expect it will be, I'll take him to see the detective in charge, he will spill what he knows about Miss McCoy, and the rest of the week is ours."

"Promise?"

Anthony turned his head toward the channel at the sound of a boat engine. "Ah. Here comes our taxi."

The boat was a shiny little craft made of varnished teak, a replica out of the 1950s. Standing at the helm with the divided windscreen pushed open, the pilot slowed and put the engines in reverse. Water frothed, and the boat bounced against tires bolted to the pilings. A slender, light-haired man in baggy pants and a faded blue work shirt stepped onto the dock and ran to secure the lines at bow and stern. He went back aboard to position a carpet-covered step stool, then once more jumped to the dock.

"M-Mr. Quintana and Ms. Connor? I-I'm sorry to be late. The boat man isn't on duty, you know, with the . . . con-construction and all. Mr. Greenwald said t-t-to tell you . . . there was an . . . a-accident with Billy. They took him out by air ambulance . . . a-about an hour ago."

Anthony exchanged a look with Gail, then said, "Is he all right?"

"Oh . . . we think so, b-but they might not get back from the hospital till tomorrow, and . . . Mr. Greenwald said he'll call you when he can. I'll take you to the Inn." The man reached for Gail's suitcase.

"Wait," Anthony said. "What kind of accident? What happened?"

The man lifted his shoulders. "I-I guess you should talk to Mr. Greenwald."

"I'm Billy's attorney and I would like to know what happened to my client."

"Well . . . he tried to . . . to hang himself. With a rope. Someone saw. They cut him down."

"Where is he? What hospital?"

"Mmmm-Mariner's. In Tavernier."

"I'm going to call Martin." Anthony thumbed through the display on his cell phone and hit a number, then turned and walked away. Privacy. The attorney closing the door to his office.

Gail glanced at the strange little man. She smiled politely. He returned her smile, then lowered his eyes.

Anthony came back. "There's no answer. I need to drive to the hospital. Would you take Ms. Connor to the island and pick me up later?"

"Sure. No problem. Use that same . . . n-number you called before."

Gail held onto Anthony's hand. "Do you want me to come with you? I'd like to."

"No, go get settled in. Have some dinner." He quickly kissed her cheek. "I'll be back as soon as I can."

Under the low roof of the boat, two cushioned bench seats faced each other. Gail sat on one of them and looked backward at the shore as the boat left the marina, went past the breakwater, and picked up speed. The American flag fluttered at the stern. The lights of Islamorada receded.

Gail thought about Billy Fadden. Nineteen years old, putting a noose around his neck. Why? There had been nothing in what Anthony had told her — which hadn't been much — that had remotely hinted at a suicidal client.

Holding onto an overhead rail for balance, she made her way toward the front. The pilot sat clutching a wheel made to resemble antique brass. His narrow shoulders were hunched up, and his eyes were fixed on the empty ocean as though he expected a killer whale to surface. He adjusted the boat's direction to stay precisely between the channel markers. Gail noticed that he was wearing green gardening gloves with leather palms.

"May I?" She indicated the seat to the left.

He looked up at her. "Sure."

The boat dipped into a trough, and Gail dropped into the copilot's seat. She tugged at her hem. "Sorry, I didn't catch your name," she said.

"Arnel Goode." He smiled. "E-E-Everybody calls me . . . Arnel."

"Hi, Arnel. You can call me Gail." She pointed toward the pinpricks of light in the distance. "Is that the island we're going to?"

"Yes. Lindeman Key."

"What do you do there?"

"I'm the caretaker," he said. "Also the gardener. And the plumber and the pa-pa-painter. Whatever they need." His soft voice was nearly lost in the purr of engine and rush of water on the hull. His fair hair was thinning on top, and his skin reflected the amber glow from the lights on the instrument panel.

"Are you from here?" Gail asked. "The Keys, I mean?"

"Indiana. It was too cold. I don't like . . . s-s-snow."

"Do you think Billy's going to be all right?"

"I think so." He stared ahead for awhile, then glanced over at Gail. "You know who cut him down? Joan Sinclair. She lives o-o-on the island."

"Oh? Who is she?"

"You don't know . . . who she is?"

"No, I don't."

"She's a famous movie star."

Gail shook her head. "I don't think I've heard of her."

"She was nnn-nominated for an Academy Award in 1963. Best supporting actress. She played Carlotta Sands in *The Edge of Midnight*. She didn't win, b-but she should have. She . . . she was in seventeen other movies. And on TV. She was in two episodes of *Sss-star Trek*."

"Really. Tell me how she saved Billy's life."

Arnel Goode allowed his eyes to move only briefly from the black water ahead of them. "Billy was on her dock, and there's a place to hang up big fish. You know? Miss Sinclair was taking a . . . a walk and heard noises and . . . and she saw him, so she cut him down and called me to . . . c-come

30

help her. We p-put him on my golf cart and I took him to the hotel."

Gail murmured, "How lucky for Billy that someone saw him." She thought of asking *why* Billy had done it, but that information would be better coming from Anthony. "I didn't know you had a famous actress at the hotel."

"No, she . . . lives in a house on the other side of the island. Her real name is Lindeman. Her gr-great-grandfather built the house out of mahogany. There was a big hurricane in n-n-nineteen thirty-five and it swept away everything but the house. That's where she lives."

"I'd love to meet her."

"Well, no, she doesn't accept visitors. Do you like plants? At the resort we have rare orchids and a hundred kinds of p-p-palm trees and a lot of native species."

"It sounds like paradise," Gail said. "I'm not much of a gardener. Everything I buy seems to drop dead in the pot."

Arnel pointed through the windscreen. "Here we are."

Gail rose up on one knee. Lindeman Key appeared just ahead like a fantasy of a tropical island. Coconut trees curved along the shore, and the fronds of taller, more stately royal palms moved slowly in the wind. Among them a high metal roof gleamed with moonlight. Lights along the seawall reflected in the black mirror of a small harbor. Several small boats were tied to the dock. Gail could see the figure of someone standing there. A woman.

The boat stopped underneath a white canvas awning that announced in gold letters, THE BUTTONWOOD INN. Arnel shut off the engine and pushed open the windscreen to scramble through to the bow and toss a rope. He jumped off and hurried toward the stern. Gail picked up her hat and purse. Arms out for balance, she stepped carefully over the gunwale. The soft, warm breeze was perfumed with flowers.

The woman on the dock made a quick figure eight around a cleat and tugged it tight. Her permed and frosted hair was pinned rather severely into a tortoise-shell clip. Her clothes were no less severe: white camp shirt, navy-blue skirt. Her legs were bare, her narrow feet in a pair of brown sandals.

Seeing only one passenger get off the boat, she turned a quizzical look toward Arnel, who was unloading the bags.

"M-Mr. Quintana went to the hospital. I'll pick him up later."

The woman walked over to Gail. She

had a firm, quick handshake. "Welcome to The Buttonwood Inn, Ms. Connor. I'm Martin's sister, Lois."

"How do you do. This is such a beautiful place."

"Thank you. We've done quite a lot with it recently." Lois Greenwald was in her early forties. She might once have been pretty, but time or the burdens of business had dragged down the corners of her mouth and sketched worry lines in her brow. Her thin lips were filled in by pink lipstick too pale for her sun-browned skin. "You've heard about Billy, I imagine. I apologize that we've had to cancel dinner. Would you mind if I have a tray brought to your room?"

Before Gail could respond, Lois Greenwald led her to a two-seat golf cart with a gold Buttonwood Inn palm tree painted on the side. Arnel Goode was loading the suitcases. They all got in, and Ms. Greenwald pressed the accelerator. She had a straightness to her spine that connoted extreme tension, and Gail assumed she was worried about her brother's stepson. Her wispy bangs lifted in the wind as the cart hummed forward.

"Have you heard anything from the hospital?" Gail asked.

"Martin called a little while ago. Billy's fine." Ms. Greenwald seemed less concerned about Billy than the inconvenience he had caused.

The narrow road went parallel to the shore, passing cottages hidden behind palm trees and decorative plants. Landscaping lights showed the way. Presently they arrived outside the main building, a white clapboard structure with a picket fence and wraparound porch. Gail followed Lois Greenwald's quick strides up a walkway paved with antique brick. The front garden was a profusion of multicolored crotons and bromeliads, bougainvillea tumbling across lattices, and miniature palm trees set among thick green grass that had to be a bitch to maintain. And not a blade of it growing in the cracks. Gail heard the wheels of the suitcases rattling behind her, then thumping up the steps to the porch.

They went through a door of beveled glass, then into a decorator's dream of a seaside mansion, with antique fishing rods up one wall, paintings of sea birds on another, and a staircase to a second floor. Sofas and chairs were grouped in congenial arrangement around a coral-rock fireplace for that one week of winter when warmth was needed.

"This is lovely," she said, looking around.

"I've put you upstairs. You should find it comfortable. There's a view of the ocean."

The stairs were carpeted with a pattern of palm fronds. At the top, a hall ran left and right, with doors set at intervals in floral wallpaper and white woodwork. Lois Greenwald unlocked a door to a room with a four-poster bed and wicker furniture. French doors opposite revealed a small terrace, the tops of palm trees, the moonlit ocean.

Gail noticed that Arnel had come upstairs with only her bag. She ventured to ask, "Have you put us in separate rooms?"

"Mr. Quintana asked for a cottage. I assumed . . ."

"No. We're together."

"I apologize. Obviously there's been a misunderstanding. Arnel, take Ms. Connor's bag to Mr. Quintana's cottage, will you?"

Gail smiled at her. "Thanks. Sorry for the inconvenience." She turned toward the door, but heard Lois Greenwald ask her to wait.

The sound of the wheels faded down the corridor.

Resting one hand in the other at the

waist of her dark-blue skirt, Ms. Greenwald stood for several seconds without
moving. Her deep-set eyes were that indis-
tinct color between green and gray. She
was not quite as tall as Gail, but her
bearing belonged to a woman accustomed
to delivering orders.

"I would like to know something," she
said. "Is Billy a suspect in Sandra McCoy's
death?"

Surprised to be asked about the case,
Gail could only reply, "I . . . I'm sure he
isn't. They're just gathering information."

"Are they?" The rise of Ms. Greenwald's
brows made fine lines across her forehead.
"When Martin told me he'd contacted Anthony Quintana again, I knew it had to be
serious. He wouldn't bring him here for
nothing. You don't find it all just a little
strange, what happened tonight?"

"Excuse me?"

"Billy trying to kill himself the day before
he's supposed to give a statement to the
police? You don't find that interesting?"

Confused, Gail managed to ask, "Are
you saying . . . you think he murdered
Sandra McCoy?"

After a moment, Lois Greenwald sighed.
"I'm *asking* what the police think. On
Sunday we reopen for business. We have

36

thirty-two guests checking in, and the following weekend we'll have fifty-six. Do you have any *idea* what would happen if people start saying there's a killer running loose at The Buttonwood Inn? We'd see it all over the news. The phone would start ringing with cancellations. Suspicion is enough, never mind guilt. If you know something, I'd appreciate hearing it."

"No, I — Look. Why would they suspect Billy? He was here at the hotel at the time the girl was killed."

"He wasn't *here,* he was at Joan Sinclair's house."

"The famous movie actress," Gail remembered.

"Famous?" Lois Greenwald smiled. "In her own mind. She was washed up thirty years ago. Billy was supposedly over there watching Alfred Hitchcock movies. I hope it's true, but who knows? Joan would lie for him if he needed an alibi."

Finally Gail's mind registered what this woman had said before. "What did you mean . . . Martin contacted Anthony *again?* What was the first time?"

"The arson case."

"Excuse me?"

"You don't know? When Billy was fifteen he set fire to a waterfront house on Plantation Key, a total loss. He said it was an accident, but he told a friend of his that he did it on purpose. The police arrested him for arson. Teri insisted on hiring Anthony Quintana, never mind that his fees cost us a fortune. But he got the job done, didn't he? By the time he finished, Billy's friend couldn't remember his own name. We had to pay off the homeowners under the table, and the case never got to trial. Anthony Quintana is quite the lawyer, isn't he?"

It took Gail a few seconds to reply. "Yes, he is. But I don't work for him."

"What do you mean? Aren't you his law partner?"

"No. I'm a lawyer, but we don't practice together. He's my fiancé."

"Your . . . fiancé. Oh." Lois Greenwald managed an apologetic smile. "I'm so sorry, Ms. Connor."

"It's all right. It's fine. Could you show me to the cottage, please?"

"Of course."

Head still reeling, Gail followed her hostess toward the stairs. She wanted food, a drink, a hot shower. She wanted to ask Anthony what the hell was going on.

3

Still unconscious, with a blood-alcohol level making the meter spin, Billy Fadden had just been put in a private room at Mariner's Hospital. Anthony Quintana stood at the end of the bed watching Billy's mother gently kiss his face and brush his hair off his forehead. The blond streaks in his hair hadn't been there four years ago, nor had the chain tattooed around his left bicep or the dark stubble of beard. An IV line dripped into a vein, and a plastic brace held his head straight. The staff had secured his wrists and ankles to the bed frame in case he woke up and decided to throw himself out a window. Fortunately for Billy, he hadn't put on much weight. He was still too scrawny to snap his own spinal cord.

Anthony could recall having lost only one client to suicide. The man had written a note confessing to his wife's murder, placed it in an envelope on his desk marked "For my lawyer," then had put the barrel of a shotgun into his mouth and pulled the trigger.

Billy had not written a note. He had called the police directly.

Martin Greenwald had announced this mind-bending news fifteen minutes ago, escorting Anthony upstairs from the lobby. Before attempting suicide, Billy had called the Monroe County Sheriff's Office and confessed to killing Sandra McCoy. A homicide detective was now waiting at the end of the hall, presumably so that he and Billy could continue the conversation.

"Teri?" When she looked around, Anthony said, "We have some decisions to make. I need to talk to you and Martin for a few minutes. Not here. I don't want to wake Billy."

Her large brown eyes were swollen. "I can't leave him. You go, Martin. Is that okay?"

"Sure, honey." He kissed the top of her head, and she vanished for a second into his ample embrace. "We'll be right outside."

Teresa Flores had come over on the Mariel boatlift in her teens, had married early and unwisely, then had met Martin Greenwald. Martin had made more money on Wall Street in the 1980s than a man could reasonably use. His first wife was dead, his adult daughter attended university in London, and Martin had nothing to do but play at running a resort and hope his heart held out long enough for him to enjoy it. Teri was a dark-haired beauty; Martin was fourteen years older, bald and nearsighted. While she dazzled the guests, he stayed in the background with his palm trees and solar energy projects. He and Teri were clearly mismatched and completely devoted. Anthony didn't know how they had lasted. The burden of a stepson like Billy would have made most men think twice, no matter how attractive the mother.

Crossing the hall Anthony noticed that the detective had not moved from his position near the nurses' station. His name was Jack Baylor. They had met on the last occasion Anthony had been called here to extricate Billy Fadden from trouble. The cop stood with a shoulder against the wall, a pistol on his hip.

Anthony led Martin into the empty room across the hall. They left the door open and the end of Billy's bed in view. The spindly chrome legs of a visitor's chair creaked when Martin sat down. He had lost weight in four years, but he was still a

41

big man. His face sagged, and for a moment he closed his eyes. "Thank you for coming."

"Martin, are you okay?"

"Me? Sure. Teri's taking this so hard. We thought Billy was getting better. It's completely out of left field. All the literature says you're supposed to see signs." With slow deliberation Martin removed a square of cloth from his shirt pocket, unfolded it, and took off his glasses. "Suicide is the second leading cause of death among young males fifteen to nineteen, did you know that?" He wiped the lenses. "What a tangle that boy's mind is. I don't know what's going on in there, but I can't believe that he committed murder. For the love of God, why would he say he *did?* Teri's about to fall apart, and I don't know what to do next. Tell me what I'm supposed to do."

From the other chair, Anthony reached over and gripped Martin's forearm. "Take care of yourself and your wife. Don't worry about anything else right now. You and Teri will stay the night, I suppose. Get some sleep if you can. You particularly, my friend. Listen. I have had clients who confessed to crimes they didn't commit. The reasons are often complex, and I don't

42

want to speculate about Billy, but it does happen."

"Are they going to arrest him?"

"They'll need more than a bare confession. Do you know if they have anything?"

"They didn't say." Martin was still cleaning his glasses. His brows were heavy and dark. "That detective. Jack Baylor. What a son of a bitch. Teri and I were waiting outside the emergency room, and Baylor came in. He told us Billy had confessed. I thought it was some kind of sick joke. Teri went into hysterics. I had to pull her away from him."

"All right. I'll speak to Detective Baylor. Is there a chance Billy might wake up before morning?"

"Not likely. They say he's down for the count."

"Good. Do I need to remind you how to deal with the police? For now, tell them nothing. If he does wake up, keep them away from him. Tell the staff not to let anyone in his room. Do you understand?"

Martin nodded. "I know the drill." He slid his glasses back over his ears.

Anthony said, "How do I get in touch with Billy's therapist?"

"You don't. He's no longer in the area. I hate to admit this, but Billy stopped going quite a while ago. He refused, and Teri didn't have the strength to fight him. I let him get away with it because he seemed to have improved so much." Martin smiled. "What's that river in Egypt? Denial?"

Anthony smiled in return, then said, "Let me call Sharon Vogelhut. She knows Billy from before, and with your permission I'll call her tonight and ask if she can be here first thing in the morning. In light of Billy's statement to the police, he should be evaluated immediately. I have to tell you, it's going to get expensive."

Martin waved the thought away. "Call her."

"I also want to talk to Joan Sinclair about the night that Sandra McCoy died. When did Billy arrive at her house and when did he leave? If she'll make a statement to the police, our troubles may be over."

"That's right." Martin nodded. "By God, that's right, isn't it?"

"Did you speak to her yourself about Billy?"

"Teri did. Joan called her and said he was at her house watching old movies the night of the murder. I imagine Billy asked her to call, but it never crossed our minds he had anything to do with Sandra's death. He rode over to the marina with Sandra that afternoon, but he didn't see her afterward."

"I didn't know that."

"Sandra left work a little early. She took the shuttle about four-thirty, and Billy rode with her. She kept her car in our employee lot. Billy took his mother's car and ran some errands. Sandra was coming out of the video store about the same time Billy was getting home. He went right over to Joan Sinclair's house."

Anthony glanced at his watch: nearly ten o'clock. "It's too late to call her now. Can you get me her number?"

"It's in the office. Lois can get it for you. But don't expect Joan to answer her phone. The procedure is, you leave a message, and she decides whether to call you back. Sometimes she does, sometimes not. I believe she will because Billy is involved. She and Billy seem to click."

"I could drop in."

"No, better not do that." Martin chuckled, and the woeful expression on his face lightened. "I recall the last time I went over there unannounced. I said, 'Joan, it's me,' and she says, 'I know who you are, now get off my land till I send you an engraved invitation.' "

"*Coño.*"

"Joan likes her privacy, that's all. Sometimes reporters show up looking for interviews, but that doesn't happen much anymore. She used to be something of a cult figure. She played lady vampires in a couple of pictures with Vincent Price back in the late sixties. Billy has the videos if you want to see them."

A movement in the corridor caught Anthony's attention. A thin, ropy man in blue jeans and sneakers walked past and stopped at the open door to Billy's room. "Who is that?"

Martin turned in his chair. "Billy's dad. I'd better go."

By the time they had gone back across the hall, Kyle Fadden was arguing with his former wife. "Why didn't you call me, Teri? You don't think I have a right to know about this? I had to hear it from Lois. She's the one who called me."

Through her teeth Teri said, "Be quiet, will you? He needs to rest."

Anthony had never met Kyle Fadden. Four years ago he had been in the county jail in Key West on a DUI. Gray hair hung from under a faded ball cap. On the back of his T-shirt a big fish circled toward a baited hook.

Martin said, "Kyle."

Fadden turned around.

"He won't wake up till morning," Martin said. "Why don't you come back then?"

"Don't tell me when I can see my son." He pushed past to lean over the bed. "What is this? Why is he tied up?" Fadden had the creased, sunbaked skin of a man who worked on the water. Sweat stains darkened the band of his MERCRUISER logo cap. "Why is he still unconscious?"

"He still has a lot of alcohol in his system," Martin said.

"Aw, Christ." Fadden shot a glance toward the ceiling. "He's been drinking again? Did you know about this, Teri?"

Her dark eyes snapped with anger. "How can you talk? I smell the beer on your breath."

"One beer. Don't get so high-and-mighty. How come you never told me he was depressed? You never noticed?"

"All right, you've seen him. Why don't you go?"

"I have a right to be with my son, don't I?"

Anthony said quietly, "Mr. Fadden, there's nothing you can do here. You should come back in the morning."

Fadden stared at him. "Who are you, his doctor?"

47

"I'm a friend of the family."

"That's nice. They call their friends and not the boy's own dad."

"Do you want security to show you the way out?"

Fadden's eyes lit up — a man who would assert his rights by throwing the first punch. "Screw you."

Stepping between them Martin said, "Kyle, it's my fault nobody called you. I promised Teri I would, and I didn't get to it yet. I apologize." Martin touched the back of a chair. "Do you want to sit down? Billy's going to sleep all night, but you're welcome to stay with us. The doctor makes his rounds at eight o'clock. Or if you'd rather, I'll call you as soon as Billy wakes, and you can come then."

Fadden stared at Martin Greenwald. "He's not your son."

"I know that, but I care about him too."

"Yeah, see where that got him. This boy has it too easy. He needs some *rules*. Look at that hair. It's ugly. I wouldn't put up with it. Flunks out of school, can't hold a job. Nobody tells me a damn thing." Fadden stared down at his son for a minute. "He's going to be out all night, huh? I'm beat. Might as well come in the morning."

"That's fine. It's up to you."

"Okay. If he wakes up, tell him I came by." Fadden looked at Teri as though he had more to say but they would get to it later. He shouldered past Anthony and went out. Anthony leaned into the hall to make sure Fadden kept going, then pulled the door shut. He wondered how Martin had managed to be so meek without choking on it.

Sighing with relief, Teri held out an arm for Martin, then wrapped herself in his embrace. She smiled at Anthony. "Friend of the family? It's true, you are. Martin told a little fib tonight, isn't he sweet? I didn't tell him to phone Kyle. That was my job, and I didn't do it. I put it off. What a coward."

"No, you're not, honeybunch. You're the best."

"Kyle won't come tomorrow. You watch. He'll make some excuse."

"Now, now, don't let him get to you." Martin gave her a squeeze. "You know what? Anthony and I had a nice talk. He's got some cards up his sleeve, and I think everything's going to be just fine."

"You do?"

"I'll tell you about it. Right now we ought to let him get to the hotel and have some dinner."

"Oh, of course!" Teri's smile shone through. "Gail is going to be mad at us for keeping you here so long."

"No, no. She's very understanding." This was sometimes true. It depended on the pressures of her job, the state of her stomach, the position of the moon.

"Tell her we're sorry we weren't there to greet her. We'll see her tomorrow." Teri stood on tiptoe to kiss his cheek. "*Gracias por todo*. We owe you so much."

Anthony found Detective Baylor in a waiting room down the hall pulling a knob on the snack machine. A pack of cheese crackers clunked into the tray at the bottom. Baylor retrieved them, then tore open the cellophane. "*Buenas noches,* counselor. I had a feeling you'd be showing up."

Glancing at the other people in the room, Anthony said quietly, "Are you planning to spend the night? Billy isn't going to talk to you."

"We'll see. If he wants to unburden his conscience, I'm here to listen." Baylor ate one of the cheese crackers and dusted the crumbs off his short mustache. He was a trimly built man with a gleam on his holster, the kind of cop who would have a police scanner in his off-duty vehicle.

"What did he say in his phone call to your office?" Anthony asked.

"I didn't speak to him myself, but we've got it on tape." Baylor chewed as he talked. "Let's see. Quote, 'This is William Fadden. I'm the one you're looking for. I'm the one who killed Sandra McCoy. It was me.' The sergeant told him to hold on. Mr. Fadden then said something to the effect of, 'I'm sorry. I didn't mean to.' Then he hung up."

Anthony waited as if Baylor would say more. "And? What other evidence do you have against him?"

"I'm not going to share that information at this time."

"You have nothing. A statement from a suicidally depressed teenager is worthless. It's obvious what he was doing: using the police as another way to hang himself."

"Oh? How about, 'I'm a violent, murdering, sociopathic little dirtbag, and I can't live with the guilt anymore'? Soon as Mr. Fadden comes out of it, we're going to ask him some questions. He's over eighteen this time. I'm willing to bet he'll talk to us. I'd also lay odds he's going to tell you to take a hike."

"Stay away from my client," Anthony said.

Baylor thumbed another cracker out of the pack. "I knew Sandra McCoy. She used to wait tables at The Green Turtle. Nice little girl, hard worker. Her parents are dead, and she came down here to take care of her grandparents. A damn shame about Sandra. Somebody grabbed her right out of the parking lot. He pulled her into some bushes and strangled her with a rope. Twisted it hard enough to crush her larynx. Then he took her to the rock quarry on Windley Key. He laid her out with her head hanging over the edge and cut her throat, almost decapitated her. Looked like somebody had poured a couple of gallons of paint down the rocks. Then he shoved her over the side and left her for the land crabs to pick at. By morning her eyes were gone. The only bright spot being that this occurred post-mortem. Oh, by the way, those little details haven't been released to the public. I thought you'd be interested."

No one else in the waiting room appeared to be listening. Anthony said quietly, "Did Billy mention those little details in his phone call?"

Jack Baylor came closer. "You know what makes me sick? This didn't have to happen. If Billy Fadden had paid for being a teenage arsonist, if he'd been put in a place where he'd gotten some real psychiatric treatment, as opposed to the Dr. Feelgood that you and his mommy sent him to, Sandra McCoy would still be alive. You ought to think about that, counselor. Take a good look at it sometime."

4

Stirred from sleep by a noise at the edge of her consciousness, Gail awakened with a start that sent papers sliding off her lap. Momentarily bewildered, she found herself lying on a sofa looking at a ceiling fan with woven bamboo blades. Footsteps sounded on wood. She sat up and the room righted itself. A shape moved past the window. The door opened, then banged against the brass security bar.

"Who is it?"

"It's me, Gail, who do you think? Open up."

Finger-combing her hair, she hurried across the room and let Anthony in. "I fell asleep. Is it late? How's Billy?"

"Out cold from too much alcohol, but he'll be all right. No permanent damage."

"That's good. Are you hungry? I saved you some leftovers."

"No, I ate a sandwich. Is there anything to drink?"

"I'll get it. Scotch?"

"Please." He pivoted, studying the room. "This is smaller than the one I had last time."

"It's perfect," Gail said. There were wooden shutters at the windows, a high beamed ceiling, furniture that could have come from a Jamaican sugar planter's house. The minibar had been made from an old china cabinet, and painted pottery brightened the shelves.

When she gave him his drink he noticed her robe and slid a hand over the silk at her shoulder and sleeve. "That's new. I like it."

She held it open and showed off the nightie underneath. "You bought it for me."

"Ah. So I did. Why don't you take it off and get in the shower with me?"

"If you let me scrub your back."

"You have a deal." He put an arm around her and she lifted her face to be kissed. His mouth was cool from the ice in his drink, but she liked the taste of him.

"Anthony, I ran into Lois Greenwald tonight. Martin's sister?"

"Yes, I remember Lois." He sat down on the end of a rattan chaise to take off his shoes.

"She thought I was your law partner. I don't know where she got that idea, but she started going on and on about Billy. She said that four years ago he was arrested for arson, and you were his defense lawyer." Gail waited for Anthony to say something. He picked up his glass from the coffee table, which had been crafted from polished teak, perhaps the planks from an old sailing ship. "Well? Is it true?"

He shrugged and took a sip of his drink.

"Why didn't you tell me about it?"

"Why should I? It has nothing to do with why we're here now."

"Well, I was standing there like an idiot without a clue what she was talking about."

"And now you know."

"No, I don't. What happened?"

"Gail, *por favor*, not tonight. It's late." He walked away, drink in one hand, shoes in the other. Lovely brown leather shoes that he had bought in Spain, where he'd gone last year after they'd split up, to avoid having to talk to her.

The bedside lamp was on, softly glowing. The four-poster bed had a tent of mosquito netting that could be let down, which was of no possible use unless one opened the windows and ripped out the screens.

56

"Your clothes are in the armoire," Gail said. The huge piece of furniture took up half of one wall.

He opened the doors. "Yes, I see. Thank you." He unbuttoned his shirt and jerked it free of his pants. His waist was slim and hard. Muscles moved in his back.

Gail leaned against the armoire. "Lois thinks the fact that her brother has brought you here again means something. She wanted to know if Billy's a suspect. I think she really believes that his suicide attempt is an indication of guilt. She started talking about losing business if people think there's a killer running around loose on the property."

Anthony laughed. "Lois Greenwald invented the word neurotic. Believe me, Billy is no threat to anyone except himself." He tossed his shirt over the back of a chair. "How is the bathroom? The last time I stayed here, my room had a Jacuzzi."

"How can you be sure Billy is harmless? He burned down somebody's house."

"He was arrested, not convicted. He said it was an accident, there wasn't enough evidence to proceed, and the charges were dismissed." Anthony unbuckled his trousers.

"Then why did you advise the Greenwalds to pay the homeowners? Didn't they collect on their insurance?"

He gave her a look. "I do not pay off witnesses."

"I *know* that. But why did you —"

"Billy was responsible. Whether the fire was an accident or deliberately set, he was responsible. Insurance didn't cover it all, and Martin and Teri paid the difference."

"Before guilt was decided."

"Yes. So what?"

Gail's temper flared. "It doesn't sound like an accident. Lois told me he confessed to a friend. She said the reason the case didn't get anywhere was because the witness changed his mind. She implied that you intimidated him."

"Intimidated? I set him down for a deposition! He wouldn't show up. I never spoke to the boy."

"That's not exactly a lack of evidence, is it?"

"*Ay, Dios mío.*" Anthony let out a breath between his teeth, a habit she found particularly annoying. He took off his pants and tossed them in the direction of his shirt. "Billy said it was an accident, I have no reason to doubt his word, and therefore the answer is no. I was his lawyer, not his mother. I had an ethical duty to protect

58

the legal rights of my client. Any lawyer who cannot grasp that concept should find some other line of work."

"Stop preaching at me, Anthony."

He slid out of his low-cut gold briefs. "It is easy to criticize another lawyer's judgment when you are standing on the outside."

"I wasn't —"

"I did what was necessary to defend my client. Why can't you respect that? I have been a criminal defense attorney for seventeen years, and occasionally I know what I'm doing." Holding up his hands, he said, "*Ni una más.* I'm tired. I'm going to take a shower and go to bed. Are you coming or not?"

He reached into the armoire for one of the resort's plush terry-cloth robes, which he threw over one shoulder as he headed for the bathroom.

Gail followed but had no intention of getting into the shower with him. She had bathed earlier in the tub, which was half the size of her car. The bathtub took up one corner, the shower another. Anthony reached in and turned a knob, creating a fall of water like tropical rain. There was no curtain, only the depth of the shower itself to prevent splashes from hitting the floor outside. The toilet and bidet had their own room, discreetly out of sight. The vanity was a long slab of marble. Standing there naked, marble at the level of his hipbones, Anthony rummaged through his toiletries bag for a razor. Scented soap. Pumice stone.

"Anthony?"

"What?"

"Are you having second thoughts about marriage?"

Their eyes met in the mirror. "Why do you ask me that?"

"Tell me the truth. I can take it."

He let out a breath. "I still want to marry you, Gail." The top of the mirror was steaming up. His dark head, her blond one, were becoming obscured in mist. "I love you."

She threaded the belt of her robe through her fingers. "We don't talk about it anymore. Marriage, I mean."

"What is there to talk about? We decided on June, no? I wanted to do it sooner, but you said stop pushing, I'm too busy, wait until Karen is out of school, so I said, well, all right, I won't bug her about it anymore." He raised his brows. "You want to get married sooner?"

"No. June is fine."

"*¿Qué te pasa?* You said June."

"I know I said June!"

He spread his hands. "Then why did you bring it up? Are you going to come in with me or not?"

"I'll just wait here till you've finished."

"*Haz lo que te dé la gana.*" Telling her to suit herself, Anthony vanished into the cloud of steam rolling out of the shower, and she heard him humming an old disco tune. It sounded like the Bee Gees.

A door with glass jalousies led to the deck, and she pushed it open and went outside, a cloud of steam rolling out with her, then dissipating in the faint breeze. She caught the scent of jasmine. The sky was deepest blue, touched by moonlight and dotted with stars.

Finally the shower went off, and Gail leaned against the open door. The shower enclosure was visible, and so was Anthony. Water had run from his chest to his groin and down his legs, making the hair lie flat and dark. "Give me a towel." She tossed him one, and he wrapped it around his waist and took another to dry himself. He pressed his face into it. He had left his jewelry on, a gold watch, a heavy bracelet, three rings. He drew the towel down his face and looked at her. His eyes were so

61

dark they could seem black, and they did now, underneath thick, straight brows. He smelled faintly of scented soap.

"You want to know why I handled the arson case as I did."

"What I want is for you to stop treating me like a weekend girlfriend."

He looked at her for another moment, then put on the hotel robe. "You know very well I don't think of you that way." He lightly kissed her lips. "Come outside with me."

They stood at the railing. "The last time I was here, the landscaping wasn't this full. Martin has done a beautiful job. Did you know that the lights are all solar powered?"

"Really."

"Each cottage has a panel on the roof." He leaned on his elbows and smoothed his damp hair. It fell into curls at the back of his neck. The moonlight gleamed on the white robe and lit his eyes when he turned to look at her.

"I was going to talk to you, Gail. I am sorry that Lois got to you first. She doesn't like Billy. She never has, or Teri either. Lois was born in the Keys and she stayed here. Martin left but came back after nearly dying in New York of a heart attack, and she took care of him. He put her in charge, and no one can say she hasn't done a good job. She took it from a second-class bed-and-breakfast to a small resort featured in travel magazines. Then her brother remarried a young woman, an attractive woman with a difficult son. Lois was demoted, one might say. Martin and Teri are very much in love. It's rare, no? Martin is a fine man. A good father to Billy, but Billy can't see it. Where did I put my drink?"

In the bedroom Anthony went through the shelves of the armoire for a pair of the satin boxers and soft cotton T-shirt he liked to wear to bed. He dropped his jewelry on the dresser. His drink was completely diluted, so he went to the living room to make another.

Gail moved her legal files off the sofa and curled up on one end. "Tell me about Billy."

"Ah, Billy. I don't know who he is anymore." Ice clanked into Anthony's glass. "Four years ago, I could tell you, but now? He's intelligent. A dark sense of humor. His childhood was lousy. Give me a criminal defendant, I give you a lousy childhood. His father is a fishing guide named Kyle Fadden, they say a very good one, but during his marriage he was a drunk and an

63

abuser. Teri was too loyal to leave, or lacked the courage. There were two sons. Billy was eight years old when his little brother Jeremy, age six, drowned in the canal behind their house. It was Billy who discovered the body."

"Oh, no. That's horrible. Where were their parents?"

"Teri was a waitress on the night shift. Kyle was at home working on his car in the garage. It was an accident. No one was to blame, but it didn't matter, the family fell apart. Fadden spent time in jail for a series of DUIs. Teri lost her job. The house went into foreclosure. Billy got into trouble. Shoplifting, fighting at school. A psychiatrist put him on Ritalin and antidepressants. But now the story takes an upward turn. Teri was hired to clean rooms here at the resort, and Martin noticed her. He had been a widower for six years, and he fell very hard. So did Teri. He was the first man who had treated her with respect and kindness. She got a divorce and married him. Kyle didn't take it well, and Billy was caught between them."

Anthony came over to the sofa, and Gail pulled him down beside her. She sat on her folded legs and stroked her fingers through Anthony's hair as he talked.

"When his mother remarried, Billy was . . . I think eleven. Martin sent him to a high-priced hospital in West Palm Beach. He began to settle down after that, making fairly decent grades, staying off drugs. And then came the arrest for arson. The Morgans had hired him to mow their lawn. Billy said the gasoline spilled in the garage, caught fire, and spread out of control. That was his story, and he stuck to it. However, he made an inculpatory statement to a friend of his from high school, Richie Moffatt, who turned him in. Based on his priors, and the fact that he was a couple of months short of his sixteenth birthday, the state wanted to charge Billy as an adult. Do you know the maximum for arson?"

Gail shook her head. "Twenty years?"

"Thirty. But since Billy was so young, the prosecutor was willing to offer ten. Ten years in prison. What was I to do? Go to trial and cross my fingers? I hired a couple of very good investigators. Ah, the things we learned about Richie Moffatt. He was seventeen. Billy danced with his girlfriend at a party, and Richie wanted to fight him, but someone dragged them apart. A motive to frame Billy? Perhaps. Richie was the contact at Coral Shores High School for

65

party drugs. Rufinol, Ecstasy. He would buy the stuff on Miami Beach. My investigator took some photographs of Richie in action. None of this is a defense to arson, but it adds a certain perspective, no? Richie knew what we had. I set him down for a deposition, and he didn't show up. Twice. Richie told the prosecutor he'd made a mistake in saying that Billy had confessed. And the Morgans had received complete restitution for their losses. So. The case was dismissed."

Gail couldn't decide whether to be appalled at such maneuvers or envious.

Perhaps reading her thoughts, Anthony took her hand. "You asked me if Billy was guilty of arson, and I said I didn't know. I didn't care then, and I don't care now. He was a seriously disturbed kid facing years in an adult prison. I couldn't let that happen. What about Teri? She would have lost her only remaining son. Do you understand?"

Anthony was asking for more than a judgment on his ability to make a first-degree arson case go away. Gail nodded. "Billy had a good lawyer. He's very lucky. I'm sorry I jumped all over you." She couldn't resist adding, "If you'd told me before, we wouldn't have argued about it."

"You're right. I should have told you." He set his empty glass on the coffee table. "Billy has put himself into another situation. Before he went off to commit suicide, he called the police to confess to the murder of Sandra McCoy."

"*What?*"

"Martin told me at the hospital." Anthony held up a hand to stop her from speaking. "Billy was lying. It was a delusion. Or a joke or a way to hurt himself or his parents. But definitely a false confession. I think so."

"You think so. Wonderful. What are you going to do now?"

"Get a statement from his alibi witness. Billy was watching videos that night with a woman who lives on another part of the island. That is all it was, believe me. This woman is probably in her sixties."

"Yes, I heard about her," Gail said. "Joan Sinclair, the famous movie actress."

"Who told you?"

"That guy with the stutter who drove the boat. Arnel something. He's such a fan, he can probably name all her movies. Anthony, you might have a problem with Miss Sinclair. Lois said she might have made up an alibi because Billy asked her to. Supposedly they're pretty tight."

67

"Yes. It could be a problem."

"You'll have to find out."

"Tomorrow," he said, "but first I need to be at the hospital very early to speak to Billy before the police do. A psychiatrist is coming to see him, and then, after all that, I'll pay a visit on the actress. Do you know what kind of movies she was in? Vampire movies."

"I heard she was nominated for an Academy Award, but I don't think it was for sucking blood. Unless she played a lawyer."

Anthony smiled. "Well, she became a cult figure as a female vampire."

"Oh, great. Just don't let her near your neck."

"Vampira and a client with tattoos and spiked hair." With a groan Anthony let his head fall into his hands. "It's all going to go away tomorrow."

Gail laughed. "Buy some garlic and a wooden stake before you talk to her."

"Yes, I will, and a cross." His smile lingered as he continued to look at Gail, and his gaze grew intense. Shifting closer he opened his mouth over hers, slid his tongue inside, bit her bottom lip, then nibbled his way down the side of her neck. *Te voy a chupar la sangre.*" With a growl, he pushed her over on the sofa and stretched out between her legs. His breath scorched her ear. "*Te voy a devorar.* I'm going to eat you up."

"All of me." She put her hands under his shirt and dug her nails into his back. "Until there's nothing left."

"Quisiera casarnos aquí mismo en los cayos."

Pushing him up by the shoulders, she said, "What was that?"

His eyes shifted on hers. "I said . . . No, you tell me. What did I say?"

"Something about getting married here. Is that what you said? Here in the Keys? You mean . . . before we go home?"

"You want to?"

"Very funny."

"You know something?" He pulled her arms from around his neck. "They might still do that at the Inn." There was a writing desk under the front window. Anthony crossed the room and opened the leather-bound book that contained information about the resort. "Where — Ah. Here it is." He came back reading a brochure. Its cover showed a beach, a palm tree, a man in a tux and a woman in a white dress. They held champagne glasses and gazed rapturously into each other's eyes. WED-

DINGS AT THE BUTTONWOOD INN.

Gail fell back on the sofa. "Oh, my God."

"Look at this. They could give us a preacher, a live band, a dinner, a cake. Here's a good one. Sunset wedding on the beach. What about that?" He whistled. "The prices! Wait. We save money this way, no big reception for all our friends and relatives in Miami."

"Your client almost killed himself! The Greenwalds aren't going to host a wedding, even if the resort were open for business, which it isn't."

"Billy's going to be fine. All right, we can get married at the branch courthouse in Tavernier. Uh-oh, there's a three-day waiting period. Three days. That means . . . *Coño.* Saturday. You wanted to be back in Miami on Saturday. Well, we could be married by a notary after midnight on Friday, have a very short honeymoon, and you can make it to Miami in the morning in time to pick up trash with Karen. What do you think?"

Gail smiled up at him. "I'm sure she'd understand. 'Oh, Karen, guess what? While we were in the Keys, Anthony and I got married, and we're moving to his house.' "

"Sweetheart, if you're going to share a bed with me, don't you think it's better to be married to do it?" As she started laughing, he shook his finger. "We're setting a very bad example for your daughter. I feel terrible about it. We can't put it off any longer."

"Yes, we can. We have to."

He shrugged. "Whatever you say." He tossed the brochure onto the end table. "Are you sure about June? Maybe we should wait until Karen graduates from high school. I don't want to rush you." He gave her a look, tilting his head to match hers. He pursed his lips in a kiss. "*¿Qué pasa, bonboncita?*"

"I don't know when you're serious."

"Yes, you do. *¿Tú me quieres?*"

"Of course I love you."

"I love you too." He leaned over and brushed his mouth across hers. "Tell me what I'm serious about doing now. *Dime dónde quieres tu primer beso.*"

Where did she want the first kiss? She told him. And the one after that, and the next . . .

The bed was solid mahogany, too heavy to creak or thud on the floor. With no other guests at the resort, who could hear

71

the noises they made? Making love in a strange bed always made it more erotic, Gail thought. These pillows were firmer under her hips, the sheets felt crisper, she slid across them in a different way.

They opened the windows to hear the night sounds and feel the air that drifted languorously across their heated skin. Crickets sang in a steady rhythm. From far away came the drone of a boat. She sank into the mattress like floating on the surface of the sea. She drifted near sleep but not into it. Anthony was still awake. She could tell by the way he occasionally let out a sigh. She scooted closer so that her cheek fitted nicely between his shoulders. "Hey." She put her arm around him. He kissed her hand and held it close. She could feel his heart beating. "What's on your mind?"

He was silent for a time, then said, "I spoke to the detective in the case tonight. He says that Sandra McCoy's throat was slashed to the bone. The intention may have been to let her blood drain out before she was pushed into the quarry."

"Oh, God."

"I don't believe Billy is capable of that."

"He couldn't have done it. He has an alibi. Remember?"

"Yes. An alibi." There came another long silence. "Four years ago the prosecutor offered us a plea as the case began to fall apart. A youthful offender boot camp until Billy turned eighteen, then three years of probation. I said no. After Richie failed for the third time to show up for his deposition, and the prosecutor saw the case going down in flames, he said, 'You know, Billy needs some help. Plead him guilty and I'll agree to probation on the condition that he gets some court-supervised therapy.' I refused. Billy was already seeing a psychologist, and I didn't want to burden him and his mother with having to report to the state. So he walked away without a scratch. I went back to Miami and forgot about him. And here we are."

Gail sat up. The moonlight shone through the windows on Anthony's face. "Oh, sweetie, you don't think you're to blame for what he did to himself, do you?"

"I don't know, Gail."

"Of course you aren't." She kissed his shoulder. "If only we could be perfect. If we could see into the future. So many things went into making Billy who he is, and to want to end his life. He's so lucky you're here for him. What other attorney would care as much?"

73

Anthony rolled over to his back. He traced a line across her cheek, down her neck, and finally to her breast, which he cradled as if it were a flower. *"Tú no sabes lo mucho te quiero."*

Her body warmed under his touch, and suddenly all her arguments seemed petty. She wanted this man. Waiting another eight months made no sense at all. Too much could happen in eight months. She would be thirty-six then. He could get tired of waiting. They could die in an car crash. Any number of awful things could happen, and then it would be too late.

Her eyes stung. "The answer is yes."

"Your Spanish is slipping. I didn't ask you anything. I said, 'You don't know how much I love you.' "

"You mean to tell me you don't remember the question?"

"What question?" He watched the path of his hand as it traveled to the other breast, circling lazily.

"Do I want to marry you before we go home? Do I want to live with you? Can I somehow explain it to Karen? The answer is yes. Yes, yes."

He frowned. "You want to get married in the Keys?"

"Oh! I knew it. You're so rotten! You didn't mean a word."

"Yes, I did."

"You did not. You were counting on me to say no. Admit it." She grabbed a pillow and swung it at him.

"*Ay, niñita.*" He was laughing. "All right, I didn't think you would say yes, but I am glad you did."

"Swear?"

"*Te lo juro de todo corazón.*" He made an X over his heart. "I want you for my wife. I have no second thoughts, Gail. Don't ever say that to me again. And don't tell me tomorrow that you've changed your mind. You wouldn't make it back to Miami alive."

"I won't change my mind."

5

At 6:30 a.m. the clock radio buzzed. Gray light was filtering through the shutters. Anthony groaned and swung his feet to the floor. Gail didn't move. How long had he slept? Four hours?

A shower helped. Putting on his suit jacket, he walked over to the bed. "Gail. Wake up, sweetheart." Her eyelids fluttered. "Do you remember what I asked you to do this morning? Gail?" He straightened his cuffs.

"Yes, general." Still tangled in the sheets, she saluted. "Leave a message with Joan Sinclair to call you."

"Good. I hope to be back before noon."

He kissed her and was out the door and down the steps to the white sand path that wound toward the main building. She would not be sleeping for long. The carpenters had arrived, and the yowl of power saws and pounding of hammers came from

76

the unfinished cottages nearby.

In the hotel kitchen, the cook gave him a freshly baked cinnamon roll and juice. Lois Greenwald was finishing her coffee, waiting for him. It took a moment to recognize her. She had lost weight, too much of it. Before, her hair had been short and brown; now it was frosted and tied back in a ponytail. She wore lipstick and mascara. He wondered if this meant she had found a man. Or perhaps not. Her shapeless black linen dress reached nearly to her bony ankles.

"You don't mind eating that on the way, do you?" She picked up a straw purse and an overnight bag from the large wooden table and headed for the screen door. She pushed through, and Anthony caught it before it could bang shut.

He followed at a quick pace to the harbor, from where she would ferry him to a marina near the hospital in Tavernier. Half a dozen boats were tied to the L-shaped wooden dock. Lois stepped into a runabout with a blue canvas top and tossed the overnight bag onto one of the seats. The bag contained a fresh set of clothing to be delivered to Billy Fadden. Lois went to untie the docking lines.

Facing north, Anthony could see the

low-lying profile of Upper and Lower Matecumbe and Plantation Keys. The sea glittered in the early light. He suddenly remembered the courthouse in Tavernier. The marriage license.

"*Ay, Dios.*" They would have to apply for a license *today,* Wednesday, to be married before they went home. What had they been thinking? Of course he wanted to marry Gail, he loved her with his soul, but to bring her back as Señora Quintana and leave her at her mother's house? It would look ridiculous. The entire idea was insane.

"Mr. Quintana."

He turned around. Lois Greenwald had put on a white ball cap with a Buttonwood Inn logo. Her ponytail stuck out the back. "Ms. Connor must have told you we talked last night. I thought she was your law partner. Sorry about that." A shadow cut across Lois's sharp nose. "I wanted to know what's going on with Billy, if they have any evidence besides his confession."

"Not to my knowledge. And I wouldn't call it a confession."

"Statement, then. Whatever. The problem is, the police think he did it, and God knows what they're going to find on Billy if they look hard enough. They can arrest people on pretty slim evidence, isn't that so?"

Anthony finished his juice and tossed the cup at a metal trash basket bolted to a piling. "It happens."

"Is there a chance this is going to get complicated?"

"There is always a chance." He unwrapped the napkin from around his cinnamon roll. He pulled off a piece, avoiding the raisins. It was still warm.

Lois asked, "How soon can you get it taken care of?"

"By the weekend, I hope, but one can never be sure. Mmm, this is delicious."

Her bright pink lips pressed together for a moment, nearly disappearing entirely, before she said, "Look. I'm going to be real up-front with you. Don't expect the fees you got last time. We can't do it. We've put everything into remodeling the resort, including our names on the dotted line at the bank. If tourism is still down this year, we're screwed. You're already getting deluxe accommodations and meals for yourself and Ms. Connor, and that's worth a thousand dollars a day, in season. Now you're bringing that psychiatrist back down here for Billy. Martin told me about it this morning. Is that really necessary?

Does she still charge two-fifty an hour, or has it gone up?"

Anthony smiled as he took another bite of cinnamon roll. "Forgive me, but I don't discuss my cases with anyone but my clients. I've been hired by Teri and Martin."

"Oh, please. Where do you think the money comes from? It's all out of the resort. Do you have any *idea* how much Billy has cost us already? Teri doesn't have a dime. Whatever she wants, Martin writes a check. We had to pay two hundred thousand dollars to the Morgans after Billy burned their house down. Now he's confessed to *murder,* and we're supposed to reopen in five days."

Anthony raised his brows. "As I said . . ."

Lois went on. "Whether he did it or not is beside the point, they'll go after him. I'll be shocked if it's not on the evening news. 'Suspect named in McCoy case.' "

"Ms. Greenwald."

"Fine. Just get it over with." Lois jerked on one of the bowlines to free it from the cleat on the dock.

Anthony finished the last of the roll, dusted his fingers, and tossed the napkin away. Food and drink were included in his fee. He wondered what Lois would say if he asked for a bottle of Dom Perignon at dinner tonight.

Heading toward the stern, Lois passed him, then spun around and came back. Her skin was imperfect. The blotches of red on her cheeks could have been painted there by nerves. "Must you rely on an alibi from Joan? What if you get the psychiatrist to say that Billy was on drugs when he called the police? What about that?"

"Why not rely on Joan?"

"Because . . . I'm not sure you can."

"Meaning what?"

"Meaning she has no friends, she doesn't go shopping, she doesn't go out to a restaurant. She's like a ghost. You never see her. If she answers the door at all, she's wearing a ratty, feather-trimmed negligee with half the feathers missing. We send dinner over there occasionally, but she wants the tray left on her porch."

"The woman prefers her own company."

Lois folded her arms. "Well, Joan's nephew thinks she's nuts. His name is Doug Lindeman. He's a partner in the law firm that handles our business. Joan was a Lindeman before she went to Hollywood. We bought the island from her brother, Doug's father. Doug wants to file a petition for guardianship this week."

81

"A guardianship," Anthony repeated.

"I assume that's not good for Billy's alibi."

"To put her competency into question? No." Anthony felt a little frisson of unease. "How old is Joan Sinclair? Or do you call her Joan Lindeman?"

"She refuses to answer to Lindeman." Lois rolled her eyes upward. "She's a star. Joan is sixty-two. Doug and I are close friends. I could ask him not to go ahead with it. What do you think?"

"I think that's an excellent idea," Anthony said.

Lois started the big outboard engine and freed the last line securing them to the dock. Anthony had barely sat down when she hit the throttle. Once out of the harbor, the bow rose, then the boat settled onto a plane, streaking toward Tavernier.

At the hospital Anthony walked past Detective Jack Baylor, who lowered his cup of coffee and watched him. Baylor was wearing a different shirt, which meant he had given up the vigil at some point last night. In the hall near Billy Fadden's room Anthony spotted Dr. Vogelhut. The wheels of her chair reflected in the shine on the floor.

She was writing in a small notebook. Anthony touched her shoulder, and she looked up at him over her reading glasses. "Hey, handsome." She tilted her face so he could kiss her cheek. Her short gray hair feathered becomingly across her forehead.

"It's good to see you, Sharon, and thank you for coming so early."

"I left the house at five-thirty. It's marvelous. You miss all the traffic that way."

"Did you notice Detective Baylor?"

"Oh, yes. I spoke to him. He remembered me. I told him that Billy Fadden couldn't be trusted to know his own name at present."

Anthony waited for an orderly to pass by, then nodded toward the door to Billy's room, which was closed. "How is he?"

"He's got a ferocious hangover, like where you blink and the shock waves vibrate your skull. But how is he? I don't expect another suicidal episode, at least for the time being. I gave him a little Xanax. I'm also putting him on Paxil for depression and anxiety, and Topomax to help stabilize his moods. His folks will keep an eye out. If he says or does anything worrisome they'll call me. Otherwise, we have an appointment at my office next Tuesday afternoon. My schedule is jammed till then. It's the best I can do."

She turned the wheels of her chair. "Come on, let's find a place where we can talk." There was a bend in the corridor, and they went around it.

Sharon Vogelhut had been in forensic psychiatry for thirty years, the last ten of it fighting multiple sclerosis. The disease had slowed her movements, but not her mind. Four years ago Anthony had hired her to do a psychological evaluation of Billy Fadden. She had spent many hours preparing for a trial that had never materialized.

Finding a plastic molded chair along the wall, Anthony pulled it closer and sat down. "What did you get out of Billy?"

"Not much." Dr. Vogelhut consulted her notes. "He says he doesn't remember calling the police. He was aware that he attempted suicide but thought he used a gun, until I pointed out the neck brace. I asked him why he tried to hang himself, and he said, 'I don't know.' I asked about his relationship with Sandra McCoy, were they intimate? He said, 'We were just friends.' I asked if he knew how she died. He said no. I asked if there were any problems with his mother, his stepfather, his dad. No. Does he take drugs? No. Does he drink? No."

84

Sharon Vogelhut turned more pages in her notebook. "I asked about school. He dropped out of the community college two weeks ago. 'How did your parents react?' He said they didn't care. Then I spoke to his mother. She says Billy had a problem with drugs at one time, but not anymore. He drinks, but not excessively. She seemed shocked that he attempted suicide, and she blames herself, although she can't explain why she should. She tries to insulate Mr. Greenwald from Billy's problems because she doesn't want to put stress on him. He's had a couple of heart attacks. I think the real reason is, she feels responsible for Billy's behavior. I asked how she felt about Billy's dropping out of school. She said it was probably for the best, given his grades, but Billy's father had yelled at him about it over the weekend."

"Martin Greenwald or Kyle Fadden?"

"Kyle. Martin doesn't rate with Billy. It's Kyle's disapproval that gets to him."

"Ahhh."

"Don't draw any conclusions just yet. A fight with his father may have been the catalyst, but probably not the root cause. Billy is depressed, granted. He attempted suicide. But why would he confess to murder?"

"You believe he lied."

"That's the wrong word unless he *knew* his statement was false." Dr. Vogelhut took off her glasses and tapped the stems together. "It's strange, Anthony. Four years ago, I ruled out any physical anomalies. I'll review his history, but let's assume that what was true then, still is. He wasn't bipolar or schizophrenic, and I see no indication of that now. There could be a substance abuse issue. At fifteen he was smoking marijuana regularly. I'll run some tests, but I don't think that's where the problem lies. Before, when Billy and I had our sessions, I got the sense that something happened to him way back, a trauma that he had pushed so far down he wasn't even aware of it. I started getting weird little vibes." She fluttered her fingers. "I have no hard facts, but I think — and I could be wrong — that this event is starting to work its way to the surface."

"The death of his little brother," Anthony suggested. "You told me that Billy felt guilty about it. He thought it was his fault that Jeremy drowned. When Sandra McCoy was murdered, his guilt came back and he confessed to murder. Is that possible?"

"Possible, but here's the thing. Billy isn't

86

repressing his brother's death. At fifteen, he talked quite freely about it. In fact, it's unusual how clearly he recalled the details. No, I'm looking for an event that he *doesn't* talk about."

"Sexual abuse?"

"Not likely. Teri denied it, and the interviews with Billy didn't show anything. There was physical abuse by his father, and many, many instances of emotional abuse. At this point, I just don't know." Sharon Vogelhut turned her warm eyes toward Anthony and smiled. "If only you hadn't worked so darn fast on that other case, I'd have had time to dig deeper. Do me a favor. Find out about this young woman who was murdered. What was she to Billy? I want some background before I see him again, and his mother doesn't have a clue."

"I'll call you." Anthony added, "Has Mr. Fadden come by this morning?"

"Not since I've been here. He knows about this, doesn't he?"

"He knows about the attempted suicide, but not the confession."

"Oh, dear. Someone should tell him. You do it, if possible. I'd be interested in his reaction." She put her glasses and notebook in her bag. "Now I really have to fly.

By the way, who gets the bills, you or the Greenwalds?"

"Send them to me," Anthony said. He would find a way to route them to Martin, bypassing Lois. What she didn't see, she couldn't complain about.

Anthony knocked on the door and went in. "Good morning."

Someone on the staff had removed Billy's restraints and had changed the neck brace for a soft cervical collar. The IV was gone. A breakfast tray, still untouched, had been left by the sink. Billy's mother folded the sports section, which she had been reading aloud.

"Look, honey, it's Mr. Quintana."

Billy gave no sign of recognition. His platinum-streaked hair had been combed to one side, as only a mother would do it.

Anthony set the overnight bag on the floor by the bed. "Lois sent you a change of clothes."

Teri told him they were still waiting for Billy's doctor to check him over so they could go home. Anthony asked if he could talk to Billy privately. Teri said she would go down to the cafeteria to find her husband.

When they were alone Anthony said,

"How's your headache?"

"Fine." Billy was looking out the window. The blue squares on the hospital gown matched the shadows under his eyes. His left hand was bandaged. Anthony hadn't noticed it last night.

"What happened to your hand?"

"I don't know." His voice had deepened to baritone in four years. A stubble of beard darkened his skin. Who was this young man? The connections they had developed were gone. Anthony hardly knew how to approach a client who might slide back into suicidal depression, but there were things to say.

"Billy, let me tell you why I'm here. Your mother and Martin have asked me to help you. You called the police yesterday and told them that you murdered Sandra McCoy. I don't believe you did. First, there's no physical evidence that connects you to the crime, and second, you told your mother a week ago that you were watching movies with Joan Sinclair the night Sandra died. Is that what happened? Were you with Miss Sinclair?"

"I guess so."

"You guess so."

"I don't remember."

"And you don't remember making the

phone call to the Monroe County Sheriff's Office."

"No. Maybe they're lying."

"I am afraid not. They have it on tape. There's a homicide detective outside named Jack Baylor. When we take you out of here, he's going to ask you if you want to talk to him. Say nothing. If you do speak, it should be, 'I'm not talking, speak to my lawyer.' Do you understand that? Billy?"

He closed his eyes. "Yes. I understand." The drugs were slowing his words.

Satisfied that the boy was not going to throw himself into the arms of the police, Anthony said, "You can talk to Dr. Vogelhut or to me about this, but no one else. Not your mother, your father, your friends. That's important. All right?"

"Yes."

"I want you to tell me about Sandra McCoy. Her friends, her enemies, how you knew her, who she was. We'll talk later, not now. Sometime today I'll ask Joan Sinclair to confirm where you were the night Sandra died. Then I'll take her to see Detective Baylor. Should I expect any problems?"

"Problems?"

"Will she confirm you were with her?"

"I guess so."

90

This was like talking to an empty bed. He said, "Is Joan Sinclair going to meow like a cat at the police station?"

Billy finally looked at him. He had his mother's brown eyes. "What?"

"I've heard she's eccentric. Crazy. Over the edge."

"Bullshit. Joan's not like other people. She does what she wants to. That doesn't make her crazy."

"I'm glad to hear it."

"Do you think I'm crazy?" It was a challenge, not a question.

"If you try to hang yourself again, I might."

That failed to arouse a smile. "Yeah, I did that because the gun wasn't loaded."

"What gun?"

"Martin's. It wasn't loaded."

"You had a gun?" Anthony doubted the truth of this. "Where is it now?"

"Still there, I guess."

"On the dock?"

Billy frowned, concentrating. "That's weird. I just remembered . . . shooting at the dogs. We don't have dogs."

"Are you sure you had a gun?"

He hesitated. "No. I'm not sure."

"We'll ask your stepfather if it's missing."

Billy tugged at the cervical collar, ripping loose the Velcro tabs, wincing as he pulled it from around his neck. A line of bruises purpled his skin. He tossed the collar to the chair by his bed. "I didn't kill Sandra. I don't care what I allegedly said to the cops. We were friends."

"Good friends?"

"I guess."

"She bought liquor for you? Beer?"

Billy looked at him. "Yes. So?"

"Anything else?"

"Heroin, crack, and Roofies. Jesus, man. No, nothing else."

Anthony let it go for now. "Did you ever have sex with her?"

Seconds ticked by. Billy noticed his bandaged hand and held it in front of his face to see it better. He picked at the tape holding the gauze. His hands were masculine but small, with bony wrists.

"May I take that as a yes?"

"Yeah. We did."

"A lot?"

"Not a lot to me. To you maybe. But she started going out with this guy."

"Does this guy have a name?"

The square of gauze came up, attached on one side. His palm showed a laceration, some stitches, the bright orange of antiseptic. "Yeow. How'd I do this?"

"Who was Sandra's boyfriend?"

Billy pressed the tape back into place and let his arm fall off his chest. "She wouldn't tell me."

"Did you fight about it?"

"It wasn't a fight."

"When did you and she *discuss* it? Do you remember? How many days before she died? And where did this discussion take place?"

He stared out the window. "We were at Holiday Isle, in the parking lot. It was on Tuesday night. She died on Thursday."

"Did anyone see you and Sandra in the parking lot?"

"Some girl named Penny. Sandra got in her car and left."

"Penny what?"

"I don't know."

The police would soon have the name. Believing they had a confession, they would reinterview witnesses and ask specifically about Billy Fadden. "Did you hit her? Answer me. I don't want to find out from the cops."

"It was a slap. That's all. It didn't hurt her, she just got mad. When she came to work the next day, I apologized. She's like, okay, it's okay, forget it. I didn't kill her. I

93

didn't." A tear trailed down his cheek, and Billy slowly lifted his hand and wiped it away. Whatever Dr. Vogelhut had given him was having an effect.

"You left the island with her the day she was killed, didn't you?"

"Yeah, we took the shuttle to the marina. She got in her car and left. Then I got in my mom's car . . . and did some errands and things."

"Did you see Sandra again that night?"

"No."

"And you arrived home about eight o'clock?"

"Yeah." Billy swallowed as if to ease a pain in his throat. "I didn't kill her. I wouldn't do that. I wouldn't. You believe me, don't you?"

Anthony remembered what the detective had told him. How she had died. The unspeakable violence of it.

Billy's eyes swam up to focus on Anthony's face. "It wasn't me. I swear."

He put a hand on Billy's shoulder. "It wasn't you."

"Mr. Quintana." His mouth twisted as he held back a sob. "I'm really glad you're here."

6

The Buttonwood Inn was one of Holtz and Lindeman's biggest clients. Calling ahead from her boat, Lois Greenwald had felt no hesitation in asking to see Mr. Lindeman immediately. He took her into his office and shut the door — such a masculine office, wood and leather, a big desk, neat rows of law books on the shelves. There were two chairs at right angles in a corner. Douglas sat with one leg over the arm of his chair, foot slowly swinging. Deck shoes, no socks. Navy pants. Yellow knit shirt, open collar, gold chain shining on his neck. Lois had been making a mental inventory as they talked.

She said, "I think Billy's so-called alibi is a crock of bull. He wanted Sandra, I could see it written all over him, but she wouldn't give him the time of day, and the frustration drove him wild, a boy his age, you know how they are, so oversexed and violent. Even if they arrest him, they won't

95

convict him. We'll give Anthony Quintana our last drop of blood, and Billy will walk. Again."

Doug's brow furrowed. "So . . . how long do you want me to wait?"

"Let's say until the police are no longer interested in Billy."

Doug shifted in the chair, dropping his foot to the floor. "Come on, Lo. That could take weeks. What's going to happen to Aunt Joan in the meantime? I'm worried about her."

"She's in no danger of starving to death. She's not going to hurt herself." Lois touched Doug's arm and felt the springy blond hairs under her fingertips. "I need your help. Someone from *Condé Nast Traveler* will be here next weekend to write an article. If you file the guardianship, and if we lose Joan as an alibi witness for Billy, I might as well board up the hotel right now."

He rolled his head toward her on the back of the chair, and she could almost make out a smile on his lips. "Don't you think you're overstating this just a tad?"

She held his gaze for several seconds. "How much do I ever ask of you, Douglas? I was the one who persuaded Martin to retain this law firm, when there are a dozen with more clout, and the first time I come to you with a real problem, you make excuses. How about a little appreciation? You told me we have a special relationship. Is that true or isn't it?"

He scooted down further in the chair, frowning, nibbling on his thumbnail. A big man, six-foot-two. Big hands and feet and long legs. His thighs were curves of hard muscle. He sat with his knees apart, displaying himself, and Lois wondered if this was a sign. He had said he cared for her, but so far he hadn't done much to make her believe it. Douglas was seven years younger, but age didn't matter when two people were fated to be together.

They had known each other since childhood. She had dated his older cousin, Teddy, in high school. Lois had noticed, even then, that Doug was beautiful. Gold-streaked hair, blond eyelashes, green eyes. Freckles on his face. He was thirty-six years old, and he still had freckles. His lips were round and pink and shiny. Lois would dream of his mouth on her body, and she would wake up, the sensations were that real. Doug knew how she felt about him, but he said he needed time. He was still getting over the death of a woman from Miami he'd been in love with since law school. Jennifer. She had died in a car crash three years ago. Doug wouldn't give her last name, though. He wouldn't talk about her. He said it hurt too much. And yet he kept a framed picture of this Jennifer person on his desk, which annoyed Lois greatly.

Stretching, Doug extended his arms. Muscles rippled. He locked his hands behind his neck. Lois had seen him in a swimsuit. He had blond hair on his chest, and his nipples were pink and shiny, like his mouth. He said, "I might wait to file the papers if you do something for me. Testify at the guardianship hearing."

"I don't want to do that," Lois said.

"Because?"

"It would look bad. The judge would say I was trying to get Joan off the property so Martin could have it. Anyway, she's not *that* crazy, not to where the men in white coats would take her away."

"That's not going to happen." Doug smiled. His teeth were slightly crooked, which made him look vulnerable and boyish. "Aunt Joan will go to the best place available. I'll make sure of it. She's all the family I have left, Lo."

"Martin wouldn't want me to get involved. He feels sorry for Joan."

"Then I guess you've got a choice to make." Doug kept looking at her, and Lois fell into his eyes like sinking into deep water. She couldn't breathe. Doug covered her hand with his, big and heavy and warm. "Lois, if you won't testify, the judge might not grant the guardianship. I want you and Martin to have the property, honey, but if I don't have the power to sign a lease, what can we do?"

They needed the property for its deep water access. The Buttonwood Inn's harbor was too shallow, and the state wouldn't let them dredge. Joan had a deep-water dock. Two years ago she had said she would give it to them, then she had said no, even though Lois had gone over there and practically begged her. Joan had screamed through the door, *I said no, now get out!* Martin was content to let it go, but if they didn't have deep water, they could never accommodate bigger boats.

"We need the dock," Lois said, "but I can't testify against Joan. I can't."

Doug leaned so close she could smell his cologne and count his eyelashes. "Have you seen the house lately? It breaks my heart, how Aunt Joan lets it deteriorate. Do you remember how beautiful the house was when my grandparents lived there?

Teddy brought you out to visit, didn't he?"

"Yes. It was a beautiful house. The chandeliers and the fireplace and the oriental carpets. We used to sit on the porch and watch the moon on the ocean, and the stars —"

"I want to restore it, Lo."

Her heart leaped. "Would you live there?"

"I'd be there on weekends. We'd be neighbors, wouldn't we?" He smiled, and his lips shone. "I need you to make it happen." He took her hand and smoothed her fingers over his. He pressed his lips to her skin. She wanted to moan, to cry. Joy, exultant and giddy, surged through her body. She leaned toward him and rested her head on their joined hands.

"Yes, Douglas. Yes. If you need me, all you ever have to do is say so."

"And could you . . . check on Aunt Joan a couple of times a week for me? Could you do that?"

Lois raised her head. "Check on her?"

"You know. See how she is. Take a look around."

"Joan won't let me in. She doesn't like me."

"You could take her a casserole or something."

"Why do I have to check on her? Let Arnel Goode do it. He's over there nearly every day."

"Listen to me, Lois. Somebody has to say to the judge, 'Why, yes, Your Honor, I visited Ms. Lindeman many times. It's so sad. She recites all the lines from her movies, over and over. She smelled like she hadn't bathed in a week. There was nothing in the fridge but caviar, beer, and moldy take-out from the hotel restaurant. The condition of her house was shocking! There are liquor bottles, roaches, garbage everywhere. She thinks that space aliens are watching her through the TV, and the FBI is tapping her phones.' "

"I can't say that."

"Yes, you can. Sandra was going to."

Sandra. Lois felt the cold wind of betrayal sliding across her neck. A few times, sitting in her car across the street watching for a glimpse of Douglas, she had seen Sandra McCoy come into this office, and it wasn't to deliver legal papers from the resort. Lois had imagined them on that couch over there, or on the carpet. Maybe Sandra had straddled him as he sat in that very chair, her tarty red hair swinging across his face. The girl had no morals. Twenty-two years old. They could go after any man, girls like that, and make a man lie about it. At the resort, Sandra had made her sly little smiles whenever Doug Lindeman's name had come up, and Lois had wanted to slap her.

"Were you involved with Sandra McCoy?"

Douglas blinked, then smiled as if he hadn't heard correctly. "What do you mean? Did I have sex with her?"

Sex. He could have phrased it some other way, but he had used *that word*. "Were you? Why else would she agree to spy for you?"

"Lois. For God's sake. Sandra didn't help me because she *liked* me. I paid her. She was planning to move to Miami. Anyway, I've been completely celibate since . . . you know."

Lois looked toward his desk, where a framed picture of the woman named Jennifer smiled back at her. "Doug, you need to get past this."

He nodded and let out a breath. "I'm trying to."

"Don't you think that by having that picture on your desk, you prolong your attachment to her?"

"My therapist says it helps me face my fears."

"Your therapist isn't doing shit for you."

"Lois, I can't talk about it now." Doug dropped his face into his palm.

"Let me help." She rubbed his shoulder. "Tell me what you want from me. Anything."

With a gasp he noticed his watch. "Damn! I've got a client coming in. Lois, I'm sorry to do this, but. . . ."

Lois looked up at him for several seconds, then said, "Someday, Douglas, when you're ready, I'll be here for you."

"I'm aware of that." He backed across the room. "Thank you, Lois. Call me in a couple of days, let me know what you find out from Aunt Joan."

"I'll keep in touch." Lois lifted her face, expecting him to kiss her cheek. He did, but she turned her face and he kissed the corner of her mouth before he could pull back. At the end of the hall she turned around and looked at him. Her long black dress hung straight from her shoulders, and the fish printed on it swam around her body in irregular rows. A few strands of hair drifted across her high forehead, and her mouth was a pink line across her face. Doug lifted a hand, then shut the door.

He wiped his fingers over his mouth as he walked to the window and tilted one of

103

the slats in the blinds. The light blazed on the white gravel parking lot. A few seconds later a dusty Jeep Cherokee appeared, waiting at the edge of the highway. The rear tires spun, and it shot across traffic. It dodged other cars parking at the grocery store and went to the back under a shade tree, circling around so that the windshield faced the law office. The sun glared on the glass.

The miniblind gave a metallic snap when he let it go.

The bitch was stalking him.

He'd first noticed this about a month ago, looking to see if Sandra had arrived yet. Across the highway, headlights in the parking lot had swept across a dark green Jeep and he had seen Lois Greenwald's face at the driver's window, staring out. It hadn't really grabbed his attention until he noticed she was still there an hour later, as Sandra was leaving.

A year ago, Martin Greenwald had been dropping hints about wanting new lawyers, so Doug had flirted with Martin's sister. A goof, a joke, some innocent flattery. He'd never imagined she would take him seriously. Now she was circling, closing in. He went to his desk, picked up the framed photograph, and shoved it into a drawer.

The photo had come with the frame. One of these days, Lois Greenwald was going to take a closer look and figure it out.

Doug didn't like waiting to file those damned papers, but he didn't have much choice. It would mean a delay, but he could deal with it.

His father's people, the Lindemans, had been Conchs, original settlers, scavengers of shipwrecks, smugglers of rum. Lindemans had helped put the railroad through in 1912, and Lindemans had died in the storm that had swept it away. Their bones were buried at the foot of the 1935 Hurricane Monument. A few had hung onto the rocks by their fingernails. They had survived. They had stayed and prospered. Doug planned to get the hell out. He invented daydreams about leaving the Keys. Walking away, not looking back. Clients asking his secretary, *What about my case?* Fuck your case. Fuck everything. Drive to Miami International Airport, leave his car with the keys in it, fly to Hawaii, no forwarding address.

Soon. Oh, Christ, let it be soon.

Doug went down the hall to Thomas Holtz's office.

The old man didn't usually get to work so early. He spent too many hours with his

105

pals in one bar or another to get here before ten, most days. Doug's father, who
had died a drunk, had been one of those
pals. Graduating with mediocre grades
from a third-tier law school, Doug had
leaned on Tom to take him in.

Tom Holtz was sixty-eight, a barrel-
shaped man with white hair and glasses.
Broken veins reddened his cheeks, and
gold glinted on his molars. His wood-pan-
eled walls were decorated with ancient
civic-award plaques, fading color snap-
shots of himself in fishing tournaments,
and amateurish seascapes done by his late
wife. If Doug had thought he would end
up this way, he would do what Billy
Fadden had done, but get it right.

"Hey, Tom. Here's a news flash for you."

Doug told him about Billy Fadden's
confession, how he'd tried to hang himself.
It looked bad, but the kid had an alibi. He
claimed he'd been watching movies at
Aunt Joan's house. Doug, as a favor for the
Greenwalds, would hold off on filing the
guardianship papers until this was cleared
up. Otherwise, the sheriff might not believe
Billy's alibi, if they thought Joan was incompetent.

Tom asked a couple of questions,
making Doug go over it again. The old guy

was slowing down. He couldn't hold a thought anymore. Finally Tom nodded. "I'm mighty relieved, to tell you the truth."

Doug said, "It's not off. We're just going to wait a while."

"Are you sure this is the right thing?" Tom leaned back in his chair. His hard, round stomach strained the buttons on his shirt. "I agreed to act as attorney of record because I wanted to see Joan get some help, but there's got to be some other way. If we say she's incompetent, it'll wound her pride."

"She can't live alone anymore, Tom. You know that."

Tom shook his head. "Have you asked what Joan wants? Have you even considered it? You get to a certain age, you need to feel you still have some control. She doesn't want to leave Lindeman Key. Maybe she needs to have her house fixed up. Some paint. New kitchen, new windows. Make it pretty for her."

Doug paced across the office, hands in his pockets. "That's a waste of money. She doesn't own it, Tom. She has a life estate. My dad set it up that way. When she dies, her interest goes to Martin Greenwald."

"Yes, yes, but that isn't going to happen for a long time. Here's what you do. Fix the place up and send somebody out a couple of times a week to clean house and look after her. Wouldn't that work?"

"Tom —"

"The woman who took care of Mary when she was so sick. A good woman, very reliable. I've still got her number."

"Aunt Joan would never go for it."

Tom held up a hand. "We'll personally introduce them. She'd like this woman. What if I go talk to her and explain things?"

"You haven't seen Aunt Joan in two years. I'm telling you, she's different. She's gone downhill, Tom."

"How do *you* know? When's the last time you were out there?"

"Not lately. She won't let me in because she's under the delusion that I'm going to steal something. There's nothing *to* steal. Her house is a junk heap."

Tom swivelled to keep focused on Doug's progress across the room and back in the other direction. "How do you know so much? Sandra McCoy? Is that who you mean?" He was satisfied to see Doug's head snap around.

Doug said, "She liked Aunt Joan. I asked her to see if she was all right."

How in hell had he opened his office to a

man like this? Tom said, "Let me tell you something. It's not right to keep Joanie in the dark. She ought to be told. I should do it myself."

"Stay away from my aunt."

The tone was so sharp that Tom jerked. "What?"

"Stay away from her. She's not to find out until the court orders an investigation and they send somebody out there." Doug stopped directly across from where Tom sat, still stunned. Doug spoke slowly, as if to a child. "If you tell her, Tom, she'll get the place cleaned up. She'll have time to bathe and put on a nice dress. She'll convince them she's perfectly sane, and she isn't."

"She is! She's fine. At least she was, last time I saw her. Don't pretend you give a damn about Joanie. I looked the other way when Sandra McCoy came around, and you telling the cops that you hardly knew her. You're a liar. If I decide to drop in on Joan, you'd best not interfere."

Doug leaned on Tom's desk, his muscular, curly-haired arms making pillars for his chest. His face was white with anger, and the freckles were brown dots. "Don't threaten me with Sandra, you pervert. What were *you* doing with her? Keep away

109

from Aunt Joan. Do you understand me? Are we real clear on that?"

Doug went out, and Tom stared at the empty doorway. He sat for several minutes without moving. Confusion and shame overtook him. His chest ached. He couldn't breathe. He sobbed once, then held it back with a knuckle pressed against his lips. Sandra had told Doug. They must've had a good laugh. But it hadn't been so terrible, what he'd done. He wasn't a pervert. He had never touched her.

It had started when Mary was dying. She had a woman to come in and help her so Tom could get out of the house. The smell of medicine and bandages and the sight of her body hadn't driven him away, though that had been bad enough. No, he hadn't wanted to be there when she died. He'd prayed to come home and she'd be gone.

He had done some damage to his liver those last weeks. He'd been to every last bar in the Upper Keys. He was leaving The Green Turtle Inn at closing time and ran into Sandra McCoy coming across the parking lot in her waitress outfit, little black shorts and a red top. He took a hundred dollar bill out of his wallet and asked her to show him something sweet. And she did. She laughed, lifted her shirt and the bra with it, then grabbed the money and ran for her car, her long red hair swinging behind her. A few days later he waited for her to finish her shift, and it happened again. They started finding places to park. A day came when she took everything off, but he never asked to touch her, and she never offered to let him.

It stopped when he and Joan Lindeman got back together. Then Joanie changed her mind. *Please, darling, let's not torture ourselves with regrets. Think of me fondly sometimes, won't you?* It had sounded like a line from one of her damned movies, and that was the last he'd heard from her. Eventually he stopped trying.

A few months later, Tom waited for Sandra to get off work. He followed her to her apartment. She asked to borrow money for some new clothes. Tom gave it, knowing damned well he'd never get it back. Then she had needed money for this or that, and he'd given it to her. One day Sandra had told him not to bother coming around again. He'd wanted to ask her if the reason was Doug Lindeman, but he hadn't asked. It didn't matter. He was tired of girls. He felt old. He was old. An old man.

All his life, he'd thought he was happy. He'd told himself so often he'd believed it.

When Joanie had said she loved him, the lies had vanished like smoke, and he could see that he'd been waiting for her all his life. What they'd had once, they could have again. Tom had to make her listen. She needed him, needed somebody who wasn't going to stand by while her nephew picked her bones clean and ruined her last good years.

His door was open. Tom got up and closed it. He took a bottle out of his credenza and poured himself a drink to steady his nerves. He smoothed his hair and sat at his desk. Joan's number was in his Rolodex. Tilting his glasses to see, he punched the numbers one by one as he held the receiver close to his chest. He raised it to his ear and listened to the ringing on the other end, hoping she would pick up. She didn't. Her machine came on.

He could have repeated the message from memory, the same one she'd had for years. The voice was dark and smoky and bored. "Hi. If you don't know who this is, you've got the wrong number. If you're selling something, hang up *now*. Otherwise, leave a message. If I feel like it, I'll get back to you."

Beep.

"Heyyyy, Joanie, guess who? It's Tom

112

Holtz. Been thinking about you. Wondering how you're doing." Tom put his forehead in his hand and stared down at his desk. A draft of a last will and testament. A receipt from the dry cleaner's. He made it rock on its fold. "I've missed you, Boo-boo. Missed you more than you know."

There was only an empty electronic silence on the line.

"Call me, Joanie. We need to talk. It's serious, and I want you to call me back. Use my cell phone number. It's still the same. Don't call the office. But you will call, won't you? Soon?"

He swung his chair around and stood up. "Dammit, Joanie, I'm coming to see you. How about a late lunch? Say two o'clock? I'll bring some sandwiches. Champagne! Wouldn't you like that? Don't worry about getting all dolled up. It's just Tom, and he thinks you're perfect."

In his own office, Doug Lindeman carefully hung up the extension. He could feel everything starting to spin away from him. The old man was about to screw it up. There was no time left, none. He'd have to think of something fast.

As the boat picked up speed coming out

113

of the marina, Kyle Fadden automatically scanned the sky to the southeast. Rolling out of bed this morning he'd done what he always did, turn on the NOAA weather station. The low pressure south of Cuba yesterday had become a tropical storm. This time of year it could head this way and get nasty. The sea was still a cauldron of heat, feeding whatever storms might pass over it. It would take a couple of days to get here, if it did. At present the sky was empty of anything but sea gulls and a couple of fighter jets streaking toward the naval air base at Boca Chica.

Fadden had three customers in the skiff, businessmen from Ohio with shiny new rods and reels, who had informed him they were here for the pharmaceutical sales conference at The Cheeca Lodge. The charter had come up at the last minute, these guys suddenly deciding they wanted to go fishing for snapper. Fadden had almost said no, having told his ex-wife he'd be by the hospital, but he needed the job, and he could just as easily make a phone call to check on Billy. So he'd bought some sandwiches and sodas at the market and put bait in the live wells. The salesmen brought a cooler of beer. They were the kind who would want him to bait their hooks, entertain them with stories about Colombian drug running, and say cheese in the photos.

The wind whipped through his hair and buffeted the bill of his cap. Fadden turned north between Upper and Lower Matecumbe Keys, taking Tea Table Channel toward the mangrove islands dotting the shallows in Florida Bay. Once under the bridge, he followed the network of troughs through the turtle grass, staying away from the places that could snag his propeller. He had a 150-horse Mercruiser, and it was running ragged, burning oil. The rings were about shot. The boat was eighteen feet of fiberglass with a console in the middle, a casting deck at the bow, and live bait wells aft. A flat canvas top provided some shade. He had designed the boat himself, and an old guy in Marathon had built it for him. Even fully loaded, it could run on dew.

A couple of miles northeast of Shell Key he slowed, cut the engine, and drifted between two mangrove islands. Using the electric motor he raised the engine to get the propeller clear of the water. The salesmen roused themselves from their seats and went about baiting their hooks. Their voices carried over the water and echoed off the trees. Fadden threw out some chum to attract the fish. Ordinarily he wouldn't do this, but these ignoramuses wouldn't know the difference. They did know what a fish was, and they didn't want to wait all day for a strike. Fadden expected a good tip for his efforts.

He stood on the casting deck with the pole while the men spread out along the gunwale, two of them getting their rods tangled. Fadden told them to quiet down. The only way he'd been able to keep from knocking a few people overboard lately was thinking about his new boat, his in just a few more weeks. He had refinanced his two-bedroom, one-bath stilt house in Marathon to put a deposit on a thirty-six-foot Silverton for deep-sea charters, ten years old but only a hundred hours on the rebuilt engines. He could keep himself together by thinking about running that baby to Cabo San Lucas, Grand Cayman, maybe take it as far as Puerto Rico, and with men who appreciated his talent, not a bunch of yahoos like these.

Fadden leaned on the pole, lifted it free of the sand, then gave another push. Shafts of light came through the mangroves and danced on the white patches on the bottom. The water was transparent, and the skiff hung suspended above brain coral, purple sea fans, jellyfish, and undulating turtle grass. Small hogfish and red drum scattered in flashes of silver as the boat drifted toward them. Fadden watched for something worth going after.

The skiff glided closer to the mangroves, into their cool shadow. The tide gurgled through the mangrove roots and ticked on the sides of the boat. A white heron spread its wings and lifted up from a branch. With no breeze coming through the mangroves, the water was calm. He set the pole, pushed, then lifted it free, drops making circles. He noticed some turbulence and pointed toward the entrance of a trough. "Okay. Cast over that way."

The boat tipped dangerously before the men laughed and rearranged themselves. Cursing silently, Fadden helped himself to a beer out of their cooler. He had just popped it open when he felt his cell phone buzzing in his shirt pocket. He took it out. The display said HOLTZ AND LINDEMAN, P.A. He thought about not answering it, but he wondered why Doug would call him this early.

"Yeah."

Doug told him he'd just heard about Billy. He had run into Lois Greenwald, and she had told him about it.

Fadden said, "He's okay. I was by the hospital last night. Listen, I'm on the water right now with some people."

Then Doug asked what he thought about his son's confession.

"What are you talking about?"

Billy had called the police just before his suicide attempt. He'd told them he murdered Sandra McCoy.

"You're shitting me."

The salesmen looked around at him. Fadden turned his back. Anger and confusion boiled in his brain. A confession? Teri hadn't said anything about it last night. Nothing. She'd left him standing on the outside, as usual.

It didn't make sense. Billy? Sandra McCoy? How could that be?

Then he caught up to what Doug Lindeman was saying. An alibi. Billy watching movies with Doug's aunt that night. And Doug wanting to do the best thing for Billy. God knows, they had to help him out. So Doug would wait to file the guardianship till after Aunt Joan talked to the police and got Billy cleared. So for now, everything was off.

All Fadden could say was, "I'll call you later." He disconnected and dropped the cell phone back into his pocket.

For several minutes he stared, unseeing, into the distance. Heard the swoosh and click of fishing rods, the men's low laughter.

Billy hadn't done it but he had confessed. What had gotten into him? Billy had always liked to act out, to grab attention for himself. But this was over the top. Before the divorce, Fadden had made him toe the mark. His mother had babied him and excused his behavior. Obviously that hadn't changed. What it looked like to Fadden was a boy pushing the limits to see if there were any.

Taking a long drink of beer, Fadden thought about the phone call from Doug Lindeman. He'd said he wanted to help Billy. Some joke. That was the last thing Doug Lindeman would care about. If he was holding off on the guardianship, there had to be some other reason. Fadden didn't know what it was, and that bothered him. If he asked Doug about it, he would lie. Fadden felt like he was treading deep water, and something was coming up from the bottom about to bite him clean through.

"Hey, guys. We have to go back." The salesmen looked at him. "It's an emergency with my son. They just rushed him to the hospital. I'll give you a refund or we can come out again tomorrow. Your choice."

They were pissed off but trying to hide it, glancing at each other from behind their sunglasses. They reeled in their lines. Fadden poled out of the shallows, lowered the engine, and cranked it. Uneven vibrations radiated outward in the water, and blue smoke poured from the exhaust. One of the men started opening beers.

Standing at the console, Fadden swung the boat southeast. Soon the skiff was skimming the surface. He pointed the bow at the red-and-white lighthouse at Whale Harbor. Gulls and cormorants lifted out of the way. The bottom was a blur of turtle grass, cap rock, and sand.

The outlines of what he would do had begun to form in his mind. He had to get out to Lindeman Key. He had a right to see his son, didn't he? Teri had ripped him off for everything else, but he still had Billy.

7

The veranda at The Buttonwood Inn, spacious enough to hold fifty people at breakfast, was occupied by only one. Gail Connor's table overlooked the lawn, the coral-rock path winding through it, beds of flowers, and a small, deserted beach. Empty lounge chairs were stacked under a thatched hut. No one lay in the cotton rope hammock. The ocean was a vast sheet of twinkling blue that vanished off the curve of the globe. Not a person or sail or even a bird moved across her field of vision. She thought of the woman at the other end of the island. What would it be like to look out day after day on such emptiness, and hear no human voice but one's own?

Anthony had just called. He'd been checking to see if she had left the message for Joan Sinclair to call him. Gail told him she hadn't forgotten, she'd obtained the number from the housekeeper and made the call an hour ago. Maybe Miss Sinclair was out taking a walk, or her phone was turned off. Maybe she slept during the day and roamed by night. Not in a mood for humor, Anthony had asked Gail for the number so he could try it himself.

Chin propped in her hands, Gail was disappointed with her lack of success. She had been sure her message would produce a response. This elusive actress, as rarely glimpsed as a Florida panther, should have taken notice of Billy Fadden's name. They were friends, were they not? Joan Sinclair had cut through the rope when he'd hanged himself. Why couldn't she return a phone call?

Gail had left the cottage a little while ago dressed in shorts and a souvenir T-shirt from Key West, as though this were a real vacation, as though she might take the walking tour of the resort and identify the various species of native plants, or see if there were someone around who could unlock the sports center and lend her a mask and fins. No chance of that. She was wanted back at the cottage. Her computer and her files were waiting. There were clients to contact, opposing counsel to yell at, a complaint to draft in an auto accident case, and God only knew what else her secretary had thrown into her briefcase. On one hand, the urgent, grinding, and nit-picking demands of a law practice, along with the queasy fear that if these matters were not handled *immediately,* her career would fall into ruins. Or she might just walk over to that little beach. How pleasant to kick off her sandals, dig her toes into the warm sand, and stretch out in the ham-mock. But not by herself. What was the good of playing hooky without a coconspirator?

She wet her fingertip and picked up a toast crumb from the tablecloth, a soft sea-foam green. The coffee cup was empty. The waitress had gone to fetch more, and Gail thought she could afford the time it would take to drink it.

What bothered her at the moment, aside from the awareness that she was, in fact, playing hooky, were the two words that Anthony Quintana had not said in his phone call. *Marriage license.* She recalled that he hadn't said them when he'd left this morning, either. She had been half asleep but remembered his quick kiss and pat on the bottom, his request that she call Joan Sinclair. There had been no reminder that they had to apply for a license *today,* or forget it.

On the phone just now, Gail had almost brought it up, but Anthony had been pre-occupied. He wouldn't have wanted to hear his fiancée nagging him about wedding plans.

What wedding plans? A notary, assuming they could find one, a hurried ceremony after midnight on Friday, then up before dawn, driving back to Miami, husband and wife, and then? And then? What a dumb idea, getting married *here*.

Gail took her cell phone out of her shorts pocket and pressed the speed-dial button for her mother. If Irene hadn't already gone to one of her various charity organization meetings, she would be in the kitchen tidying up after breakfast with Karen. She considered it her life's mission to put some meat on that girl's bones. There had been some success: Karen had started her period and sprouted some size-AA curves on her chest.

Irene's cheerful voice invited the caller to leave a message.

"Hi, Mom, it's me, checking in. We're having such a great time. You would love Buttonwood Key. Anthony's in Tavernier with his client right now, and I'm just about to get down to work. I'll call Karen after school. Love you."

For a while, two summers ago, Gail and Karen had lived with Anthony in Coconut Grove. A breakup, though temporary, had ended that arrangement. They had moved in with Irene, to the house where Gail had grown up. Karen seemed happy there. She had made friends in the neighborhood, and her grades had improved. There was someone to supply milk and a sandwich when she got home, listen to the latest school gossip, keep her uniform pressed and her room dusted, and ferry her to soccer practice and Scout meetings and the preteen group at church. It was horrifying to think of not having Irene around. As horrifying as not having Anthony.

He was intent on getting married *ahora mismo*, right away. If she dared to point out that it might be better to wait, his eyes would darken. He would accuse her of trying to back out, and did she want to marry him at all? Yes! She loved him, ridiculously so. After Karen's father had walked out, Anthony had made her feel wanted again. Not just wanted, *desired*, with a passion so hot her bones had melted.

Gail heard a sudden crack, a whoosh, a thump. She leaned over the railing and looked toward the front of the hotel. At the base of a tall, curving coconut palm, a man with a pole saw was picking up a cluster of coconuts. He had apparently cut them down before they could fall and conk an unsuspecting guest on the head. He heaved them into the back of a miniature electric-powered truck. The truck bed was already loaded with palm fronds that draped to the ground like the tail of a peacock.

He wore a hat and his back was turned, but something about the narrow shoulders and shapeless khaki pants was familiar. This was the man who had piloted the boat last night. Arnel. He knew Joan Sinclair. Gail dropped her napkin on her chair and hurried across the veranda and down the steps, then doubled back along the path. She was too late; the hum of an electric cart faded around the corner of the building.

A voice came from above her. "I have your coffee, Ms. Connor. Are you leaving?"

"No, I wanted to speak to someone, but he's gone."

The young woman who had served breakfast was caramel-skinned and brown-eyed, with the friendly detachment common to exclusive hotels. Her knee-length shorts and crisp white shirt had the look of a British island colony. She poured more coffee from a porcelain pot as Gail returned to the table. The coffee was delicious, the Canadian bacon had been juicy, the omelet fluffy, and the toast warm, even in the silver toast rack. The breakfast dishes were sunny yellow with ocean waves around the edges. A lush purple vanda orchid bloomed from a basket on the table. This was perhaps too much fuss for one person, but Gail, who usually wolfed cold cereal before running out the door in the morning, could hardly complain.

She lifted the lid of a gold-rimmed sugar bowl. "You're going to spoil me. I'm not really a guest, you know."

"I know. That's all right." The woman stood there with the coffee pot. She hesitated, then said, "I heard they're bringing Billy back this morning. They say he'll be all right."

Gail didn't feel she could elaborate. "Yes, that's what I heard too." She smiled at her. "What is your name?"

"Emma." Her short, straight hair was parted neatly on one side, and little gold earrings adorned her ears. "I'm the only one in the kitchen, except for the housekeeper. It's a good thing she cooks, because I don't. The chef will be here Saturday, and all the wait staff Sunday morning. Would you care for anything else?" Gail said no, thank you, but Emma lingered. "You're here for Billy, aren't you?"

"Yes. Well, Anthony Quintana is Billy's attorney. I'm . . . helping out." Gail could not bring herself to say, *I have nothing to do with Billy, I came along to sleep with his lawyer.*

Emma said, "My husband's sister is a deputy sheriff. She told me about Billy calling them yesterday. And what he said? It's not true. It can't be. I don't know why he said that. Maybe he was drinking. He does drink some." Emma shook her head. "But he's such a good person. Miss Greenwald has this rule, we're not supposed to fraternize with the guests or the owners. Billy doesn't care. He's like, 'Hi, how're you doing?' Sometimes he helps out, if we're super busy. He wouldn't hurt anybody, I know he wouldn't. He and Sandra were always joking around. Well. That's all I wanted to say. I hope you can straighten this out."

"Wait. Emma, may I ask you something? Did you know Sandra McCoy?"

"Not well, but yes, I did. She came here about a year ago, and she worked in the office for Miss Greenwald, taking reservations off the computer, answering phones, filing, stuff like that."

"Which Ms. Greenwald? Lois or Teri?"

"Lois. Teri is Missus Greenwald, and Martin is Mister." She laughed. "We just call them by their first names, except in front of Lois or with guests, and you aren't a guest."

"How did Sandra get along with everyone here?"

"All right. Nobody had any reason to kill her, if that's what you mean. I heard she was going to quit because Lois was mad at her." Emma quickly added, "But Lois drives everybody hard."

Sensing there was more to this, Gail said, "Yes, I've met Lois. Why was she mad at Sandra?"

"Because Sandra wouldn't kiss her butt. Lois doesn't own the resort, but she acts like it. Everything has to be perfect. She'll take money out of your pay if a guest complains about service. She wanted us to wear white gloves at dinner, but Teri said no. They argue a lot behind Martin's back. Teri's real sweet. Martin stays out of the business for the most part. He just plays with the new water system and works on his orchids and palm trees. You didn't hear me say that."

"What about Sandra's life off the island? Did you know any of her friends?"

"Actually, we didn't have that much contact." Emma shook her head. "Sandra was in the office, and Lois doesn't like her staff associating with the kitchen people, excuse me very much."

"I see. How can I meet Joan Sinclair? Is there some trick to it? She doesn't return phone calls."

"Sorry, I can't help you with that either. I only saw her one time when she came to dinner with a man she was dating, and that's been . . . ohhh, two years at least. I think they split up. She hasn't been back since then, as far as I know."

"What does she look like?"

Emma lifted her eyes in the direction of the ceiling fan, remembering. "About as tall as you, but sort of big on top. Brown eyes, gray hair — not *at all* like grandma-gray hair. You'd never guess her age. All those actresses get face-lifts. Billy let me borrow one of her movies to take home. *Bride of Nosferatu.* She still looks like that. Older, and lots of makeup, but you can tell it's her."

"How was the movie?"

A smile broke through. "Kind of lame."

"Do you ever hear people say she's mentally unstable?"

"No." Emma shrugged. "She's just this

130

lady who likes to be by herself. The state the world is in, I don't blame her. A few times a week she orders dinner, and somebody takes it to her. Our chef is really good. Too bad you won't be here when he comes back. Sandra used to drop off Joan's food sometimes and run errands, like to the pharmacy or the grocery store."

"That was nice of her."

"Oh, she got paid for it."

"By Joan?"

"She got paid *twice*. Sandra was always looking out for herself. She wanted to save enough money so she could move to Miami Beach. She goes, 'I'm going to get me an apartment on the beach and go out to clubs every night of the week.' Dream on, I've been there, but Sandra had her mind made up, how great it would be. So she charged Joan, plus she got paid by Joan's nephew. He's a lawyer in Islamorada. He gave her a thousand dollars just to run errands, no lie. Sandra said they wouldn't find out because they didn't speak to each other."

"Who, Joan and her nephew?"

"Yes. His name is Doug Lindeman. She's a Lindeman too. She was born in the Keys, did you know that? She came back and moved into the old family home, and her nephew never did go over there, not till recently, so of course she's not all of a sudden going to welcome him with open arms. She wouldn't let him in. That's why he asked Sandra to keep an eye on her. That's what Sandra told me."

Emma glanced over her shoulder. "Well, I need to get back to work. We're starting lunch. Teri and Martin are bringing Billy home in a little while. And please, if there's anything I can do to help him, you just ask me."

Before leaving the cottage, Gail had glanced at a map of the resort. She knew from having studied Anthony's road map in the car yesterday that Lindeman Key was a slender finger of land about half a mile long. On the resort's map, only the western half appeared. The rest of the island vanished off the right side of the page, marked by the words PRIVATE PROPERTY.

Gail put on her straw sun hat.

Instead of taking the direct route to the cottage by going back through the hotel, she went down the steps of the veranda. She planned to follow the path along the southern shore, which would take her, she thought, past the orchid house and koi pond, then to the opposite shore, which faced Islamorada. From there she could easily find her way to their cottage, the second to last in a meandering line of twelve.

Through the dense foliage came the faint *pop . . . pop . . . pop* of an air hammer, probably a carpenter attaching paneling or lattice. On her way to breakfast she had moved aside for a cart loaded with five-gallon paint cans, then another carrying rolls of carpet. All that activity was a hundred yards away. On this side of the island, she was alone.

She took off her sandals and walked to the water. Too shallow for waves, it lapped at her ankles, warm as a pond. She couldn't dig her toes in. The gritty white sand had worn thin in places, and the rock showed through. Beaches were not natural to the Keys. A pile of new sand had been dumped on the shore, probably from a barge, and workmen would have to spread it. Gail came back onto the grass, then to a path of carefully tended, hard-packed sand that took her past several empty cottages, all on stilts. The path curved out of sight of the water.

Small signs had been placed at the base of various trees and palms with their Latin and common names, but Gail didn't take

133

the time to read them. She noticed the inconspicuous black plastic pipes and spray heads that would provide rain when it failed to fall naturally. There were landscaping lights along the path and electronic devices to trap mosquitos. She came to a painted arrow pointing to the orchid house, but continued straight to see where the path would end. It narrowed, and she ducked under some branches from a tree she had no hope of recognizing.

Left to itself, the island would revert to wilderness. Without fertilizer and water, the grass would burn off, and the fragile exotic species would wither, choked out by buttonwood, white mangrove, strangler fig, and poisonwood. A gruesome name. Gail wondered if any remained on the island, and if lizards and snakes were hiding in the underbrush. Hopping for balance, she dusted her feet and put her shoes back on. Soon the sandy path became rock, and the grass turned to sparse, springy clumps. The breeze dropped away, and sweat dampened her forehead and neck.

Unsure of her precise location, Gail had no fear of getting lost, as the island was small, and all routes circled back toward the hotel at the western end. The path seemed to turn more north, and presently joined with a wider path. Gail soon came to a chain-link fence so thick with vines that she couldn't see through it. From a gate hung a metal sign, POSTED, NO TRESPASSING, PRIVATE PROPERTY. But the gate was open a foot or so, pushed inward toward the tangled woods beyond.

This was where the map had ended. *Terra incognita.* Joan Sinclair's domain.

A big padlock dangled open from the latch. Gail walked closer to the gate and looked through. The tracks vanished into the trees, which arched overhead in a dark tunnel of leaves, vines, and twisted branches.

Gail took out her cell phone and picked through the buttons until her next-to-last call showed on the screen. She hit REDIAL. Waited. After the fourth ring she heard the alto drawl of a woman who couldn't be bothered.

"Hi. If you don't know who this is, you've got the wrong number. If you're selling something —"

"Oh, come *on.*" Gail disconnected. Joan Sinclair had to be home. She was always at home. Maybe she kept her phones off. If that was the case, it could be days before she called back.

Gail took off her hat and went sideways through the gate.

The land on the other side seemed to rise slightly, then dip, and at that point the tracks diverged. One way left, the other up a gradual slope. Reasoning that a house would not be built on low ground, Gail continued straight. The thickets opened up to a sort of clearing. Even with the hat, she squinted in the merciless sunlight. A breeze came up, and the long grass bent and shivered. Gail spun around when a bird cawed behind her, then laughed at her own skittishness. She continued along the rocky trail, which presently split into three. Right, left. Straight. The land continued to rise.

She came to woods, but here the underbrush had been cleared, and the trees opened up on an area that had known the careful hand of a gardener. There were groupings of thatch palm and native mahogany, pink oleander and yellow lantana. The ground was soft with shredded mulch. She rounded a thick stand of traveler's palm and saw the house directly ahead. It seemed to rise up and up, two stories of dark clapboard resting on concrete pilings, with gabled windows in the roof.

Shade trees surrounded the house, their heavy limbs draped with air plants and fern. Walking around to the front, Gail could see down a slope to the ocean. There was no beach, only heavy rocks for a breakwater and tangles of mangrove. If ever the house had enjoyed a clear view of the sea, it had been lost to the overgrowth of foliage.

At the bottom of a long wooden staircase, Gail looked up at a porch, shuttered windows, a screen door, and behind it the dark, fan-shaped glass of an entrance door. There was no noise from inside. Her eyes traveled to the second floor, a balcony, and windows with closely drawn curtains. Not a movement. At a distance the house had appeared sturdy. A closer look revealed abandonment and decay. The balcony supports had been patched with cheap lumber, the window putty had dried and fallen out, and the eaves were rotting. Decorative lattice had been put up to hide the pilings, but this was falling away.

At the foot of the stairs, Gail put a hand on the ball-shaped finial post. A crack ran through it, and a leaf had caught there. She picked it out as she considered what to do next. Bang loudly on the door? Admit defeat and let Anthony handle it?

A muffled ringing reached her ears. Gail took out her cell phone and saw the name

137

on the screen. Irene Strickland. She leaned against the finial post, a foot on the bottom step.

"Hi, Mom. . . . No, you didn't have to call back. . . . I'm *fine*. . . . Nothing's wrong. In fact, Anthony asked me if I'd like to get married down here. . . . Yes, before we come back. Isn't that insane? . . . I told him yes. . . . I know, I know. . . . We didn't discuss it, but we'd probably move back into his house, which I don't think Karen would appreciate. . . . I can't tell him that, Mother, after I've already said yes. . . . Of course I want to, just not *now*. . . . There's no way he's going to admit he made a mistake, and if I try to suggest anything so reasonable as waiting for a couple of months, we'd be on our way to the courthouse within five minutes. . . . Oh, you don't *know*. He is so sensitive."

She noticed a movement to her right and jumped, taking a breath. A man in a straw hat was looking back at her. The boat pilot. Arnel Goode. How long had he been standing there?

Cell phone at her mouth, Gail said quietly, "Listen, I can't talk right now. Call you later. . . . Love you too."

Arnel Goode held his hands up to show he intended no harm. "I-I didn't mean to scare you, but you shouldn't be here. This is Miss Sinclair's property."

"I know, I'm sorry, Arnel." Gail took her foot off the stairs. "I need to speak to her. I've been calling, and she doesn't answer."

The man wore gardening gloves, and rings of perspiration darkened the underarms of his dust-covered, long-sleeved shirt. The weather wasn't cool enough to require so many clothes, but his pale skin appeared fragile, susceptible to sunburn, which explained the hat. "Wh-Why do you want to speak to her?"

"I really can't discuss it. Do you work here too? I thought you worked for the Greenwalds."

"And for Miss Sinclair."

"Is she home?"

"Yes, but . . . she — she doesn't get up this early. We better go." Arnel started to move away, expecting Gail to follow.

"Could I come back later? Well, it's Anthony Quintana who would see her. Perhaps I would come too, but he's Billy's lawyer." The man's blue eyes stared blankly back at her. "Remember Mr. Quintana?"

"Yes."

With a sigh, Gail came closer. "All right. Billy was watching videos with Miss

Sinclair the night Sandra McCoy was killed. The police think he did it. We need for Miss Sinclair to tell them Billy was with her, so they'll leave him alone. That's what we need to see her about."

He nodded, the hat brim moving slowly up and down.

"She saved Billy's life, and I'm sure she'd want to help him again. You would, too, wouldn't you?"

Arnel glanced quickly at the house. "She d-d-doesn't like visitors."

More firmly Gail said, "Whether she likes it or not, we have to see her. We aren't movie fans looking for an autograph."

He noticed a weed and bent down to pull it. His hat was fraying at the crown. "Okay. When she wakes up, I'll ask her to call you."

Gail said, "How will you know when she wakes up?"

"She always calls me. I have a cell phone." Arnel shook dirt off the roots of the weed.

Looking at her watch, Gail said, "It's just after ten. Will she be up by noon?"

"I think so." He took a step toward the corner of the house, arm extended. "You wa-wa-want a ride back to the hotel?"

Seeing she would get nothing else here,

Gail said, "Yes, if it's no trouble. Thanks."

They went across the yard, around a thick hedge of oleander, and toward a storage shed made of concrete blocks. Arnel's little electric truck was parked just beyond. Gail hadn't noticed it earlier. A rake leaned against the rear of the truck. Apparently he had been dumping the contents of several black plastic lawn bags into a mulch pile. From within the eight-foot square of landscaping timbers came the heavy, pungent smell of decaying vegetation.

Arnel went over to the truck to take the last of the lawn bags out. He had been polite but not friendly. Gail had questions but didn't know how to approach this man. Was he mentally slow? Or had his halting speech made him shy?

She smiled at him. "This is a lot of work. Do you do all the gardening around here?"

"For Miss Sinclair I do." Arnel propped the rake on the lawn bags and dusted his hands. "At the Inn, there's a . . . yard crew. I help out."

He got into the truck and Gail sat beside him, holding on to the bar that supported the roof. Glancing sideways, she studied the face of her companion, as much of it as she could see under the hat. His small nose

141

and chin made him seem young, but a closer look put his age past thirty-five. The hands on the steering wheel were encased in blue striped gardening gloves.

Motor whining, the truck made a circle out of the yard. Gail watched the house vanish behind the trees. "How long have you worked for Joan Sinclair?"

"Fifteen years."

"Really. How'd you get the job?"

"Mr. Greenwald hired me . . . at the resort, but one day I w-w-went over to Miss Sinclair's house and said I could help her and . . . she didn't have to pay me. She said okay."

"You don't still work for free, do you?"

"Oh, I couldn't t-take money from Miss Sinclair. She depends on me."

Gail smiled back at him, hiding her indignation. Joan Sinclair was using this pathetic little man's adoration to get free handyman service. "I guess movie stars are pretty demanding."

"Oh, you bet. Do this, do that. I told her to buy me a . . . a cell phone so she could call if she n-n-needs anything. She used to have a mansion and . . . servants. She was a star. But in Hollywood, people took advantage, and they sta-abbed her in the back. When you're f-f-famous, they want

142

your soul. That's what she says."

The truck rattled down a slope and around the sun-whitened trunk of a fallen tree.

"Why doesn't she ever leave the island?"

"Because her f-f- . . . her fans are always after her. They won't leave her alone." His brows were as blond as the wisps of hair falling across his forehead. "She doesn't stay in her house all the time. She likes to work in her garden and catch fish off the dock. And . . . she goes to the f-family graveyard so she can put . . . flowers on the graves."

This was more than slightly strange, Gail thought. The woman never left the island except to visit the dead. "Does she do this often?"

"What?"

"Go to the graveyard."

He shrugged. "Not too often."

"How does she get there?"

"I take her. Or Mr. Greenwald does."

The truck bounced over some ruts, and Gail held onto her hat and braced herself with a foot on the dashboard. She remembered something Emma had told her on the veranda. "Joan has a nephew, a lawyer in Islamorada. Doug Lindeman?" Arnel nodded. "I've heard she won't talk

143

to him. Do you know why?"

Arnel watched the path ahead of them, and for a while Gail thought he would refuse to answer. Finally he spoke. "He wants to . . . p-put her in a . . . a home for old people. She said no. She isn't old. This island is her home, why should she leave?"

Gail made a note to herself: She would suggest that Anthony give Doug Lindeman a call before he went to see Joan Sinclair. As a family member, Lindeman would have an opinion about his aunt. It wasn't likely to be good. "So . . . Doug is her only relative?"

"Now he is. Her other nephew Teddy died in f-f-federal prison in Atlanta. Lung cancer."

"Why was he put in prison?"

"He sold drugs."

"Here? In the Keys?"

"Yes. Cocaine."

Gail abandoned any thought of asking for details.

Arnel slowed and stopped as they came to the chain-link fence marking the property line. He got out and opened the gate fully, got back in, drove through, then went back to secure the padlock.

On the Buttonwood side, tires glided smoothly on combed sand, and the little

144

truck hummed around a pond of water lilies, then over an arched wooden bridge painted Chinese red. They came down the other side to a sweeping view of the Keys across sparkling turquoise water. After the wild tangle of the eastern end, the resort seemed as tame as Disney World. They turned west. In only a minute or two they would be back at the hotel.

Gail heard her cell phone softly jangling in her pocket. She ignored it. She asked Arnel, "Did you know Sandra McCoy?"

"Not too good."

"Didn't you see her when she came to Miss Sinclair's house?"

"Mostly she came when I was working over here."

"Well, do you know if Sandra had a boyfriend? Did you ever see her with a man, or hear any talk about her?"

Clear blue eyes, and such a vacant look in them. Then he said, "Tom Holtz, but I don't know . . . if he was her boyfriend. He's pretty old. I saw him go in her apartment."

Gail turned around on the bench seat. "Who is Tom Holtz?"

"A lawyer for the Greenwalds. He and D-D-Doug Lindeman have an office together. I had to take Sandra home one

145

night, real late. Her car was getting fixed, so . . . I took her home from the marina in the van. She lived in a-a-a duplex apartment on Plantation Key. When we got there I saw Mr. Holtz's car parked on the corner. I said, 'What's he doing here?' Sandra said, 'M-M-Mind your own business, Arnel.' She went in her apartment. I went around the block, and I saw her let him in."

"Then what did you do?"

"I left."

"When was this? Do you remember?"

He thought about it, then said, "A-A-About a month ago."

"Did you tell the police? When they were investigating Sandra's death, I mean."

"They didn't ask me any questions."

And why should they? A man like Arnel Goode. She let the facts of his story play in her mind. It could mean nothing. It could mean everything. "Is Tom Holtz married?"

"No. His wife passed away." Arnel's brow furrowed in alarm. "Ms. Connor? Don't . . . don't tell anyone. I d-d-don't want to . . . m-m-make problems for Mr. Holtz. He didn't kill Sandra. What I think is . . . somebody g-g-going to K-Key West, a criminal ju-just out of jail, saw her, a p-p-pretty girl like that, and he k-kidnapped her and then . . . and then he killed her. It

146

wa-wa-wasn't anybody we know."

Gail put a calming hand on his arm. "I'll have to talk to Anthony Quintana about this, but only him. I won't tell anyone else what you said."

The truck swerved left, then braked to a stop. They had arrived beneath a portico alongside The Buttonwood Inn.

Arnel said, "Well. Here we are."

Gail stayed in her seat. "Would you mind talking to Mr. Quintana?"

"I have a lot to do."

"When will you have some time?"

Arnel stared at the knees of his shabby khaki pants. "I said enough already." He put the little truck into reverse, and Gail reluctantly got out.

"You'll talk to Miss Sinclair, won't you? And tell her to return Mr. Quintana's call? Will you tell her?"

He nodded.

"Don't forget."

"I won't."

Gail watched him wheel backward, then hurtle away with a spurt of sand from under the tires. Her phone rang, and she reached into her pocket. The display showed Anthony's number.

She put the phone to her ear. "At last! Where are you?"

"We're about to leave," he said. "We'll be there in half an hour." Gail could hear the low rumble of a boat engine in the background.

"Good," she said, "I have a lot to tell you."

"That makes two of us," he said.

8

The Greenwalds had a friend with a cabin cruiser who agreed to take them, along with Anthony and Billy, from the hospital to The Buttonwood Inn. Traveling half a mile offshore, the boat followed the line of the highway past Plantation Key, then Windley and Upper Matecumbe, before veering in a more southerly direction. It was a choppy ride, as the wind had risen since morning. Standing up as they approached the island, Anthony could see the line of royal palms along the seawall, the high roof above the trees, then the harbor, several small boats, and Gail under the awning on the dock. The skirt of her blue dress fluttered, then swirled around her legs. Even at this distance he could make out a white flower in her hair. He lifted a hand, and she waved back.

A supply boat was already in the harbor unloading boxes and crates. The Greenwalds' friend found a place for his boat, and a young man in a white Buttonwood Inn shirt helped tie up to the dock. The four passengers got off, and within a minute the boat was on its way back to Tavernier.

Anthony made the brief introductions, and Gail warmly smiled and shook their hands. What did she see? A man and woman in rumpled clothes, pale and exhausted; a gaunt and scowling teenager with a neck brace and bleached hair. The family got into the golf cart for the ride to the Inn. Anthony and Gail walked, taking the path along the shore, stepping aside for a cart loaded with boxes. The racket of hammers and saws had been replaced by air compressors and paint guns. The noise faded as they approached their cottage.

"Are you hungry?" he asked. "They're going to bring us some lunch. Teri called ahead and arranged it."

"My God. If I'd been through what she has, I'd make my guests fend for themselves. Have you heard from Joan Sinclair yet?"

"No, nothing."

They climbed the staircase to the porch, which was shaded by the roof overhang and a trellis laden with pink bougainvillea. Gail had left the windows open, and the soft breeze came through. Hanging up his suit pants in the armoire, Anthony noticed the draped mosquito netting and the soft duvet on the four-poster bed and thought of lying down for awhile. Instead, he made a call to Douglas Lindeman's office. He wanted to know if Lois Greenwald had persuaded Lindeman to delay filing the guardianship. When the secretary answered, she said that Mr. Lindeman would be out of the office until later in the afternoon.

Anthony thanked her and left his number and a brief message that referred only to Lois Greenwald. He punched the disconnect. *"Carajo."*

He put on shorts and walked into the living room barefoot, buttoning his shirt. Gail handed him a beer. The flower in her hair was real, a white hibiscus with a yellow stamen. She had tied it to a small comb that held her hair back from her face. He kissed her cheek. "That's a pretty flower. *Tú eres bellísima.*"

He had registered the fact that Gail had said nothing about going to the courthouse today. No hint, no reminder. There could be only one explanation: She had since changed her mind. Left alone all morning to work on her files and make phone calls, she had said to herself, *What were we thinking?*

Anthony decided to ask if this was the case. "Gail, *mi amor* —"

At that moment the golf cart arrived with the same young man who had driven the Greenwalds to the Inn. He bounded up the steps with an ice bucket, then went back for a tray laden with covered dishes. Gail told him to put everything on the table outside, such a lovely view of the ocean from here, she said.

They sat at a round teak table. The sun winked through the palms and put flashes of light on the turquoise and yellow plates, the lemon slices in the pitcher, the flowers that Gail had found in the yard. Stomach growling, Anthony dug into his lunch. The mango chicken salad had been lightly seasoned with ginger. *Delicioso.* He decided to wait until after they ate to discuss this business of getting married.

They talked about Sandra McCoy. Who had she been? Baylor had described a "nice little girl," a hard worker, a member of the First Methodist Church, caregiver for her grandparents. The same girl who had bought liquor for Billy Fadden and had had sex with him. A hard-edged girl who had been sleeping with another man,

152

possibly married. Billy didn't know who; she'd refused to tell him. Sandra wanted to move to South Beach, and she needed money to do it. She had collected a thousand dollars from Douglas Lindeman to run errands for his aunt. A lot of money for running errands.

The clash between Sandra and Lois Greenwald could be worth looking into, but the most intriguing fact, if true, had come from Arnel Goode. Late at night, a couple of weeks before her death, he had seen a man going into Sandra's apartment.

Four years ago Anthony had met him. His name was Thomas Holtz. He was one of the Greenwalds' attorneys. Holtz handled the negotiations with the owners of the house that Billy had burned down. Anthony remembered a stout white-haired man, a widower in his sixties, a regular in fishing tournaments, a lawyer not too hungry anymore, coasting on contacts with local bankers, realtors, and members of the chamber of commerce. His reason for entering Sandra's apartment at that hour could have been perfectly innocent. Could have been. Then why had she told Arnel Goode to mind his own business?

Anthony's watch had swept past one o'clock. "Joan Sinclair should have called

153

by now. You said she gets up at noon."

"That's what Arnel told me. Why don't you call her again?"

"I've already left three messages." Anthony stabbed the last piece of mango with his fork. "If she doesn't call within an hour, I'll go over there. I should talk to Teri and Martin first." He laughed. "I thought this would be simple. I would take Billy to the police station today, perhaps tomorrow, the detective would say, 'Oh, you have no information, thank you for coming, good-bye,' and then you and I, *mi querida,* would spend the rest of the week lying on the beach. This isn't what you expected, is it? I am sorry."

For several seconds Gail looked at him as if waiting for him to say something else. Her finely arched brows seemed suspended over a question. Her eyes had flecks of gray, like stones, like clouds. He had no idea what she was thinking.

He pushed his empty plate away and reached for his dessert. Some kind of iced cake. He poked at it with his fork and discovered a raisin, which he flicked aside. "Before I see Joan Sinclair, I should find out more about her. And Sandra McCoy. I want to hear what Lois has to say about Sandra."

"It seems," Gail remarked, "that you

have your afternoon filled."

He swallowed the mouthful of cake. "What would you like to do?"

Her smile was directed at the ocean. "Well, I brought a lot of work with me. I should get some of it done. In fact, I should be in there right now."

She rose from her chair and went to get the tray the porter had left on a bench near the top of the stairs. She brought it back and began to clear the table. The pitcher thudded onto the tray. Glasses, salt and pepper shakers. Silverware clanged on the dishes. She snapped the crumbs off her napkin.

"Gail." He held out a hand. "Come here." He pulled her closer and put an arm around her hips. "Do you want to apply for the marriage license today? Tell me. What are we going to do?"

She sent a cool little smile down at him, a drop of melted ice. "I think we've more or less decided, haven't we?"

"We'll go now if you want."

"If *I* want?" She laughed. "You were certainly enthusiastic last night. Oh, it doesn't matter. We don't have to do this now. You have Billy Fadden to worry about."

He shrugged. "If you want to do it, we will."

"Do *you* want to, Anthony?"

The white hibiscus was falling from her hair. He reached up to straighten the comb it was tied to. "Of course I do, *querida*. I love you. I want to marry you. There is nothing I want more. But this week is not such a good time."

"I suppose so."

"Do you agree or not? That way, we don't have to rush. You won't worry about Karen missing the wedding —"

"You're right. We'll wait."

He turned her hand over and put a kiss in her palm. He was both relieved and unsettled. He had disappointed her. It couldn't be helped.

"I guess we're back to June," she said.

"Whatever you want."

"June is fine."

He pulled her onto his lap and felt the pressure of her hipbones on his thighs, the warmth of her body. "*Mamita,* you know I love you." He pulled her face down to his. "*Soy tuyo.*" Her lips were sweet. He tasted icing in the corner of her mouth.

A cell phone was ringing. It took him a moment to disengage his thoughts. He turned his head toward the door. "Whose is that?"

"Yours."

He scooted her off his lap and dashed inside, through the living room and into the bedroom, where he found his cell phone chirping for the fourth and last time before it would switch to voice mail. "Yes?"

"Mr. Quintana?"

He knew this voice. He had heard it three times already today — not a British accent, but not exactly American either. His ear, more tuned to Spanish, couldn't place it.

He noticed Gail standing in the doorway.

"Yes, this is Anthony Quintana. Miss Sinclair?"

Gail came quickly across the room and tried to put her ear close to his. He held up a hand and turned around. "Thank you for returning my call."

There was a slow inhalation, then the soft snap of a cigarette being pulled away from her lips. "God *knows* you left enough messages. Let me guess what you want to ask me. 'Was Billy Fadden with you the night the McCoy girl was murdered?' Yes, he was. As I told his mother last week, Billy and I were watching Hitchcock films from eight-thirty until two-fifteen the next morning. Do you want a list? *The Rope*, *Vertigo*, and *The Birds*, in that order."

"Would it be possible," Anthony asked,

"to discuss this in person?"

"Surely that isn't necessary. I've told you what you wanted to know."

"And I am grateful, but you need to tell it to the police, and we need to decide the best way to do that."

A pause. "I can call them. I'll call them right now if you like."

"I'd rather you didn't. Let's discuss it. I'm free at the moment. I can come to your house."

"Now?" Another pause. "Sorry, but it's not convenient."

"Name a time. Forgive me, I must insist. The police suspect Billy Fadden of murder. Only you can save him."

After a long silence, he heard an exhalation. "Very well. I'll be at home at nine o'clock this evening. Come then. The gate will be open."

Click.

She was gone. Anthony put his cell phone back on the dresser.

Gail raised her brows. " 'Only you can save him'? That's dramatic. What did she say?"

"Come at nine o'clock."

"Thank God. I was afraid she'd told you to get lost. How did she sound? Coherent?"

"Completely."

"That's a relief," Gail said. She put a hand on his arm. "I want to go with you."

He shook his head. "Miss Sinclair doesn't expect another person."

"Did she specifically say, 'Come alone'?"

"Gail . . . no. She might refuse to talk to me at all. I don't want to risk it."

"If she doesn't want me there, I'll leave. It's better if I go with you. It's a test. If Joan Sinclair can't handle the two of us, how can she go off the island and discuss a murder case with a roomful of police officers?"

"*Ay, Dios mío.*"

"You know I have a point. Admit it."

"All right, but sweetheart, what is your connection to this case? What do I tell her? 'This is Ms. Connor, my fiancée. She wanted to meet you.' "

"Don't patronize me, Anthony, as if I were some giggling *fan* of Joan Sinclair. You did enlist me to call her today, remember? She knows who I am. I've left enough messages. I'm trying to help you."

"Thank you, but I'd rather handle it myself."

"Why?" Gail looked at him intently. "Because you don't want anybody to find out you were wrong. You're afraid you might have screwed up last time with Billy.

You're afraid you walked him when he should have been pushed into intensive therapy, and as a result, something worse has been created. He tried to kill himself. Not only that. He might have committed murder."

"He isn't guilty."

"Are you sure?"

"Gail, I don't make guarantees about my clients, but I am certain that Billy Fadden is innocent. There's no evidence against him."

"He confessed."

"Falsely."

"He killed Sandra because she started going out with someone else."

"He has an alibi."

"Maybe." Gail waited, then said, "But you don't *know*, do you? You don't, and it's going to eat at you, and you'll start brooding and worrying and be impossible to live with, and we'll both suffer."

"Do you think I *want* to know if my clients are guilty or not?" Smiling, he looked at her a while, then averted his gaze out the window, to the riot of green past the open glass louvers. "I don't care about that. Anyway, the truth is hard to hold on to. You think you have it, then it bites you. I don't even ask."

"Who are you lying to, me or yourself?"

"It's an accommodation I make that keeps me sane," he said. "That and a good billing department at Ferrer and Quintana."

"What are you going to do between now and Saturday, interview all these people yourself? Why don't you hire me? We'll get it done in half the time, then we can play."

"What do you mean, hire you?"

"Let me work on the case. I know how to investigate a case, and I *do* happen to care, for your sake at least, whether Billy Fadden is innocent."

"This was supposed to be a vacation."

"Really? When do we see each other? When you come to bed? Sorry, that's not enough." She went to the closet and pulled out her suitcase. She laid it on the floor, unzipped the top, and started tossing her shoes inside. "You're going to be busy, and I could work so much more effectively at my office. Have you seen that stack of files in the living room?"

"What are you doing, Gail?"

"If there's no good reason for me to be here, I might as well go back to Miami."

"How? Swim?"

"Arnel can take me to the marina. There must be a bus going north."

He sighed. "All right. You can help me work on the case." She turned around and looked at him, swinging her hair off her face. He said, "Don't forget whose case it is. You check with me before you do anything. Is that clear?"

"Perfectly." She tossed a high-heeled black sandal back into the closet. "How much are you going to charge me for your services?"

"Oh, my fees, I nearly forgot. Let's see. For you, five dollars an hour."

"*Qué barato*. That is cheap. I would have given you ten."

She held out her hand. "I need a retainer. Come on, let's have it. I don't work for free."

Anthony took out his wallet and gave her a twenty. "That's four hours. I expect you to turn in a time sheet."

Smiling, she tucked it into a side pocket of her dress. The dress was thin cotton that followed her curves. He bent to press his lips to her chest, just at the edge of the low neckline. Her scent filled his head.

"I wouldn't really have left." She put her arms around his neck. "Not unless you told me to. Maybe not even then."

"I know. *Te quiero. Nunca te diré que te vayas.*" He kissed her. "I will never tell you

162

to go. I did it once, to my shame. Not again. Ever."

She outlined his mouth with her fingertip. "Scratchy."

"I'll go shave."

"No, wait. Kiss me again. Do it just like that."

After a minute she pulled away. Her breaths came as quickly as his. "You have to talk to the Greenwalds. When?" She undid the top button of his shirt. Then the next.

"They can wait." He plucked the flower from her hair and tossed it onto the bed.

9

They took the white sand path leading behind their cottage, catching only a glimpse of the cottages tucked into the trees, the white clapboard and pastel gingerbread trim winking through the foliage. A soft breeze brought the scent of frangipani and jasmine. The quiet was broken only by birds and the rustle of palm fronds. The carpenters had left, or had traded their power tools for paintbrushes.

Anthony had called ahead to let Teri and Martin know they'd meet them on the patio behind the Inn. As they walked Gail read the tags on the trees. Golden raintree, cassia, royal poinciana. Lignum vitae, with wood so dense it would sink. Gumbo-limbo, nicknamed "tourist tree" for its peeling red bark. Ylang-ylang, perfuming the air with delicate fragrance. Gail was not the gardener her mother was, but many of these species were in Irene's back yard.

Cycads, fuzzy red chenille plants, variegated ginger. Heliconia made vivid splashes of red and orange in the dark green shade.

They walked around a croquet green, then past a chess set with pieces three feet tall. There were nooks where a person could sit and read, and chaises for dozing in the sun. Holding Anthony's hand as they walked, Gail wondered what it must be like to own such a place, as the Greenwalds did. It was all very nice for a week or maybe two, but beyond that? . . . If she had to *live* here, she might soon find herself slumped sideways in a chair, drooling.

A gust of wind teased her sun hat, and she reached quickly to keep it from flying away. They walked past the spa, whose entrance was a Zen courtyard paved in black slate. The few leaves that had drifted there seemed placed by the designer's hand. A hammered brass egret dipped its beak into a long narrow pond. At the other end, a fountain splashed musically against the rocks.

For a shortcut to the hotel, they cut across the grass, went through a break in the hedge, and came out behind a two-story building, the fitness center, as best they could tell. They were about to round the corner when they heard low, angry voices. A man, a woman.

Anthony held up a hand. Gail took off her hat and shifted forward to see through a thatch palm.

The woman was Teri Greenwald. The man . . . Gail had never seen him before. He wore shorts and a billed cap, and gray hair touched the collar of his shirt. His wiry body was tight, as if ready to leap. Teri blocked his way up a staircase leading to a porch on the second floor. They were arguing about Billy.

"I gave up a fuckin' five-hundred-dollar charter trip to come over here."

"If you'd wanted to see him so much, why didn't you come to the hospital this morning like you said?"

"It's not my fault. The water pump went out on my car, and I got stranded."

Gail whispered, "Is that Billy's father?" Anthony nodded.

Kyle Fadden's arms were corded with muscle, and his right hand opened and closed. He might have wanted to slap his ex-wife for old time's sake. Gail knew it was bad manners to eavesdrop, but she waited for Anthony to back away. He didn't. Neither did she.

Teri's eyes flashed fire. "You can't just

166

show up whenever you want to. This is private property."

"What are you going to tell him, Teri? Huh? 'Your dad was here to spend some time with you, but I threw him out.'" Fadden grabbed her elbow. "I'm going up there to see my boy."

Anthony went around the corner, then stopped as if surprised to see anyone here.

"Oh, hello," Gail said, following.

Kyle Fadden turned and gave the intruders a cool stare.

Teri took a breath. "Kyle, this is Anthony Quintana, Billy's lawyer. And Ms. Connor. Also a lawyer."

Fadden had a screw-you smile. "Two lawyers. Billy must be in trouble."

Anthony walked over to Teri. "Is everything all right?"

Fadden said, "I'm here to see my son. He's expecting me."

"Go ahead," Teri said. "You want to see him, go."

Anthony stepped in front of him, getting close enough to demonstrate the difference in height. "Mr. Fadden, before you do, I want to speak to Billy. It won't take long."

"Why?"

"To remind him not to talk about the McCoy case. That's all. And I would ask

167

you, as his father, to avoid that topic. If the police know that you've been here, they might ask you questions. You understand." Without waiting for a reply, Anthony trotted up the stairs.

Kyle Fadden turned around, smiling, spreading his arms, unable to challenge Anthony and showing the women it didn't matter. "Okay. No problem." Teri stared at the brick pavers in the courtyard. She had changed her rumpled dress for cropped linen pants and a white top. Her black hair gleamed in the dappled sunlight. Billy's father settled a shoulder against the clapboard side of the building to wait. Gail noticed the triangular leather case on his hip. Her own ex, who had gone fishing on weekends, had once pointed out to her what the pros carried. The case would contain a scaling knife and needle-nose pliers for removing hooks. Gail assumed that the bigger the pliers, the bigger the manhood.

When Fadden spoke to Teri again, he had calmed down. "Billy's not going to try this again, is he? Try to kill himself?"

Teri gave him no more than a quick glance. "We don't think so. He has an appointment in Miami on Tuesday with a psychiatrist. Her name is Sharon Vogelhut. If you're interested."

"Yes, Teri, I'm interested. Maybe I should go with you." Her dark eyes fixed on him. "Maybe not. Could you give me a call after? Let me know how it went?"

"If you like."

Kyle Fadden hooked his thumbs in his belt and gazed up at the windows. "This is a wake-up call. I blame myself somewhat. You know, the divorce and everything. I want to be around more often. I want to take him fishing. Diving. Whatever. You know. Do some father-son bonding. I think it'd be good for Billy. Is that okay with you?"

Teri stared at him as if he'd just told her he'd been baptized by immersion and wanted to share the experience with their son. She said, "It's up to Billy."

Listening to this, Gail became confused. She had understood that Kyle Fadden was a monster, a wife-beater, a child abuser. But her sympathy had begun to shift in another direction. This was Billy's father. He was making an effort. People did change.

She put her hat back on. No one spoke.

The door upstairs opened, shut. Anthony took his time coming down, making Kyle Fadden wait at the bottom. When Anthony was out of the way, he went up without a backward glance.

Teri closed her eyes. Anthony said quietly, "Let's find a place where we can talk."

They crossed the courtyard. Teri lifted the latch on a white wooden gate, and they walked onto the patio behind the hotel, paved in big squares of coral rock, shaded by a trellis draped with passion flowers.

Freed of the possibility that someone might overhear, Teri let out a cry of exasperation. "I don't believe him! I looked out the window and there he was. He never comes here!" Her voice was quick and light, with only the faintest trace of the accent she'd brought from Cuba.

"Where is Martin?" Anthony asked.

"Resting. I didn't tell him you called. Martin has been so good, so supportive with Billy, but I don't want to put too much on him. This isn't his problem, it's mine."

Gail found this attitude very strange. Did Teri expect that her husband would run out of patience? Was she afraid what he'd do if he saw Kyle Fadden on his property? Martin Greenwald had not seemed like the kind of man to lunge against his chain if his wife's former husband showed up. Unlike Anthony. But who knew?

Anthony was saying, "Teri, I've persuaded Gail to work with me. She's an ex-

170

cellent attorney, and I hope you feel no hesitation talking to her."

She gave Gail a warm smile. "None at all. Come on, let's go sit by the pool." As they walked, Teri slowed her steps, turning sideways to speak. Her hair fell from a center part to just below her shoulders, thick and glossy. Her lipstick shone, and liner accented her eyes.

"Kyle sounds so sincere, doesn't he? He is — until he has to follow through on his promises. Bond with his son? I'm sorry, but I'm not impressed. If it happens, then I'll believe it." She went on about Billy's desire to see his father, the times that he had gone to his house in Marathon and Kyle hadn't been there.

They arrived at the lagoon-shaped pool, which overlooked the ocean. Ferns softened the white rocks marking the perimeter, and arbors made shady places to sit. A small thatch-roofed hut for drinks and towels had been freshly painted in wild Caribbean colors. Teri gestured toward a blue metal table with four chairs tilted up against it. "We can sit over there. Please let me get you something to drink. There's a phone by the bar."

They said they didn't want anything, thank you.

171

"What a view," Gail said, sweeping off her hat, lifting her face to the sun.

"Oh, yes. I love it. It's paradise. Martin and I travel occasionally, mostly in the summer, but we're happiest right here. He bought Lindeman Key in 1988. The hotel was only one story, basically a fish camp. We have old black-and-white photographs in the library. You should let me show them to you."

Anthony had pulled out their chairs. "*Por favor,* ladies."

Teri hooked her arm through Gail's as they walked toward the table. "When it's all done, I want you and Anthony to come back and really enjoy yourselves. I feel terrible that we've had to leave you on your own." Except for the narrow straps of her snug white top, her shoulders were bare, her skin like amber honey. From a gold chain hung an antique locket with a filigree case.

Sitting down, she beamed at Anthony. "You're my savior! You too, Gail. You wouldn't believe, last time Anthony came here — he told you about it? — he fixed everything. He saved the day. That's why I know Billy's going to be all right."

Anthony and Gail exchanged a brief glance as he took the chair between the

172

women. He folded his sunglasses and set them on the table. The sun wasn't so bright here in the shade, and the shadows of palm fronds moved on the terra-cotta deck.

"Gail and I are going to see Joan Sinclair tonight. Tomorrow we'll take her to the sheriff's office, if she will go with us. There could be a problem. Douglas Lindeman is planning to seek a guardianship alleging that his aunt is incompetent. Lois told me this morning. Did you know about it?"

"Yes, she mentioned it a few weeks ago, but we haven't heard anything lately." The mild curiosity on Teri's face turned to alarm. "Oh, my God. He can't do that."

"Lois said she would ask him to delay until this is over. I've left a message at his office, but he hasn't yet returned my call. Where is Lois?"

"Still with the contractor in Key Largo, I believe. I'm sure if Lois asked Doug to hold off, he will. That law firm gets a lot of business from us. Do you want me to call her now?"

"A little later, if I don't hear from Lindeman. What's your opinion of Joan Sinclair's mental state?"

"She's fine. When she called me about Billy, I didn't have the slightest doubt about it."

"When was the last time you actually saw her?"

Teri dug her fingers into her long black hair and swept it off her forehead. "Let's see. Last Christmas! Has it been so long ago? I took her a nice wine and cheese basket from Martin and me. She said thank you but didn't invite me in. Billy knows her better than I do. He never said she had problems. I'm sure she's perfectly fine."

"Why do you think that Doug Lindeman intends to allege she's incompetent?"

That brought a blank look. "Well . . . I hadn't really thought about it."

"So you don't know where he's getting his information? I ask because we've heard that Lindeman and his aunt don't speak, and he hasn't seen her for a long time."

"That's true," Teri said.

"We also believe that he paid Sandra McCoy to check on Joan for him. Perhaps Sandra's observations caused him to question his aunt's competency. Is that possible?"

"It could be."

"Who hired Sandra to work here at the resort?"

"Lois did. She knows Sandra's grandmother. She wanted someone completely

174

trustworthy, someone who could follow orders. Well, *that* didn't work out. Lois said she was going to fire her as soon as she found someone else."

"Was there any particular reason?"

Teri rested her chin on her fists. Her long nails gleamed, a perfect French manicure. Even nearing forty, she was petite and curvy, with a small waist to go with the Latina hips.

"Lois didn't say, and I didn't ask her. I don't interfere in what Lois does, unless it gets too silly, like wanting our employees to use the back halls and stay out of sight of the guests. I'm not criticizing! She's done *wonderful* things with the resort. Martin and I couldn't do it without her."

But you'd like to try, wouldn't you? Gail was beginning to pick up on the hostility between wife and sister-in-law that Anthony had alluded to last night. Having met both of them, Gail could understand it. Lois had been overshadowed by this woman in every way but one: power.

Anthony asked more questions about Sandra McCoy, but Teri apologized and said she didn't know much about her, as Sandra had worked for Lois, and Teri didn't have much to do with running the hotel. That was Lois's territory.

Drifting at the edge of the conversation, Gail gazed at the ocean glittering in the sunlight. Two cabin cruisers passed each other, their engines barely audible. A double-masted sailboat tilted in the wind. This morning Gail had turned on the news in time to see a satellite image of the Caribbean, a big red-and-yellow splotch right under Cuba. The storm was expected to intensify today and turn east on Thursday, pushed by a cold front coming through Florida. There could be thunderstorms in Miami. Gail wondered if the Biscayne Bay cleanup would be rained out.

Gradually she became aware that Teri was talking about Sandra's activities the afternoon she died, a few more details to add to those that Gail had heard. Billy taking Sandra to the Blue Water Marina around four-thirty then staying in Islamorada to buy some parts for his boat. He had returned to Lindeman Key by eight o'clock that night and had gone directly to Joan Sinclair's house. Sandra McCoy had rented a video at Movie Max at seven-fifty-two p.m. She'd been grabbed in the parking lot.

"Did Billy talk to anyone at the marina who could verify what time he left?"

"I don't know," Teri said.

Anthony said he would find out.

The sky had been clear this morning, but between the palm trees Gail could see clouds floating lazily westward. If the school trip was called off, Anthony would ask her to stay through the weekend. Gail thought she would go home on Friday as planned, even if it was raining buckets in Miami. She had promised Karen. Anthony wouldn't like it, but he wouldn't force her to make a choice: me or Karen. Even so, Gail could hear them already. If she wanted to stay: *Mom, you promised you'd be here Friday night!* If she wanted to go: *Why do you let a twelve-year-old call the shots?*

Teri was explaining about Billy's movie collection.

"He records them off the satellite dish. He has over a thousand videos. Seriously! Martin installed a dish outside Billy's apartment that gets about a hundred foreign channels. He has movies from all over the world."

Anthony wanted to know how often Billy went to Joan's house to watch movies.

"Not often. You'd have to ask Billy about that."

"Does she invite him? Or does he just drop in?"

"I'm not sure."

"Do you know if Joan Sinclair drinks? Has Billy ever mentioned she has a problem with alcohol?"

"I know she *drinks,* but he didn't say she had a *problem.*"

"What I am wondering," said Anthony, "is whether she might have been drinking on the night of October third."

Teri vigorously shook her head. "Oh, no, she wasn't drunk that night, or she wouldn't remember what time he got there or when he left."

"Does Billy drink when he goes to see her?"

She raised a shoulder as if warding off the question. "Probably. Yes. I thought . . . it's better here than with his friends, where he could flip his boat and drown. I was trying . . ." Anthony's brown eyes were on her, but he said nothing. Teri pushed her hair behind her ear. "I didn't know he drank so much. He said he didn't. He won't let me in his apartment. 'Mother, would you please leave me *alone?* ' " She bit her lip. "That was a mistake. I've made a lot of mistakes."

Anthony said gently, "There is time to put it right again."

"He's all I have. Martin . . . I love Martin, but Billy is my life." Teri stroked her fingers slowly through her hair, again and again. "I don't know him, isn't that funny? My own son. Who is he? He plays music, he watches movies, he rides around in his boat. He never said he was so unhappy he wanted to put a rope around his neck and kill himself."

Gail reached across the table and took her hand.

"I'm all right." Teri pressed her fingers to her cheek to catch a tear, then laughed. "We're going to be fine. We have you now, don't we?"

Someone shouted out from behind them, "Hello there!"

They turned around.

A man with white hair was coming toward them from the bar. He carried a small wicker picnic hamper. A bright red knit shirt stretched across his belly. He wore white slacks and a belt with nautical flags on it. Clip-on sunglasses hid his eyes.

Teri shifted to see around Anthony. "It's Tom Holtz. Hi, Tom."

The man was unhappy about something. "Where might I find Martin?"

"He's taking a nap. Can I help you, Tom?"

He set down the hamper and introductions were made. Anthony stood to shake

179

Holtz's hand. Holtz nodded at Gail, then kissed Teri on the cheek. "I sure was sorry to hear about Billy. Doug told me. He's all right, though, isn't he? You brought him home?"

"Yes. He'll be fine."

"Glad to hear it." Tom Holtz's forehead was deeply creased, and above the clip-ons, his eyebrows were tangles of white wire. Broken veins reddened his nose and cheeks.

"Sit with us, Tom."

He put both hands on the back of a chair. "I need to ask you something, Teri. Is Martin trying to get hold of Joan's property?"

Teri glanced at Anthony, then back to Tom Holtz. "What do you mean?"

Frowning, Tom Holtz said, "He's always talking about needing more room for his palm trees. And I know Lois wanted to build over there. Joan didn't want to sign a deed, but Doug might, if he were the guardian of her property. Did Martin ask him to file a guardianship?"

"Why, no, Tom."

"Huh." His perplexity was still evident. "Well, then, what is Doug doing it for?"

Anthony said, "Lois went to ask him to delay the guardianship. Do you know if he agreed to do that?"

"He did. It's off for now. I had agreed to be the attorney of record because I thought it would be the best thing for Joan. Well, today I said count me out. Joan doesn't need an assisted living facility, she needs someone to give her a hand. I was just over there talking to her. *Trying* to talk to her." Glancing down, he gave the wicker basket a tap with his foot. "There's some cold champagne and a couple of sandwiches in there. I wanted to surprise her. She wouldn't let me in. I had to talk to her through the screen door. I told her about the guardianship. She was plenty ticked off, and I don't blame her."

Gail looked at Anthony, whose face showed his irritation.

Holtz picked up the hamper. "Hey, listen, Teri, let me put this stuff in the fridge. I want to go on back over to Joan's. She's got to see reason."

"Wait." Anthony stood up. "Tom, I'm going to ask you a favor. Gail and I have an appointment to see Joan at nine o'clock tonight. It's regarding Billy. He was at her house when Sandra McCoy was murdered, and we need to discuss it with her."

"That's right, Doug told me about it. Joan's the alibi witness."

"Correct. Let her talk to the police and

get this out of the way before you see her again. I want her completely focused on Billy. Do you understand?"

His eyes didn't show behind the clip-on glasses, but he nodded. "All right. I get the point. Do me a favor. Tell her you ran into me. Tell her . . . I'm still her friend and I care about her. I want to make sure she's happy. Would you let me know what she says?"

"Certainly."

"Thanks. Teri, good to see you. I'll be thinking about that boy of yours." The glasses turned toward Gail. "Miss . . . ah . . ."

"Gail Connor."

"Good to know you, Ms. Connor."

Anthony said, "Tom. Let me walk you to . . . where are you going? Did Arnel bring you here in the shuttle boat?"

"No, I came in my boat."

"I'll go with you to the harbor." Anthony pushed his chair in and smiled quickly at Gail and Teri. "I won't be long." He put on his sunglasses.

After the men had left, Teri looked quizzically at Gail.

"I think he wants to ask Mr. Holtz about Joan."

But Anthony would be asking more than

that. Gail knew he had a question about Sandra McCoy. He wouldn't say who had witnessed Thomas Holtz going into Sandra's apartment late at night, two weeks before her murder. He wouldn't ask if it were true. He would state it as fact and wait for the explanation.

"Gail, your ring is gorgeous. Let me see it."

She extended her left hand across the table. "The diamond was Anthony's. I liked it, so he had it reset for me."

"Oh! It's perfect. When are you getting married?"

"Probably next June."

"That's too far away!"

"Well, I have a daughter. Karen is twelve, and I'm so busy with her and my job, and I just don't have time to think about a wedding right now."

Teri's eyes lit up. "We do weddings here at The Buttonwood Inn all the time. Sunset weddings are the most popular. Your daughter — Karen? She'd love it. To girls her age it's a fairy tale. Gail, if you and Anthony want to get married here, it would be our pleasure, on the house, plus the party afterward."

"Teri, no, it's too much."

"You and Anthony already have plans?"

"Well . . . not really, but —"

"Let it be my little thank-you for taking care of us." She squeezed Gail's hand. "You think about it, okay?" Her eyes shifted in the direction of the Inn, darkening as though she could see through the trees to her son's apartment. "I wonder if Kyle has left. He shouldn't stay too long. Billy's very tired."

"Let's go, then."

As they walked back around the pool, Gail remembered something she'd been meaning to ask about. "How did you happen to hire Anthony? Did you know each other before? In Cuba, I mean."

"We knew each other, but he left long before I did. It's more like my family knew his, and we sort of stayed in touch that way."

"You're from Havana?"

"No, a little dirt-road town in Camagüey Province, way out in the sugarcane fields. We knew his father's side, not his mother's. Do you remember hearing about the Mariel boat lift?" When Gail nodded, she went on, "That's how I left, in 1980. I had a boyfriend, Nestor. He was in trouble with the police, and he had to get out, so I went with him. I didn't tell my parents, or they would've stopped me for sure. We hitched a ride to the port. He had false ID papers, and I pretended to be his wife. They put us on a boat, about a hundred people, all crammed together, whole families and factory workers and petty criminals and a couple of homosexuals and this one old man who couldn't stop crying. I hung over the railing all the way, throwing up. We got to Key West about midnight. We were filthy and tired, and all I owned was what I had on, shorts and a top, and a pair of tennies.

"Nestor's aunt lived there, and she sponsored both of us. Nestor and I broke up a year later, and he went to Miami. I don't know where he is now. I stayed in Key West and worked in a restaurant about twenty hours a day. I met Kyle. We got married and moved to Tavernier. What can I tell you? Love. Hormones. We were okay for a while but things changed. We didn't have much money, and then the kids were born, and there was even less. Kyle had a temper. I learned to be very quiet, believe me. Where could I go? What would happen to my kids? Kyle said he loved them, but his idea of discipline was to take off his belt. Most of the time I kept them out of his way. That sounds weak to you, but you don't know, unless you're in a situ-

185

ation like that, how hard it is to leave. I was trapped. Nobody was going to come for us in a boat and take us out of there."

Teri stopped herself and lifted her eyes to meet Gail's. "I had two sons. Jeremy drowned when he was six. He fell into the canal behind our house."

"Yes, Anthony told me. I'm so sorry."

Wordlessly Teri grasped her gold locket and inserted the tip of a fingernail in the side. It clicked open to reveal two small photographs. Billy — before he bleached his hair. And another, much younger boy. A beautiful, smiling child with lustrous brown eyes.

"That's Jeremy," Gail said.

"Yes." Teri pressed the locket to her lips before closing it. "I wasn't there when he died. Kyle called me at work. 'Come home, Jeremy's dead.' There isn't a day that goes by that I don't think of him. Not one. That was eleven years ago. He's right here." She put her fist over her heart. "Billy found him. He tried to save him, but it was too late. Billy was different after that. He had nightmares. He would wet the bed, and Kyle would yell at him and take off his belt. Those days were the worst of all. You should have seen me, so skinny! *Flaquita*." Teri held up her little finger.

"Kyle and I lost our house and we moved into a trailer. We walked around like dead people. He wasn't as violent but he drank a lot. I found a job here on weekends." She laughed. "Yes! I used to clean rooms at The Buttonwood Inn. Clean rooms and help in the kitchen. I wore a maid's uniform. I didn't mind. No, it was wonderful. And the best thing about it? I met Martin.

"Kyle says I destroyed our marriage. That's a laugh. It's true I slept with Martin before I divorced Kyle, but he should beg *my* forgiveness. He drove me away. He doesn't give a damn about Billy, it's only a way to get to me. That's why he came here, not for Billy but to show me what a terrible mother I am, that it's *my* fault what happened. But Kyle never calls Billy to see how he is. Never. Billy calls *him*. Kyle treats him like dirt, but Billy thinks he's God. Explain that to me. Martin offered to buy him a new boat, but Billy refused. He'd rather have the old one Kyle gave him, that hardly runs. I'm so afraid Billy will leave. He's only nineteen. He could go if he wants to, but he's incapable of living on his own.

"My sister-in-law would love that. She keeps trying to get rid of him. Billy should live with his father and learn to be a fishing guide because it's obvious, isn't it, that he isn't cut out for college. She told Martin to rent him an apartment on the mainland because our guests don't like to see tattoos and spiked hair, do they? It just doesn't fit the image of refinement we want to project. What a hypocrite. She used to smuggle marijuana when she was about Billy's age. Yes! She had her own boat, and she and Teddy Lindeman brought in bales of it. He was Joan Lindeman's other nephew, besides Doug. Lois only did it for a couple of years, but Teddy went on to cocaine, and they got him. He recently died in prison. So for Lois to be preaching to Billy about the image of The Buttonwood Inn makes me want to scream.

"Lois and I don't fight openly. We used to, but Martin couldn't stand it. He told her, 'Don't make me choose between you and my wife.' So she shut up about me. Now she's going after Billy. It was Lois who let Kyle know that Billy was in the hospital. It's obvious why she did it, to cause trouble. Her life was perfect until Billy and I showed up. She told Martin not to marry me because I only wanted his money, which was a filthy lie.

"I try not to bother Martin with this. He was so good when they arrested Billy four years ago. You know about it, don't you? It was an accident, but Anthony told us to go ahead and pay the owners of the house and tell them we were sorry it happened. Anthony saved Billy from going to prison, but now they suspect him of murder. I keep wondering, when will Martin decide it's enough? If he sent Billy away, I'd have to go too. I would.

"I have to remind myself, it's going to be all right. It has to. You and Anthony and Dr. Vogelhut will take care of Billy, the resort will reopen for business, and everything will be wonderful. Do you know it hasn't been twenty-four hours since all this happened? My head is spinning. I'm going to check on Billy, then maybe take a nap. I'd love to have you and Anthony join us for dinner, but we wouldn't be good company, I'm afraid."

"No, we couldn't anyway," Gail said. "We have to see Joan Sinclair tonight."

"What about tomorrow? We'll be recovered by then." Teri put her arm through Gail's. "May I ask Arnel to take you to Joan's house? You don't want to lose your way in the dark."

"We'd appreciate it, thanks." Gail said, "Arnel is a funny guy. I can't figure him out."

189

"Yes, I know what you mean," Teri said. "At first, I thought he was, well —" She touched the side of her head. "But he isn't. He's just very quiet. Plus the little problem with his speech. I don't even notice it anymore. He works hard and keeps to himself. I never worry about him around the guests. He's very smart. He fixes the engines and helps Martin with the palm trees. When he was a boy he lived on a farm."

"Indiana," Gail remembered.

"Arnel came here because of Joan Sinclair. That's the truth! He has every one of her movies. He found out where she was, and he hitchhiked all the way and begged us to give him a job so he could be near his favorite movie star."

"I think she takes advantage," Gail said. "He says she doesn't pay him."

"That I don't know about, but we pay him, and he stays in the caretaker's cottage for nothing. He can eat in the kitchen anytime he wants to. Don't feel bad about Arnel. He's very happy here."

Nearing the hotel, Teri led Gail through a gate in a wall of antique brick that seemed to be held up only by the banyan tree whose roots had dropped down over it like melting wax. Inside was the back entrance to the kitchen. A cart path entered through wide gates and ended in a circle. Men from the supply boat were carrying boxes and crates into a concrete-block storeroom. Cases of liquor and wine; boxes of linens and paper goods; new mattresses and rattan dining chairs still in their plastic wrap. There was no white clapboard here; this wasn't part of the fantasy.

Teri pointed to the gates. "If you go that way, you get to the main road. Your cottage is just a little bit farther."

"Thanks. We'll see you tomorrow," Gail said.

"Wait a minute, I want to tell you something." Teri walked her toward the gates, away from the men unloading the boxes. "It's about Joan. Do you want to hear it?"

"All right."

"I was in love with Martin, but I wasn't going to say so. I was nobody, one of the girls who cleaned the rooms. I could see that he noticed me, but he was so . . . so *American*. So proper. One day I took some mail over to Joan Sinclair — I used to do that for her — and she said, 'What's eating you?' So I told her, and I started to cry. She fixed me a martini — I hate martinis, but I drank it, and she said to tell Martin that I loved him so much that I had walked out on my husband, and what was he going

191

to do about it? Joan told me, 'A woman who ain't got the brass won't get her man.' I said no way could I do that. But a week or two went by, and one day I went to Martin's office. I closed the door behind me and said I was going to leave my husband for him, and if he wanted to marry me, okay, but if not, I was in love with him anyway, and I would sleep with him."

Teri laughed. "My God, the look on his face! He had to sit down. He said he felt the same, but he didn't believe I could love a man so much older, and with a bad heart. I said, 'No, you have a good heart, the best.' It's so crazy, isn't it? Joan came to our wedding. It was here at the hotel. She sat in the back and left before the reception. Nowadays we don't see her at all. I wish she had married Tom. They would have been happy together."

Saying good-bye, Teri gave Gail a warm embrace. "You and Anthony shouldn't wait too long. Things happen, you know."

The hotel staff had left a little gold box of chocolates on the nightstand. Gail took the box and her cell phone out onto the front porch and propped her bare feet on the railing. She bit into a mocha cream just as the phone was picked up on the other end.

"Hi, Mom, it's me. What's new?"

Her mother asked why she was calling again the same day. Was something wrong?

"Nothing's wrong, we're having a wonderful time. In fact, I'm sitting here with my feet up, looking at the water and eating Godiva chocolates and thinking very hard about getting down to work. . . . Anthony's not here at the moment. If he were, I wouldn't get *anything* done. . . . I called to ask if you'd seen the weather report. Looks like it might rain all weekend. I wonder if the Biscayne Bay clean-up has been canceled. Could you call Karen's school for me and find out? They would know, wouldn't they?"

Irene said she had already called. If the clean-up was canceled, the children from Karen's school, along with their chaperones, would be sent instead to Camillus House to make sandwiches for the homeless.

"Oh, damn. . . . No, it's just that I was hoping to stay over till Saturday afternoon. Mother, I wonder if you could possibly —"

No. So sorry, but no. There was an appointment at ten to have her hair done. Then a luncheon for Friends of the Opera. Then she wanted to visit Verna, who'd gone into the hospital again, and it didn't look good this time —

"Oh, God, I'm so sorry. Poor Verna."

A thought flashed into Gail's head. Karen could sleep over with Molly Perlmutter on Friday. Molly's mother was one of the volunteer mothers, too, and she wouldn't mind taking Karen. The girls were best friends. And if Irene could just drop Karen off at Molly's house —

Guilt slammed the door on that idea. Gail took her feet off the railing and put the chocolates aside. She told her mother to please give Verna her love, and tell Karen she'd call her later.

"I'll be home Friday night. Love you."

10

Anthony Quintana stood on the Buttonwood dock waiting for Thomas Holtz to answer the question just put to him. The old man's mouth was tight with indignation. He glared from behind his clip-on sunglasses.

"I was in the neighborhood, so I stopped by her apartment to say hello. What kind of crime is that? If you're implying I killed her, I resent the hell out it."

"You were not 'in the neighborhood,'" Anthony said. "You were parked outside her apartment waiting for her to come home. Listen. I'm trying to save Billy Fadden's skin. Who would you rather talk to, me or the police?"

Holtz slung his picnic hamper into his boat. Sun had dulled the fiberglass finish, and mildew spotted the seat cushions. "I never touched her in a sexual way. Hell, I never touched her in a *non*sexual way."

"What did you do with her?"

"Nothing! We did nothing." His voice faded. "She — She let me look at her."

After a pause, Anthony said, "Without her clothes on." Holtz nodded. "You gave her money for this."

"Yes."

"How long had you and she . . . had this relationship?"

Holtz passed a hand over his forehead. "I don't know. Three years. Except for when Joan and I were together."

"How did it start?"

"My wife was dying. Sandra . . . it was a little joke. I gave her some money and said . . . I said, 'Lift up your shirt.' " Holtz cleared his throat. He had shaved badly, and white hairs dappled his cheeks. "She was a waitress. It was in the parking lot behind the restaurant. We were both having a little fun."

"When did you start going to her apartment?"

"Not at first. She lived with her grandparents. Later on she got a place, but I didn't like going there. It made me nervous. Usually we sat in my car."

"Did she come to your office?"

"God, no. Not for that. She came on business for Buttonwood, but Doug handles most of that, so I didn't talk to her. I didn't avoid her, I just . . . all that other stuff was in a different place."

"You never had intercourse with her?"

"No. Look, I never hurt the girl. I certainly didn't kill her." Holtz steadied himself with a deep breath. "The night she died I was having some drinks at Papa Joe's. Ask the bartender, he knows me."

"When was the last time you were with Sandra?"

"That time I went by her place and somebody saw us, according to you. I know who it was. Had to be whoever dropped her off. Who was it? Arnel Goode?"

"I can't say."

"It was Arnel. Wouldn't you know it? The last time I'm there, someone spots me. The last time. She let me in long enough to tell me it was over. She said she was tired of it. Well, so was I. I was tired of the money going out."

"Did she have other men?"

"Others?"

"Did she make a habit of giving sex for money?"

"It never occurred to me."

"What about a boyfriend? Billy said she was having sex with someone. Who?"

Holtz shrugged. "I don't know. We didn't discuss it."

"What about Doug Lindeman?"

"Doug?" Holtz sputtered. "No way. She was a kid. I mean . . . Doug has a woman in Key West he's involved with. And one in Miami. And he has his hands full with the ladies he runs into at the resorts. Doug has a full life, you might say."

"Apparently so. Sandra never mentioned being interested in anyone?"

"We never talked about personal matters. We hardly talked at all. Girls that age don't have much upstairs, do they?"

Holtz was lying, but Anthony decided not to push. He changed directions. "You were going to be the lawyer of record in the guardianship case. Why do you believe that Joan Sinclair is incompetent?"

"I never believed that, but I could see she wasn't taking care of herself. I thought we could get Joan some help, at least wake her up. I'll tell you something, Quintana. I'm living dangerously today. Doug ordered me to stay away from Joan. He didn't want me giving her a head's-up, what he was doing." Holtz laughed without humor. "It's too late now. She knows, and she's not happy."

Anthony asked if Joan Sinclair had written a will.

"Not that I know of," Holtz replied.

"A person judged incompetent can't write a will, isn't that so?"

The man's heavy white brows drew together. "If you think Doug's after her money, you're wrong. Joan doesn't have any. Her house and land go to Martin Greenwald when she dies. The money she made in Hollywood, she lost. She's not a wealthy woman. You'll see that when you meet her tonight."

"And there is no cash or jewelry hidden under her mattress?"

"It must've dropped out of the sky, then."

"What does she live on? She's too young for social security."

"There's a dribble of royalties from her movies and TV shows, about eight thousand dollars a year. Her agent sends me the checks, and I put them in her bank account. I've been doing this for Joan ever since she came back from California. When we split up — and it was her decision, not mine — she never asked me to give back her deposit slips." Tom Holtz had more to say; unsure whether to say it, he looked at Anthony awhile before he spoke.

"Joan gets some money from . . . oh, I guess you'd say from a trust set up by her

199

nephew, Teddy Lindeman. His dad was killed in Vietnam. Joan and Teddy were pretty close."

Anthony remembered what Gail had told him. "Teddy Lindeman was convicted of cocaine smuggling and sentenced to federal prison. He died of lung cancer."

"That's right, this past June. He got ten years instead of twenty because he cooperated with the government. He gave me enough to take care of Joan until he got out, but there's not much left. When it's gone, it's gone. Doug doesn't know about it. No one does."

Where Teddy Lindeman had obtained the money, Anthony could guess. It had almost certainly been in the form of cash, and probably delivered in a briefcase or a gym bag. "How much did Teddy give you?"

"A hundred thousand. He told me to give her ten a year. I've been the family lawyer for a long time. Teddy trusted me to handle it properly. I mail her an accounting every quarter. I figure out her taxes. I don't charge her anything." Finally Holtz began to worry if he had said too much. "If you'd forget you heard this, I'd appreciate it."

"Of course."

"You wanted to know what she lives on," Holtz said. "That's it. I'd pay out of my pocket if she ever needed anything, but she has a history of pushing me away." He looked out at the Keys on the horizon as if puzzled to find himself on this side of the water. "She jilted me twice. The first time we were kids, and she decided to seek fame and fortune in Hollywood. I was crazy about that girl. God, how I loved her. I was in law school when she gave my ring back. We could've had a good life together, but she said she just had to give acting a try. Joan had some early success, but it fizzled out. Twenty-five years later, she dragged herself home, not in too good a shape, either, what I heard. Over the years I'd see her in town, and we'd say hello, or she might drop by my office to sign something, but that was rare. When Mary, my wife, passed away I grieved, but she'd been sick for a long time. One day I got the nerve to call Joan. I said, 'Hi, guess who? And guess whose birthday this is? Yours. How about I take you out for a steak dinner?' She said, 'You old son of a bitch, it was last week, but I forgive you. You come on over with those steaks, and we'll grill out on the dock and watch the sun go down. And bring me some champagne. Something expensive.

I've just turned sixty, and I damned well deserve it.' "

Chuckling to himself, Tom Holtz glanced down at the wicker hamper in his boat. "I took her some Perrier-Jouet with the flowers on the bottle, same as I brought her today. She was waiting on the dock in a pair of old blue jeans. Her hair was gray. I expected a glamorous movie star, but she was just herself. Joanie. That's all. She said, 'Tom, I've been on this god-forsaken rock long enough to find out who I am. If you're looking for Joan Sinclair, you might as well get back in your boat and shove off.' I said, 'No, you'll do just fine.' A couple of months later I asked her to marry me. She started packing her things. Then a week later, she called me and said she'd changed her mind. I still don't know why. I shouldn't have backed down. I should've — Hell, I should've marched over to that damned house and dragged her out of it."

Spent, he rested his fingers on his forehead and let out a long sigh. "Maybe there is something wrong with her. I'll tell you one thing, she doesn't need to be put in an institution. That is not going to happen."

Footsteps sounded on the planks in the dock, and Anthony turned around. Kyle

Fadden, his billed cap pulled low, had just walked over to a fishing skiff tied a few yards away. He untied the lines, pretending not to see the two men standing nearby.

Holtz whispered, "Who is that fellow?" He flipped up his sunglasses. "I know him as well as I know my own name."

"Billy's father, Kyle Fadden."

"So it is." Holtz called out, "Kyle! What brings you here?" Walking stiffly, sway-backed, he went over to find out. His clip-ons were upside down on his forehead.

Fadden gathered up a line and tossed it to the deck of his boat. "I came to see Billy."

"Oh, Jeez. Sure you did. He's doing all right, though. I ran into Teri. She said he's okay."

"Yeah, he's okay."

"Do you fellows know each other?" Holtz held out an arm in Anthony's direction.

"We've met," Fadden said, untying the other line. He gave Anthony a quick nod, then stepped onto his boat and turned the key. His engine coughed and sputtered to life, then settled down to a throb.

Holtz spoke loudly to be heard. "When are we going out for some yellowtail?"

"You know my number." Kyle Fadden

gave them a salute and turned the wheel. The boat rumbled away from the dock on a widening wake and the faint blue haze of exhaust.

"He's a damned good guide. A natural fisherman, best I've seen. I don't go out like I used to, though. I passed Kyle off to Doug. Doug's only problem is, he doesn't put in the time. Well. I'd better get back. Untie that line over there, will you?"

Bending to take the line off the cleat, Anthony said, "Tom, I have a question. It's about the case four years ago, when Billy Fadden was arrested for arson."

Tom Holtz stepped into his boat and felt around in his pants pocket for his keys. Anthony repeated, "Billy was arrested for burning down a house in Islamorada."

"Yes, I remember. What's the question?"

"You know the owners, the Morgans. That was why Martin asked you to handle the settlement negotiations with them."

"They've moved away," Holtz said.

"All right, but four years ago you knew them. Correct? Were you aware of any dispute or argument existing between the Morgans and someone Billy knew? His father, for example?"

Thomas Holtz stood with his arms folded over his stomach. The sunglasses were still up, and his eyes registered confusion. "That's a funny question. I'm not sure I follow."

How to explain to this man? How, when his own mind was teeming with contradictions? Anthony said, "I believe that the fire was an accident. Billy was filling the gasoline tank while the lawn mower was running. A stupid thing to do, but he was fifteen. However, Billy had at that time some severe psychological problems — as he does now. You are aware of all this. The Morgans were on good terms with Billy, but were they angry at someone Billy cared about? A friend? His mother or father? Even Martin Greenwald?"

Holtz stared back at him.

Anthony said, "If it wasn't an accident, where is the motive?"

That brought a short laugh. "Why did he burn their house? I'll tell you why. He wanted to see something go up in smoke, and Hal and Betsy's house was convenient. They never did anything to that boy. They were the sweetest people you'd want to meet. I'm sorry to say this, but Billy Fadden scares the hell out of me. He never showed the slightest remorse for destroying a home and everything those people took a lifetime to accumulate."

205

Standing at the wheel, Thomas Holtz turned the key, and the engine sputtered to life. He let it run, then turned back to Anthony.

"I hope that Billy was with Joan when Sandra was murdered. I pray he was, but I'm not going to stand here and say he couldn't have done it. He confessed. Maybe he's psychotic, and he *thought* he killed her. Maybe he's playing with us, and he confessed to see if he could get away with it like he did last time. Let me tell you. He could have strangled Sandra just like he spilled that gasoline. No more thought behind it than a desire to see what it feels like."

At the cottage, Anthony stood at the bottom of the steps, a hand on the stair rail, feeling curiously fatigued. What was it? Lack of sleep? His age catching up with him? Not that, because only last week he had run up four flights of stairs at the federal courthouse to avoid a slow elevator. What, then? He wondered if fatigue was a sign of something more ominous. He felt his pulse. Normal.

Disgusted with himself for such thoughts, he trotted up the steps. He found the front door open for the breeze and Gail at the desk in the living room. Her files were stacked beside her, and her fingers flew on her laptop keyboard. He picked up the Godiva chocolate box and raised the lid. Empty.

"You didn't save me any?"

"Not one. And they were *so good*." She lifted her face to be kissed. "I'll make it up to you later."

He tossed the box back on the desk and took a look at her computer screen. She was working on a complaint in a commercial lending case. "How exciting."

"Well, you weren't around, and I needed some fun." She saved her work and turned around in her chair. "What did Tom Holtz have to say?"

"He admits he was the man Arnel saw, but he says he didn't kill Sandra. He has an alibi. We could check it out, but I believe him."

"They were sleeping together?"

"Not exactly."

"Meaning . . . what?"

"For three years he paid Sandra to let him see her naked. He never touched her."

With a grimace Gail said, "Oh, that's *bizarre*. Three years? If he didn't touch her, what did they do?"

"I did not ask."

Gail reached for Anthony's shirt and pulled him closer. "Did she talk dirty to him?"

Against her lips he murmured, "I'm sure she did. What do you think she said?"

"She said . . . 'Oh, Daddy, you make me soooo hot.' "

"Not bad. Keep going."

" 'I want to roll you in sugar and lick it off.' "

He smiled. "Sugar?"

"Okay, then. Melted, amaretto-flavored, bittersweet chocolate."

"*Qué sabroso.*"

"I could turn off the computer."

He kissed the top of her head. "No, keep working. I'll tell you everything later. Right now I'm going to find someone to take me to Islamorada. Doug Lindeman is in his office. I want to ask him about his aunt before we meet her."

"You're going by yourself?"

Anthony gave a little shrug. "It doesn't take two of us to ask one question."

Gail's blue eyes stared up at him.

"Sweetheart, you want to help me, and I sincerely appreciate it, but go ahead and finish your work. I don't want to hear you complaining that you never have enough time."

Her mouth opened, and a little laugh of disbelief came out, before she said, "Anthony, do you ever *listen* to yourself? That is the most condescending, patronizing —"

"*Ay, Dios mío.*"

"It's not that I'm *insisting* on going with you, but it would be nice if you *asked.*"

"Gail, I don't have an appointment. Lindeman hasn't returned my phone calls. To try to see him will probably waste the rest of the afternoon, and you told me you had to work. Didn't you tell me that?" She said nothing. Anthony let out a breath. "Do you want to go with me, Ms. Connor?"

"I'd love to. Thank you." She stood up and put her arms around his neck. "Since you've been so agreeable, I'm going to share a totally useless piece of information with you. This is from Teri. Her sister-in-law, the lovely and charming Lois Greenwald, used to smuggle marijuana. She and Doug Lindeman's cousin, Teddy, who later went to prison for importing cocaine."

"*No me digas.*"

"Don't you love it? I'm billing you a whole hour for that one."

Anthony called Martin Greenwald to see about getting to Islamorada. Martin said he would take them himself. They agreed to meet in the lobby in half an hour.

This gave Gail and Anthony time to change into something they could wear to a law office without looking like tourists. Having expected to do nothing serious on this trip, Gail had only her sleeveless dress with the tropical flowers. It wouldn't have worked in the city, but it would do for the Keys.

She put on her makeup and related her conversation with Teri Greenwald, a woman whose life had veered between horrific and hopeful and now hung suspended while her son was suspected of murder. How her sister-in-law plotted to ruin her. How she loved her husband but feared she would lose him to a heart attack or to a fate nearly as bad: indifference. He would grow tired of it all.

Touching up her mascara, Gail could sense Anthony's attention wandering. As she described Teri's quandary, Anthony searched through his shaving kit for his comb. He wasn't in the mood for domestic drama.

Anthony said the main goal at present was to find out why Douglas Lindeman thought his aunt was incompetent. If he had a good reason, it meant trouble.

Sooner or later, even if Joan Sinclair swore that Billy had been with her when Sandra McCoy's throat was cut, the police — or even worse, a jury — would wonder.

Anthony leaned closer to the mirror and turned his head slightly. The gray was beginning to show at his temples. He noticed Gail watching him and went back to his list of things to do. Find someone at the Blue Water Marina who remembered seeing Billy Fadden get into his boat and head south toward Lindeman Key between seven-thirty and eight p.m. on October third. If Billy couldn't get an alibi from Joan, he would need a backup. And lastly, since Gail had brought her camera, she could take some photographs of the crime scene.

Anthony put away his comb and turned off the bathroom light.

When they reached the lobby of the hotel, Martin Greenwald was just coming down the stairs. He was dressed for going out in a boat, wearing shorts and leather deck shoes. Gail thought his hangdog face looked a little more rested than it had three hours ago. His heavy eyebrows lifted when he saw her, and he took her hand.

"Teri says you're working with Anthony

211

now. He's calling in reinforcements, is he?"

"We have a lot to do before tomorrow," Anthony said. "If Joan Sinclair will make a statement in the afternoon, we hope to get Billy cleared at the same time. Martin, do you own a gun?" He explained what Billy had said this morning, that he might have tried to shoot himself with Martin's gun, but wasn't sure. He could have imagined it.

Martin said he had a rifle upstairs and a .38 revolver in the office.

"Would you mind checking to see if the revolver is there?"

They followed him around a corner past the front desk, into a side hall, then through a door into an uncluttered room whose color scheme ranged from gray to paler gray. A glossy, poster-size photograph of The Buttonwood Inn at sunset, taken from half a mile out, provided the only clue that this office was not in a government building. A woman of about sixty with glasses sliding down her nose sat at a desk with a calculator. She glanced up, said, "Hi, Martin," and went back to her work.

Lois had a telephone at her ear, walking back and forth as far as the cord would allow. Her dress was long and loose, with a pattern of white cartoon fish to relieve the funereal black. She was saying, "Yes, I understand. It's no problem at all. . . . We'll run the credit through immediately. Goodbye. We hope to see you another time." She hung up. "Damn it."

Her brother asked her what was going on.

She smiled at him. "Oh, some of the guests are a little nervous about the weather. Don't worry. We've transferred most of them to other open dates. And no, I'm not returning any deposits."

Martin nodded absently, less like the owner than an outsider, as comfortable here as he would be if he'd stumbled into the ladies' room. He said, "Lois, I need to check on something in the back, all right?"

"Certainly." Lois followed him with her eyes, then said to Anthony, "I'm sorry that our regular shuttle service won't resume till Sunday."

"Not a problem," Anthony replied.

When Martin came back, he asked Lois if she had seen his gun, the .38 they kept in the file drawer.

"No, Martin, I haven't. It's not there? Where else would it be? We keep that drawer locked."

"Billy found the key," Martin said.

"My God." Alarmed, Lois clutched at her heart through the fabric of her dress. "Well, get the gun back from him. Martin, what's he going to do with it?"

"Calm down. He doesn't have it. He took it with him last night to Joan's dock and dropped it somewhere, or threw it. He can't remember."

"We have to find it."

"We will, we will. As soon as I get back, I'll take a look. Let me have the keys to my boat, will you?"

"Martin, don't go." She put her hand to his cheek. "You should rest. You've been up all night. I can take them to the marina." Even with more than ten years between them, their faces echoed in the prominent nose and thin lips. Under the blond streaks her hair was brown, and his was the same shade, though it was going gray and he'd lost most of it.

"I'm fine," he said. "It would do me good to get some fresh air."

In reproachful silence she went to a desk in the far corner and opened a drawer.

Gail murmured to Anthony, "Could you guys go ahead to the boat? I'd like to talk to Lois." Anthony raised a brow. "I'll be right there," she said.

He glanced at his watch. "Five minutes."

Returning, Lois handed her brother a key ring with an orange plastic float attached. When the men were out the door, Gail said, "Lois, I know you're busy, but I have a question about Sandra McCoy."

"Are you working for Mr. Quintana? You said you weren't."

"Well, now I am. He asked me to help out."

"Please don't tell me we have to pay you too."

Gail smiled at her. "Anthony's taking care of my fees." She glanced at the woman still clicking away on a calculator. "Could we talk privately?"

Lois led her to the same office from which Martin Greenwald had emerged a minute earlier. Lois's desk was as plain as those in the front office. A bulletin board on one wall tracked cottages, rooms, and reservations in multiple colors of ink. Lois remained standing, a hint for Gail to ask her question then be off.

"We've found out that Joan Lindeman's nephew, Douglas, paid a thousand dollars to Sandra McCoy to run errands for his aunt. What he was probably doing was gathering information to use against Joan Lindeman in the petition for guardianship. Were you aware of this?"

Lois Greenwald blinked a few times, then said, "A thousand dollars? I wasn't aware of the amount. I was aware that he asked her to take care of Joan, in a manner of speaking. Delivering meals. Seeing if she needed anything."

"Do you happen to know how long Sandra had been doing this?"

Lois's pale green eyes went blank for a moment before she said, "About two months, perhaps a little longer."

"So that works out to five hundred a month."

"Yes," Lois said, "it does. What is your point?"

"That it's a lot of money for running errands."

Since hearing about Tom Holtz's strange relationship with Sandra McCoy, Gail had realized that this had been a girl with a creative approach to morality. A girl who, according to Billy Fadden, was going out with a man whose name she wouldn't divulge. So who was this guy? Maybe the one who was paying Sandra McCoy an exorbitant amount for her services — whatever they were.

"How old is Douglas Lindeman?"

"Thirty-six. Why do you ask?"

"I was wondering if perhaps there could

have been something between him and Sandra. Of a romantic nature, I mean. Is that possible?"

With a small laugh of surprise, Lois Greenwald said, "No. It's not possible. Doug and I are very close. We're engaged, in fact. He wasn't involved with Sandra. I would know, believe me."

"Oh, I'm sorry, I didn't realize —" Gail smiled an apology even as her mind groped to find where her theory had gone wrong.

"Douglas lost his fiancée last year, and he's still in mourning." Lois whispered, "I'm helping him work through it. He says I'm indispensable to his recovery."

"Really." Gail studied the deep lines in Lois Greenwald's sun-splotched skin, the bony knobs of her collarbone.

"We aren't *officially* engaged, but I'm sure it will happen for us. Do you believe in fate, Ms. Connor?"

"I . . . suppose so."

"I have a psychic reader in Key Largo that I go to. She says that when two people are meant to be together, they will be. Doug and I are destined to spend the rest of our lives together, so if he needs a little extra time to work out his issues, I can be patient."

"Well. Congratulations," Gail said, though

217

unsure if this was the proper sentiment in the circumstances.

"Thank you." Lois Greenwald's face softened with pleasure, and a blush tinted her angular cheekbones.

Gail thought of something else. Time was pressing on her, and Anthony might already be picking out what words he would toss her way when she got to the boat, but she couldn't keep from asking Lois, "Two years ago, Joan Sinclair was going to sell her property to your brother, but she changed her mind. Do you know why?"

"Her life estate," Lois corrected. "She doesn't really *own* the property. No, I haven't the slightest idea why she decided not to sell. Martin was heartbroken. He had planned to have a palm nursery and garden. We wanted to put in walking paths and some very exclusive cottages. It would've been beautiful." After a pause, Lois added, "I think Joan did it for spite. This whole island used to belong to her family. She can't stand the fact that her brother sold it to Martin instead of leaving it to her."

There was a clock on the wall behind Lois, but Gail didn't want to look.

"It's my understanding that Sandra's

work here wasn't satisfactory. And you were planning to let her go? What was the problem?"

Lois had a cold little smile that could have scooped ice cream. "She was lazy. Devious. Flippant. She dressed too provocatively for the Inn, these short little skirts that showed her navel! I was within a few days of firing her. She thought she was doing us a favor, working here. She was routinely late. Sometimes she'd call Billy to come pick her up. He would've jumped off the roof if she'd said to. He was always tagging around after her, always watching. What do you think was going on in his head? I'm very much afraid that you and Mr. Quintana are going to end up right where you started. Billy said he killed her. Maybe he meant it."

Thirty seconds later, running down the front steps of the hotel with her purse bouncing and a shoe in each hand, Gail silently repeated the question that she hadn't asked, wouldn't have dared to ask, even if there had been time.

Where were you, Lois, when Sandra McCoy was dragged into the dark and murdered?

11

Anthony sat with Martin Greenwald under the white canvas top of a twenty-eight-foot Sea Ray twin inboard. Employees at the resort were few this week, but Martin had found one, and had told him to bring the boat down from its lift in the boathouse. The young man was waiting on the dock, ready to let go the lines as soon as Ms. Connor was aboard.

The boss wore a faded khaki fishing hat secured under his chin by a wooden knob, a long-sleeved shirt with air vents, and a fraying pair of hiking shorts. His legs were tanned nearly as dark as his deck shoes, whose leather laces were pieced together. Except for the Rolex and expensive prescription sunglasses he might have been mistaken for one of the local fishermen. His speech was laconic, his movements deliberate and slow. Creases scored his long, solemn face. Those who didn't know him might think he lacked a sense of humor.

Martin was telling Anthony about Joan Sinclair's trips to the Lindeman family graveyard. He had last taken her there in the spring.

"There's a routine for this, you see. We leave the boat at the marina, and then we go by the florist to pick up some roses. She buys them wrapped in cellophane, and not a few of them, every last rose in the shop. She says, 'Why don't you have *more?* Is this *all?*' and the clerk says, 'Well, Miss Sinclair, if you had called first —' Joan likes the red ones best. Then we drive over to the graveyard. I sit on a bench under a tree outside the fence. She dresses like a widow at a Mafia funeral, right down to the black gloves and stockings and a hat with a veil. She crosses herself, and she's not even Catholic. You'd swear it's a movie."

"Where is this graveyard?" Anthony asked.

"Go past Mile Marker 86 and turn into the Bay Harbor Resort. You'll see it from the road. Old man Lindeman, Harry and Joan's father, used to own the property, and he sold it on condition the graveyard be kept up. He's buried out there. It's a pretty little place, about half the size of a tennis court."

221

Something caught Martin's attention. He looked through the crack between his sunglasses and the brim of his hat. "That woman sure has a lot of energy."

Anthony turned to see Gail in her pink dress rushing along the path from the hotel. At the dock she put on her shoes, balancing on one foot, then the other. She smiled and waved. Anthony lifted his arm and tapped his watch. When she reached the boat he helped her aboard. "You said five minutes."

"No, *you* said five minutes." She apologized to Martin for running late.

"As long as you're running, it's okay," he said. "Sit there next to me. Make that ugly boyfriend of yours sit in the back." Anthony took the seat directly behind Gail's. She made an air kiss in his direction. Martin turned one key, then the other, and the engines purred to life.

Crossing to Islamorada, he kept the boat moving slowly, steadily toward shore. Martin was rarely in a hurry. The wind teased Gail's hair around her face. She chatted with the captain about palm trees. He had recently acquired a *Pelagodoxa henryana* from the Marquesas Islands, very rare. The baby was only two feet tall, but was doing nicely. She might also enjoy the sealing-wax palm, with its shiny, bright-red leafstalk.

Gail showed an interest in the subject that Anthony had not known she possessed. Raptly she listened to Martin explain the difference between *pinnate* and *palmate* leaf structure. Anthony sat so that the sun warmed his back and he could look at Gail's face. He loved looking at her: the soft skin, the dusting of gold at her hairline, delicately arching eyebrows, a small chin, and a nose that turned up. Her upper lip protruded slightly farther than its mate, and at any moment her mouth could curve into a smile. The light made her squint, but she held her sunglasses in her lap. Anthony wondered if she did this to let Martin Greenwald see her eyes, which were the blue-gray of dawn, a color any man could admire. An irritating thought.

He slid his hand up her arm and caressed the back of her neck.

Martin recommended a lady palm for her office. Better still, a *Chameadorea metallica*, a hardy but well-mannered plant. He would give her one to take home.

She said, "Martin, when we saw Tom Holtz today, he mentioned that you had planned to grow palm trees on the other side of the island. Do you still want to?"

"I wouldn't mind, but Joan Sinclair is living there, you know. I was going to start a nursery for rare species, but it would have been more of an ego thing than a sensible investment. We've put the money into improvements in the facilities instead."

"What about Lois? She had hoped to build on the other side?"

"Yes, some two-story guest houses, but development laws have been tightened to the point that's no longer possible. Last winter Lois worked out a deal to lease the dock, but Joan backed out. I said never mind, what's the point of getting excited about things you have no control over?"

"Why did Lois want her dock?" Gail asked.

"For bigger boats. Our harbor is only four feet, which is plenty for boats like this one, but the big boys could scrape bottom. Sailboats are out of the question. The state won't let us dredge, but over on Joan's side, it's ten feet, with a natural channel out to the Florida Straits."

"You have shuttle service to the marina. Don't people leave their boats there?"

"They do, but they don't like it. Would you? While you're cruising, the boat is your home. You don't want to leave it at the marina, pay them a docking fee, and move your stuff into a cottage. You'd rather tie up to our dock and pay three hundred a day for full use of The Buttonwood Inn facilities."

"I see. The resort makes more money that way?"

"Not from the dockage, particularly, but if we can accommodate yachts, we attract a different class of people. There are many, many people with serious money. If you're in that group, and you want a tropical island experience where you can feel safe, where the food is first-rate, and there's a major city not too far away, and you can spend U.S. dollars and not get ripped off, and also — forgive me — where you don't have to worry about impoverished people begging for handouts — If you want all that, where do you go? That attitude may not be popular, but there it is. Lois wants the dock, but Joan refuses. For myself, honestly? I don't care. I've been around people with that kind of wealth, and they tend to expect too damned much. Hell, I'd have to shave every day and wear socks."

Gail smiled.

"Now, what are all these questions about?" Martin asked, glancing at Anthony as well. His gentle humor was coupled with quick intelligence.

Guessing where Gail was going with this, Anthony let her answer, but it was not the direction he had expected.

"We're looking for the reason Doug Lindeman wants a guardianship. If he controls his aunt's property he could sell it or lease it to you."

"Oh, I don't think that's going to happen. Joan Sinclair might be eccentric, but is she legally incompetent? I doubt it."

"Let's assume a judge did grant the petition. Wouldn't Doug make you a very good deal? He'd do it for Lois, wouldn't he?" Gail looked around at Anthony, triumph in her eyes. "Doug is in love with her."

"*Coño.*"

Martin laughed. "Where did you hear that?"

"From Lois. I just talked to her." As Martin shook his head, Gail added, "She didn't actually use the words 'in love,' but that's what she meant. She said they were probably going to get married."

"Good God." Martin lifted his hands from the wheel, then let them drop. "I knew she had a thing for Doug Lindeman, but not that it was reciprocal. My sister is full of surprises."

Gail turned her head toward Anthony and raised her brows. He read her mind: It

226

could have been Lois's idea to file the guardianship, and Doug had gone along. It was a theory, but not one they could use. The question remained: Would the police believe Joan Sinclair if she provided an alibi for Billy?

A pelican glided across the bow. Martin pulled back on the throttles, slowing the boat as they neared the marina. He said, "I'm going to drive to a doctor's appointment in Key Largo. I should be back around five-thirty, and if you want to hitch a ride home, give a call and I'll wait for you. Otherwise, we'll send someone to pick you up."

Gail stood to see through the windscreen. "Martin, I've got a question about Sandra McCoy. Maybe you can answer it."

"I'll try," he said.

"Why was Lois going to fire her?"

"You've got me already. Ask Lois. Whatever happens in the day-to-day operation of the resort, that's her bailiwick. I really didn't know Sandra. I've learned that if you have a manager, it's good policy not to become too familiar with the employees. They start running to you to intervene." He steered the boat around the breakwater. "I work in my garden. I put on some classical music. I don't get ulcers."

Gail had come to a dead end. Frowning, she put on her sunglasses and watched as Martin wound his way through the maze of boat slips. They passed a smaller boat, and Martin raised a hand to its occupants, who waved back. The boat moved steadily toward the Buttonwood Key dock, where a marina worker was waiting to help them tie up.

"Martin." Gail looked at him over her sunglasses. "When Detective Baylor came to the resort investigating Sandra's death, did he want to know where everyone was when she died? Did he ask about that?"

She was out of reach, or Anthony might have yanked her back into her seat. He had an idea what the next question would be.

"Oh, sure." Martin was concentrating on the steadily diminishing distance between dock and boat. He adjusted the wheel. "They wanted to know when Sandra had left that day, who she went to see, who her friends and enemies were. I couldn't offer them much."

"Where did Lois say she was at the time?"

Martin looked around at Gail, then back at the dock just in time to throw the throttle into reverse. Water churned at the rear of the boat.

Anthony let out a breath between his teeth.

She heard; her eyes shifted toward him behind her sunglasses. She started backpedalling with Martin. "I'm filling in the blanks, that's all. If Joan Sinclair gets Billy off the hook, the police will start looking for someone else. We should be prepared. We need to know who was where in case they start asking."

The boat dipped when a man stepped onto the bow to retrieve the line. Martin shut down the engines, removed the keys, and slid them into his pocket. He sat once again and turned toward his companions. He laced his fingers and spoke in his quiet, unhurried way.

"Teri and I were having dinner in our apartment upstairs between seven o'clock and eight, at which time the housekeeper came to clear the table. You may ask her if you wish. Lois was in a meeting at Doug Lindeman's office until shortly after eight o'clock, after which she returned to the resort. I spoke to her around nine-thirty when I went down to the library for a book. I understand that you would like to direct the police away from Billy, but I did not retain you to accuse another member of my family." Behind the dark glasses, his eyes were on Anthony.

"No one is accusing Lois," Anthony said. "You asked me to help Billy. To do that, we need to know at least as much as the police do."

Weighing that, Martin said, "I expect to be kept informed. If you have anything to say to Detective Baylor, I want to know about it first."

"That may not always be possible, Martin. You aren't the client. Billy is."

He looked for a while longer at Anthony, not liking what he'd heard, but finally he pushed himself out of his captain's chair. "All right. I'll be back later. Call and let me know if you need a ride."

They stood beside Anthony's Cadillac under the long awning set aside for The Buttonwood Inn. Gail couldn't see his eyes behind his sunglasses but it was obvious he had something to say. His lips were pressed together to hold it in. He was waiting for Martin Greenwald to get into a Jeep Cherokee and head out of the marina parking lot.

She spoke before he let go. "Anthony, before you say anything — You and I both suspect that Doug Lindeman was sleeping with Sandra McCoy. What if Lois Green-

230

wald was so jealous that —"

"*Oyeme.*" He held up a forefinger to silence her. "You shouldn't have raised the issue of Lois's guilt without first discussing it with me."

"How could I? I just talked to her!"

"Then you say nothing. You *wait.*"

"Anthony, I wanted to have Lois's alibi before we talk to Lindeman. You'd have done the same."

"You don't make that decision! I do!" He ripped off his sunglasses to glare at her, dropped them, then glanced around as he picked them up, to see how many boat owners or fishermen were watching this petty display of temper. No one.

Gail said, "If you didn't want me involved, you shouldn't have hired me. Since you have, I expect to be treated as an equal partner, with due respect for my abilities as a lawyer and as a person with some intelligence."

"Five dollars an hour! *¿Qué tú crees?* This makes you an equal partner?"

"You're a lucky man we aren't still on the boat. I would probably shove you overboard."

"You start questioning my client without any warning, without asking me —"

"Martin Greenwald isn't your client.

231

Billy is. Did you not just say that to Martin?"

"You were wrong, Gail. Admit it." He lowered his head to look at her straight on. With one finger he pushed her sunglasses down the bridge of her nose.

She felt her fingernails dig into the straw of her handbag. She thought of hiring a boat to take her back to The Buttonwood Inn. No, a bus to Miami. She smiled at him. "I remember now why I didn't take a job at your law firm last year when you offered. It's your attitude. Your way or no way."

"Screw my attitude, you were wrong. Admit it."

"Okay. Fine. I was wrong."

"Thank you."

"And screw you for being such a jerk."

They looked at each other.

She said, "Are you going to be mad at me the rest of the week?"

He put his sunglasses back on and took his car keys out of his pocket. "Forget it. Let's go talk to Lindeman. We don't have much time."

"You still want me to go with you?"

"What do you think?" He opened her door for her. "Talk to me on the way. Tell me what other surprises you have."

"I think that was it," she said.

The fog of rage had lifted far enough for her to see that Anthony wasn't angry that she had been *wrong* in her theory. He was ticked off about having to take the heat from Martin Greenwald. He could have deflected it off on Gail, but he hadn't. When he got in the other side, she said, "Thank you for not screaming at me in front of Martin. You aren't a total jerk."

"Gracias." He started the car.

"Are we — Excuse me, are *you* going to follow up with Doug Lindeman on this issue of Lois and Sandra?"

Anthony sat there with the engine idling. "I want to know one thing from Lindeman. Is Joan Sinclair crazy? If she is, I won't waste our time taking her to see Detective Baylor. Maybe Billy has somebody else who can vouch for him, maybe not. I will send my investigators here next week, and they can interview everyone and his dog. This wasn't supposed to be complicated. I don't want to get involved any further in this fucking case. It was supposed to be a vacation, and I don't know what I'm doing here. You were right, wanting to leave on Friday. Tonight we see Vampira, tomorrow we talk to the police — or not — and after that, we thank Teri and Martin for the very

233

nice time and get the hell out of here."

Gail turned and put her hand on his arm. "Anthony, what's wrong? Do you want to go somewhere and talk about it?"

"*No, no, y no.* I want to get this over with."

Holtz and Lindeman, P.A. was in a one-story, concrete-block building on U.S. 1. Gravel bed with cactus for landscaping. Tile roof, blue awnings over the windows, and a carport at one end with four spaces. In the space marked LINDEMAN, a silver BMW with a rusting dent in one fender. A vanity plate: KEYSLAW, no doubt meant to read "Keys Law," but it made Gail think of shredded cabbage.

Douglas Lindeman had wavy, sun-bleached hair, a mouth too ripe for his short, upturned nose, and freckles, lots of them. His office had the expected book-shelves, corner seating area, two client chairs, and a desk, behind which sat the lawyer. On the wall to his right hung a stuffed fish that looked like a blue plastic pool toy. Gail had never seen the point of this; the equivalent of a stuffed moose head, she supposed.

Her attention went back to the man at the desk. Yellow knit shirt, gold necklace, a nice chest. A little soft around the middle, but Gail was accustomed to Anthony's middle, so she was picky. Doug Lindeman could have been the former star quarterback at the local high school, who got his excitement these days driving up to Miami with his buddies for lap dances at the strip bars on South Dixie Highway.

She tried to imagine him and Lois Greenwald naked together in bed, and couldn't see it. She wondered if Lois had unusual talents. Anthony had told her on the way here that Doug Lindeman liked to hang out at the upscale resorts to pick up female tourists. She doubted that Lois knew about it.

Gail tuned back in just as Lindeman was saying, "My great-grandparents built that house out of solid mahogany. Aunt Joan spent time in the house as a kid, I guess that's why she decided to live there. On breaks from law school I'd go out to visit her. You asked what she was like. Sorry to be so blunt, but she was a drunk. Skinny, foul-mouthed, stumbling around the house, babbling about her movies and her lousy directors and her lousy ex-husbands.

"My Dad said, 'Joan came home to die.' She didn't die, which surprised us all, but I think the alcohol affected her brain. You'll see. She sits in her house with the curtains drawn and watches movies. She's afraid to go out in the daytime. I'd be interested to know what you find in her refrigerator. It makes my stomach turn to see that fine old house go to ruin."

Doug Lindeman leaned on his elbow. His arms were as freckled as his face. "There's a guy that helps her out, Arnel Goode, but he's useless. Have you met him yet? You have? He's a weird one, isn't he? Get this. Aunt Joan told me why Arnel stutters. When he was a kid his family owned a farm in Indiana. He saw one of the farm workers fall into a grain auger. That's a big pipe with a steel screw inside that moves the corn from place to place. Aunt Joan didn't go into details, but you can imagine what came out the other end of the auger. She said Arnel couldn't speak at all for months afterward."

Gail and Anthony exchanged a look.

Lindeman said, "Don't get me wrong. I like Arnel. He's completely devoted to Aunt Joan, but this is the person she's relying on for her sustenance and care? He's a handyman, not a nurse. He told me he does what he can, but she's not always easy to get along with. I tried to see Aunt Joan a few months ago to make sure she was okay, but she told me to go away. God, it was so sad. I hate to see her like this. She needs some help, she really does. I'm not going to put her in a hospital. I want to find a nice apartment for her with people her own age."

He noticed his watch and stood up. "Golly, look at the time. I hate to do this, but I've got a client coming in soon."

Not moving from his chair, Anthony glanced over at Gail. "Is there anything you want to ask about?" His eyebrows lifted, inviting her to go ahead, what the hell, nothing to lose.

"Well, I was wondering about Sandra McCoy. You knew her, didn't you?"

"Yes, she worked for The Buttonwood Inn."

"You asked her to run errands and keep an eye on your aunt. Sandra told one of her coworkers that you paid her a thousand dollars, and I'm assuming you paid her in cash, over a space of about two months. Is that right?"

Lindeman focused on Gail. "I don't know. Possibly. That amount of money isn't so much when you're talking about peace of mind. I can't get out there as often as I'd like, and frankly, I was worried about Aunt Joan. I'm still worried."

"How did you happen to hire Sandra?"

"Well, I needed someone already at the resort. I'd met Sandra, and she seemed like a responsible young lady. Lois Greenwald gave her a good reference, so I asked her to help me out. She already knew Aunt Joan and was very sympathetic."

"How did that work? I know that Sandra often came here to your office on business for The Buttonwood Inn, delivering papers and so forth. Is that when you paid her?"

"I . . . I guess so." He spread his hands. "Is there some point to this?"

"I'm just trying to figure things out. Excuse me for asking such a personal question, but . . . did you and Sandra have more than a business relationship?"

He stared at Gail, then made a single laugh. "No."

"Sorry. I suppose the police interviewed you after her murder?"

He let out a breath, showing how patient he was. "Yes, they did. They talked to everyone who knew her. Everyone except for Billy Fadden." He looked at his watch again.

"One other thing," Gail said. "Could you tell us where you were when Sandra was killed?"

Frowning, he ran his tongue across his

lower lip, then laughed and looked over at the only other male in the room for support. "What's going on here?"

"I think she's asking for your alibi," Anthony said.

"Oh? I think it's time for both of you to get out of my office." Doug Lindeman stood directly over Anthony, whose eyes were turned upward, though he remained casually slouched in his chair.

Anthony took his cell phone out of his pocket and unfolded it. "Martin Greenwald's number is on speed-dial. Martin is a big client of yours, no? He'll take the call. Ask him if it's all right if you talk to us."

Lindeman backed off. "Great. I have nothing to hide. I was in trial in Key West all day. I drove back, had something to eat, then came here to finish some work. Lois Greenwald came around seven o'clock to go over some contracts, and she left at eight-fifteen. I turned off the lights, locked up and went directly home. I got there at eight-thirty. All right?"

Gail looked at him. "You were with Lois Greenwald."

"That's what I just said."

"What is your relationship, exactly, with Lois?"

"Relationship? She's my client."

"There's no romantic involvement?"

"What is it with you? I said she was my client. I do not get *involved* with my clients."

"Really. She said you were. She said you were practically engaged."

Doug Lindeman's full, rosy mouth hung open. He laughed. "Yeah, well, she's . . . we're friends."

"I must have misunderstood her," Gail said.

"I guess you did."

They stood at the edge of the quarry looking down into a weedy, brush-choked pit about twenty feet deep and fifty yards across. White coral rock thousands of years old had been blasted, hacked, and broken away in great cubes, then hauled out to be sliced into decorative slabs called keystone. The quarry had shut down in 1962. The state had turned it into a geological site.

Behind the visitors center a hundred yards or so east, out of view from where they stood, were some rusted tracks and an even more rusted steam engine. Men had pounded steel pikes into the rock, gouging a long trough so the block could be cracked away from the side.

Sandra McCoy's body had been found

here on the desolate western side of the pit. A ranger had supplied a map and marked the place. Anthony walked to the edge. Gail kept her distance, fighting the irrational urge to look behind her.

The sun had dropped below the tops of the trees but still shone on the pit floor and on the opposite wall. She could see across to the bright water of Florida Bay and a scattering of low mangrove islands. She wondered if, in the days since the murder, the rain had washed the blood away, or if streaks of it still darkened the rock.

Sandra's body had been positioned with her legs pointing away from the pit, shoulders just at the edge, her head back, throat exposed. Already dead. When the knife had sliced through her neck, the blood had not spurted but flowed. She had been found crumpled at the bottom in a patch of weeds, discarded like a soda can or a cigarette pack.

Still looking down, Anthony peered through the viewfinder and pressed the shutter.

Gail had shown him how, no real trick to it. When they got back to the cottage, which she hoped would be soon, she could download the card to her computer and bring up the image on the screen.

Taking shots of the video store had been easy. Movie Max was the last of four small, glass-fronted stores in a building set back at an angle off the highway. She had captured the parking spaces in front, a few shade trees, and at the far end of the lot, a hedge. Sandra McCoy had left her car in the last space. She had gone in for a video, come out, stuck the keys in the door, and he . . . someone . . . had grabbed her. No one had noticed the video bag and her purse on the ground until late the next morning.

The rope had gone over her head too fast for her to scream. He had dragged her around the end of the building and finished the job. His car would have been close by. He had probably driven to the access road just west of the rock quarry and carried or dragged her through the woods, a distance of only twenty yards or so. Why here? He could have taken her body anywhere, could have left her in the mangroves. She'd have been reduced to bones in a week. But he had brought her here. He had laid her out on these rocks like a sacrifice, her sightless eyes staring up at the starlit sky, and her throat slit open, the blood pouring out, a long quiet flow.

"Anthony, are you about finished?"

He raised the camera and took a couple of shots across the rock pit, then turned and picked his way over the weedy ground to where she stood.

"Did you see anything?"

"Some crime scene tape. The brush is trampled. That's all."

Gail turned off the camera and put it back into her purse. "Let's get out of here. This place gives me the creeps."

Arriving at the Blue Water Marina, they spotted a man in old hiking shorts and a khaki fishing hat seated among the patrons at the bar outside the restaurant. Anthony parked the car under the awning near the Buttonwood dock, and they walked back across the lot.

Martin saw them and lifted a hand in greeting. He was halfway through a mug of beer. Anthony asked if there was time for him to talk to the marina manager. Unspoken but understood was the reason for this: Anthony wanted to find out who had been on duty the night of October third. Had anyone seen Billy Fadden around seven-thirty p.m. getting into his boat and heading for home?

"Go ahead, take your time," Martin said. "We'll be right here." Someone moved down one stool, and Gail slid in next to Martin. A waitress bustled through the screen door of the restaurant with a basket of peel-and-eat shrimp, which she gave to a man at the end of the bar. Martin asked Gail if she was hungry. Gail said she would have a beer, and the bartender tilted a frozen mug under the tap.

Martin told her he'd just heard one of the fisherman bitching about losing a charter. "They say the storm is right on track for the Upper Keys, unless it veers off at the last minute."

"It is going to become a hurricane?"

"No, no, don't worry. They're not going to start ordering evacuations, but we'll get some heavy rains and wind on Friday. I've talked to Lois. She's already putting every hand to work battening down the hatches. We'll have to delay the opening."

"Oh, that's bad."

"It's not bad. Bad is the roof blowing off the hotel. This is inconvenient."

"What about your nursery?" Gail grabbed a napkin to blot the foam off her lips.

He answered with a shrug. "Palm trees are made for this weather."

"Martin, I want to apologize to you."

"Why?"

"I shouldn't have asked about Lois the

way I did, making it sound like we suspected her."

"No need to apologize," Martin said. "I've had some things on my mind, and I took it badly. You go ahead and do your job. I won't interfere."

"Well, we talked to Doug," she said. "He confirmed that he and Lois were in his office discussing business at the time in question."

"What did he say about Joan?"

"He thinks Joan is loony."

"I thought he would."

Gail took another sip of her beer, crisp and cold. "Martin, forget what I said about Lois and Doug being involved in any way. I must not have heard her correctly. Please don't mention it to her. I'd die of embarrassment."

But Gail had heard correctly. And either Lois had wildly misunderstood her relationship with Doug Lindeman, or she was delusional. Anthony said it didn't matter; it was Lois's problem, and they should leave it alone. Gail thought he was right, but it bothered her. She already felt sorry for Teri. Now this.

"I won't say a word." Martin had finished his beer and was signaling the bartender for another.

Gail said, "Should you be drinking? Oh, God, listen to me. I'm sorry."

"You're right, I shouldn't. This is my last one. I've just been to see my doctor."

"Not bad news."

"The old ticker is wearing out. They want me to go to Miami next week for some tests. The cardiologists are talking about raising the hood and replacing a couple of parts. I'm not in any imminent danger of falling off this bar stool, don't look so alarmed." He smiled at her, then said, "I hope you don't mention this to Anthony. Above all, not Teri. You and I will have a mutual pact of silence."

"Martin, are you talking about a *transplant?*"

"Heavens, no, just a valve or two. A couple of new pipes. The first ones they bolted in there aren't holding too well." He looked through the open bar to the water beyond. "It's a pretty day, isn't it? We'll need umbrellas tomorrow."

His sunglasses hung from a cord around his neck, and she could see his deep-set hazel eyes, sad and beautiful, under thick, dark brows. Once he had been a powerful man; it showed in his bones and the way he carried himself. The king was dying — or believed he was.

"Teri has to know," Gail said. "She's your wife. She loves you."

He finished a swallow of beer and set down his mug. "That's precisely why I don't want to tell her. She has too much on her mind already with Billy. We've been through some tough times with him. This is about as bad as it ever was. I hope that psychiatrist can offer some guidance, because I'm at my wit's end. This is something I've tried to fix, and I have failed completely.

"He doesn't like me. I can't fish as well as his father can. I don't push him around, so how can he respect me? He wants to stand on his feet like a man and he can't do it, and he's frustrated to hell and back. Oh, I remember what it's like, being that age.

"What I fear most is that Teri will be hurt. Billy's going to break her heart, and there's not a damned thing I can do about it. I've succeeded at everything else most people put value on. I made my first million at twenty-six. That's true. And I didn't lose it and make it back, I kept it and made even more. Oh, it was great fun stomping the opposition, scooping up deals. We had a fantastic apartment on Central Park West, and I rarely saw it. My daughter wouldn't speak to me. My wife was about to divorce me when she got sick. She died a year later. I went to her funeral and was back at work the next day.

"I was thirty-eight when I caught that first whiff of mortality. It wasn't a bad attack, as these things go. The biggie came at forty-one. Lois flew up to take care of me. She browbeat my doctors for six months of recovery. I couldn't go back to work. It would have killed me. She told me Lindeman Key was for sale. So I bought it.

"The only way I got the deal I got — and it still cost me a bundle — was by agreeing to take the property subject to Joan's life estate. Her nephew, Teddy, talked Harry Lindeman into it. I think it was so Teddy could continue to enjoy the property, too, that's what I think, because he and Joan were pretty tight, but Teddy got himself busted by U.S. Customs and went away for ten years. He never got out. He died in prison."

Gail said she had heard about that.

Martin looked into his beer mug, turning it around and around on the varnished teak bar. "Lois and I had big plans at first. A megaresort with a timeshare condo on the eastern side. Very bad idea. Joan's being there saved me from that.

Now I've gone green. I'm working to get everything low impact, totally solar powered, making all our own water. The world will have to go that way eventually. If not, we're all in trouble. You know, Gail, the good thing about nature is that it reminds us we are not in control. The storm is coming, and my trees will be blown away or not, and my heart will go when it decides to, and that's all right. I've learned something: We don't choose our fate, it chooses us.

"I don't know why Teri loves me. I don't know, but I'm grateful, as I'm grateful for the sunshine. Lois gets the resort when I'm gone, but Teri will have enough to live very well and to take care of whatever Billy might require. I don't expect to go tomorrow, but I tread very lightly. I know the odds.

"My beautiful wife. Teri wants another child, can you imagine that? She's young enough, but I put her off. She has enough on her hands with Billy. Wouldn't that be a rotten joke to pull on her? Give her a child and then keel over? I want her to be able to find someone else when I'm gone. I think that's the best gift I can give her. She loves me, but it would be a tragedy if she loved me too much."

Gail felt a knot in her throat. This was so sad. Martin was afraid to tell his wife he was sick because she was young and beautiful and she might stop loving him. Teri was afraid he would see how unworthy she was. Teresa Flores, a Cuban refugee, a maid, a nobody. Her first husband had beat her, and her younger son was dead. If only she had been home instead of working, she might have saved him. She wasn't good enough for Martin Greenwald, so she created an illusion for him, the perfect wife. They were miles apart. Martin would never know who she was or how desperately she loved him. Each of them, an island.

When Anthony finally came back, Gail was so mired in gloom that he had stolen a sip of her beer and was talking to Martin before she realized he was there.

She gathered that Martin had asked him if he'd had any luck.

Anthony was saying, "There were two men on duty that night. Neither of them remembers what time Billy left. They can't even remember if they saw him."

"What do you do now?"

"Now we talk to Joan Sinclair and we cross our fingers."

12

At the fence dividing the properties, the cart left the landscaped grounds of The Buttonwood Inn and entered the woods on the other side. The headlights made a circle of light that bounced over the rutted path. Shadows swirled in the trees. Gail sat in the front with Billy Fadden, leaving the rear seat to Anthony. They came to a clearing. The sky brightened and dimmed as clouds drifted across the moon.

Billy looked tense and unhappy, and Gail saw him wincing when they lurched out of a hole. He had not volunteered to play chauffeur. He said Joan Sinclair had asked him to. She wanted to see with her own eyes if he was still alive, or if she had cut him down off the beam for nothing.

The cart reached a smoother patch of ground. Gail asked, "Do you visit Joan often?"

"Not really." Billy added, "Not like I used to."

"Why?"

"I've heard it all."

"All of what?"

"Her stories. What Hollywood was like thirty or forty years ago."

"That could be interesting."

"Well, it's not. We used to talk about how movies were made. She made me watch *Citizen Kane* about ten times in a row, and she took it apart. But she's changed." Billy steered the cart around a fallen log. "You keep waiting for the director to say 'action.' "

"With your interest in movies," Gail said, "why don't you go into filmmaking?"

"Yeah, right."

"I'm serious."

He shook his head. "There's a million people who want to get into it. You have to know somebody."

"You know Joan."

"Like that's going to help."

Gail wondered if all conversations with Billy dropped into a black hole. She said, "Could you let me borrow one of her movies?"

"Which one do you want? I have them all."

She remembered what the waitress, Emma, had told her this morning at breakfast. "How about *Bride of Nosferatu*?"

"Okay, sure," Billy said. "It's not her best, but it's the one that got her noticed in the horror-film genre."

After returning with Anthony from Islamorada, and before dinner arrived on a tray, Gail turned on her computer, hooked it up to the phone line, and searched the Web for Joan Sinclair. She got over fifty links, most of them to very strange home pages. "Eric's House of Goth" contained a photo of a young Joan Sinclair with vampire teeth, an abundance of eyeliner, and a drop of blood on her lips. Someone called "Count Shockula" had a Joan Sinclair fan club page that hadn't been updated in three years. A site called "Women of Darkness" featured two streaming video clips: From *Black Flame*, Joan Sinclair standing outside a dungeon cell, black hair piled on top of her head, breasts straining at the low neckline of a red velvet dress. A terrified, sweating, half-naked man is chained to the stone floor watching her. She smiles. "You called me evil. Am I? Do you think so? Well, my darling, you're about to find out what evil is. Hendrik! Open the door!" From *Dawn of the Undead*, a blond Joan

253

Sinclair in a diaphanous white gown, moonlight revealing every curve. She puts a hand to her ear. "Listen. Do you hear the music? It's the voices of the dead, singing to us. *La-la-la-laaaa.*"

There were many insignificant references contained in longer articles. Joan Sinclair's name listed in the cast of a movie. Mentioned in articles about Vincent Price, Christopher Lee, Roger Corman. Joan Sinclair as scream queen and campy comedienne. Joan Sinclair as typical of, example of, or betrayal of, feminist ideals. The most comprehensive biographical data came from the online *Guide to American Film*:

Sinclair, Joan (born Joan Lindeman, Key Largo, FL, 1940?), a virtual unknown, was given the coveted role of ill-fated mob girl Carlotta Sands in *The Edge of Midnight* (MGM, John Huston, 1963), which earned Sinclair an Academy Award nomination for Best Supporting Actress. She appeared in three other major pictures (most notably Paddy Chayefsky's *Network*) but became best known for her work in horror films (*Bride of Nosferatu, The Scourge, Hell House, Black Flame, Moon of the Vampires,* and others). TV appearances include the occult drama *Dark Shadows*; *Star Trek*; and the suburban witch mother in the short-lived 1980 sitcom *Skeleton in the Closet*. Sinclair had become a cult figure and subject of parody by the time she guest-hosted *Saturday Night Live* in 1981. Her career suffered due to disputes with directors and other actors, a failed lawsuit against her agent, and arrests for drug possession. Married four (?) times, including actor Sam Jakes and British rock guitarist John Everts.

Los Angeles Times movie critic Art Hammersmith (1987): "Even in a string of low-budget bombs, Sinclair's approach was slyly comedic and self-consciously aware, forcing the viewer to go along for the ride."

Though Joan Sinclair sank into B-movie obscurity, she has a quirky and possibly underrated place in American film history. She lives in seclusion somewhere in the Florida Keys.

Such a weak bulb burned in the porch lamp that they had to feel their way up the steps. Only a sliver of light shone through a crack in the curtains. Billy lifted a hand to knock on the door but stopped when a

255

woman's angry voice came from behind it.

"— tired of arguing with you. Why shouldn't I, if I want to? Why must you always —" The voice grew too faint to make out, as though the woman had turned in another direction.

Then another voice, too muffled to indicate its gender.

Billy banged on the screen, which rattled on its hinges. The voices went quiet.

"Joan? It's me, Billy."

From inside: "They're here, would you *leave?* Get out. *Go!*"

There were footsteps fading away. Then a door slammed somewhere deeper in the house.

Half a minute later the click of high heels came nearer, and a lock was thrown back. The door opened, and the figure of a woman appeared on the other side of the screen. Soft jazz and cigarette smoke drifted out. The glow of an ember rose and brightened and for an instant reflected in her eyes. Bracelets jangled as they slid down her wrist.

Billy said, "Hi. I brought Miss Connor and Mr. Quintana."

They murmured their hellos. Joan Sinclair leaned for a moment longer against the frame, then pushed open the screen door and moved aside. "Come on in out of the snow, why don't you?" The words were spoken clearly, slowly, with an undertone of wry amusement.

She shook their hands. Her fingers were arched, the grip quick and light. Long black hair fell past her shoulders, and bangs stopped at the level of her wing-shaped eyebrows. Her nose was strong, and her lips were outlined and filled in with red. Dark blush accented her angular cheeks. She wore a loose, leopard-print sweater with the sleeves pushed up, black Capri pants, and high, backless heels with open toes. A gold silk scarf was tied around her neck.

She held up her cheek to Billy. "Kiss, kiss." With a sigh of embarrassment, he gave her a peck. She turned up her palms as though she expected something more. "Aren't you going to say 'thank you'? Or do you want me to mind my own business next time?"

"Thank you, Joan."

Joan gestured toward the bandage on Billy's left hand. "You bled all over my new blouse." She was Billy's height, but his posture was bad, and he seemed smaller. "Billy darling, when I said death was beautiful, I didn't expect you to take it literally."

She walked him toward the door. "Now scram. Your lawyer wants to talk to me."

She stood looking out as the hum of an electric cart faded, then flicked her cigarette into the yard. She locked the front door when she came in. For her age, she was stunning. The black hair had to be a wig, but a very good one. Her waist wasn't as small as in the photos from thirty years ago, but she still had the curves.

Gail looked around, getting the layout of the house: Living room ahead, hall and stairs to the right. Old furniture, a scattering of threadbare rugs on wood floors. A hanging light fixture with most of its low-watt bulbs missing. A row of candles flickering on the mantel of the coral-rock fireplace. On the other side of the living room a wide opening to another room, probably the dining room at one time, now empty except for two recliners, a big-screen television, and many posters on the walls. In the semidarkness, the outline of a door, perhaps to the kitchen. Had the other guest gone out that way? Was he — or she — still here?

"Bienvenue chez moi." Joan Sinclair's cocoa-brown eyes lingered on Anthony before moving to Gail. "Mr. Quintana brought you along as backup? We'll gang

up on him if he gets out of line. Have a seat, you two." She motioned toward the camel-backed sofa, which had been draped with a fringed, green brocade throw. Fake fur pillows had been propped in the corners.

At the other end was a pole lamp with three metal shades, and Gail clicked one after another without result. She smiled apologetically at her hostess. "It's dark in here."

Wordlessly the owner of these gloomy environs moved around Anthony to switch on a lamp at the nearer end of the sofa. The wooden base was carved into a vaguely female shape. The scarf draped over the shade allowed a soft pink light to come through. "Better?"

On the coffee table, incense curled upward from a brass burner, masking the smell of cigarettes, mildew, and unwashed laundry. A jazz trumpet was coming through the built-in speakers of a cabinet in the dining room. Gail remembered her mother had owned one of those. She walked a few steps nearer and saw a stack of phonograph albums.

"Do you like Dizzy Gillespie?"

Gail looked around. "Is that who it is? Yes, it's very nice."

"What can I get you to drink?" Joan Sinclair's breath revealed that she herself had already had one or two.

"Do you have white wine?" Gail asked.

"Wine. Wine. I have red wine. Wouldn't you rather have a martini? I make a mean martini, my own secret formula." Her voice was a breathy alto, and each word she spoke seemed to carry the weight of some hidden meaning.

"Just some club soda, then."

"She's being a good girl tonight." Dark eyes shifted to Anthony. "How about it? Want to join me in a martini?"

"All right."

"Sit down, will you? Get comfy."

The bar was on the wall near the dining room, an oak cabinet on claw feet. Over it, an ornate gold mirror tilted from the wall. The striped wallpaper was curling down at the ceiling. Joan Sinclair found a rocks glass and used aluminum tongs to drop in a few ice cubes from a metal refrigerator tray. She bent over to search behind some doors for the club soda. Her Capri pants fit snugly. She had slender legs and a round butt.

Anthony was staring at her. Gail leaned closer and whispered, "You think she's hot."

He leaned forward, resting his elbows on his knees, passing a hand over his hair. His lips barely moved. "I think Billy is in trouble."

"One club soda. Tee martoonis." Joan Sinclair's tilted image in the mirror smiled at them. "I learned to drink martinis when I was in Vegas shooting *The Runner's Club.* I got to know Elvis Presley. He wasn't in the film, but he came by the set to see what was going on. He was a lot of fun, but I'll tell you something. If he sang like he made love, he'd be a frog." She laughed.

Bottles clanked as she searched among them. "Life in the fast lane. I'm not gonna lie to you about it."

She set out two glasses.

"Okay, boys and girls. How to make a Sinclair martini. Premium gin, a wet kiss of vermouth. And a few drops — don't overdo it — a few drops of Rose's Lime. Gives it some sass." When she finished she clamped on the strainer and poured with a flourish, raising the shaker high, then down, filling both martini glasses to within a quarter inch of the rim. She brought over the drinks and some cocktail napkins on a black lacquer tray inlaid with mother-of-pearl. The napkins were printed with a pirate's grinning face and the words CAP'N

BOB'S TAVERN, MARATHON FL. Someone must have pocketed a stack of them and brought them here.

Now that her eyes had adjusted to the lack of light Gail could see that the entire room was filled with oddities, cast-offs, and assorted junk. Every surface was crammed with ancient and dusty knickknacks of the sort that remained when everything else at the garage sale had been sold.

"Where the hell are my cigarettes?" Joan found them on the end table, a pack of Salem menthols. She sat down in a rattan chair at right angles to Anthony and slid a cigarette out of the pack. He picked up a tarnished, silver-plated table lighter and clicked the wheel. She cupped her hand lightly around his. Her nails were crimson. A green stone, too big to be real, twinkled in its setting of cubic zirconias. She blew out smoke. "Thanks."

Gail sipped her club soda from a smoky-gray glass trimmed with silver. The ice tasted like it had been in the freezer too long.

Anthony said, "Miss Sinclair, we need to ask you about Billy Fadden."

She settled back in her chair and crossed her legs. "You want me to tell the police that Billy was with me when someone mur-

262

dered Sandra McCoy. He arrived here at eight-thirty, we watched three movies, and I sent him home around three-thirty in the morning. And I'd like it if you called me Joan."

"All right. Joan. When we speak to Detective Baylor, it's important that you remember as much as you can and that you tell the truth."

"I swear." She held up a Scout salute and took a sip of her martini.

"May I get some details about your evening with Billy?"

"Go ahead."

Anthony picked up his drink. "Tell me again the movies you watched, and in what order."

"*The Rope. Vertigo. The Birds.*"

"How do you know precisely what time he arrived?"

She pointed to the mantel clock, whose hands showed 9:06 p.m., the correct time by Gail's watch. Joan said, "He knocked on my door at eight-twenty-seven. Close enough?"

"Good. Did you and Billy have anything to eat or drink?"

"He brought a six-pack of Red Dog beer with him. I had a few drinks. We shared a bag of pretzels."

"What was Billy wearing? Do you recall?"

She took a long drag on her cigarette, making an O, careful not to smudge her lipstick. She exhaled to the side. "Jeans and a dark green T-shirt. Hog's Breath Saloon, Key West."

"Did you already have the movies here, or did he bring them?"

"They were here. I have every important American picture through 1980 and a lot of the British stuff too. They're filed alphabetically in my viewing room. Name one, I'll tell you the director, the actors, and the year." She tapped her cigarette over the square, cut-glass ashtray. A corner was chipped off. "I have an excellent memory."

"You do. It's amazing." Anthony nodded slowly.

She asked him, "Where did you get that accent?"

"In Cuba. I left there when I was thirteen, but I haven't had too much luck with my English."

"You speak wonderfully. It's very sexy. You're a very sexy guy. Don't get mad at me, Gail, it's true, and I am ever so envious." Joan Sinclair smiled over the rim of her martini glass. "You're a lovely couple. Do I see an engagement ring?" Gail showed her. "Oh, my. Sparkle, sparkle. When's the big day?"

Gail glanced at Anthony, then said, "We're not sure. Probably next spring."

"Good God." She laughed. "What the hell are you waiting for, permission? I married my second — no, my third husband a week after I met him, and it lasted for years. But that was back in the old days, when you couldn't just shack up, or people would talk. Times change, *n'est-ce pas?*"

Hiding a smile, Anthony sipped his martini.

In the dining room, the music grew to a crescendo of trumpet and drums, then blared to a stop. There were some clicks, then silence.

Gail said, "Miss Sinclair, I mean Joan . . . I'd like to ask you about Sandra McCoy. I suppose you knew her pretty well. She was here often, wasn't she? Helping you out, running errands, and so forth? Do you have any idea who would have wanted to kill her?"

Black-penciled eyes narrowed. "No, I don't."

"Did she talk to you about herself? Did she have a lover?"

"I wouldn't know." Joan took a quick puff on her cigarette, then snapped it away from her lips. "Let's get something straight. Sandra was a two-faced little bitch. She didn't come to *help,* she came to spy on me. I thought she was all right because she was a friend of Billy's but she was working for my nephew, Douglas Lindeman. I went upstairs and caught her opening drawers. I told her to get out. Douglas is trying to have me put away. How's that for a kick in the pants? I just found out. Someone came to warn me."

"Tom Holtz," Gail said.

"Do you know Tom? Of course you do. Everyone in the Keys knows Tom. We've been close friends since we were kids. Tom and Doug are lawyers. They have an office together. That's how Tom found out."

Gail said, "We spoke to Doug about it this afternoon. He says he's concerned about your welfare, but we're not so sure."

"My welfare? My ass. He wants my house! He wants to get me out of my house."

"Why do you think —"

"Because he's going to sell it to Lois Greenwald." Joan crushed out her cigarette in the ashtray. "She's another bitch. She'd better watch her step around *me.*" Then just as quickly as her rage had appeared, it vanished. Joan Sinclair let out a breath and

266

adjusted the long row of bracelets adorning her arm from wrist to the edge of her leopard-print sweater. She had pale skin, and the tendons and veins showed through, evidence of her age. Even a good manicure couldn't disguise the knobby fingers.

She spoke, and her voice belonged to a woman who had seen too much of life, too many sorrows, too much pain. She put a hand to her heart. "I left because this was the dullest place there ever was. I've come back for the same reason. All I want is to rest. The world has no joy for me now. People who swore they loved me, betrayed me. Gone. Everything is gone. I don't have much time left, dear God, but at least let me rest."

Gail could only stare helplessly. She glanced at Anthony and saw the same look of stunned pity on his face.

The sly smile reappeared, and Joan Sinclair twirled the end of her little gold scarf around her finger. "I am playing with you, my darlings. Ethel Barrymore, *The Bells of St. Ann's*, 1937. Of course you don't know it. Waaa-aay before your time. Mine too." She took another cigarette and held it between her fingers. *"S'il vous plait?"*

267

Anthony lit it for her, throwing Gail a look as he did so. He was clearly as confused as she about this woman's state of mind. Smoke drifted around Joan Sinclair's head, barely moving in the closed and claustrophobic air of this house. Gail realized that the stereo had been going for a while. Not the same record. She heard a piano and the slow, sensuous voice of a female singer she had heard somewhere before, but the name wouldn't come.

Bracelets clinked as Joan gestured over her shoulder. "Ms. Connor, there's a telephone on that little table in the hall, see it? The cord is long enough to reach. Bring it over here, will you?"

There was indeed a telephone by the stairs, a model so old it had a dial, not buttons. Gail said, "Do you want to call someone? I have a cell phone we could use."

"Fine. Call the sheriff's office. Let's get this over with. Who am I supposed to talk to? A detective somebody."

Anthony said, "Detective Baylor, but we're not going to call him tonight. I mentioned this to you. We're going to see him tomorrow."

"What do you mean, see him? At his headquarters? I'm not going to a police station. I've *been* to police stations, and I don't like them. He can come here."

"No, it's better if you go with us. Don't worry. It won't take long, I promise you. Martin Greenwald will take us there and back in his boat. You would be gone no more than two hours, probably less."

"Did you explain who I am? I'm Joan Sinclair. Why can't they come here? The detectives are supposed to come to the person's house. Isn't that the way it's supposed to be?"

Anthony made a little shrug. "In the movies, perhaps, but in this particular case, I am asking you to go with us."

"You said you spoke to Douglas. You're working with him, aren't you? That's what's going on here. It's some kind of trick."

He leaned closer and put a hand on her arm. "Joan, please. We're working for Billy. Please trust us. Nothing will happen to you."

"I don't like to leave my house. Someone might break in."

"No one will break in. If you're worried, tell Arnel Goode to watch it for you."

"Arnel is worthless," she said. "He's worse than Sandra McCoy, sneaking around, eavesdropping, telling me what to do."

Gail asked, "Was that Arnel who was here earlier, just before we came in?"

Nodding, Joan let out some smoke and extinguished her cigarette. "I told him to help me get ready. I needed the dishes washed, the floors dusted. He wouldn't leave. He wanted to play bartender. God knows what he wanted. I am getting so tired of Arnel."

"He's not still here, is he?"

"He went out the back door, and I locked it."

"Does he have a key to your house?" Gail asked.

"No. I have the key. The *only* key." Joan lifted an eyebrow. "I'm not *afraid* of him. Arnel is . . . he's like a child. A puppy. He has no one but me. It's *Douglas* I'm afraid of. The last time he was here he tried to push his way through the door. He put his foot inside so I couldn't close it. I screamed. I told him I would call the police. He laughed at me. He said I was a crazy woman and I should be put in a mental hospital. I couldn't believe he would even *think* of such a horrible thing, but Tom told me it was true. Now you see why I can't leave here. No, not even for Billy. I'm sorry, you tell Detective . . . Detective Baylor that he has to come *here*, to see *me*."

Anthony gently took her empty glass from her, put it back on the lacquered tray, and reached for her hand, enclosing it in both of his. She stared at his hands, then at his face. "Miss Sinclair, I am going to be very honest with you. You are a woman who appreciates honesty, I think."

"Of course I am. I can't stand people who *lie* to me, and there have been so many of them, you have no *idea*."

"Well, then. Here is what we are up against. Billy is in trouble. I explained to you already, he confessed to a murder he didn't commit. I don't know why, and probably he doesn't either, but the fact is, he is the main suspect in Sandra McCoy's murder, and the police want to talk to him. But first it would be extremely helpful for *you*, Joan, to tell Baylor what time Billy arrived at your house and when he left."

Her eyes were pinned hypnotically to Anthony's, and she leaned toward his soft, resonant baritone.

He said, "Yes, the police could come here. If I asked them to, they would. However . . . and please listen to me before you say anything. You've been living in this house for so long that you don't see it as other people do. It's so disorganized, so dark and cluttered, that if the police came

271

here, they could believe your mind is the same. They would say, 'Look at this place. How can we trust what she tells us? There is something obviously wrong with her.' I'm not saying it is true, only that they could *think* it is true, and if they do, what have we accomplished for Billy? Do you see?"

"Is it so bad?" Her long black lashes brushed her cheeks, and she pulled up her shoulders as if to hide in them. "I used to have *maids* and people to *do* things for me. I lived in the most beautiful home. It had marble floors."

"I'll give you another reason to be brave," Anthony said. "Your nephew. He believes you're unbalanced. He's going to file a petition for guardianship to say you're incompetent. Joan, come with us tomorrow. If you tell Detective Baylor clearly and calmly what you've just told us, you do two things. You prove that Billy is innocent. You also prove that Douglas Lindeman is wrong about you."

Her dark eyes filled with intelligence and resolve. "The lousy bastard. He never was any good."

"Will you go with us?"

"Maybe. You have to do something for me. I need a lawyer. My goddamn nephew is trying to steal my house, and I need somebody on *my* side. I'll pay you." She reached out to grip Anthony's arm. "I have money. I have four thousand dollars in the bank, and my agent sends me royalties every six months."

It wasn't so much, Gail thought. Joan Sinclair must indeed have come down in the world if she thought that four thousand dollars was a lot of money.

Anthony said, "I am sorry, I don't know anything about this area of the law, but Ms. Connor does. Don't you, Gail? Gail Connor is one of the toughest lawyers in Miami. She scares me, she's so tough."

Gail looked at him, then said, "I'd love to help you, Miss Sinclair. It would be an honor."

"Good. I like women with brains. In my career I refused to play syrupy, mealy-mouthed housewives or idiotic sex kittens. No way, no how. A woman has to stand up for herself in this world or she gets walked on. Right?"

"Absolutely," said Gail. "And don't worry about fees. I'll send my bill right to Mr. Quintana."

"You've got a deal." Joan Sinclair stood up with her empty glass. "Who wants another drink?"

"Thank you, but no more," Anthony said. "It's been a long day, and we —"

"Oh, sit *down*. You just got here." She wobbled back to the bar in her high heels and opened the gin. "What time should I be ready to go tomorrow? Warning. I don't get up early."

Anthony said the afternoon would be all right. He would arrange something with Detective Baylor and let her know, and the boat could leave from her dock.

Gail ventured to ask, "What do think you'll wear?"

Joan Lindeman turned around and looked at her. "I have an extensive wardrobe."

"Well, I just thought . . . since you haven't been off the island in so long —"

"I do get out, Gail, I just don't blab it to everyone. Sometimes I ask Arnel to take me for a ride. It's beautiful here. The sun, the ocean, the stars. I didn't always appreciate such things. I was only nineteen when I left. I couldn't wait to get out. I went to California with two thousand dollars that I borrowed from my father. He said, 'When it runs out, start waiting tables.' To hell with that. I was destined to succeed. Thank God I didn't know how many people with talent go to Hollywood and fail."

"How did you get your start in the movies?"

As soon as the words spilled off her lips, Gail knew she shouldn't have asked. It was late. Anthony was exhausted.

"I succeeded because I knew I could." The ice cubes rattled in the cocktail shaker. "Does that sound arrogant? Too bad. When you've got it, you've got it, and the only thing separating them that do and them that don't, is not lettin' nothin' stand in your way. I didn't wait around to get lucky. I worked my ass off. I took classes at the Film Institute. I didn't eat, but I had money for school. My boyfriend was a stunt double, and he got me onto the Paramount lot. I stayed out of sight and watched the actors and listened to the director. I slept with a casting agent. I did what I had to, and I'm not going to apologize for it. He got me a nonspeaking part in *The Time Machine*, a *wretched* picture. They used about fifty girls in blond wigs, and everybody looked exactly alike. I did a couple other things, then *finally* got a part where I could open my mouth. What was it called? Who cares?"

Joan Sinclair carried her drink across the room, stopping halfway. "You ever see a sound stage? My first time was such a

275

thrill. Cables and equipment, and the actors, and dozens of people running around. The ceiling is so high you can't see where it ends. 'Give me a number three warm gel on Miss Sinclair!' 'A little more to the right!' Then here comes the camera, ro-o-oolling toward me on a dolly. My first line: 'Hello, Mrs. Potter, how's Jeff doing today?' I was brilliant.

"Word got around that John Huston was looking for a girl for *The Edge of Midnight*. I *wanted* that part, I would *die* for that part. I saw him in the hall at the Institute, and I said if he didn't let me try out, I would kill myself. He'd been thinking of Natalie Wood, but she was too sweet, and when they saw my test, they cast *me*. It wasn't easy. It was the hardest thing I've ever done. I had a voice coach and an acting coach, and they were tearing their hair, but when the picture was done, I *knew* it was good. The reviews! 'Joan Sinclair . . . a stunning newcomer . . . she sets the screen aglow.' Except for this one cretin I insulted at the premiere. He said I had the talent of a potato. I called him up and told him to kiss my ass. After that he went out of his way to trash me whenever he got the chance. Petty, petty, petty.

"I didn't care. I was nominated for an

Academy Award. Best Supporting Actress. They threw us a party the night before, all the nominees. Everybody was there. Audrey Hepburn congratulated me. She said, 'I hope you win. You were wonderful!' Then the awards ceremony the next night. I arrived in a limousine, naturally. Photographers and flashbulbs, and lines of police and screaming fans. Smile and wave, wave and smile. All the reporters ask the same dumb questions. 'How do you feel?' 'Do you think you'll win?' I didn't win. Margaret Rutherford won for *The V.I.P.s.* Can I be a bitch and say she didn't deserve it? Yes, I can. She didn't deserve it, I did, but they gave it to her because she was old and that was her last chance.

"After *The Edge of Midnight* I was besieged with offers. Columbia wanted me, MGM wanted me, Fox wanted me — if I'd take a deferred percentage of the profits. The studios are such thieves. They never show a profit! The studio execs didn't know what the hell they were doing. When *Runner's Club* came out, they publicized it like a goddamn romantic comedy. It flopped, so the next picture, they hardly spent anything on advertising, and that one flopped even worse. As if the studios

277

weren't bad enough, my agent screwed me over. Mike Nichols wanted me for *Carnal Knowledge* but they were only paying SAG wages, and my idiot agent turned down the part without even telling me about it! They gave it to Ann-Margret."

Joan flopped into the rattan chair. The blues singer on the stereo sang softly, *It's been so, so long . . . since my man's been gone . . . and my tears come down . . . like rain.*

"I could've saved my career if I'd learned how to pucker up and kiss ass. You have to work at being a phony. Go to the parties, doesn't matter how bored you are. You go and you make small talk and you smile. I knew it was horseshit so I stayed away. They called me cold and stuck-up. The other actors snubbed me. The tabloids said I was having affairs with *everybody.* Probably true."

She finished her drink. "Then I got a part in *Bride of Nosferatu.* I had no money and no pride, so why not? After it came out Vincent Price called me up and he asked me to costar in his next picture. I *adored* Vincent. He taught me not to be so goddamn serious. I played a vampire princess in *The Scourge.*" Joan Sinclair narrowed her eyes and lowered her head.

278

" 'No man holds de rrrreins off my soul, nor vvoman either, nor beast, nor Gott. I am guided by my own desires.'

"The critics haaaaa-ated it." She laughed. "I had a damn good time doing those silly pictures. I got lots of fan mail, made lots of money. A lot. Don't know where it went. I had a TV show, a sitcom. Oh, God. Forget that. Cancelled after four episodes. I did *Hollywood Squares*. I was on *Saturday Night Live*. John Belushi and I did *Samurai Vampire*. Big deal. Then what? . . . I don't remember. This and that. I got married again. Unmarried. It wasn't pretty. They evicted me . . . from my goddamn apartment and nobody . . . would take a phone call. Kick in the pants, huh? . . . What do you do? . . . So I came home." She blinked. "I could've stayed here. I could've married Tom, but I didn't want to. I wanted to be a famous actress . . . and I did it, by God."

Her eyes closed, and her glass tipped in her hand. Anthony reached out to catch it before it fell.

13

It could have been the flutter of bird wings that awakened her, or the soft rustle of palm fronds against the windows. Or rain. Yes. A light, steady tapping on the leaves. Gail opened her eyes and noticed the clock on her nightstand. The numbers came into focus.

"Oh, my God."

She pushed Anthony's arm off her waist and rolled out of bed, nearly tripping over the sheet before she managed to wrap it around herself. The sky was so overcast it hardly seemed possible the sun had come up.

From his pillow Anthony mumbled, "*¿Qué pasa?*"

"Stupid clock. The alarm didn't go off." She found her cell phone on the dresser and hit the speed dial for her mother's house. "I have to call Karen. The bus might not have come yet."

"Go in the living room," he said.

When Irene picked up, Gail said, "Hi, Mom. Has Karen left already? . . . I know, I'm sorry, but we got back so late last night, and I must've hit the wrong buttons on the alarm. . . . Was she mad?"

Not mad, Irene said. Disappointed.

Anthony put his pillow over his head.

"What did she say? No, wait, let me guess. That I don't care. I'm so mean, I'm the worst mother, running away on vacation, ignoring her —"

"Gail!"

She turned her back and said quietly, "When Karen comes home, would you please tell her I'll try again this afternoon? This is so ridiculous. She has my number. There's no reason she can't call *me*. She just *won't*. It's like unless I call her, I have somehow failed this test of motherhood that —"

"*¡Es de madrugada! ¡Hazme favor, sal de aquí con el teléfono!*"

"Anthony, please!" She spoke into the phone again. "Sorry. *Señor* Grouch needs his IV of *café cubano* before he can be civil in the morning. I'll call you later." She disconnected. "Anthony, don't yell at me when I'm talking to my mother."

"Why didn't you go in the other room?"

"You told me you had to get up early."

"Not this early." His hair curled in all directions. Squinty-eyed, he bunched his pillow under his neck. "When are you going to stop letting Karen pull your strings?"

"Look. I promised her I'd call. I said, 'Karen, I *promise* to call you every day.' "

"And yesterday you didn't have time. Too bad."

"If I make a promise," Gail said, "I try to follow through. Karen needs to know she can rely on me."

"You promised to call her because you feel guilty about being here with me."

"Oh, please."

"*¡Es verdad!*"

Gail sat on the edge of the bed. "You're probably right. I need to stop feeling guilty. Why should I? We've been working." Dragging the sheet with her, she crawled over to Anthony. "I'm such a bad person. I don't want to make sandwiches for the homeless. I want to lie on the beach with you."

"I'll tell you something. I'm ready to get out of here. If we finish this case today, let's go back. We'll get a room at the Fontainebleau tonight, and you can have your wish."

"I don't think so. It's going to be raining on Miami Beach."

"Good. We'll sleep. *Shhhh.*"

Gail settled into his arms. "Do you think Joan Sinclair is going to come through for Billy?"

"Yes, I do. I had my doubts at first, but she isn't crazy. Eccentric, yes, but alert and in full control of her faculties."

"So Billy is innocent."

"You sound uncertain."

"No, but . . . I wish we knew the rest of it. Why he confessed."

"Let his psychiatrist figure it out."

Gail put a kiss on the corner of his mouth. "I should try to be more like Joan Sinclair."

He laughed. "Why?"

"Not as she is now. I mean as she *used* to be. Not Joan the actress but Joan the person, before she turned nutty. She sat through *Citizen Kane* ten times with Billy Fadden. Who else would give him ten minutes? Well, his mother, but mothers don't count. I loved what you told me, how Joan let her hair go all gray, and she wore blue jeans when Tom came to dinner with champagne. I hope I have the courage to do that. Will you love me when I get old and gray?"

"Siempre, mi vida." He yawned into the pillow. A moment later his eyes opened. "What time is it? I have to meet Billy at ten o'clock."

"About eight-thirty, I guess. Why do you have to meet Billy?"

"We're going to be very well prepared before we talk to the cops." Anthony raised up far enough to grab his watch off his nightstand. He frowned at it, closing one eye.

"You need your eyes checked," Gail said. "I've noticed you squinting."

"No, it's too dark in here to see."

"Give me that." She glanced at his watch. "Eight-twenty-two. Uh-oh. Anthony needs glasses. *Caballo viejo,*" she said. The old horse, out to pasture, the name he used for his grandfather, when the old man wasn't around to hear it.

"*¿Caballo viejo?*" Anthony put his watch back on the nightstand then moved down in the bed until their faces were aligned. *"Ven a montar este caballo."* He had a horse he wanted her to ride. He took her hand and put it under the covers.

The pause in the rain would not last long. Heavy masses of clouds lumbered across the sky. Brief shafts of sunlight hit the water in sparkling patches that quickly dimmed and were gone. The sea was an empty plain of murky blue.

From his position on the dock, Anthony turned toward shore and spotted movement in the bushes. Billy Fadden was still looking for his stepfather's .38-caliber revolver. Martin had been unable to find it yesterday before nightfall, and Anthony had suggested that Billy have a look. The boy came out from behind a tangle of low branches and poked the weeds with a stick. The blond spikes in his hair had fallen, and his jeans were soaked.

Anthony had just finished talking to Billy about the meeting with the police, set to take place four hours from now. Billy had been in a dark mood, unable to focus, his responses not going much beyond "Uh-huh," "Yeah," and "I guess." Anthony assumed the medication was having an effect, though it was hard to know what was going on in Billy's head.

He might have imagined throwing the gun away. He remembered shooting at dogs that night, but there were no dogs on the island. He said he had tried to shoot himself, but the gun wasn't loaded. Or maybe it was loaded, and he had dropped it somewhere else with six rounds in the chambers. Loaded or not, if the gun had landed in the water, or in the thick and undulating mat of decaying turtle grass near the seawall, they would never find it. Anthony decided to give this five more minutes.

He stepped further onto the dock, which was shiny with rain. Bird excrement dripped down the pilings where pelicans sat, ready to push off if he came near. Seagulls skittered away from his feet, rose in a flock, and wheeled away, quickly becoming gray dots against a grayer sky. He walked around a pile of rotting lobster traps and stopped to look up at the beam from which Billy had hanged himself. It was eight feet off the dock, supported by two heavy vertical timbers. A rope from one of the lobster traps had made the noose.

That memory had come back. Billy had told Anthony this morning that he remembered trying to kill himself, and he remembered calling the police and confessing to murder. Anthony had asked him why. Billy had shrugged. He didn't know why.

Studying the beam's height, and guessing at the distance between the dock and the rope, Anthony wondered how Joan Sinclair had cut him down. What had she used? Had she been out taking a walk and by luck had a knife in her pocket? Anthony made a mental note to ask her.

He noticed at the end of the dock an old lawn chair and a small plastic table. Ideal for a young man who wanted a place to get drunk or smoke a joint after dark. The road was two miles away, and water closed in on all sides. One could easily feel so isolated in this dreary place that suicide might not seem an irrational idea.

A raindrop hit his shoulder, then another. There was a curtain of rain a few miles east, moving this way.

"Mr. Quintana!"

Billy stood at the other end of the dock, a gaunt figure in a white T-shirt and jeans. His reflection shone dully in the wood. He lifted his hand to show Anthony what he'd found. A gun.

Anthony retraced his steps. "Let me have it. I'll give it to Martin." He took out his handkerchief.

"Hang on." Sitting on his heels, Billy laid the revolver on the dock. Water had pooled in a depression in one of the boards. Careful of his injured hand, he used the other to splash dirt and bits of grass off the wood grips. The barrel was dark gray, about two and a half inches long. Standing, Billy wiped it dry with his T-shirt. "Is it ruined?"

"I doubt it." Anthony checked the chambers. Empty. He spun it, clicked it shut, and wrapped the gun in his handkerchief. "It just needs a cleaning." The gun fit in his trousers pocket.

Billy raised his head and glanced toward shore as though startled.

"What did you hear?"

He smiled hesitantly. "Nothing." He crossed his arms over his chest. His shoulders twitched as though someone had put a cold and unwanted hand on his neck.

Anthony looked at him. "Tell me what you heard, Billy."

"Dogs barking. Kind of far away. You don't hear them, do you?"

"No."

Billy bent over as if in pain and pressed the heel of his hand against his ear. "Oh, man."

Anthony gripped his arm. "Do you need Dr. Vogelhut? I have my cell phone."

"Don't call her, I'm okay." He was trembling. "They aren't real. I know they aren't."

"Do you hear them a lot?"

"Not a lot. Sometimes not for a long time, then they'll come back. It's usually if I'm tired and I'm trying to go to sleep. It's pretty funny, you know. Like being awake and having a dream at the same time. It's like there's this wall between what's real and what's not real, and things can break through it. Black dogs. Why can't it be something else?" He laughed. "You know what it means? It means death. They use them in the movies. They put in black dogs to signify death. Joan told me, and now whenever I see it, I go, 'Uh-oh. Metaphor! Bzzzzzt!' "

Anthony was caught between wanting to get this kid out of here and wanting an answer. "Whose death do they signify for you? Yours?"

"My brother." Billy took a breath that seemed to scour his lungs. "Yeah. I'm pretty sure about that. When he drowned, the rottweilers were running all over the yard barking. Big dogs. Huge. It's so real. I can hear their tags jingling on their choke collars. So when I hear them barking . . . when I *think* I do, then I feel like if I looked in the water right now I'd see Jeremy. But he isn't there. Is he? He isn't." Billy's face twisted. "Would you . . . this is stupid . . . would you look? Just tell me he isn't there. I'll be okay if I know for sure."

Billy's terror was so real, so palpable and immediate, that Anthony could nearly believe that if he looked over the edge of the dock there would be a six-year-old boy in pajamas, floating face up, eyes wide and staring, his body moving slightly, bumping against the barnacle-encrusted piling.

Not letting go of Billy's upper arm, Anthony moved toward the edge. He saw gray-green water and bits of sea grass. Occasional drops of rain made circles that wobbled on the surface and vanished.

"It's all right, Billy. There's nothing."

"I knew that." He forced another laugh.

Among the many facts that Anthony had heard about Jeremy's drowning, he could not recall the dogs. "Did your family have rottweilers?"

Billy stared back at him for a few seconds. "No."

"You said they were in the yard, running around and barking."

"They couldn't have been ours. Mom doesn't like dogs. Maybe they were at the house next door. I don't remember." His voice dropped to a deep, portentous monotone. " 'Black dogs of death. Scream and scream again. Coming soon to a theater near you.' " He turned toward the shore, and as he did, looked over the edge of the dock as if to assure himself he could do it. He stopped, and his eyes became fixed. His mouth went slack.

With a low moan he sank to his knees.

"Billy!" Anthony grabbed him to keep him upright. "Lean over. Get some blood in your head." The boy was skinny but had enough dead weight to threaten to send them both into the water. Anthony pulled him back, wishing he had followed his first instinct, to get Billy away from here as quickly as possible.

"Breathe!" he ordered.

Billy mumbled, "Goddamn. Didn't want to do that. Sorry." He took some breaths and sat up. He moistened his lips. "I want to tell you what I saw before I forget. It's really interesting, you'll like it. A mermaid. It's the second time I saw the chick. She was out here two days ago when I had my party. I saw her off the end of the dock. She's got red hair and a green tail. She's holding the moon in her hand. I look at her, and she looks back and she opens her eyes and smiles at me, but she's *dead*. Whoa. What's Dr. Vogelhut going to say about that one? My brother turning into a mermaid. I guess I am nuts."

"Can you walk?" Anthony asked.

"Yeah." He got to his feet. "I am so tired of this shit."

"You'll be okay. You're seeing Dr. Vogelhut on Tuesday."

"Tell her not to put me in the hospital. No thanks. Been there, done that, bought the T-shirt." He laughed shakily.

A few steps took them off the dock and onto the path. The way was narrow, and they had to dodge through the brush before reaching the clearing where they had parked the cart. Rain had caught up to them, falling not hard but steadily. Anthony swung into the passenger seat and waited for Billy to get in.

Billy didn't move. Strands of blond hair reached to his thick, dark eyebrows. A drop of water slid down his forehead. "The mermaid was real," he said.

"The mermaid?"

"She was *real*. I'm not making it up. I remember. She was a lamp on the dock behind our house. She was made out of concrete. I remember her hair hung down and hid her breasts. She had a white plastic ball in her hand. Like this." Billy extended his arm and turned up his palm. "The light was turned on when Jeremy died. That's how I saw his body in the dark." Billy's eyes pleaded with Anthony to believe him.

Anthony nodded. "All right. Get in, let's go."

"You think I'm lying."

292

"I think you don't know what is real and what isn't."

Saying no more, but clearly feeling betrayed, Billy got into the cart and turned the key. They jerked forward, skidding over the weeds as they turned in a tight circle back toward the resort.

Gail was in the middle of a phone call to her secretary when she heard Anthony's footsteps coming up the stairs. He came through the screen door with wet shoulders and rain on his face. Gail gave him a quick kiss as he went to the bedroom to change clothes.

On his way he dropped a couple of takeout bags on the table by the sofa. Gail went over to see what he'd brought. Sandwiches. And tucked in beside them, a video. Still talking to her secretary, she took it out. A copy of a video, to be more precise, with a color copy of the original box taped to this one. *Bride of Nosferatu*, starring Edward Steele, introducing Joan Sinclair, a gloomy castle behind them. The bride was a blond with dark eyes and a heart-shaped face, the kind of face that could look either innocent or evil. She stared from the cover of the box as if she wanted to take a bite out of Gail's neck.

The vampire was older with streaks of white over his ears. The points of his teeth showed on his lower lip. Hers were also visible, but not long and yellow, like his. They were cute, little-girl-vampire teeth. It was creepy and perverse, Gail thought.

"Miriam, go ahead and do a draft of that complaint and e-mail it to me. I'll take a look at it tonight and get the changes to you in the morning, okay?" She disconnected.

Anthony came out fastening the gold cuff links in his dress shirt. He had changed into his suit pants too. Time to play lawyer. Noticing the video in her hand, he said, "That's from Billy. Do you want anything to drink?" Anthony went to the minibar.

"No, thanks. Listen to this. 'The vampire Count Nosferatu kidnaps the beautiful Katerina on the eve of her wedding and soon discovers that she has a blood-lust even greater than his own. To satisfy his new bride's raging thirst, Nosferatu opens his castle to travelers on the lonely road through the mountains.' " Gail said, "Ooooh. A husband trying to satisfy his wife. This might be good."

"We'll watch it later. Help me clear off the table, *por favor, bonboncita?*"

They couldn't eat outside today; the deck was too wet. Cool damp air came through the screen. As Gail unwrapped sandwiches, Anthony told her that Billy Fadden had found the gun.

"So he didn't imagine it after all."

"Oh, no, if the gun had been loaded, his death would have been very real. I took it back to the office. Lois said she would lock it in her desk."

Gail asked how his talk had gone with Billy. If Billy would be nervous talking to Detective Baylor. And what would Anthony do if Joan Sinclair bombed in her performance —

"Anthony, are you listening to me?"

He was frowning out the window. "I want to ask your opinion about something."

She put down her sandwich. "All right. What?"

He told her what had happened to Billy on the dock.

"Oh, my God," Gail said. "He saw his brother's body?"

"It's even more strange. He saw a red-haired mermaid holding the moon. She was dead, but she looked at him and smiled."

"Oh, Anthony."

"Billy said she was real. Not at that moment, but real in the past, in the time his brother drowned, and he and his parents were living in the house in Marathon. The mermaid was a *lamp*. It was on their dock. That's how he was able to see Jeremy in the water that night."

Anthony pushed away from the table, turning sideways in his chair. "Gail, I just spoke to Teri. She said there was no mermaid. They had a dock, but the only light was an outdoor spotlight. There was no mermaid on any of the neighbors' docks, and no rottweilers in their yards. No black dogs. But he hears them barking."

Gail looked back at him, speechless.

"Aha, you see? This kid is having delusions, and I'm supposed to convince the cops he had nothing to do with a murder? How can I? He's not going anywhere near Detective Baylor today. We take Joan Sinclair and that's it. Let Sharon deal with Billy. She's the psychiatrist."

"But you can't leave it alone," Gail said.

"Yes, I can."

"No. You can't." She put a finger to his lips. "Let me say this. You asked my opinion, remember? I think Sharon Vogelhut was wrong when she said Billy's suicide attempt wasn't connected to his

296

brother. They *have* to be connected. Billy found Jeremy's body in the canal. That means he'd been looking for him, that he felt responsible for his brother. When Billy found him dead, he blamed himself. His father had already taught him how bad he was. Don't you see? Two days before Sandra died, they had a fight, and Billy hit her. He felt bad about it. His guilt about his brother came back, and he called the police to confess, but he's mixing it all up in his head. Sandra's murder and his brother's accident."

Anthony finished the last of the beer in his glass, then set it down. "What if it wasn't an accident?"

That horrifying thought took a few seconds to work its way into Gail's mind. "He couldn't have."

"Why not? He's been a bad kid all his life. That's what they say, isn't it? He burned a house down for fun. Murdered Sandra McCoy for a thrill. He could have pushed his brother into the canal because he was jealous."

"You don't believe that. Billy adored his little brother. He found him floating and couldn't save him. That's enough to make anyone crazy."

Anthony squeezed his forehead. *"El loco*

soy yo." He was the one going crazy.

Gail took his hand away and looked intently into his face. "Billy didn't burn that house down on purpose, and you didn't somehow enable him to kill Sandra McCoy."

The rain fell steadily outside, and the light was dim through the screen. Anthony's eyes were dark, almost black. "We were going to get out of here this afternoon."

"Never mind. We'll stay through Friday. If you need to stay longer, do it. I'll ask Mother to drive down. It's not that far. Don't worry about me."

He leaned over until his cheek was against hers, his lips at her ear. "You know something?"

"What?"

"You are worth more than five dollars an hour. I should give you a raise."

14

The Islamorada branch of The Monroe County Sheriff's Office was located in a concrete-block building about the size of a double-wide trailer. The waiting room contained some molded plastic chairs, but Gail was too nervous to sit. Anthony stood by the window looking out at the highway. He appeared calm, but he was jingling the change in his pocket. They had dropped Billy off at Mangrove Mike's Café half a mile down the road and told him to sit there and drink as many sodas as it took for them to get back to him.

Gail walked around and read the posters about law enforcement and drunk driving. Two men busied themselves filling out a form, one giving instructions, the other writing. A middle-aged woman with a long ponytail was reading a paperback thriller, combating boredom, waiting for who-knew-what.

A uniformed officer sat behind glass at the other end of the room. Gail happened to walk by as the officer got up and opened a door. He left a narrow space through which Gail glimpsed an auburn wig and the back of a double-knit, black-and-white checked suit. A hand with long red nails lifted to take a cup of water from the edge of a desk. A heavy faux-gold bracelet dangled from her wrist.

Joan Sinclair had made an attempt to dress the part: society matron testifying in a courtroom drama, but Gail could almost smell the mothballs. A boxy little suit and black turtleneck sweater, kid pumps, and sheer black hose. The lenses of her Dior sunglasses had immense tortoise-shell frames. Joan hadn't removed them in the fifteen minutes since Detective Baylor had ushered her inside.

Baylor was out of sight but another man leaned against the desk with his arms folded across his sport shirt, a holstered pistol on his belt. Did they believe Joan Sinclair's story? Gail could glean nothing from his expression.

The officer came back, closed the door, and sat down again behind the glass panel. With her view blocked, Gail wandered over to Anthony. She had made him change out of his conservative suit into pleated slacks and a sport jacket so she wouldn't look silly by contrast in her short pink dress.

"What do you think? Joan's been in there a long time."

He said, "I was thinking about a room at the Fontainebleau."

"Lovely," she said, "but we can't skip out on the Greenwalds' dinner."

Teri had called to remind her, and Gail had said she hadn't forgotten, though of course she had. Teri wanted to do a special thank-you dinner, since they were leaving tomorrow afternoon. It remained to be seen if there was anything to thank them for.

The door to the waiting room opened, and Detective Baylor stood aside to allow Joan Sinclair to go through it. She walked with a little swing to her steps. A penciled auburn brow, the same shade as her hair, rose over the frames of her sunglasses, and a smile flitted across her lips. She reached into her bag and pulled out a silver-plated cigarette case and a disposable lighter.

The woman with the pony tail looked over her paperback, which slowly dropped to her lap. "Excuse me, but . . . aren't you Joan Sinclair?"

Tapping her cigarette on the case Joan said, "Yes, I am."

"Oh, my God, it's Joan Sinclair." The woman stood up, glanced excitedly around the room as if to share this amazing news, then rushed back to her purse. She fumbled for a memo pad, a pen. "Would you mind signing an autograph? If it's not too much of an imposition —"

Joan purred, "Not at all. I'd be delighted."

Baylor said, "Miss Sinclair?" He pointed to the sign. "No smoking."

Hollows appeared in her cheeks when she tightened her lips, but she put her cigarettes away.

"Counselor, could we speak to you a minute?"

Anthony told Joan Sinclair to have a seat. "Gail, come with me."

They went through the door, and Baylor closed it.

"My associate, Ms. Connor."

Baylor made a quick nod in her direction. "Ms. Connor." He was a man around forty with a light brown mustache, short hair, and an open-collar knit shirt. A badge was clipped to his holster. He tilted his head toward the other man, whom Gail had glimpsed earlier, and introduced him as Sergeant Miller.

He led them to a cubicle. There was only

one chair, which Baylor rolled under the desk to get it out of the way. Everyone remained standing. The narrow window gave a view of the rain-soaked parking lot and some patrol cars.

"That's quite an actress," Baylor finally said. "She almost had me convinced."

The other detective smiled.

Baylor said, "Miss Sinclair is a nice lady, and kind of a local legend around here, so I won't accuse her of lying. I'm going to give her the benefit of the doubt and say that Billy Fadden confused her. Maybe he was at her house. I can buy that. But no way did he get there at eight-thirty. You didn't encourage this little show, did you, counselor? I'd hate to have to arrest you for obstruction of justice."

Aware of being on the periphery of this conversation, Gail ventured a glance at Anthony, wondering if he was as utterly shocked as she. Only a slight narrowing of his eyes revealed his emotions. He asked the question that Detective Baylor was clearly waiting for. "What time did Billy arrive at Joan Sinclair's house, since you seem to have some source of knowledge I am not aware of."

"Oh, probably closer to nine-thirty, ten o'clock." Baylor put a hip on the desk and swung his foot. "We've talked to a few more people since your client's confession. We can put Billy Fadden at Movie Max Video with Sandra McCoy around eight o'clock. She left a little later than we'd initially thought, probably eight-fifteen, and Billy left shortly thereafter. Let's see now. Motive. Two days prior, Billy and Sandra had a fight in the parking lot at Holiday Isle. He accused her of double-timing him, and he slugged her. If you'd like to bring him in so we could talk to him, the welcome mat is out. Maybe he's got some explanation that could clear this up."

"Who are the witnesses?"

"Can't tell you."

"What time did Billy leave the video store?"

"We're not sharing our evidence at this time," said Baylor.

Anthony glanced out the window, mulling the facts over in his mind. He said, "He stayed around for a while, didn't he? If he had followed Sandra out the door, you would be all over him by now. You wouldn't have bothered to speak to Joan Sinclair. Did you hope she would make a mistake? Say the wrong thing and implicate him?"

Baylor unfolded his arms and stood up.

"We're going to get a search warrant for every Buttonwood vehicle that Billy Fadden has access to. We want to take a look at his boat, his room at the hotel, and the general area. This would be a whole lot easier if we could secure the Greenwalds' consent. I think a lot of Martin Greenwald, and Teri's a good woman. I'm sorry what they've had to go through. Talk to Martin. See what he wants to do. We'd like to avoid embarrassment for everybody."

Anthony said, "You want to search, go talk to a judge."

Taking them back to the waiting room, Baylor paused with his hand on the door knob. "Tell Billy to keep his toothbrush handy. He's going down. Ain't nobody you can pay off this time, counselor."

The rain had stopped, though the pavement was shiny and the air cool and damp. Traffic hissed by on wet tires. Walking toward the car, Anthony clutched his umbrella as though he might like to strike someone with it. Joan Sinclair paused to light a cigarette. Gail waited for her.

Exhaling smoke, Joan said, "Well? What did they say? Was I all right?" Her eyes sparkled with triumph behind the big amber-tinted lenses. "Douglas can't use

Detective Baylor against me, can he? If
Douglas does go through with that
damned guardianship, you can call Baylor
as a witness for *me*. He was very nice. I
don't like cops, as a rule, but I think I impressed him. Come on. What did he say?"

Anthony opened the rear door of his Seville. "I don't allow smoking in my car."

"That's why they make ashtrays, dear."

"Put it out." A muscle twitched in his
jaw, betraying his mood.

With a sigh, she dropped her cigarette to
the pavement and rotated the toe of her
pump on it. The shoes were old, with
pointed toes and sharp heels. Gail noticed
with some dismay how ropy this woman's
calves had become. The years had not
been gentle with her body. Only the face
was still young, or seemed so, with face-
lifts and makeup to assist the illusion.

Gail opened her own door.

From the backseat Joan Sinclair said,
"What's eating *him?*"

Anthony got in and turned on the engine
for the air conditioner. The windshield was
fogged. He turned around and shifted so
he could look at her directly. "Miss
Sinclair. You want to know what they said.
They said you were lying. They have a witness who saw Billy talking to Sandra at the

video store at eight-fifteen. He could not have been at your house at eight-thirty. What time did he arrive?"

"I don't know exactly."

"Guess. You have a good memory."

With an elaborate shrug, hands lifting, she said, "Nine-twenty?"

"Did he say he had seen Sandra?"

"No, he didn't."

"Did you offer to lie, or was it Billy's idea?"

She was a silhouette against the back window. "I'm loyal to my friends, which is more than I can say for some people."

Letting out a breath between his teeth, Anthony put the car into gear.

Joan said, "Billy didn't kill Sandra."

"How do you know?"

"He was completely normal when he got to my house. There was no blood on his clothes. He wasn't nervous. I didn't notice anything wrong, and I have a sixth sense about people. He didn't do it."

"Why did you lie? If we'd known the truth, we could have worked with it. Now Billy looks guilty, and you look like a conspirator."

"Yes, I lied. I would have done anything, *killed* if necessary, to keep them from desecrating his grave."

Anthony's eyes moved to the rearview mirror. "What grave? Is that from one of your movies?"

"*The Moon of Stonehenge.* I filmed it in England with Christopher Lee in 1967. I was quite good in that part."

"*Me vuelvo loco.*" The tires spun on gravel when Anthony backed out of the space.

Joan Sinclair scooted forward on the seat and put a hand on his shoulder. "Anthony, darling, as long as we're on the subject . . . Do me a favor. Take me to Plantation Key. Do you mind? It's up the road just a few miles. I want to buy some flowers and take them to my family cemetery."

"We're going to the resort," he said.

"But I tried to help Billy. God knows I tried." She pulled a tissue from her purse.

Gail said, "We're not in a rush to get back. I'd like to see the cemetery."

Anthony shot her a look.

"Oh, come on. Aren't you in the least curious?"

They collected Billy from Mangrove Mike's, then went by the florist that Joan Sinclair designated. She bought every rose in the shop, $263.52. She smiled at the clerk. "Send the bill to Tom Holtz." The

308

woman replied, "Yes, ma'am, I know. Just sign here, please."

Gail assumed that Holtz would pay the bill out of the money he gave Joan from her late nephew Teddy's trust fund. The money would run out soon. And then what?

Joan told Billy to put the flowers in the trunk.

They all got in, and Anthony turned in the other direction on U.S. 1. The windshield wipers swept away the mist churned up by the car ahead of them.

Billy asked Anthony what had happened at the sheriff's office. Anthony replied he would talk to him about it later. Gail noticed Billy look toward Joan Sinclair, but Joan only reached over and patted his hand.

A mile down the road they passed Movie Max Video. Neon lights shone in the window. Gail saw the place where Sandra had left her car. If the police were right, she had rented the video but had stayed to talk to Billy. She'd finally left about eight-fifteen. Billy had left later than Sandra, or the police would have been all over him. Whom had they talked to? Someone at the store. It wouldn't be hard to find out.

Gail remembered that Doug Lindeman

and Lois Greenwald had been discussing business at his office, located half a mile west of Movie Max. Lindeman said they had left at eight-fifteen. Lois would have driven past the video store on her way to the marina. She might have noticed Sandra coming out. Martin Greenwald had seen Lois at the resort around nine-thirty. An hour and fifteen minutes. It didn't take that long to get back to the island.

Out the window Gail saw the Whale Harbor Inn, then a bridge over a channel, then Holiday Isle, a sprawling complex with hotel, marina, restaurants, and outdoor bars. The parking lot was almost empty. Wrong time of year, bad weather, and a storm coming this way. Two weeks ago in that parking lot Billy Fadden had slapped Sandra McCoy. The friend of Sandra's — Penny something — who had witnessed this had just talked to the police. Gail wondered if she could be found. Friends confided in each other. The girl might have something to say about Sandra and Doug Lindeman.

The road took them past the Windley Key state geological site. Someone had driven this way with Sandra's body, then had turned off the road — Gail saw the opening in the brush — and had dragged or carried her to the quarry. Could Lois have done that? It would take more strength than most women possessed, not only to twist a rope hard enough to break bones, but to drag a body through dense foliage on a moonless night.

Another bridge put them onto Plantation Key. Joan tapped Anthony's shoulder and told him where to turn left.

The Bay Harbor Resort owned several acres of rocky ground dusted with short, brittle grass. The hotel was a plain, two-story, flat-roofed building on the bay side of the highway. Sailboats and powerboats were tied at the docks. They drove along a sandy road that led to the eastern edge of the property, where a slight rise in the land was marked with several shade trees and some headstones.

The Lindeman graveyard was about twenty feet square with a black iron fence around it, painted and rusted and re-painted. More than a century ago a pioneer family named Lindeman had chiseled out rock to a depth of eight feet and filled it with sand. There was a brass historical marker announcing this, as well as the fact that the resort had promised to take care of the graves "in perpetuity." There were thirteen of them. A few were enclosed in low walls of coral rock or concrete. The oldest headstone was a wide piece of cracked granite with the names Hiram and Felicity, who had died in the 1890s. Six graves were dated 1935, victims of the hurricane. There were three very small graves with angels or lambs carved into the headstones. One grave was marked with four concrete paving stones laid in a row, no name at all.

The gate squeaked when Joan went through it. Billy followed with the armload of flowers. He gave one of the packages to Joan and laid the rest on a mildewed concrete bench. She turned back the cellophane and took out a long-stemmed rose. The color was too red, too lurid against the gray and unhappy backdrop of headstones, heavy clouds, and threatening rain.

Anthony motioned for Billy to come with him and Gail. They walked to a tree a dozen yards away. There was a bench, but too damp to sit on. As Joan Sinclair put the roses on the graves, crossing herself, saying her prayers, Anthony told Billy what the police had said.

Avoiding eye contact, Billy stared out at the bay as if following the lone sailboat motoring toward the harbor, sails tightly furled.

"I told you in the beginning, Billy, there is one thing I demand: Don't lie to me. When I ask you a question, I want the truth. Did you see Sandra at the video store?"

"Yeah."

"Tell me what you were doing there. I don't want to hear it in the state attorney's opening argument at your trial."

Looking at him coldly, Billy said, "You think I killed her."

There was only a slight hesitation before Anthony said, "No. Talk to me, Billy."

"I went to rent a movie."

"What did you get?"

"There was nothing worth watching."

"I am not surprised. You have a thousand pirated videos in your room, and Joan has more than that. I ask you again. What were you doing there?"

Billy clenched his teeth. "I bought some weed, okay?"

"From whom? Don't tell me 'some guy.'"

"His name's Chip. If anybody finds out they'll fire him. That's why I didn't tell you before."

"Ah. At last the truth, or closer to it. I'm going to accept that for now. What time did you get there?"

"I got there as Sandra was leaving. We said hi, then she came back in."

"After she had already rented her video?"

"Yes. After."

"Go on."

"We talked for a while, then she left. It was about . . . I don't know, ten after eight, eight-fifteen. I hung out with Chip —"

"Back up. Did you and Sandra smoke a joint together?"

"Yes."

"Where? In the store?"

"We went out the back door."

"Were there any customers?"

Billy shook his head. "Nobody was there, just Chip. He's the night manager."

"All right. What happened then?"

"Sandra left, I hung with Chip for a while, and I left at eight-thirty. I drove to the marina, got in my boat, and went home."

"Did you talk to anyone at the marina? Any other boaters?"

"No. I just got in my boat and left. I don't know when I got to Joan's. Nine o'clock, I guess. That's what time she expected me."

"Joan told me you got there at nine-twenty."

314

Billy thought about it. "Oh, yeah, I had a six-pack in my apartment, and I went and got it. I walked over to Joan's. She opened her window upstairs and said to wait on the porch because she was still getting dressed. If she says it was nine-twenty, I'll go with that. I didn't look at my watch. I had a beer and waited for her to open the door. The rest is just like I told you."

"Is it the truth this time?"

"You fuckin' figure it out." Abruptly Billy walked toward the water.

Anthony drove his fist into the other palm. He laughed. "I love clients like this."

"What about that friend of his, Chip? If the police find out he's selling drugs, couldn't they lean on him? He could say that Billy left earlier. He could lie."

Anthony's eyes shifted to Gail, and he smiled as though she were particularly naive. "Chip could be lying now to protect Billy. Or to protect his own ass so Billy won't turn him in. We can't be sure what time Billy left Movie Max, can we?"

That question left Gail with the sickening feeling that the truth had once again skittered away from them. She noticed Anthony's attention shifting to something behind her, and at the same moment a car door slammed.

A portly, white-haired man had parked his Lincoln next to Anthony's black Seville, and he was coming across the ragged grass. Thomas Holtz. Lifting a hand to acknowledge their presence, he headed for the graveyard, stopped, and changed directions for the tree under which they stood. He propped his red-and-white golf umbrella against the bench.

Holtz said, "I thought I'd find you here. The florist called me to make sure I'd okay what Joan spent. I always okay it." Through his heavy glasses he gazed at the woman still placing flowers on the graves. If she had noticed him, she gave no indication. Holtz said, "Sometimes I park out by the road and watch her, or I buy a drink over there at the bar and sit by a window. I'm feeling brave today."

Holtz turned back to them with a big smile. "So. How'd it go with Billy? You said to leave Joan be till you got Billy taken care of. Are we in the clear?"

"We're working on it," Anthony said. "If you want to talk to Joan, be my guest."

"I'm going to ask her to marry me. What do you think of that?"

Gail and Anthony exchanged a glance.

Gail said, "I don't know if she would. She doesn't want to leave the island."

316

"That's true," Holtz said. "That's why she turned me down before. She had an emotional attachment to Lindeman Key, and I was trying to break it, you see? Not this time. I'm going to do it on her terms. We're going to fix that house up, add a deck, a pool, anything she wants."

Tom Holtz looked from one of them to the other as if they had voiced some objection. "She can't live alone anymore. She's got to be sensible. I've already talked to Doug about it. I said, 'Doug, you can forget that guardianship, buddy, it's all over. I'll be taking care of her from now on.'"

Then Holtz fell silent, turning his gaze once more toward the graveyard. "I love Joanie Lindeman. I've loved her for forty-five years." Swinging his furled umbrella by its wooden handle, Tom Holtz went to speak to her.

"*Ay, Dios mío,*" Anthony said.

The gate squeaked, and Joan froze, giving a little glance over her shoulder. When her old lover came nearer, she bent to pluck another rose from its cellophane package. She remained sitting on her heels in the sand, head bowed, while Tom Holtz talked. She stood up and carried her roses to the next grave. He followed.

They were too far away to be overheard.

Tom Holtz opened his umbrella and held it over her as she continued to put red roses on the graves. The rain was no more than a slight drizzle, and none at all came through the leaves.

"Look at them. You can see how much he loves her," Gail said.

"Is everyone crazy here?"

"Maybe it will work." Gail leaned against Anthony's side and felt his solid warmth. He put his arm around her. She murmured into his ear, "You know what we could do?"

"Tell me."

"Let's go to the courthouse in Tavernier and apply for a marriage license. It's four-twenty. We might make it. Billy and Joan won't mind. We don't have time to get married in the Keys, but at least we'll have the license. It's something."

"I think you're serious."

"It's the sanest idea I've had lately."

Anthony turned to look at her. "Yes, you are serious." He laughed softly. "What would you tell Karen?"

"I'd tell her . . . Anthony and I are getting married. Next week, next month, whenever it's convenient. I love him very much. Please be happy for us."

His hand was warm on her cheek, and a smile slowly lit his eyes. "Tomorrow on our way to Miami. We'll do it then. No backing out."

"You either," she said.

He made an X over his heart. *"Te lo juro."* He kissed her to seal the promise.

Leaves rustled, and a drop of water came through, then another. Anthony opened his umbrella. It was not raining hard, but thunder rumbled to the east. A gust of wind sent shivers through the tree, dislodging more raindrops. The wind swept the empty cones of cellophane toward the far side of the fence, where they flattened against the bars. Joan Sinclair ran to pick them up. Tom Holtz shouted at her to leave them, but she grabbed one and then another. He gamely tried to keep up, and the big red-and-white umbrella bobbed and swayed over her head. When she had gathered them all, Tom opened the gate and they hurried toward the cars.

"Where's Billy?" Gail asked. She looked toward the bay. He was sitting under a palm tree with his back to them. "Go get him."

Anthony cupped his hand and shouted, "Billy!" There was no response. "He doesn't hear me. I should let him stay there. He can swim home."

"Go get him, Anthony, before he gets struck by lightning." Gail ran toward the car. She waved to Tom Holtz, who was just closing his door, starting the engine. Anthony sprinted across the field with his umbrella.

Gail got in and swept her hair out of her eyes. The clouds had not let go yet, but a few drops spilled out, spattering the windshield as if someone had thrown them.

In the backseat Joan Sinclair was repairing her lipstick, looking slightly cross-eyed into the mirror of a scuffed, gold-colored compact. Her sunglasses were pushed up into her bangs.

Gail asked, "Did you have a nice talk with Tom?"

Joan blotted her lips on a tissue. She looked into the mirror again and cleared a smudge from the corner of her mouth with her little finger. "He asked me out to dinner tonight at The Buttonwood Inn."

"Really?"

"Really." Brown eyes fixed on Gail for a moment before she tossed her compact back in her purse and put her sunglasses on. The lenses were clear enough on the bottom for Joan to see out. It seemed more an affectation than warranted, given the heavy overcast. Joan took out her cigarettes and lighter. "I need a smoke. Shoot me."

Gail barely noticed. "What did you say to Tom? Are you going out with him?"

The interior lights came on as Joan cracked the door open. "I said I'd think about it." Joan's cheeks went hollow as she inhaled. "I'm fond of Tom, but my God, what would I do with a man in my life? I've had so many." She made a deep chuckle. "And enjoyed every one." She blew smoke toward the crack in the door.

"Joan, do you mind if I ask you something? Why did you change your mind about marrying Tom two years ago?"

She paused with her cigarette at her lips. "Arnel talked me out of it."

"Arnel?"

"He said it would be a mistake."

"Why did he say that?"

"He said Tom would be like all the others, wanting me because I'm famous. He said Tom is a drunk, and I would be sorry. Arnel's uncle was a drunk. His parents were dead, so he was sent to live with his aunt and uncle, and his uncle beat him. It was terrible for him."

"Tom never hit you, did he?"

"No! Tom has been nothing but a gentleman. Arnel is selfish, selfish, selfish. Al-

321

ways whining, demanding, trying to make me feel guilty. 'Don't leave me, Miss Sinclair. Please.' It makes me sick."

"This sounds very strange. Joan, is he . . . all right? Mentally?"

"Why wouldn't he be?" Joan replied.

The rain had begun to fall faster, drumming on the roof.

Gail asked, "Is it true that he saw a man killed in some farm machinery when he was a boy?"

"I beg your pardon?"

"Douglas told us that Arnel saw a man ripped apart by a . . . what was it? A grain auger, and that's why he stutters. Is it true?"

Smoke drifted toward the door. Joan said, "Yes, it's true. His uncle. He deserved it." Rain dripped inside the car, and Joan slammed her door shut. "I don't want to talk about Arnel."

The opposite door opened and Billy slid across the seat. He ran his fingers through his hair, lifting it straight up again. Anthony wrestled his umbrella inside. The shoulders of his jacket were dark with rain. He turned around and looked at Joan's cigarette. She opened the door long enough to throw it out but offered no apologies.

Anthony glanced at Gail, who had allowed this travesty, then started the engine.

By the time they reached the far end of Upper Matecumbe Key, the wind was still blowing in gusts, but the rain had let up. Anthony parked under the long awning that belonged to The Buttonwood Inn. There were not as many vehicles as three hours ago; the staff was being shuttled off the island. The van was there, and the Jeep that Martin had taken to Key Largo to have his heart checked, a Mercedes with a vanity plate that said TERESA-G, and two other sedans. Consent or not, the police would soon have their forensics people crawling all over them with their tweezers, magnifying glasses, and vacuum cleaners, looking for traces of Sandra McCoy's DNA.

Anthony locked his car and they walked to the dock, where Billy had tied Martin's Sea Ray. With no extra hands to spare at the resort, Billy had brought them over. The plastic rain panels were in place to keep the seats dry. Billy jumped aboard to help Joan cross the gunwale in her high heels. She vanished below. On the ride to Islamorada she had stayed in the cabin to keep her hair from getting mussed.

When Billy extended his hand to Gail she said, "Just a second," and dragged Anthony away to speak to him.

"Let's go see if the guy at the video store is there. We should talk to him."

He shook his head. "I'll send my investigators on Monday."

"Don't you want a statement before he changes his mind?"

"Gail, a lawyer does not question a potential state witness. You know that. What if he says something to incriminate Billy? We could be forced to testify against our own client."

"How likely is that?"

Anthony stared at her. "It isn't proper."

"Fine. I quit. I'm no longer your associate. You wait outside, and I'll ask the questions."

"The boat is leaving. How do we get back to the resort?"

"I don't know, we'll . . . we'll call for the shuttle. Arnel can pick us up. Or Tom Holtz can take us."

Anthony lifted his eyes.

"We have to," she said.

He told Billy to go ahead without them.

15

There was so little space in Movie Max Video that two people could not pass each other in the aisles without turning sideways. To brush against the sagging shelves was to risk a cascade of videos and DVD boxes onto the dusty, chewing-gum-speckled carpet. Handwritten signs marked the various sections: the sparse collection of recent releases, long shelves of foreign and independent films, and a great quantity of out-of-date Hollywood movies that could be rented for a dollar-fifty each. Time-faded posters were taped to the walls, and a video game blinked silently in a far corner.

Beyond confirming that his name was Chip, the night manager exhibited a remarkable lack of recall. He said he remembered nothing about Sandra McCoy's visit to the store on the night of her murder. Chip was not impressed by the fact that the two lawyers standing on the other side

325

of the counter were working for a young friend of his.

"Was Billy Fadden here that night too? I can't recall." Perched on his cushioned stool, Chip concentrated on entering returned videos into the computer.

Anthony Quintana had seen witnesses like this, the kind who would venture across the line into petty criminal activities just far enough to make ends meet. They stayed off the police radar screen. This man was in his late twenties with sun-bleached hair, a faded Hawaiian shirt, and a boating tan. Nothing about him would warrant a second glance.

Two teenagers came in, jangling the brass temple bells over the door. Anthony waited until they had walked past on their way to the video game before he said, "I want to know what time Billy Fadden left here. It's not a hard question. Billy hasn't given you up as his source — yet. You should want to keep it that way."

Chip's fingers paused over the keyboard before he finished his entry. "Billy didn't leave here for at least fifteen minutes after Sandra. She left at eight-fifteen, he left at eight-thirty, give or take."

"Did the police suggest to you that you were mistaken, and that Billy left earlier?"

"They suggested, but I told them he left when he left. It was obvious to me that he couldn't have killed her. Sandra was long gone by the time Billy took off." Chip glanced to the back of the store to see where his customers were. "The cops told me he confessed. Is that true?"

"No," Anthony said. "They were playing with you."

That produced a short laugh. "Typical."

"Did you hear what he and Sandra talked about?"

"I don't remember anything specific. I told the detective there was no shouting, no threats. It was a friendly conversation. Billy didn't rush out of here to follow her."

"How well did you know Sandra?"

"I knew her to say hello to, that's about it. She didn't come in here often."

"Did you ever see her with a man?"

"Not that I recall . . . but she wasn't the kind of girl to be alone, if you know what I mean."

During this conversation Gail had been going through a box of old videos for sale. She looked over at Chip and gave him a little smile. "Do you happen to remember what movie Sandra rented that night?"

"I can check the records." Chip tapped on his keyboard. "McCoy, McCoy. Here it is. *Bride of Nosferatu* with Joan Sinclair. She asked for it by name."

"Why that particular video?"

"Who knows? Oh, I do recall one thing she said — that it was probably the last video she'd be renting from us."

"The last video?"

"She was moving to Miami Beach and buying an apartment right on the water. So she said." Chip shrugged.

"*Buying* an apartment?" Anthony asked. "Or renting?"

"Buying. As in . . . purchasing?"

"Did she say where she was going to get the money?"

"No, and I didn't ask." The bells over the door jangled again when the teenagers went out. "In the Keys, people mind their own business. That's one of the benefits of living here."

Gail asked, "Do you have that same video in the store now?"

"I believe we do. The police found it in the parking lot and gave it back." Chip came around the counter and walked to the section marked HORROR. A small plastic skeleton and a bat dangled from the sign. Chip studied the densely packed shelves for a few seconds before locating *Bride of Nosferatu* and handing it to Gail.

On the box a young Joan Sinclair gazed hungrily at the viewer. Gail turned the box over and read the other side as though she expected to find something she had missed before.

Chip said, "If you give me your credit card information, you can rent it."

She smiled and gave it back to him. "No, thanks. We have this one."

It was almost six o'clock, and heavy clouds lumbered northward. A beam of sunlight broke through with such force that Anthony had to pull down the visor. Reaching into his pocket for his cell phone, he told Gail to call Arnel Goode to come pick them up at the marina. "You'll find his number in the directory."

Anthony let his head fall back on the head rest. Had it been only two days since they had arrived here? Not even two days, and he was exhausted. Why? Lack of sleep? More likely the lack of progress. It didn't bother him particularly that Billy Fadden's alibi witness had lied, or that Billy had lied, or that the video store clerk's statement couldn't be trusted either. Such things happened too frequently to be surprising. What irritated him was the looming certainty of an arrest, and his own inability to prevent it. Jack Baylor would scratch around until he found some combination of facts that he could take to the state attorney for a first-degree murder indictment. Billy had confessed; they would start there and work backward, discarding the facts that didn't fit the conclusion.

Tonight the Greenwalds expected them for dinner at The Buttonwood Inn. Anthony had hoped to have some good news. Instead, they would all sit there and discuss the weather.

Gail said, "I left him a message to call us back."

"What?"

"Arnel didn't answer, so I left a message. Want me to call Martin?"

"No, I don't want to bother Martin." Anthony turned into the Blue Water Marina and brought his car to a stop under the Buttonwood awning. *"Carajo."*

"Call Billy, then," she said.

"I've seen enough of Billy Fadden."

"How about Lois?"

"Forget it. Come on, I'll pay someone at the marina to take us." He opened his door.

"Wait. What about Tom Holtz? If he's having dinner with Joan at the hotel tonight, he can take us. We can ask him about Sandra McCoy." Gail's blue eyes were alight with an enthusiasm that Anthony found incomprehensible.

He said, "Ask him what?"

"Where Sandra got the money to buy a place on South Beach. She must have said *something* to him, don't you think?"

"Gail, I can't bring it up in your presence. He doesn't know I told you about his relationship with Sandra. It would embarrass him."

"I see. Well . . . call him anyway. We need a ride."

"It's only six o'clock. Tom wouldn't be going to dinner this early."

"For God's sake. What's his number?"

"Give me the phone, I'll do it," Anthony said.

There was no answer at Holtz's office. Anthony got his home number from information, and Holtz picked up on the second ring. He said it would be no trouble to come by the marina, which was on the way from his house on the bay side of Lower Matecumbe. "I'll be there as soon as I can," he said. "Go have a drink."

Anthony would have been content to tilt the seat back and close his eyes until Holtz appeared at the dock, but Gail said she was cold and wanted some tea. Through a crack in the clouds, the setting sun put an orange glow on the windows of the restaurant. The weather had kept the boaters at home, so the place was nearly empty. The booths were of knotty pine, and a net in the ceiling had caught all manner of glass floats, life preservers, plastic lobsters, and assorted nautical junk. Behind the bar was an immense, bubbling aquarium with reef fish as bright as neon. They found a booth overlooking the water and were able to see the rain-misted spot of land called Lindeman Key.

When the waitress came to the table, Gail ordered a basket of fried shrimp.

Anthony objected. "We're going to have dinner at the hotel."

"Oh! That means you don't want any of my shrimp. I get to have them all to myself." She asked the waitress to bring some hush puppies too. "I'm starving."

"Just coffee for me," Anthony said, and handed the waitress his menu. Slumping against the corner of the booth, he squeezed his eyes shut and rubbed his forehead.

"Do you need some aspirin?"

"No."

"Eat something. You're such a grouch when you're hungry."

He said, "They're going to arrest Billy. No matter what I do, they will arrest him. There will be an arrest and a trial . . . and probably an acquittal. Yes, I think I could pull that off. I never tell my clients, of course, because you never know what a jury will do. But assume an acquittal. By then, Billy will have been in jail for six or eight months, if he hasn't hanged himself. No, no, that won't happen. He'll be on suicide watch."

Anthony felt Gail's slender fingers curl around his wrist.

"You're doing all you can," she said.

"He *confessed*. I could kick him from here to China. Even if he's acquitted, people will believe he's guilty. He'll have to move. Where should he go? Miami is a very forgiving city. He could live on South Beach, like Sandra wanted to do."

"Anthony —"

"Or he could stay on the island. Yes. He could become like Joan Sinclair, half-mad, a hermit, watching movies day and night. What gets me is that I *don't know*, I have not the least idea, if he is guilty. No idea. If you're a defense lawyer, most of your clients are guilty of something, maybe not what they were arrested for, but they aren't exactly innocent, and you can live with that. It's part of the job. But Billy Fadden . . . I don't know what to think about Billy."

"You need him to be innocent," Gail said. "If he isn't, you're going to know for sure that you screwed up his other case."

Anthony brought her face into focus. Gail Connor had a way of going straight to the heart of an issue, like an ice pick.

"Don't give me that look," she said. "Anthony, it doesn't *matter* what happened four years ago. Maybe you made a mistake, but maybe you did exactly the right thing. Quit being so hard on yourself."

He turned around to find the waitress. "What is she doing, grinding the coffee beans herself?"

Gail sent him a chilly smile. "I wonder how long we would last as real law partners? A month? We might last a month, if one of us had to go out of town for a three-week trial."

He let out his breath and lifted his eyes to the ceiling.

"I wish you wouldn't do that," she said.

"Do what?"

"Sigh like that and roll your eyes. I don't like it."

"Eat something," he said. "I think you're hungry."

The waitress appeared with the coffee on the same tray as Gail's shrimp basket. The aroma made Anthony's stomach growl, but if he asked for one, Gail would have something to say about it. She ate as if he weren't there. Her teeth nipped each shrimp down to its tail, and the grease made her lips gleam. "Mmmm."

The waitress came by to refill his coffee cup. Anthony reached for the sugar and noticed that the rain had started again. Then he saw a man hurrying across the parking lot with a red-and-white striped umbrella. "It's Tom Holtz."

"Already?"

Tom Holtz spoke to the bartender as he passed by, then came to the booth and slid in next to Gail. "Hello again, folks. Do you believe this lousy weather?" She held out her hand, but he put a kiss on her cheek. Holtz's face glowed, and aftershave wafted across the table. He wore a blue jacket and yellow-checked shirt, ready for his date with Joan Sinclair.

Scooting further toward the window, Gail said, "Tom, you've been around the Keys all your life. I'm going to describe something, and tell me if you've ever seen it."

"I'm game," he said with a chuckle.

"It's an outdoor lamp made to look like a mermaid, and she's holding a globe that lights up. Have you ever seen anything like that?"

"Made out of poured concrete?"

"Yes, that's right. You've seen it?" She exchanged a glance with Anthony.

"Those used to be real popular around here. Concrete mermaids, pelicans, sharks, dolphins. Most people bought the mailbox versions, though. There was a guy up in Key Largo that made them. He had a store on the highway. He's been out of business for . . . oh, twenty years, at least. Why are you asking?"

Gail's disappointment had begun to show halfway through his rambling response.

Anthony said, "Billy Fadden had a dream about a mermaid like that, a red-haired mermaid holding a white globe. He said it was real, but we thought it was something he invented. Apparently he was right. They do exist."

The waitress, a thin woman in jeans and a marina T-shirt, arrived with Holtz's drink. "Here you go, Tom, one gin and tonic. Y'all want anything else?" She rested her tray on a hipbone.

"Have a drink," said Holtz. "It's on me."

"No, we're fine," Gail said.

"Bring me a scotch on the rocks," said Anthony. "Single malt if you have it." His mood had lifted. "Put everything on my check." He took one of Gail's shrimp and dredged it through the cocktail sauce. "Think back about ten years. Do you remember seeing a mermaid lamp? And if so, where you saw it?"

Holtz slowly shook his head. "Nothing comes to mind."

"Ah, well."

Gail moved closer and rested a hand on his coat sleeve. "Tom, thank you so much for coming out of your way to rescue us. I thought we were stranded." She had a lovely voice, warm and soft, and the old man smiled back at her. She said, "You know, I *promised* to call my daughter this afternoon, and I'd better do it now while I have the chance. Would you gentlemen excuse me?" As Thomas Holtz struggled to get his bulk out of the seat to make way for her, Gail grabbed her purse and gave Anthony a look that clearly said, *Talk to him before I get back.*

"A fine girl," Tom Holtz said, watching her walk away.

Anthony took another of Gail's shrimp. He repeated the basic elements of the conversation with the clerk at Movie Max, coming around to Sandra McCoy's plans to buy an apartment on South Beach. "You can't get into a South Beach waterfront condominium for less than a quarter million dollars. At her age, and probably with not such good credit, she would need at least a hundred thousand down. Was it bullshit?"

"How do I know?"

"Say she was serious. Where would she get the money?"

Holtz concentrated on fishing the lime out of his glass with the cocktail straw. "The only thing I heard from Sandra was how broke she was. Maybe she all of a sudden found a sugar daddy."

With a nudge of impatience, Anthony asked, "When we talked yesterday you said you didn't know if she and Lindeman were sleeping together. Were they or not?"

"Of course they were. I never caught them in the act, but I know her style. Doug's no better. He doesn't usually mess around in his own neighborhood because he's afraid Lois Greenwald would find out." Holtz saw the expression on Anthony's face and laughed. "Doug's stringing her along to keep the Buttonwood account. One of these days she'll see the light. Poor woman."

The waitress brought Anthony's scotch. When she was gone, he said, "Do you think Sandra was blackmailing Doug? She could have made trouble with Lois."

"Hell, no. I'll tell you what I think. It's all about Joan Lindeman's property. That's what the son of a bitch wants. He wants Joanie's property, and Lois Greenwald wants Joanie's property, and they're in on it together, and so was Sandra. That damned guardianship was an attempt to take over, don't you see? Lois Greenwald gets her deepwater dock, and she pays Douglas off for sending Joanie to a group home. Maybe Martin's in on it too."

"I doubt that." Anthony dropped another shrimp tail into the basket. He wondered if Sandra had fabricated the story about buying a place on the beach to hide the truth: She could only afford a squalid little studio apartment with a view of a parking lot. Either way, it was obvious that Douglas Lindeman wanted something from his aunt, and Anthony didn't believe it was the dock.

"You said that Joan has no cash or valuables in the house. How do you know this?"

"Joan told me. She had no reason to lie about it."

"Perhaps." Anthony drank his scotch. He said, "What about the money from Teddy Lindeman? He gave you a hundred thousand dollars, payable at ten thousand a year. Is it in the bank, or did she take it out and hide it somewhere in her house? See what you can find out from her tonight."

"No, Doug can't be after Teddy's money because I never told him about it," Holtz said. "Joan wouldn't have either. She doesn't trust him."

"Lois Greenwald. Could she know? Teddy used to be her boyfriend."

"Oh, they split up a long time ago. Twenty years or more."

"We heard that Lois used to smuggle marijuana."

"That's the story. She and Teddy started off together, but she got out when he moved to cocaine." Holtz laughed. "You wouldn't believe it to look at Lois now, would you? A dried-up broad like her, running bales of pot? She should've smoked more of it, might've improved her personality."

"Was Doug Lindeman involved in that?"

"Not at all. The DEA took a lot of supposedly upstanding citizens off to jail, but Doug was clean. The government seized everything Teddy had — house, cars, boat, bank account. I liked Teddy. He was a sensible man in most ways, and he always talked about retiring early. He never flashed his money around. He provided for Joan. They were very close. What a tragedy. I'm sorry about Teddy, I sincerely am."

Not a tragedy, Anthony thought. A very bad choice, for which Teddy Lindeman had paid a heavy price.

Munching another shrimp, he calculated how much money Joan Sinclair could have saved. If she had filled jars and shoe boxes with every dollar that Teddy had provided for her, and Douglas had found out, there still wouldn't be enough to justify filing a guardianship so he could get his hands on it.

Anthony was forced back to the idea that Teddy's money wasn't what they were looking for. Joan was hiding something else in her house. This could explain her reluctance to leave home.

"Tom, are you certain that Joan has nothing of value? Jewelry, gold, rare coins —"

"I don't know. It's possible. Maybe she didn't trust me either." Holtz's eyes were watery behind his thick glasses. "I can understand that. People have used her. She's been through hell. I told Douglas today,

341

'You leave her alone. I'm taking care of Joan from now on.' And I mean to do it."

Looking past Holtz, Anthony could see to the front of the restaurant. Gail stood at the bar watching the fish in the aquarium. When she glanced around, Anthony shook his head. Wait.

Tom Holtz finished his drink, pushed his glass aside, and leaned on his arms. "Listen, Quintana. I thought Billy killed Sandra. If he left the video store when you say, then I was wrong, and I'm sorry. I'm so sorry that I'm going to tell you something I should've told you before. On the day she died, Sandra came by the office and asked to see Doug. It was shortly after five o'clock, and the receptionist had just left. Sandra was all excited. 'Where's Doug? Where's Doug?' I told her he was in Key West and he'd be back around seven for a meeting with Lois Greenwald. She asked to use the phone. I was curious, so I listened in. He didn't pick up, so she left a message. She said she had to talk to him, it was important, and to call her as soon as he could."

For a moment Anthony sat without speaking. "Did you ask Douglas about it?"

"A couple of days later. He said he never got the message."

"Why didn't you tell the police?"

Holtz's face sagged. "He was my partner. Is my partner. There was that thing with Sandra . . . you know. Why stir up trouble? Anyway, Doug was with Lois Greenwald at the time of death. At least I thought he was."

"Would Lois lie for him?"

Tom didn't reply. He didn't have to.

Anthony reached over to grab his arm. "Tom, you have to tell the police what you heard. I want you to talk to Detective Baylor immediately. Tell him everything. We can call him right now. I have my cell phone —"

"No, no, no." Holtz lifted his hands. "Let's not get all carried away."

"Carried away? The police could arrest Billy Fadden for murder at any moment. You must tell them, Tom. Tell them they have another suspect."

"Maybe I'm wrong, then what?" Holtz couldn't look at Anthony straight on.

"You can't worry about being wrong or right, you simply tell them the truth."

"All right, I'll . . . I'll call them tomorrow."

Anthony was about to press for some assurance of this, but a slim figure in a pink dress caught his attention. Gail was coming back. As she reached the table she looked down at the remains of her shrimp basket. "You finished *all* of them?"

Tom Holtz fixed on her a steady but unfocused gaze that quickly became so vacant that Gail glanced at Anthony to provide some explanation for this. He could only shrug.

Holtz spoke. "Jesus, Mary, and Joseph. I just remembered where I saw it. How could I forget?" He put a hand to his forehead. "What's the matter with me?"

"What are you talking about?" Anthony asked.

"The mermaid."

Thomas Holtz wouldn't say *where* he had seen the lamp, only that he was sure that he had seen it, and that unless someone had taken it down, it was still there. Would they like to find out? Anthony checked his watch, a useless gesture since Gail was already dialing Teri Greenwald's number to say they might be a few minutes late.

Holtz had tied his boat at the Buttonwood dock. The canvas top was up but did little to keep out the rain, which was falling steadily, pushed by gusts of wind into the cockpit. Holtz suggested that Gail sit below in the small cabin, but she refused.

He found some extra raincoats. Gail's was so large it could have served as a tarpaulin. Her face peered out from the voluminous hood. Anthony stood between the two seats.

"Hang on. We're going to run around the back side of Upper Matecumbe to Plantation Key." Holtz flipped on his running lights. By now the sun had set, and the world had turned a uniform gray without delineation between sky and sea. Past the marina's breakwater he made a sharp turn to starboard. The boat hit a trough, and a wave splashed over the bow. Gail shrieked and slid out of her seat to the deck.

As Anthony helped her up he yelled over the noise of the engine, "Tom! Forget it! We'll come back tomorrow."

Holtz waved him off. "It's not as rough in the bay!"

They sped under the bridge at Tea Table Channel then into water only marginally less choppy. Ten minutes of this pounding took them by the Bay Harbor Resort. Holtz pointed. "See those trees? That's the Lindeman cemetery." It had grown too dark to make out the headstones or the wrought iron fence. Holtz guided the boat around a mangrove island, staying out of the shallows, then came around between two channel markers.

They headed directly for the dark, wooded shoreline, toward lights that indicated a residential area. The channel became a canal branching left and right. The turbulence of the open water was gone. Holtz slowed the boat, and the engine noise dropped. Gail flipped back the hood of her raincoat to see out. Anthony used his handkerchief to mop the water off his face. He tasted salt.

The houses were large, the seawalls long, the yards well-tended. The homes rose two or three stories, constructed on concrete pilings for possible storm surges. Some of the lower areas were enclosed, some not. Expensive motor yachts and sailboats were tied to the docks. The uncurtained windows of one home revealed a woman coming downstairs and a man sitting on a green leather sofa watching television, taking his socks off.

"I feel like a voyeur," Gail said. "Where are we?"

"Anthony knows. Don't you?" Holtz kept his eyes on the canal.

"Not at all."

"The house I'm going to show you used to be the only one on this street, but that was ten, fifteen years ago. This area has been built up since then."

Holtz turned the boat left. They moved slowly along the narrow inlet, which would come to a dead end fifty yards ahead. Their view of the last house was blocked by an immense sport fisher whose upper deck was swaddled in rain panels. A glow fell across the water. They came around the sport fisher and saw where the light was coming from — a white globe held in the lifted hand of a mermaid on the seawall. Her curled tail rested on a pedestal of ocean waves, and long blond hair hung over her breasts.

"There she is," said Holtz.

Gail said, "It can't be. Billy's mermaid had red hair."

"Oh, this is the one, all right." He glanced around at Anthony, and the light in the mermaid's outstretched hand shone in his glasses. "Is it coming to you yet?"

"I have never seen that thing before. I am sure of it. I would remember."

"Then you didn't walk around to the back. You drove by and didn't get out of your car. This is Periwinkle Street. Does that ring any bells?"

Anthony stared at the angle of the house on the lot, the placement of the garage

347

under the main floor, the line of palm trees along the west side. He did know this house. The last time he had seen it, the roof was a heap of scorched timbers and broken tile.

It was the house that Billy Fadden had set on fire.

Tom had something more. "Guess who used to own it."

"The Morgans —"

"No, before the Morgans. I'll tell you. Teddy Lindeman. Teddy lived here before the government sent him to prison." Holtz grinned at the astonishment on Anthony's face. "Ain't this a small world?"

16

Kyle Fadden had just poled his skiff out of sight behind the boathouse at the Buttonwood harbor when his phone rang. He unzipped his waterproof jacket to get to it and saw the name on the lighted screen. Holtz and Lindeman, P.A.

"Yeah."

"Hey, buddy, what's going on?"

Fadden carefully laid the pole back in the chocks. "Nothing much. Waiting to hear what the plan is."

"That's why I called. What happened with Billy at the police station today? Did they get it all cleared up?"

"I don't know yet. I'm going to talk to him."

"Where are you?" Lindeman asked.

"I'm home drinking a beer. Watching TV."

"Okay, good, stay there. I don't want you on the island, not until your kid's lawyers are gone. We're filing the guardianship in two weeks. I've got a judge who can give me an emergency hearing within a few days after that. So we're back to the original plan. Okay?"

"What do we do in the meantime?"

Lindeman said, "We wait. I'll call you."

"When might that be?"

"Next week. Just wait for my call."

Fadden reached for the edge of the concrete seawall to keep the boat from drifting. Water splashed along the hull.

Lindeman said, "Did you hear me?"

"Yeah. I'll wait for your call." Fadden turned his phone off and slid it back inside his jacket.

When Billy got to the harbor, he expected to see his father's boat tied to the dock. The lights were dancing on the surface, and wind rattled the awning over the loading area. His father had said he wanted to talk to him. Billy guessed it was about the meeting with the police. He didn't feel like getting into that, but he couldn't see any way to avoid it.

A figure in a ball cap and a green rain jacket stepped out from behind the boathouse, walking around it and down to the seawall.

"Hi, Dad."

His father smiled and gave Billy's shoulder a firm pat. "How're you doing?"

"Fine."

"Everything went okay at the sheriff's office?"

"My lawyer didn't let me talk to them. Joan talked to them, but I didn't."

"Well? Do they still think you did it?"

"My lawyer doesn't want me discussing the case with anybody."

"I'm your father."

Billy crossed his arms. "Yeah, well, my lawyer told me not to."

"Okay. Whatever you say." His father reached into his jacket for his pack of cigarettes and lit one. "Hey, listen, I ran into Doug Lindeman today. He said he's worried about his aunt when we get that big rain tomorrow. He says her roof might be leaking. He wants me to take a look at it."

"Her roof? I never saw any leaks."

"Doesn't mean there aren't any. We're going to get quite a storm, Billy. That poor old lady in there by herself, rain coming through. Doug wants me to make sure she's all right."

Billy wondered why Doug Lindeman cared about Joan's roof, and why he called Kyle Fadden to fix it. Kyle was a fishing guide, not a carpenter, though he'd built

351

an addition on his own house. Doug Lindeman probably knew that because they went fishing together. Lindeman was a lawyer; he was soft. Kyle Fadden could do anything with his hands.

His father said, "Let's go on over and take a look."

"Now?"

"You know her, Billy. We'll say it was your idea."

"My roof is fine," Joan said at the door. She was looking through the crack, still wearing the clothes she'd had on this afternoon at the police station, her black-and-white suit and her red wig. She had a drink in her hand.

Billy's father said, "Miss Sinclair, you've been a good friend to my son, and it would be my honor to help you."

"I can't have people going all over my house. I need to get ready for Tom. He's taking me to dinner at the Inn. I have to get dressed."

Billy felt his father give him a nudge. He said, "It won't take a minute. If Dad sees any leaks, he won't even have to come back inside. What would you do, Dad, put a tarp over it?"

"That's absolutely all, Miss Sinclair.

Billy says you have a long ladder. I'd just throw a tarp over any trouble spots till you can get it fixed properly."

She said, "I really don't see the need."

Billy said, "What if the wind tears off some shingles? The rain could come through on your movie collection. You don't want that to happen."

"Oh, God." She turned her head toward the video room. Her wig was flat in back, like she'd been lying down. "All right, but please be quick." She moved aside so they could come in.

Billy was used to Joan's house, but when she turned on the lights he could see how shabby it was. His dad looked at the stuff on her shelves, and the dusty floor and torn curtains, and then he wandered into the dining room. He wasn't a big man, but his green jacket took up too much space. "So this is where Billy watches all those movies. That's a nice TV."

Billy said, "Hey, Dad, the roof is upstairs."

"Hold on a minute. As long as I'm here, let's see if Miss Sinclair needs any immediate assistance." He pushed open a door and walked through to the kitchen. His boots pounded on the wood floor. "Is the plumbing in good shape? Any electrical problems?"

He switched the fluorescent light on and off and on, leaving the long, bare tubes glaring down on the peeling linoleum. There were dishes everywhere, worse than Billy had seen lately, and he wanted to turn off the damned lights. His father tested the faucets, which screeched and rattled. Billy whispered, "Dad, get out of here."

"What's this door to?" He opened a narrow door on the other side of the old gas stove. The wood caught, then let go with a loud squeak. The smell of musty earth rolled up the dark stairs. "What's this?"

"The cistern is down there," Joan said, rolling her eyes toward Billy. She finished her drink. "And the roof is in the other direction."

"Dad —"

"I'll be. Haven't seen one of those in a long time." He flipped a switch but the light was broken.

"Mr. Fadden, I don't want to be rude, but *please*."

He put a shoulder to the door to close it. "All right, let's go upstairs."

Joan hurried after him, telling him not to go into her bedroom. On the second floor an old rug ran down the hall, and the

striped wallpaper was stained and spotted. Billy had never been up here except once when Joan had fallen asleep in her recliner watching a movie. The door to her room had been closed, and he hadn't dared to open it. The other bedrooms were full of old furniture and dust, and the bathroom had a tub with claw feet.

She stretched her arm across a door at the end of the hall. "This is my room. It's private."

"Look up." Billy's dad pointed. "Look at the ceiling."

A bare bulb in the light fixture showed the brown patch in the ceiling where plaster had buckled and water was dripping through. A puddle had formed on the rug. He walked to the other end of the hall, then up a smaller staircase to the attic, and they heard his boots thumping around.

He came down a minute later shaking his head. "Ma'am, you've got a serious situation up there. I'll be back later with that tarp, no inconvenience to you, I promise."

Joan leaned against the wall and put her face in her hands. "If you must."

"I'll get a pan from the kitchen," Billy said. He took his father by the arm and pulled him downstairs. Joan followed and said she would get her own pan, thank you very much, and good night.

They went out. The front door slammed shut behind them, and a lock turned.

"I don't believe you went all over her house!"

His father was smiling. "That woman needs some help, and I don't mean with her roof." He swung into the passenger seat of the golf cart.

"If she wants to live like that, it's her choice."

"You think so? Rain pouring inside, and that's her choice?"

Billy said, "I didn't know about her ceiling, okay?" He shifted to get the pills out of his front pocket. He thumbed open the little plastic box.

"What's that?"

"Ecstasy." His father's eyes fixed on him. "It's a prescription. Percodan. Okay? For pain." He turned the cart back toward the resort. The lights bounced over the ground. He felt like driving the cart into a tree.

"Slow down!" His father said, "What's the matter with you?"

"Nothing." Billy slowed down.

They got to the fence and went through the open gate. Billy thought about closing it, but Joan expected Tom Holtz to come over. Wait till he saw that kitchen. He would run the other way. Billy felt sorry for Joan. She didn't used to be so lonely and suspicious. It was depressing.

The cart rattled and jerked, and Billy's neck was killing him, but he didn't waste any time getting back to the harbor.

He stopped the cart on the seawall next to the boathouse. It was raining again.

His father took out his cigarettes and a lighter. He cupped his hand and the flame shone on his face. "That's a nice boat," he said. Martin's Sea Ray was visible in the security lights. "I guess if you're rich you can buy whatever you want."

Billy told him, "Martin has a fifty-two-foot Bertram docked in Key West."

"Imagine that."

"Give me a cigarette," Billy said.

"Since when do you smoke?"

"I smoke. You never come around, so how would you know?"

"I hope to change that, Billy. I haven't been around as much as I should." He held the flame under Billy's cigarette.

It was time for the dear-old-dad routine. His father was feeling bad because his only son had tried to kill himself. Billy exhaled smoke, and the breeze took it. Rain tapped on the roof of the cart.

His father propped one waterproof boot on the dashboard. "What are you going to do with yourself, son? You're nineteen. An adult. You need to start making some intelligent choices."

"I guess."

"Is that all you can say? Don't you have a thought in your brain?"

"Actually, Father, I've been considering film school."

"Film school?"

"Movies. Directing, screenwriting —"

"I know what the hell film school is. You just flunked out of a community college, now you want to go to film school?"

"Why not? L.A., Chicago, New York. They've got a film program at the University of Miami."

His father smiled. "With your grades?"

"They'd accept me if I transferred in from Keys Community."

"Which you just flunked out of. Who's paying for this?"

"Martin probably."

"Sure, to get you out of the way. He'd send you anywhere you wanted to go and let you fall on your ass. You aren't cut out for college, Billy. You need to learn a useful trade."

Billy didn't know what to say to that. He

was tired. He didn't want to talk anymore. He wanted his father to leave.

"I'm going to buy a marina pretty soon. That's right. I'm getting a settlement from a lawsuit. Some jackass up in Miami ran into me, and I hired a good lawyer. If you can get your act together, you can work for me. Would you like that?"

"I don't know."

"You don't know."

Billy laughed. "You're going to buy a marina?"

"In Marathon. And a boat — a big one. I'm going to do charters. You can be my first mate."

"No lie?"

"Damn straight, son. Are you interested?"

Billy crushed out his cigarette in the little ashtray bolted to the dashboard. "I guess so." It would be a cold day in July, he thought, before Kyle Fadden had the cash to buy a marina, much less a charter boat. "Sure, let me know. Sorry, Dad, but I need to get back."

"Do yourself a favor," his father said. "Don't tell Teri I was here. She'd freak out. If it was up to her, I'd never see you. All right?"

"She's not what you think," Billy said.

359

"I know what she is." The ember on his cigarette glowed orange in the darkness. "We were still married when she started cheating on me with Martin Greenwald. He had money and I didn't, end of story. She walked out on me and took you with her, and look where you're at. On pills, flunking out of school, trying to commit suicide. Jesus. Why'd you do such a stupid-ass thing? Why? And if you say 'I don't know,' I'll pop you one. Come here." His father put an arm around his neck and hugged him. Pain shot through Billy's neck and he ground his teeth together. "You dumb kid. You dumb little shit. Don't you know better?"

Billy pulled away. "Don't say that about my mother."

"It's the truth."

"Well, don't fucking say it!" Then for just a second his father's face turned to stone, and Billy flinched — which was stupid, because nothing would've happened. He was too big to get hit.

His father laughed. "Okay. The boy loves his mother."

Billy's hands were shaking. He picked at the bandage and lifted it up. The laceration in his palm looked like it was held together by dried black worms. He ripped

360

the bandage off and flung it to the floor of the cart. He wanted to get drunk and pass out and wake up in about a week or maybe never. "I have to go."

His father was looking at him. He seemed to have gotten a lot older lately. His hair had turned gray, and there were shadows under his eyes. "I love you, Billy. I don't want to ride you so hard, but . . . damn. I see you in trouble, and I can't stand idly by like some people do. You know? You need to get off this island. You need to be a man." He gently patted Billy's shoulder. Then he kissed him, and beard scratched his cheek. It was like a stranger doing it, but it was good, too, because it was his father. Billy felt like he might start crying.

"I just want you to be happy, son. You know that, don't you?"

"Yeah."

"Do you? Don't tell me you do if you don't."

"I *know*, Dad."

Finally his father got out of the cart. "Good night, son."

"See you," Billy said. He turned the cart toward the hotel.

Doug Lindeman had been standing on

the front porch of Lois Greenwald's cottage for almost ten minutes, cursing her for being late and wishing to hell he had thought to bring a raincoat, when he finally heard the sound of footsteps on the path. She came into view, pushing her umbrella through the rain-heavy branches of an oleander hedge.

"It's me! I'm sorry you had to wait." Lois pounded up the steps in her deck shoes. The hems of her slacks were wet. She shook off her umbrella and leaned it against the wall. "We've been working like maniacs getting everything done before the storm."

"It's fucking cold out here," Doug said.

"I should have told you to go in. The door's not locked."

Doug picked up the plastic bag he had dropped on one of the porch chairs.

"I'm such a *mess!*" Lois fluffed her hair. The weather had turned it to a streaky blond mop. She noticed the bag, which had come from the Wal-Mart in Key Largo. "What is that?"

"The stuff for Aunt Joan." He set the bag on the floor, which was bare wood but for a scattering of brown area rugs.

The cottage was like an extension of Lois's office in the main building. File cabinets, a computer, a desk. Her beige sofa had a lamp at either end, as inviting as a lobby at the Holiday Inn. The coffee table was taken up with stacks of papers, a calculator, travel magazines, a coffee mug with a Buttonwood palm tree. Her dark blue sweatshirt had a Buttonwood logo over the left breast. He wondered if she had a logo on her panties.

Lois walked to the other end of the room, where she had made a kitchen out of a tiny refrigerator, a hot plate, and the bar sink. Open metal shelves held some cans, a few boxes of tea, some crackers. A hall led toward her bedroom. He was relieved to see that the door was closed. He imagined a single bed, a bare lightbulb, and her clothes in gray file cabinets.

"May I fix you a drink? Some wine?"

"No, thanks, I need to get right back. I have a meeting to go to." Doug didn't want her to think he was here to socialize. Things were getting dicey with Lois Greenwald. He had kidded around with her, a few jokes, some mild sexual innuendo, but it had gone too far. *I'm so sorry, Lois, I sincerely value your friendship . . . and God knows I value the Buttonwood account, but honey, I wouldn't touch you through a biohazard suit.* He had to find a way to tell her without pissing her off. He just couldn't do it now.

Lois folded her hands at her waist and smiled at him. "You've never been to my house before. I feel like I ought to offer you something. Have you eaten?" Her lipstick was neon pink. She must have put on a fresh coat of it before coming to meet him.

Doug held up a hand. "I'm taking a client to dinner."

Her smile was still bright. "A man?"

"What? Yes. A male client. Two of them. From the bank." He laughed. "Okay, so if you could give the stuff in the bag to Aunt Joan when she comes over — Don't tell her it's from me, she'd spit on it. Say you keep nightgowns for guests who forgot theirs."

"All right," Lois said.

"Great. And if you could find a way to keep Arnel Goode from going over there tomorrow too. He could cause a problem if he saw me."

"How will you get in?" Lois asked.

"Does it matter? I'll get in."

Doug had been enraged when his law partner had informed him that he planned to take Aunt Joan out to dinner tonight. Once those two got back together, Doug's chances of getting the property were zero.

Then he realized he didn't need the property. He only needed a few hours on the property. Tom Holtz would be doing him a favor. Lois could do him another favor — keep Joan at the hotel for the weekend.

What Doug had told Lois was that he needed to get into the house to take photographs for the guardianship before Tom could make any changes. Doug had been afraid that Lois wouldn't believe him, but she had. She was in love with him. He could tell her anything.

She took off her deck shoes and placed them side by side on the floor, then curled up on one end of the sofa. She patted the cushion. "Sit down, Douglas. You've come all this way, relax for a few minutes."

He could not remember that she had agreed to do what he asked. "Lo? Are you going to help me out with this?"

"Maybe."

"Maybe? You said you would when I called you."

"Sit down, Doug."

Shit, he thought. "Lois, I need you to do this for me."

"Don't you love to sit and listen to the rain? Open the windows."

Doug turned and looked out. Rain dripped silently off the eaves. There was no view of the ocean from here, nothing but a heavy wall of vegetation that seemed to press against the cottage from all sides. As if he were suffocating, he grabbed the window crank and turned it. Damp air floated in.

He said, "I have a meeting —"

"Call and say you'll be late." The only color in Lois's face was the pink gash of her narrow lips. "Douglas. I said sit down with me. Please?"

"Just for a few minutes." He sat facing her with his back against the arm of the sofa. His knee on the cushion served as a barrier.

Lois said, "What if Joan wants to go home?"

"Tell her the storm is coming."

"If she wants to go, I can't stop her."

"Actually, Lois, you can. Talk Tom into persuading her. Don't lend her a cart. Make her a pitcher of martinis. Lock the gate. And get rid of Arnel tomorrow too. Okay?" Doug smiled. "I need your help, cupcake."

Lois leaned over to stroke his hand. Her fingers were dry and cool. She said, "I like it when you say you need me."

"When is Tom coming over? Did he say?"

"About seven-thirty. I'm skipping dinner.

I have nothing to do all evening." Lois unfolded a leg. With mounting distaste Doug watched her bare foot as it slid across the sofa. Her toes were long and white. Calluses rimmed her heel. She nudged his thigh. "Douglas, what is going on with Tom?"

"Going on?"

"Martin thinks he wants to marry Joan. Does he?"

"He's not going to marry her."

"Why wouldn't he?"

"Because she's nuts, my dear. Ten minutes in her company, he'll notice, believe me."

"What's going to happen with the guardianship? Are you forgetting about my dock?"

"The guardianship is still on. Don't worry about it." Doug looked at his watch. It was time to go.

Lois moved toward him. "You said I could have the dock."

"You'll have the dock."

"Tom is going to tell Martin not to give it to me."

"You can have the fucking dock!" Doug got up. "You will have the dock, Lois. All right? I promise. If that's what you want, it's yours."

"How, if Joan is living there?"

"You will have the dock because one way or the other, Aunt Joan will end up in state care. She will slip her gears, and someone — possibly even good old Tom — will call the police. They will take her away in a straitjacket to a mental ward."

Her eyes were fixed on him. "Are you still planning to move to the island?"

"I didn't say I was going to move here, just fix the house."

"You said you were going to live in the house. You said we'd be neighbors."

Doug was sweating. He rested his hands on her shoulders. Strands of frizzy blond hair hung over her high, tanned forehead. She raised her brows, waiting for him to speak, and lines furrowed her skin. "Yes, Lo. I'll live there. We'll be neighbors."

Her face relaxed. "Let me tell Martin. He'll be so excited."

"No, don't do that. Wait. Let me get some plans in place first. All right?"

"Yes. Whatever you want." Lois slid her hands up his chest, then down, snagging one of his nipples with her fingernail.

He jerked away. "Hey, what are you —"

"I love you." Her arms went around his hips, and she pressed her face into his stomach. Her voice was muffled. "Oh,

God, Douglas, love me. Love me."

He wanted to scream. It came out as a little laugh, and he took her arms and pushed her away. "Come on, Lois. I have to go. I have a meeting."

"You're afraid, aren't you? You're afraid to love again."

"I guess that's true. I'm not ready yet." Her hands were like snakes, crawling over him.

"I know you want me." She stood up and followed him as he backed away. "Why would you come here, to my house, to see me *alone,* if you didn't want me?"

"I need to go, Lois."

"Please, Douglas, stay with me tonight. Stay."

"I've got a meeting in half an hour, and if I'm not there —"

"Listen to me!" Her face was red, and her lips trembled. "We're supposed to be together. You said so."

"I didn't —"

"You said it, and don't think you can change your mind and push me away! I won't let you. You think I won't do anything about it, but you're wrong. I could write to all your clients and tell them what a cheat and a liar you are. I could file a complaint with The Florida Bar. I would

369

do all this for your *own good,* Douglas, but I'd rather not. Do you think I *want* to hurt you?"

He stared at her, rage choking off his ability to speak. He wanted to put his hands around her neck, feel his fingers digging in, pound her head against the floor. *Bitch. You crazy fucking bitch. I'm going to smash your face.*

Her thin pink lips turned up in a smile. "I'll help you with Joan, but you have to stop hiding your true feelings. I know you love me. Say it."

Doug's muscles ached and began to tremble from the effort of holding back what he wanted to do to her. He cursed himself for having come here. He cleared his throat. "I am starting to feel something for you. Maybe you're right."

"I am so, so right about us." She put her arms around his neck.

"Lois, please. I have to go. Look. I'm sweating. I can't take any more of this."

"Kiss me." Her pubic bone was sharp in his groin. He felt himself shrivel. She whispered, "One kiss. That's all I'm asking for tonight. We'll start there."

When he put his lips on hers, he felt her wet, probing tongue, and pulled back. "Okay. I've got to go." He patted her shoulder and fled to the door and flung it open. "Thank you, Lois. Call me when you've got Joan all squared away."

"I will. I'll call you tonight when I'm in bed." Lois's hand trailed over him as he went past. "Good night, my love."

Doug couldn't get down the stairs fast enough.

17

Kshh-kshh-kshh-kshh —

Joan Sinclair crossed her room to lift the phonograph needle from the record. The automatic return had broken a long time ago. Nancy Wilson's *Lush Life* slowed to a stop. Joan blew off some dust and slid the record back into the sleeve. Flipping through the stack of LPs, she decided on Gilberto Joao. She dropped the needle into the groove, flipped the switch to start the turntable, and closed the lid.

A few samba steps took her back across the room. She hummed the tune, unable to understand the words. She could ask directions or order dinner in several languages, but had never learned Portuguese. And one of her lovers had been from Rio too. What he had taught her wouldn't be found in any phrase book.

Picking up her martini glass she caught sight of herself in the standing mirror across the room. Her hair was in a towel, like a turban. Her skin was polished ivory. She made a slow circle, and feathers fluttered at the hem of her red satin robe. More feathers tickled her neck and floated around the wide cuffs. Matching red slippers appeared and vanished as she walked.

The chandelier was on a dimmer, and it seemed that a dozen candles were suspended over her head. Arnel Goode had grumbled about hanging a chandelier in a bedroom, but she had insisted. It was real Bavarian crystal. It was perfect for the room. The wallpaper was embossed silk, the furniture French provincial. An oriental carpet softened the parquet under her feet. A shantung silk divan was positioned by the windows so she could open the curtains and look out at the night. The four-poster bed held so many pillows that she barely had a place to lie down. Her movie posters were on the walls in gorgeous gold frames. Her refuge, her sanctuary.

She returned to the dresser and finished her martini. There was more in the ice bucket, but she didn't want to get smashed, not tonight. She pushed her sleeves to her elbows and uncapped a tube of makeup. Candles flickered in the cande-

labra, twinkling on the atomizers and perfume bottles, the gold powder box with the
long-handled puff for doing her neck and
shoulders. She didn't need a strong light.
In Hollywood she'd paid close attention to
the makeup artists, and she could have
done this in the dark. Base makeup, con-
tour, highlight. Quick, easy. The vanity's
three-way mirror let her see her profile,
right and left. She powdered lightly then
flicked a camel's-hair brush over her face.
Her eyes looked so strange, almost not
there at all. Her face was a blank. She felt
naked.

Sitting back she let her robe drop down
on her shoulders. What jewelry tonight?
Her ruby pendant? She scooted the cushioned stool back to get into one of the side
drawers. She lifted out a box and rummaged through the necklaces. The gold
was warm, sliding through her fingers. A
simple gold chain with a diamond pendant, that would do it. She fastened it
around her neck. She opened another section for the rings. An emerald caught her
eye, and she put it on, thinking of Alexei.
He'd been only twenty-three. He had worn
her out. She tossed the ring back into the
box and tried on a diamond. No, no, too
much, too flashy. Now who the hell had

given it to her? Yves or Jean-Paul?

The box unfolded. This gold locket, a congratulations for her Oscar nomination. These rubies, a gift from Sam Goldwyn to woo her over to MGM, but she hadn't listened, fool that she was. This amethyst brooch from Vincent Price. What a great guy.

A gold bracelet from Frank after a gig at the Sands. A set of Tiffany earrings from the owner of Spago. A darling pair of plain pearl earrings from her housekeeper, Maria. Lovers, husbands, friends. Even down on her luck, starving, no money to pay her rent, she couldn't have sold any of her jewels. That would be like cutting out a piece of her heart. She closed drawers and panels and pushed the box aside. No time for this now.

Makeup pencils and cases rattled when she opened the center drawer of her vanity. Quickly she outlined her eyes, drawing the line across her lid to an upswept point. She checked her profile. Perfect. She had been lucky with her looks. High cheekbones, a straight nose. Eyes dark as night. Wing-like eyebrows. She shaped them with medium brown pencil. Tonight she would be a blond. The candlelight sent shadows dancing on her cheeks.

In the mirror she saw someone standing behind her. A man at the door. She tensed before realizing it was only Arnel. She had forgotten he was downstairs.

He said, "I w-w-won't come in."

"You'd better not, or I'll have your head. What do you want?"

"Is there anything else you n-n-need, Miss Sinclair?" He had eyes like water and thin, pale hair.

She kept her back to him and leaned closer to the mirror to touch the mascara wand to her lashes. "Have you finished the floors?"

"Yes."

"Is everything put away? Did you light the candles? I wanted the roses put in the Baccarat vase. Did you do that?"

"Yes, ma'am. Yes, I . . . did everything."

"That's all, then. You may go."

But he stood there gaping at her. He was like a child, really.

"You're v-v-very . . . beautiful tonight." When she made no reply he said, "Are you g-going out?"

"You've been eavesdropping. Naughty. That is a very bad habit, and I don't like it." She outlined her mouth with lip pencil.

"Are you . . . going out with Mr. Holtz?"

"Why shouldn't I? It's boring around

376

here. I deserve to have some fun once in awhile." Joan went through four tubes of lipstick before finding precisely the right shade. Caramel Kiss.

A whisper came from the door. "I-I-I don't want you to go."

"Well, I'm going. Tom's taking me to dinner at the Inn." She put on the lipstick. "We'll have a small table by the window. Candles, an orchid. Champagne. I wonder if the band will be playing tonight. I love to dance. I'm going to wear my gold dress." Joan looked at Arnel to see his reaction. He was hanging his head.

"Mr. Holtz wants to marry you."

She pretended surprise. "Does he? Would you hate it very much if I said yes?"

"He's t-too old for you."

"Older men can be very attractive."

"He doesn't love you. He's . . . using you."

"You're wrong. Tom adores me." Joan pulled a scented tissue from the gold filigree dispenser and blotted her lips. "He would give me anything I wanted. We'll travel. We'll have parties and entertain our friends."

"P-P-Please don't do it."

"Go away, Arnel. You're always whining. Close my door on your way out."

"I don't . . . want you to get married. I don't want you to."

She screamed at him in the mirror. "Shut up! I don't *care* what you want! You won't control me, do you hear? You won't! Get out of my house!" She grabbed for something to hurl at him — a hand mirror. Bottles tipped over, and makeup scattered. She turned and drew back her arm, but Arnel was gone. She threw the mirror anyway, and it shattered to pieces in the hall. "Get *out!*" She could hear his footsteps thudding down the stairs.

18

The detour to Plantation Key had cost half an hour and put so much salt spray in her hair that Gail almost despaired of making herself presentable for dinner. Quick shower, blow-dry her hair, do her makeup, spritz of perfume, rush to the bedroom to take her black dress off its hanger. Anthony told her to hurry up, and she told him to leave her alone. A minute later she heard the TV in the living room go on.

Her dress had long sleeves, a short hem, and barely any neck at all. She fastened the skinny straps on her high-heeled sandals, checked to make sure she hadn't snagged her hose, then zipped opened her jewelry bag for her earrings. Half-carat diamond studs, Happy Valentine's Day from Anthony, smaller versions of her engagement ring. She held her hand up next to her face in the mirror, and the stones sparkled. Her makeup had come out all right, and her hair curled obediently behind her ears. "You'll do," she said to her image.

She grabbed her clutch purse, yanked open the door, and slowed down as she rounded the corner to the living room. She put a little swing in her hips, waiting for his reaction. "I'm ready to go."

Anthony nodded. He was standing in front of the television staring at the screen. It was an old movie; the colors were too vivid, and the hairstyle on the woman was way out of date. Platinum blond curls were piled on top of her head and lacquered in place. She was sitting on a stone bench in a garden at night, and waltz music played in the background. A tall man in a black suit put his hand on her shoulder. Closeup on his face: hooded eyes, chiseled lips, a beaked nose. "Come, my lovely one. Dance with me." Then to her face, which wavered between fear and guilty anticipation. "My fiancé would not be pleased." The man's smile gave a glimpse of canine teeth. "But your fiancé is not here."

"Oh, my God," Gail said. "That is so bad. What are you watching, *Bride of Nosferatu?*"

Anthony pointed. "Look. It's Joan Sinclair."

The actress rose from the bench and walked around it, putting a barrier between herself and the Count. Her waist was cinched in, and her breasts threatened to pop out of her virginal pink satin gown. "Charles and I are to be married next week. Please leave me." Nosferatu closed in. "You should not be alone in the garden after dark. It is dangerous."

A knock came at the door of the cottage, and Gail dragged her eyes away from the movie. "I think our limo is here." Billy had called earlier to say he would take them to the hotel so they wouldn't get wet in the rain.

Anthony aimed the remote and the screen went dark. He finally noticed Gail's dress, and his eyes raked over her body. "*Qué bella.* Look at this woman. I want to bite you." He put an openmouthed kiss on her neck.

At the door Billy opened a big umbrella and held it over them as they went down the steps. He lifted the rain panel aside so they could slide into the second seat. He took the front, and the cart moved along the lighted path, splashing through shallow puddles of water that had accumulated in the hard-packed sand.

Billy spoke over his shoulder. "Chip called me. He said you came by the store. Now I guess you know I wasn't lying about what time Sandra left. It was like fifteen minutes before I did."

"Yes, that's the only reason you aren't in jail." Anthony leaned closer to speak to him. "We found out — from another source — that Sandra wanted to see Doug Lindeman that night. She left him a message to call her, it was important. We don't know if he did call hcr, or what she wanted to tell him, but a couple of hours later she went to Movie Max and rented *Bride of Nosferatu.* According to Chip, she wanted to show it to someone. We think it was Lindeman."

Billy stared ahead. The raindrops made slashes in the weak light from the head-lamps. "Was he the one she was going out with? That she wouldn't tell me about?"

"Probably so."

"Well, well. Doug Lindeman. I had a feeling about him."

"Sandra was planning to buy an apartment on South Beach. Did she ever mention that to you? Or where she would get the money to do it?"

"Yeah, I knew she wanted to move away. She didn't say anything about money, though. I don't blame her for wanting to get out of here. I'm leaving, too, soon as I can."

Gail touched his shoulder. "Billy, do you

have any idea why Sandra wanted to show *Bride of Nosferatu* to Doug Lindeman? I mean, of all the movies on the shelf, why that one?"

"Not a clue," Billy said.

In the lobby of The Buttonwood Inn the coral-rock fireplace held a small, cheerful fire. Teri Greenwald laughed and said the weather had been so damp and gloomy she'd turned down the air conditioner and lit the gas logs. She took Gail's hands, drawing her closer, putting a quick Latina kiss on her cheek. "I love your dress. *Qué sexy!*" But Teri herself wore nothing as ordinary as black: She was bright as a daffodil, and her dark hair flowed like silk across her shoulders. Her tanned legs were bare, and her sandals were almost invisible. If Gail hadn't liked her so much, she would have been horribly jealous.

Teri led them to the cozy arrangement of love seats and chairs near the fireplace. Lamps gleamed on the gold frames of Audubon prints and the collection of antique fishing rods over the mantel. Tom Holtz was there, a drink in his hand. Gail had expected to see Joan Sinclair with him. Tom said he was waiting for Arnel Goode to show up and take him over to Joan's house.

There were hors d'oeuvres and bottles of wine. Martin poured the new arrivals a glass of champagne. He was drinking club soda, Gail noticed. Teri said they would have dinner as soon as this little problem of how to get everyone to Islamorada had been solved. The staff were leaving after a long day of preparing the hotel for the storm. Teri had left a message for Arnel, but either his battery was dead, or the weather had caused an interference. It could do that, as the island had poor reception from the nearest tower.

Teri picked up her wine from the low table. "Cheers. To good times and good friends."

"And to beautiful women," Martin said. "Anthony, my friend, if we don't have the most beautiful women on the planet, I don't know who does."

Teri blew him a kiss. They all raised their glasses.

Tom consulted his watch again. "Teri, why don't I just drive over to Joan's? Lend me a cart."

"No, Tom, it's too dark. Wait a little. Arnel is sure to call back."

A young woman with short, dark hair appeared from the direction of the kitchen carrying an umbrella, purse, and sweater.

Gail remembered her name: Emma. She announced that she had put everything on warming trays in the dining room. "Are you sure it's okay if we leave? I'd stay to help clean up, if you want. Really."

Teri said, "Thank you, Emma, but as soon as Arnel arrives, we'll get you and the others to the marina."

"Good night, then," said Emma. She went to join the small group waiting by the door.

Tom looked at his watch again, and Teri called out, "Billy, come over here, please." He came across the lobby. She took his hand. "Would you go pick up Joan Sinclair? Tom will ride with you. And then I want you to find Arnel. If he isn't at Joan's, he's at his cottage."

Billy said, "I just told everybody I'd take them to the marina."

"I don't want you to go out. Find Arnel for me."

"They've been waiting for half an hour already. They want to leave *now*."

Tom said, "Come on, Teri, I can drive myself to Joan's house. I haven't forgotten the way. I'd better go now because the rain has slacked off some."

From the big leather chair by the fire, Martin said, "Let Billy make the run to

Islamorada. We don't need Arnel."

"Billy shouldn't be out in this weather."

"Honey, he is perfectly capable of going to the marina and back. He's been boating in these waters all his life, and in worse conditions than this."

Billy looked around at Martin, evidently surprised that his stepfather would speak up for him. "I know what I'm doing, Mom."

Outnumbered, Teri made a bright smile. "Okay, then. Go get the keys to the shuttle, and show Tom which cart to use. And please be careful. Take your cell phone."

With a roll of his eyes, Billy headed toward the office.

"Teri, don't worry about him," Martin said.

"I'm not. I'm not worried. Everything is just wonderful." Teri closed her hand over her gold locket and held it close to her heart, a gesture as seemingly automatic as counting the beads of a rosary. One son was dead, the other in mortal danger. Teri knew what Billy had experienced this morning on Joan Sinclair's dock, the auditory and visual hallucinations, the mermaid that could have represented either Sandra McCoy or his drowned brother, Jeremy. But everything was just wonderful.

Teri got up to refill her glass. Her hand trembled, and bubbles of champagne spilled down the side. Laughing, she wiped them away with a cocktail napkin, then sat down and crossed her lovely legs.

She appeared to listen intently to her husband explain to Anthony how safe the hotel would be in a storm. He had used poured concrete on deep foundations and shatterproof glass to withstand debris flying at one hundred miles per hour. The roofs were impervious to water.

"Excuse me a minute," Gail murmured. She crossed the lobby.

"Emma, could I speak to you about something?" They went outside to the front porch. Past the landscaping lights and the little lamps that marked the walking paths, the sea and sky were so dark they gave the impression of one continuous black void.

"Yesterday morning at breakfast you offered to help if there was anything you could do for Billy. Did you mean it?"

"Of course I did," Emma said.

"Maybe you can do this, maybe not. The police say they have a witness who saw Billy and Sandra arguing in the parking lot at Holiday Isle two days before she was murdered. I would like very much to talk

387

to this person. Her first name is Penny, but that's all we know. Your sister-in-law works for the sheriff's office. Is there any way you could find out for me? Don't feel obligated, if you'd rather not."

Without hesitation Emma said, "How can I get in touch with you?"

"Call the cottage — No, better call my cell phone." Gail wrote down the number for her. "As soon as you can," she said. "We're leaving tomorrow."

"No problem." Emma tucked the slip of paper into her pocket.

The front door opened, and five people came out, led by Billy Fadden. The last in line was Tom Holtz, who had put on a shiny yellow rain slicker with a hood. He looked like an enormous grapefruit. "Ms. Connor, we'll be seeing you in a little while."

"I hope Joan hasn't changed her mind," Gail said.

"Not as of half an hour ago." He flipped up the hood of his jacket. "Save us some of that champagne."

When Gail returned to the lobby, Martin Greenwald was telling Anthony they should leave in the morning or risk being trapped until the storm passed. The forecast was dismal: There would be thunderstorms with heavy rains by late afternoon and possible wind gusts to sixty miles per hour.

"Sixty!" Gail exclaimed. "That's only fifteen short of a hurricane."

"You don't want to drive in weather like that," Martin said. "In the morning I can take you to the marina, but as the day goes on, it could be dangerous to get into a boat. If you and Gail aren't off the island by noon, you may be stuck here for the weekend. You're more than welcome to stay with us, no question there."

Sitting beside Anthony, Gail could clearly sense his indecision. They had hoped to have the entire day to follow up some leads. She said quietly, "You can stay. I'll come back for you on Sunday."

"We'll talk about it."

"Shall we go in to dinner?" Teri said brightly. "Now that everything's been taken care of, we can enjoy ourselves." She tugged on her husband's elbow. "You escort Gail to the dining room, and Anthony can take me. That's how they do it on formal occasions, no? Tonight is special. Come on, everyone."

"Gail, it would be my honor." Martin pushed himself from the depths of his chair and held out his arm.

The shutters in the dining room had been pulled down to protect the windows, but one area remained open. Glass panels looked out on the terrace and its ferny, coral-rock fountain. The room did not seem as empty as it otherwise might have, because the lights in the far corners were off, leaving the garden view illuminated. Soft jazz played on hidden speakers.

There were two tables. They sparkled with crystal and silver. Orchids bloomed from bud vases, and candles flickered. The smaller table was waiting for Joan Sinclair and Tom Holtz.

Teri directed them to the buffet, where the staff had left covered serving dishes with lobster consommé, prime rib, braised vegetables, freshly baked rolls. Teri apologized to Gail and Anthony that they had to serve themselves. Anthony said it was better this way; he could have seconds or thirds without waiting for someone to bring it. Everyone's mood was upbeat, or seemed so, as if in conscious defiance of the weather. Not only the weather. The question of Billy's fate was an even darker cloud.

As Gail knew that it must, the topic of conversation came around to that. Anthony said to expect a search warrant, probably next week. As nothing could be done to prevent it, Martin and Teri should cooperate but call him immediately. Anthony would discuss it with Billy later tonight.

"I'm sure it's going to be all right," Teri said. Her smile hadn't wavered.

Anthony talked about Douglas Lindeman's probable involvement with Sandra McCoy, and Sandra's plans to buy an apartment on Miami Beach. "We don't know where she would get the money," he said, "but it's likely that this scheme, if there was one, has to do with Joan Sinclair. Perhaps Sandra found some valuables in her house. The guardianship could be a means of removing Joan from the property. We don't know. However, we are encouraged about one thing. Tomorrow Tom Holtz will call Detective Baylor about the message from Sandra. This will help deflect suspicion from Billy."

"So Doug Lindeman is a suspect," Martin said. "Why am I not surprised?"

"When Tom returns, it's better not to bring it up," Anthony cautioned.

"I am so relieved," Teri said. "They can't arrest Billy if there's another suspect."

"We'll see how the police react to what Tom tells them," Anthony replied carefully.

"Doug Lindeman has an alibi. He was at his office with Lois, but — I'm sorry, Martin, but it's possible that Lois could have lied for him. She believes that he's in love with her."

Martin nodded soberly, understanding why she might have done so.

Teri leaned toward Gail, who sat opposite. "Lois told you that she and Doug Lindeman are going to be married? I can't believe it. Did she actually say that?"

"Teri." By speaking her name gently and firmly, Martin Greenwald told his wife that she should not bring up family matters likely to embarrass his sister. It was bad enough that Lois could have lied to the police.

Having been chastised, Teri gaily asked if anyone wanted more champagne.

Gail had to speak. "Martin, you should know about Doug Lindeman. He isn't in love with Lois. Not only was he sleeping with Sandra, he has a woman in Key Largo and another in Miami, and he goes after whatever female tourists he can get his hands on. We found out from Tom Holtz. Someone should tell Lois before she gets in any deeper."

Martin glowered at the remains of his prime rib. He had done no more than shove the pieces around on his plate. "Teri, bring me another of those delectable potatoes, will you, sweetheart?"

It was obvious she was being sent away, but she went around for his plate, steadying herself on the back of his chair. "Only one. I have to be strict with you." She kissed the top of his head.

Martin watched her go. "I'd prefer not to discuss my sister's romantic attachments at dinner, but you're right, she should be told. I haven't been entirely satisfied with Holtz and Lindeman, but I left the choice of legal counsel up to Lois. I may have been wrong, and that's all we need to say on the subject."

Gail stole a glance at Anthony, who gave her a little nod, reassurance that she had not been entirely out of line, bringing it up. Gail announced she had to have another sliver of prime rib.

What she wanted was to get Teri alone just long enough to tell her that she must stop pretending that nothing was wrong. *Talk to Martin. Tell him you need him. Tell him that Lois is trying to destroy you. If you don't, you'll lose him.*

But Gail lost her courage. "Dinner is lovely, Teri."

Teri smiled at her and was on her way

back to the table, wobbling slightly, setting her husband's plate in front of him.

Standing there silently, wondering what to do, aware that she had no right to interfere, Gail thought she heard a noise. It came from the hall. What had it been? A footfall, a shifting of clothing? Still holding her dinner plate she tiptoed to the door. The fire sent its flickering light into the lobby. Gail couldn't see around the corner to the area where they had been sitting, but she noticed through the terrace doors that the wind had picked up. The branches of a tree scraped across the glass. Satisfied that this was the source of the noise, Gail went back inside the dining room.

Sitting down, Gail said, "I wonder where Joan and Tom are?"

"Yes, where are they?" Teri stole a glance at her little Rolex, whose cheery yellow face matched the color of her dress. "Should we be concerned?"

"Not a bit," Martin said. "They're probably having a few drinks. Tom has his phone. If he were lost, he'd call us."

Teri pointed to the ice bucket. "Anthony, would you open that other bottle? I feel like having a party. Why aren't you drinking, Martin?"

"All right," he said. "Half a glass. One of

us should be able to get up the stairs tonight."

"You." Teri laughed. "You can carry me. I am such a lucky woman to have a man so . . . so macho." She pinched his cheek, and Martin winked at her.

"My God, you're a sexy wench."

She smiled and tossed her hair back over her shoulder.

Anthony stood to twist out the cork and refill the glasses. He put barely any in Martin's glass. He said he had something he wanted to ask before Joan arrived. "It's about her other nephew, Teddy Lindeman. When we saw Tom this afternoon, and he took us to the Morgan house, he said that Teddy used to own it. The house was seized by the government, sold at auction, and resold once or twice more before the Morgans bought it. Did you know about this, Martin?"

"Vaguely. I didn't think it was important. Is it?"

"I am not sure."

"Teddy died last June," Teri said. "In prison." She hiccuped. "I never met him."

Anthony asked what they knew about Teddy Lindeman's activities as a drug smuggler.

Martin ate the last of his potato. "He

wasn't a smuggler, per se. He let them use his house on Plantation Key as a transit point. Fast boats would take delivery from a ship ten or twenty miles out, bring the kilos of cocaine to the dock at Teddy's house, and dealers from Miami would pick it up. It was a surprise to me. He didn't seem the type — if there is such a thing. I knew him because he used to visit Joan fairly regularly."

"They were close."

"They were. It was Teddy, in fact, who suggested to Doug's father, Harry Lindeman, that Joan have a life estate in the property. Teddy wanted to make sure Joan had a place to live, and I suspect he wanted to continue enjoying the property himself. All that ended with his arrest."

Martin's heavy brows lifted as he focused on something across the room. Gail turned to see Lois Greenwald coming in their direction.

"Lois," said her brother, "are you sure you can't join us? There's more than enough."

"Thank you, but I've eaten." She came closer, acknowledging Gail's and Anthony's presence with a brief nod but making no indication that she saw her sister-in-law. Lois's sharp-boned face seemed to float above the gloom of her navy-blue sweatshirt. "Martin, I had a thought. Joan Sinclair shouldn't spend the weekend alone in this awful weather. I'd like to offer her the Coquina room upstairs. Do you mind?"

"It's fine with me, but I'd be surprised if she accepted."

"I'm sure she would if *you* asked her. I put some night clothes and toiletries in the room."

"Thoughtful of you," Martin said.

Lois took a key card from her pants pocket. "If you'll just give this to her?"

Teri swung her hair over her shoulder. "Lois arranges everything *before* she asks Martin."

Without looking at her, Lois replied, "When you manage this resort, you can find a better way to do things."

How brazen, Gail thought, looking back at Teri.

Martin's jaw was tight. He said to his sister, "Thank you, Lois. We'll take care of Joan."

Lois smiled. "Ms. Connor, Mr. Quintana, it's been such a pleasure having you here at The Buttonwood Inn. Next time we'll arrange better weather."

In the face of such bald hypocrisy, Gail

could think of nothing to say. Anthony allowed a slight nod and one of his noncommittal smiles.

"By the way," Martin said, "have you seen Arnel? He isn't answering his phone."

Lois came back a few steps. "I asked him to bring in your palm seedlings."

"At this hour?"

"Yes, Martin. If we get high winds and rain by morning, they could all be ruined. I know how hard you've worked on them."

"It's late. Tell him to finish in the morning."

Teri broke in. "You should have told us where he was! He was supposed to take the staff to the marina. You knew that, didn't you? I had to send Billy. The seas are terrible tonight! Did you hope he would drown?"

"Don't be hysterical. Of course not." Lois looked back at her brother. "As I was saying, Arnel is busy. I assume that's why he isn't answering his phone."

At this blunt dismissal, Teri's face flamed with anger. She twisted her napkin in her lap.

Martin noticed. "That's fine, Lois. You may go."

"Good night." Lois turned her back and

left the room.

When she had gone out of sight, Martin wearily sighed. "Teri, never mind Lois. She's had a long day. As have we all."

It may have been the accumulated tension of worrying about her son, or her position with her husband, or simply too much champagne, that caused Teri suddenly to burst into tears. She put her elbows on the table and hid her face in her hands.

"Oh, come on, sweetheart." Martin turned in his chair and tried unsuccessfully to pull her hands down. "Teri, don't be this way. Stop crying. Lois didn't mean anything."

"Stop telling me that!" Teri slammed her hands on the table. "She hates me, are you blind? She hates Billy, too, and she poisons you against us. She wants him to die! I will go out of my mind if I have to continue putting up with this!"

Martin stared at her.

"You have to choose! Her or me. Choose! Now!"

"Teri, for God's sake."

Her face twisted. Tears dripped from her chin. "Please . . . let's go away. Away from her. She's waiting for you to have another heart attack so she can take everything.

Can't you see that? Please, Martin. I have to take Billy away. I can't stay here. I love you, but I can't — I can't stand it anymore." She lurched from her chair, overturning her glass. "Shit!" She began to mop it up, then threw her napkin onto the table.

She smiled at Gail and Anthony, and her voice came out as a whisper. "I'm so sorry. Please finish your dinner. I have to go."

"Teri, come here." Martin held out a hand. "Don't leave like this."

She ran toward the hall.

"Teresa!" he thundered.

She turned. Husband and wife looked at each other across the dining room. Gail wanted to slide under the table out of sight, and Anthony had averted his eyes.

"Go fix your face and come back to dinner." Martin expected to be obeyed.

"*Vete al carajo.* Go to hell. You and your precious sister! That bitch!"

Teri vanished, and the clatter of her high heels faded.

Martin Greenwald stared into the space his wife had just vacated, and after a few moments remembered he was not alone. "I'm sorry for that. I don't . . . I don't know what caused . . . why Teri —" He carefully folded his napkin and laid it beside his plate. "Would you excuse me?"

Anthony stood up. "Martin. You will forgive me, I hope, when I tell you that if you value anything in your life, it should be Teresa Flores."

"I do. She knows that. I've told her."

"Have the nerve to tell her about your heart. She won't leave you."

"My heart?" He seemed confused, distracted, years older. "I'll be right back. No. I might not, but stay. I have to see about my wife. Excuse me."

He pushed back his chair and went out.

After a moment, Anthony sat back down. He and Gail looked at each other.

Gail let out a breath. "Oh, my God. What should we do?"

"Finish our dinner."

"Anthony, how can you say that?"

"Because I'm still hungry."

"Do you think they'll be all right? I mean, considering."

He lifted the bottle of champagne from the ice bucket and held it as though he couldn't decide what to do with it.

"Don't give me any more," Gail said. "I am so out of the mood."

Anthony was still frowning. Finally he said, "Yes, I think they will be all right."

"How?"

"They're in love. It's a momentary disagreement."

"Really."

"We've had them, if you remember."

"I remember very well." Gail pushed her glass toward him.

"His wife or his sister. What a choice. Lois has gone too far this time." Anthony smiled and filled Gail's glass, then his own. "We won't see Martin and Teri again tonight."

19

They had been arguing for so long that Tom suspected he had fallen into a loop, the same lines over and over and over. Joan had been drinking even before he got there, and he thought that might be the problem. She couldn't focus on what he was saying.

"Remember two years ago, when I asked you to marry me, and you said yes? What happened, honey? Were you afraid it wouldn't work? I'm not like those guys you married before. This is me talking. Tom Holtz. You've known me all your life."

"I don't *want* to get married." Her voice was petulant and sloppy. "I like being my own woman. I do what I damn well please."

"Okay, if you don't want to get married, we won't, but you can't live by yourself anymore. I want to take care of you," Tom said.

Joan lifted her glass, frowning when she

saw it was empty. How she could see anything in this cave was beyond him. He liked candles, but this was too much. He had tried to turn on a lamp, but there was no power to the house, or she had unscrewed the fuses.

She concentrated on putting her martini glass on the coffee table. With a sudden cry she dropped her face into her hands. "Oh, Tom. What am I to do? Tell me."

He reached out and squeezed her shoulder. "Let's quit yakking and go have dinner. You'll feel better. Everyone's waiting for us."

She had come to the door in high heels and a gold dress with shoulder pads. A little out of date, but she looked very pretty. He'd made the mistake of coming in for a drink and talking about marriage.

Tom stood and shook a cramp out of his leg. "Come on, Joanie."

Joan raised her head and stared at him from under the bangs of her Marilyn Monroe wig. "Why do I have to *leave?* You keep saying you want to take me away."

"We're just going to dinner at The Buttonwood Inn, that's all. We're not leaving Lindeman Key. I'm not going to take you away, I promise. I made a mistake before, wanting you to come live with me, but not this time. No, this is your home, and we'll get it all cleaned up and repaired. How about a nice new kitchen. Wouldn't you like that?"

"Why do people keep barging in and telling me what to *do*? Billy's father was just here. He came right in and told me my roof was leaking. Arnel can fix my roof. I don't *want* people running all over my house."

Tom had to walk to let off some steam. He was getting frustrated. "Are you afraid somebody's going to break in and rob you? Is that what you're afraid of? What've you got that's worth taking? Bags of hundred-dollar bills? Diamond tiaras? Mink coats?"

Her eyes followed him as he paced around her living room.

"Look at this junk." From a shelf he grabbed the first thing at hand, a pair of blue birds sitting on a porcelain branch. One of the birds' wings was cracked off and reglued. He turned it over and squinted through his glasses. "Taiwan. My God, Joanie. This must be worth a couple thousand bucks."

"Why are you asking me about my money?"

"I'm not *asking* about your money. I don't *care* about your money. I want to help you. Don't you understand that?"

"That's what they all say. 'I love you, baby. Where's your goddamn checkbook?' " Joan reached for her cigarettes and snorted a laugh. " 'I'm in trouble with my bookie, Joan, you gotta help me out.' Sure. 'Let's buy that new Caddy convertible, we can afford it.' 'Just one more time, then I'll quit, I swear.' "

"Can't you shut up for a minute and listen?" Tom wanted to shake her. "If you push me away, who've you got? Douglas? He wants you out of here so he can sell the property to Lois Greenwald, or whatever the hell he's doing. Joan Lindeman, I want you to stop this foolishness and come with me. Now. We're going to dinner. If you can't do that simple thing, I'm in a mood to say to hell with it, you deserve what you get."

Her cheeks went hollow as she sucked in smoke. She exhaled on a smile. "Are you threatening me?"

"Holy God, Joanie, look at yourself. Look with your own eyes. Come here." He dragged her out of the chair by an elbow. Over the bar with its collection of dusty liquor bottles, a cracked, gold-framed mirror tilted from the wall. He positioned her in front of it. A dozen or more candles of various sizes and colors wept puddles of wax into mismatched china saucers. "Take a good look. Who is this woman? Who? You're not a Hollywood movie star, you're Joan Lindeman."

She gazed triumphantly into her own dark eyes. "I know damned well who I am! I'm Joan Sinclair!"

It was too much. In an explosion of anger Tom reached out and grabbed a fistful of wig. "Can't you stop acting for once in your life? You're a sixty-two-year-old woman with gray hair!"

Denuded to her stocking cap, Joan became all eyes and mouth for a second before her face crumpled. Howling, she bent over and hid herself behind her arms. "No! No!"

Tom looked down at the wig in his hands, ashamed of his anger. "Oh, Jesus, baby, I'm sorry."

She grabbed the wig and pulled it back on. Blond curls hung sideways. "You son of a bitch, get out of my house. I never want to see you again!"

"Oh, Joanie."

"Get out!"

Tom said, "I'll make sure you're taken care of. Do you hear me? You'll go to a place where you can get some help. I'm still your friend."

Joan slid to the floor with her hands over her face. "I feel nothing for you. You've killed every last shred of love or pity, and all that's left is hatred. I hate you! I hate you!" Her voice caught in a sob, and she looked up at him. Her cheeks were splotched with mascara. "Oh, Tom . . . don't leave me!"

Carlotta Sands, *The Edge of Midnight*.

It was hopeless.

"Good night, Joanie." Bracing his back, he picked up her smoldering cigarette from the floor and walked over to stub it out in the ashtray.

She sobbed and slumped against the bar. Bottles and glasses rattled. "Tom."

Shaking his head, Tom took his jacket off the peg in the hall and opened the door. A faint rectangle of light fell onto the porch long enough for him to see rain splattering on the warped boards and twisted columns. The cart waited at the bottom of the stairs. He pulled the door shut and put on his jacket. He walked forward, feeling for the railing. Rain drummed on the tin roof and poured in streams to the yard. Tom wiped his glasses with the palm of his hand. Raindrops hit his hood with a racket like popping corn.

Easing himself down the stairs, he ex-

408

plored the treads with his toe for secure footing. At the bottom he stepped into a puddle and cursed that he hadn't thought to bring a flashlight.

He walked around to the other side of the cart, and as he started to get in, his head jerked backward. For a split second of perplexed confusion he thought that his foot had slipped or that he had caught his rain hood on a spur of exposed metal.

Then came an immense blow over his ear, and the pain shot through his spine into his legs. He struggled to turn around, to see beyond the edge of his hood. The second blow hit, sending him against the cart. Yellow and red dots swam in his vision. He cried out and lifted his arms to ward off another blow that he sensed was coming, and it did. Again. Again. He staggered away to find a telephone, aware that his collarbone had shattered and he needed someone to fix it.

Another blow put him on his knees, staring into the darkness. Warm liquid ran into his eyes. He heard a distant splash and tasted the grit of mud. Tom moved his lips, but the words gurgled in his throat like water.

20

Beyond the dark glass in the bedroom window a palm frond trembled, then swirled in the wind. Gail crossed the room to close the wooden louvers. Walking past the nightstand she turned on the lamp to make the room even brighter. She was alone in the cottage. Anthony had stayed after dinner to talk to Billy, and Gail had decided to start packing since they would be leaving in the morning. She had noticed *Bride of Nosferatu* and brought it into the bedroom to watch while she worked.

It was a cliché-ridden, low-budget horror film. Too much mist on the ground, too many candles, squeaking hinges, and footsteps echoing in stone passageways. The music track consisted of screeching violins and mallets on open piano strings. The aging male lead was a cadaverous, former Shakespearean actor of minor pedigree with a silken British accent. "Sup with me.

We shall dine on bones and drink our fill of blood." It was silly . . . and yet Gail found herself pulled into the plot, jumping at every strange noise, staying away from the bed in case something was under there to grab her ankles.

Whenever Joan Sinclair appeared, Gail stopped packing and watched her. Joan had been in her mid-twenties when the movie was made but had looked younger, with big eyes, pouty lips, and a pretty little valentine of a face that spoke less of innocence than of voracious sexuality.

So far Nosferatu had seduced Katerina, brought her to the lonely mountains of an unnamed Central European country, and had failed to satisfy her thirst. He lured travelers to his castle, one of whom, conveniently, was Katerina's former lover, Charles. He had become engaged to someone else but was still in love with Katerina.

Gail watched the movie as she laid clothes out on the bed to be folded.

Sundown, a narrow road through the mountains. Charles in the carriage with his new fiancée and a group of fellow travelers. The horses are nervous. They bolt, and the carriage careens into a ditch and breaks an axle. It will take some time to repair it.

411

Count Nosferatu offers them lodging. A warning from the coachman, but no one listens. From there, a plot littered with blood-drained corpses.

Dinner with the count. A gloomy dining room, black velvet curtains. Enter the bride of Nosferatu in a trailing white gown. She sits at the other end of the table. Shock! Charles recognizes his former betrothed. He still carries a small photograph in a silver frame of the two of them together in Katerina's virginal, prevampire days. He vows to bring her back from the legion of the undead. His fiancée, Anna, sweet as pie, has no objection to this. "You must, Charles. You must save her."

Then a long scene with Nosferatu going after one of the other female guests. Uninterested in this, Gail took Anthony's pajamas from the armoire and folded them around his T-shirts to prevent wrinkling. She didn't mind; it made him happy. He also liked his socks folded, not rolled into balls.

Anna was walking down a long, empty hallway. Footsteps tap on stone. "Charles? Charles, where are you?" Candles flutter in the wall sconces. Shadows loom. Anna senses something behind her. She turns around. It's Katerina, whose lips curl back like a dog's. Anna screams, runs away. Katerina is waiting in the next room.

Gail heard a noise at the front door and froze, then let out a breath. She called out, "Is that Nosferatu coming in to ravish me?"

A deep voice answered, "It is I." A second later Anthony appeared at the bedroom door. His head turned toward the television. "You're watching that movie. How is it?"

"Great, if you like over-the-top B-movie melodrama. Katerina has sucked the blood out of most of the men in the cast already. I'm waiting to see if Charles can bring her back from the undead."

"Who is Charles?"

"The man she was engaged to before Nosferatu carried her off."

"Ah, yes." Anthony saw his suitcase open on the floor. "What is this? Oh, thank you, sweetheart, but don't do any more packing for me. I will probably stay through the weekend."

"Why?"

"Two reasons. First, I want to make sure Tom Holtz talks to Detective Baylor. And second . . . Billy wants to see the mermaid lamp."

"He remembers it?"

"He says no." Anthony went to hang up his jacket in the closet. "Four years ago he was at the Morgans' house at least twice mowing the yard, but he says he has no memory of the mermaid being there. So tomorrow, first thing in the morning, he wants to see it for himself. Martin will take us in his boat." Anthony kicked off his shoes.

"So Martin came downstairs after all?"

"No, I called him. He was not happy to be disturbed. He and Teri were . . . busy."

Gail said, "I don't want to leave you here during the storm."

"Martin made this resort to withstand a force-five hurricane, so a little tropical storm is nothing. You need to get back, Gail. You have a date with your daughter on Saturday morning. You and Karen and stacks of bread and jars of peanut butter. Come back for me on Sunday, if you can, and if not, Martin said he could arrange someone to take me home."

She looked at him a while. "Fine." She took his socks and briefs out of the suitcase and carried them back to the armoire. "I'll see you on Sunday."

Laughing softly, Anthony caught her hand and pulled her around. "I wasn't finished. Tomorrow, after Billy sees his mermaid, you and I will go to the courthouse in Tavernier. We apply for the marriage license, you go on to Miami, and I return here. But we'll have to hurry. You need to be on the road by noon."

"The marriage license." She couldn't hold back a smile. "You still want to do it."

"Yes, *bonboncita.*" His hands slid down her back, pressing her close. "Did you think you could escape?"

"I thought *you* were trying to."

"Never. When you called Karen today from the marina, did you tell her about it?" When Gail replied with a grimace, he shook his head. *"Qué cobarde."*

"A big fat coward," Gail agreed. "I'll talk to her this weekend."

"Is that a promise?"

"I swear." She put an X over her heart. He kissed her. "Let's go take a shower."

"Soon as the movie is over. Come on, watch the ending with me."

They turned off the lights and propped pillows against the headboard as Katerina told Charles to meet her in her chambers at midnight. She would be his for eternity. But Nosferatu waits in the shadows. Charles guessed this in advance, clever man, and he carries an altar cloth sewn with garlic and wolfsbane. He throws the cloth over the vampire and weights it with crosses to keep him from escaping. The vampire thrashes and howls.

Katerina's eyes gleam with desire. Her breasts strain at the low neck of her nightgown. She moistens her lips, exposes her teeth. Charles is tempted but in a surge of manly fortitude he pulls the cork from a bottle of holy water and douses her with it. Katerina screams and writhes on the floor. Charles leaps on her and in a single thrust throbbing with metaphorical significance, plunges a sharpened stick into her heart. For a brief moment her face softens. Her eyes fix on him. "Charles." Her eyelids drop.

"*Ay, Dios mío.*" Anthony laughed.

Charles running with the body of his beloved in his arms, grabbing a torch, setting fire to the curtains on his way out. They burst into flames, no doubt soaked in gasoline by the special effects crew. Closeup on Nosferatu trying to claw out from under the altar cloth, flames engulfing him.

Anthony pointed. "No, that's wrong. You can't kill a vampire that way."

"He can come back in a sequel," Gail said.

A graveyard near a church. Overcast sky, bare trees, a small group of mourners.

Charles kisses the portrait of himself and Katerina. He tosses it into the grave. The gravedigger steps forward with his shovel. Closeup on the coffin, the photograph of the lovers gradually being covered with dirt.

Credits roll.

"Well." Anthony stared at the screen as if waiting for something more. "Did you find out why Sandra McCoy wanted to show this movie to Doug Lindeman?"

"I have no earthly idea," Gail said.

"Maybe she learned a new way of sucking blood." Anthony turned on the lamp on his nightstand and began to unbutton his shirt.

Gail got up and went over to press the rewind button. "Joan was good, though, wasn't she? Completely overqualified for this film." On the video box Joan Sinclair's sin-black eyes stared back at her. The points of her teeth made indentations in the red pillow of her lower lip. "You have a secret that you're not telling. Don't you?"

"*Señora,* are you coming with me or not?" Anthony tossed his pants over the back of a chair.

"What? Oh, yes." Gail set the video box upright. "I meant to ask you. Did Tom and Joan ever show up?"

"No, they didn't. Martin found the cart parked under the portico, where it always is, and Tom's boat wasn't at the dock. He must have gone home."

"But it's odd, don't you think, that he didn't tell anyone?"

Anthony pulled her along behind him. "Yes, very inconsiderate. I'll call him tomorrow. Now I want you to show me what you learned from that movie."

The phone had rung twice before, and Doug had let it go to voice mail, but this time he rolled over and turned on the lamp. The woman beside him lifted her head from the pillow.

"Why don't you turn off the damned phone?"

"Let me just see who —"

Lois Greenwald.

"Shit. I have to take this. It's a client." He picked up the handset. "Yes?"

"You said to call you. I was worried."

He cleared his throat. "Sorry. I was asleep. What's up?"

"Joan never came. I put her things in the room and gave Martin a key. Martin was going to talk to Joan. He could have persuaded her, but she never came."

"Crap."

"What do you want me to do now?"

Doug swung his feet to the floor. "Where's Tom?"

"He went home. His boat is gone. We didn't see him either. Maybe she went with him."

"Maybe."

"Douglas? I heard something tonight that hurt me a great deal. I want you to be completely honest with me. Do you have other women?"

"No. Where'd you hear that?"

"Is it true?"

"Absolutely not. Someone is lying to you."

He could hear her intake of breath. "Yes," she said. "Yes. You love me, don't you?"

Naked, Doug took the phone down the hall, closing the bedroom door on his way out. "Listen to me. What did I tell you? I need time. Didn't we agree on that?"

"Say you love me."

"I don't want you calling me at home in the middle of the night —"

"Say it. Please."

"Lois, I'll say it when I fucking feel like it. Okay? Jesus. Don't push me. My therapist said the worst thing for me right now is to push too hard. Grief isn't something

419

you can just turn on and off. You understand that, don't you? Honey?"

There was a long silence. Then she said,
"You have to try."

"I'm trying."

"I can help. I'd come to your house tonight if you wanted me to."

"Not tonight," he said.

"When?"

Doug pounded his head slowly, silently
on the wall. "Soon. Very soon. Maybe by
next month I'll be able to . . . you know.
God, I can't even say it."

"It's all right. Forgive me, darling."

"I want to be normal again. I don't feel
like a man anymore." He made a choking
noise, a stifled sob.

"Douglas! Please, darling, what can I do
to help you?"

"Nothing. Don't worry about it. I'll be
okay. I'm going to take a Paxil and go back
to bed. Lois? Before I come out there tomorrow to take the photos — remember? — see if you can talk Joan into
staying at the hotel for the weekend. Say
you're having a party. I need her to be
gone. Arnel too. Don't fail me, honey. It's
important to both of us."

"I won't fail you, Douglas."

"Good girl. Well. Good night, cupcake."

"Good night, my love."

Before he disconnected he heard the sound of a kiss in his ear.

The bedroom was dark, and he felt his way back to the nightstand, where he fumbled the handset onto the base.

A laugh came from the other side of the bed. "A client? Give me a break."

Doug reached for her. "Shut up and come here."

Under an umbrella in the parking lot of Sea Spires Condominium, Lois Greenwald held her mobile phone to her chest and stared up at the windows of Unit 403. Top floor, bay view. Two bedrooms, two baths, eat-in kitchen, screened patio. The same as the vacant unit one floor below. She had looked at it last week, thinking she might buy it.

Doug's silver BMW was in his assigned space under the building. There were many other cars underneath or outside in the open lot. Lois wondered if one of them belonged to a woman, and if that woman was with him right now. Teri and that other bitch, Gail Connor, had laughed about Douglas cheating on her. It was a lie. He had sworn it was a lie.

But if he'd been asleep, why was the

living room light still on?

Lois went around the building as far as she could, until she reached the seawall. The wind was whipping the water onto the rocks. She tilted back her umbrella and looked up at his patio, through the sliding doors. He wasn't in his living room. Lois walked back to her car and got inside. Rain streaked the windshield, and the building seemed to wriggle and squirm.

She slid down in her seat and took a sip of coffee from her Thermos. She would wait to see if the living room light went off. If it did, she would wait a little longer and see if anyone came out the main entrance.

21

With an electric hum and the clicking of cables, the lift arms lowered Martin Greenwald's boat into the water. Past the roof of the boathouse, the sky was gray as concrete. At dawn the rain had rattled the windows of the cottage, then had mysteriously stopped half an hour ago. Not trusting this pause to last, Gail had taken Anthony's umbrella along when she followed the men to the harbor.

Billy shut off the lift motor. His green waterproof jacket was too long in the sleeves, and the bleached spikes of his hair stuck out like wires. He passed by Martin without looking at him. "I don't need anybody to go with me. I can take my own boat." He stepped on the gunwale and leaped to the deck.

"Your boat is too small for this weather," Martin said.

"Not for one person, it isn't."

Weighty drops of rain made overlapping circles on the water. A sudden gust of wind clawed them away and swirled across the harbor to shake the tops of the palm trees.

"Here." Martin held up the keys, attached to a bright orange float, and pitched them underhanded. Billy caught them against his chest. "You drive."

"Aren't you afraid I'll capsize it?"

"That's what life vests are for. Start the engines." Martin looked around at Anthony, more amused than irritated. He stepped aboard and sat in the copilot's seat.

Gail held onto Anthony's arm. "Is he okay?"

"Billy? He's scared to death and trying very hard not to show it."

"And he still wants to do this?"

"He has to."

The thought of Billy flinging himself into the water in despair, or running the boat full speed into a bridge piling, went through Gail's mind. "Be careful," she said.

The engines churned up the murky water and left the stench of exhaust. Gail walked onto the seawall as Billy steered the boat out of the harbor and beyond the breakwater. Last night Anthony had called

Dr. Vogelhut for advice. She had told him that if Billy was still determined in the morning to see the mermaid lamp, then let him go — but not alone. Gail suspected that Billy's psychiatrist was as curious as they what would come of it.

The islands stretching along the horizon were barely visible, and presently the boat and its occupants vanished into the rain. Gail put up her umbrella and headed toward the cottage. She thought of Billy's courage and wished some of it for herself. She had been avoiding a confrontation with Karen. Yesterday they had talked on the phone, but Gail hadn't mentioned marriage plans. *Hi, sweetie, how's school going, miss you too. . . .*

Joan Sinclair drifted into Gail's thoughts. The actress in her long black wig, holding her martini and exhaling a plume of cigarette smoke. *What the hell are you waiting for, permission?*

As soon as Anthony got back, they would drive to the courthouse in Tavernier to apply for a marriage license, one step closer to the edge. Gail *wanted* to grab his hand and jump. He wasn't a stranger. He was part of her life. They had been together — with a few lapses — for more than three years. *Listen, Karen, you know that Anthony and I love each other very much. We plan to get married . . . next month. In two months. Please don't say you want to go live with your father until you try . . . until we all try to make it work out.*

Gail repeated these thoughts in different combinations of words until she reached the cottage and shook out the umbrella on the porch. Her suitcase was inside, ready to be carried down and loaded into the shuttle when Anthony returned. She wanted to wheel it back to the bedroom and hang her clothes next to Anthony's in the closet, but tomorrow morning she and Karen would be at Camillus House making sandwiches. Unless the event had been called off. Perhaps it had.

She reached into her shorts pocket for her cell phone and hit a speed-dial button. After a few seconds, Irene came on the line sounding as though she were standing in a crevasse on the moon. "—lo? . . . Hello?"

"Mom, it's me."

"— calling from, darling? Can't hear —"

"I'm at the resort. How's the weather there? . . . The *weather*. . . . I was wondering if the school project is still on for tomorrow morning. . . . If Karen's project — Never mind. Ready for a news flash? Anthony and I have decided to get our marriage license today. Isn't that wild? I don't know when we'll actually get married. Soon. Mother, I am so in love with Anthony. I can't bear to be apart from him."

The line crackled. "— so happy — love him too — tell Karen?"

"I'll be back this afternoon." Gail cupped her hand around the mouthpiece. "Tell Karen *this afternoon*. . . . Mother, the reception is awful, I can't hear a thing you're saying. I'll call later. Love you!"

She noticed the telephone by the sofa. She was on the point of trying again on a land line when her cell phone rang. She put it to her ear. "Yes?"

"It's Emma," the voice said.

"Emma." The waitress at the resort. "Right, you were going to find Sandra's friend for me."

The reception was fuzzy but she could make out that Emma's sister-in-law at the sheriff's department had come through with the name of Penny Lobianco. It was she who had seen Billy strike Sandra McCoy two days before her murder. Penny worked at a gift shop called Island Treasures near Mile Marker 85.

Having brought nothing warmer than a

shawl, Gail put on Anthony's brown cashmere sweater and rolled up the sleeves. Her sneakers were soaked by the time she ran up the front steps of the hotel. They squeaked all the way across the dim, empty lobby. She was looking for Lois Greenwald.

She found her in the office. Lois was slicing Arnel Goode apart for his shiftless attitude yesterday. How dare he abandon Martin, whose two hundred pots of seedlings had been exposed to the weather all night! Had Arnel finished putting them away? Every last one of them?

"Yes, ma'am, I-I did."

"Good. I want you to go to Everson Electric in Key West and pick up a part for the generator. We'll need it if we lose electricity. Here. All the information is on this sheet of paper."

"B-But it's so far, and I promised Miss Sinclair I'd t-take in her yard f-furniture and close her . . . shutters —"

"Arnel, who do you work for? Who pays your salary?"

"You do, b-but, Miss G-Greenwald, if I go to Key West, I m-might not be able to come back. The storm —"

"If you stop arguing, and get moving, you shouldn't have a problem. Don't use the shuttle, we might need it. Take one of the runabouts."

"What — What's the matter with the generator?"

"Arnel, if you don't like working here, you can easily be replaced. Is that what you want?"

"N-No. I-I'm sorry, M-M-M-Miss G-G-G —"

"Say it. *Ms. Greenwald*," Lois pronounced with exaggerated precision. "You can talk when you want to, Arnel. Yes, you can. I've heard you. Greenwald. Say it."

In the hall Gail listened in shocked disbelief. This was beyond the bounds of decency. It was like striking a child. She strode into the office and stood next to Arnel. She sent a chilly smile toward Lois.

The wide-open spigot of the woman's verbal abuse immediately turned off, leaving only a drip of disdain. "Yes?"

"Good morning, Lois. I need very much to get to the marina and back. I wouldn't bother you if it weren't extremely important."

Lois looked at her as though she were feebleminded. "Why didn't you ride over with Martin?"

"Because this just came up. It's regarding Billy's case," she added, but didn't

429

know why this should make any difference to Lois. "Perhaps Arnel could take me."

"I'm sorry, he can't," Lois said. "Arnel is on his way to Key West."

"But he's going to drive there from the marina, isn't he?"

"How would you get back? Arnel isn't returning immediately, and I can't pick you up."

Gail said, "I'll think of something."

"Fine. Arnel, take Ms. Connor to the marina." With a nod of dismissal, Lois Greenwald sat down and began to go over some figures on a spreadsheet.

Once Gail had retrieved her umbrella, Arnel motioned for her to follow him out the back. They stood on the landing that led down to the delivery area. He had draped his plastic raincoat over the railing. He put it on, a rumpled gray shroud that came nearly to the tops of his rubber boots.

"Where a-are you going in . . . Islamorada?"

"Island Treasures? Mile Marker 85," Gail said.

"I'll take you."

"That would be wonderful. I'm sorry to be an inconvenience."

"It's not." A smile flickered across his

lips. He took a hat out of his raincoat, shook it, and dropped it on his head. Gail noticed his hands, which she had only ever seen before in gardening gloves. His nails were gnawed to soft pink pads, probably the result of raging neuroses. Gail was not surprised.

They ran down the steps and into the rain, splashing through puddles, leaping over fallen palm fronds. Arnel's raincoat flapped like the wings of a bird. At the harbor the sea was a sodden blanket of gray wool. She followed him to a small boat bobbing up and down in the water, and she drew back. "Are we going in *that?*" Arnel reached under one of the seats and pulled out a rain poncho, which he told her to put on. He said, "D-Don't worry. I'll get you across and . . . and Martin can bring you back."

Wipers kept the windscreen reasonably clear, but Gail could feel the wind pushing them sideways. The boat nosed down, then came up, and a wave rolled over the bow, obliterated the view, and surged away.

Gail lifted her feet to get them out of the water. "I hope we have life vests!" she shouted.

"It's just a little s-s-s-s-squall passing by. We'll come out of it soon." Arnel clutched the wheel and leaned toward the wind-screen. In a few minutes, as he had predicted, the thundering noise on the canvas roof abated, and the wipers scraped enough rain away to reveal their steady approach toward the marina.

"How will you make it back?" Gail asked.

"Not in this boat, if the w-w-wind gets bad."

"Lois shouldn't have sent you to Key West!"

"Oh, well."

The little boat shuddered into a wave, and foam exploded off the bow. Gail held on and prayed.

At the marina the masts of sailboats swung to and fro, and their cables rang like bells. Arnel tied up at the dock, and he and Gail made a dash for the awning where the resort kept its vehicles. Arnel opened the door to an old panel van obviously used for running errands, and Gail climbed in.

He had just gotten in the other side when he reached into his trousers pocket for his cell phone. "Arnel here. . . . Yes, ma'am." He sighed. "I have to go to Key West. . . . Lois said to . . . A part for the generator." He glanced at Gail. "I'll try. . . . Yes, ma'am. . . . Okay." He rolled his eyes and made a mock sigh of exasperation. "Yes, Miss Sinclair, I will." He put the phone back into his pocket. "She wants me to buy her some gr-groceries and . . . more candles and another bottle of B-Beefeater. She drinks too much, but . . . try to tell her that."

"Have you got your phone set to vibrate? I didn't hear it."

He nodded. "She d-doesn't like it to ring. If I'm . . . over at her house? She says, 'T-T-Turn that . . . goddamn thing off! Can't you see I-I'm resting?' " Except for the stutter, his voice was eerily similar to Joan Sinclair's. He had mimicked perfectly the bored drawl, the Lauren Bacall accent, the smoky rasp. Why not? Arnel Goode was Joan's biggest fan. How many hundreds of hours had he spent watching her movies, memorizing her lines?

He shook out a cluttered key ring and inserted the right key into the ignition. Gail remembered something. "Arnel, you took Sandra and Billy to the marina the day she died, didn't you?"

"Sure." Arnel checked the rearview and backed up.

"Did you hear what they were they talking about? Did Sandra mention why

433

she was leaving work early?"

"No." He frowned through the windscreen. "But I think . . . she had a f-f-f-fight with Miss Sinclair."

Gail had guessed correctly. This had been the day that Joan Sinclair had kicked Sandra out after catching her upstairs in her bedroom. "Did Sandra tell you about it?"

"Miss Sinclair did. She said . . . Sandra was t-t-trying to steal her jewelry and . . . she told her to get out and don't . . . come back."

"Does Joan have a lot of jewelry?"

Arnel drove out of the marina and turned right, making no indication he had heard the question. The wipers beat on the windshield.

"Arnel? I'm trying to help Billy. Anthony and I are looking for the reason Sandra McCoy was killed. What if Sandra . . . let's say she told someone that she had seen some valuable jewelry in Miss Sinclair's bedroom."

"Told who?"

"It's just a theory. Let's suppose that this other person wanted all of it. He killed Sandra so he wouldn't have to share it with her. Or maybe he thought she was going to turn him in to the police. Whatever. So

434

does Joan Sinclair have something worth stealing?" Gail waited for Arnel to respond. "Arnel? What did Sandra see?"

His face was hidden by the slouching brim of the old rain hat. "I-I don't know."

"You just said Joan accused Sandra of trying to steal her jewelry."

"I don't know w-w-what she has. She won't let anybody in her room."

"Not even you?"

He shook his head.

"Has Joan ever mentioned having something valuable in there?"

"No."

Gail wanted some way to get past the surface, unsure whether Arnel simply didn't know or refused to say out of loyalty.

Arnel glanced at her. "How are you g-g-getting back . . . back to the marina?"

"A taxi?"

"I'll take you. If-If you won't be in the store too long, I'll take you back to the marina. Then you call Martin."

"But you're supposed to drive straight to Key West."

"A-A-Are you going to tell Lois?"

"Not me," Gail said.

"Me either," said Arnel.

★ ★ ★

It had become a custom between Gail and her daughter that whenever one of them went on a trip, the other could expect a small gift to appear from the suitcase when the traveler returned home. The gift wouldn't be expensive; humor was valued more highly than cost. At Island Treasures, suffering from low-grade guilt, Gail found two items for Karen. The silly gift was a green plastic change purse shaped like a sea turtle; the other, a piece of polished coral set in a spiral of silver wire that Karen could wear as a pendant on a chain.

The clerk was still attending to another customer, so Gail set the gifts on the counter and wandered into an alcove featuring tropical clothing for ladies. On the half-price rack she noticed a white linen dress with starfish and shells embroidered around the low neckline. Original price, $195, on sale for $100. She found a mirror and held the dress under her chin. It was beautiful, flaring from a slim waist to mid-calf with panels that would lift if caught by a breeze.

"That dress would look very nice on you." The young woman had apparently finished with her customer, a fact that was confirmed when the front door opened and shut. "I sold one to a lady who was going to get married. We have a lot of brides come in here. You can't wear a traditional bride's dress in the Keys. Well, you *can*, but who wants to sweat in all that satin?"

"It goes so well with my sneakers, don't you think?"

"Why don't you try it on?"

"I'm afraid I might end up buying it. Are you Penny Lobianco?"

"And you're Gail Connor. Emma said you'd be coming in." Penny was in her early twenties, thin as a stick with short blond hair like the fuzz on a poodle.

"Thank you for talking to me," Gail said.

"Emma threatened to slash my tires if I didn't. Just kidding."

"Billy didn't kill Sandra McCoy."

"I wasn't there, and you weren't either, so who knows?"

"You don't like Billy."

"He's a smart-mouthed geek, a spoiled little rich boy. But hey. Why be different?"

"Was Sandra sleeping with Doug Lindeman?"

"Do you think *he* killed her?"

"I think he might have, yes."

"Why?" Penny snorted. "They weren't in

437

love." Her tone put quotation marks around the word. "I mean, it's not like if she looked at some other guy Doug would get all pissy-faced about it."

"They were just having a good time?"

"You could say that."

"Did you tell the police about their affair?"

"They didn't ask." Penny smiled. "Anyway, he didn't do it."

"Do you have any theories as to who did?"

"Besides Billy Fadden, you mean? Because he flipped out when she broke up with him? And he hit her and said she was a slut whore who should drop dead?"

"Yes, who besides Billy?"

Penny sighed. "Some whacked-out freak. A sexual sadist. A jerkoff who just happened to see her in the parking lot. It happens. You do something as simple as leave your house to rent a video, and you wind up with your throat cut. I'm from Miami. I left there because I got mugged *four times,* but it's getting crazy here too. We have murders in the Keys. People are killed for no reason except it seems like a fun thing to do. I keep my doors locked, and I always look behind me at night. It could happen to anybody, especially girls with long hair, like Sandra. The psycho serial killers go for girls with long hair, it's a proven fact. That's one reason I cut mine off."

For a few moments Gail could think of no reply that would not contain the word *paranoid*. She asked, "Did Sandra ever talk to you about Joan Sinclair?"

"Jeez-o-Pete, there's a weirdo for you. The way she lives, shit all over the place, talking to herself, freaking out if Sandra wanted to come in."

"But Sandra did come in. In fact, Doug Lindeman paid her a thousand dollars to look around Joan's house. Did you know about that?"

"No, I didn't. No way I'd go in there. She said that woman used to be a vampire in the movies."

Gail asked Penny Lobianco if she knew about the apartment on South Beach. Penny said she did. Gail asked, "Do you know how she intended to pay for it?"

"She said her aunt died and left her some money in her will. That was probably bullshit, but I don't blame her for wanting out of here."

"Why do you live in the Keys if you don't like it?"

"Because everywhere else is *totally* horrible. We've still got a few good days, mostly when the tourists aren't littering the beaches and running people off the road, you know what I mean?"

"Did Sandra ever talk about Joan Sinclair being rich? Maybe she had something of value in the house? Jewelry, gold, cash . . ."

Penny Lobianco laughed. "Are you serious? The way Sandra talked, if that lady didn't have a house, she'd be on the street with a shopping cart."

This picture was so at odds with the one that Gail had been developing in her mind that she rephrased the question. "Did Sandra specifically tell you that Joan Sinclair had no money? That she was broke?"

Penny crossed her thin arms and jacked a hipbone out to one side. "I don't remember *what* she said, okay? But that's what she *meant*. Maybe she was wrong. You know, a lot of those old women get taken away by social services, and you find about fifty flea-bitten cats and a big pile of cash in their houses."

"When was the last time you talked to Sandra?"

"When? That same night your client, William the Wonderful, slapped her across the face."

Two days before Sandra McCoy had been murdered. On her last day alive, Sandra may have seen something in Joan Sinclair's bedroom that she didn't get a chance to tell her friend Penny about.

"Is there anything else you want to know?"

Gail smiled at her. "No, I guess that's it."

They walked to the cash register. Penny keyed in Karen's change purse and coral pendant. Subtotal $45.00. She looked up. "Where's the dress?"

"I don't really need it."

"Who ever *needs* a dress? It would look good on you. Plus it's marked down. Last chance."

"All right, why not?"

"One thing, though," said Penny. "You gotta lose the sneakers."

22

In the false twilight of heavy overcast, Martin Greenwald's boat proceeded slowly into a channel that Anthony barely recognized. He pointed out what he believed to be the correct turn, and Billy swung the long prow of the boat to the left. The houses along the narrow inlet were quiet; no one appeared in the yards; closed hurricane shutters indicated that many owners had not yet returned for the season. The rain came down in a slow, steady drizzle. Wind catchers hung limply from the trees, and a line of seagulls perched miserably on the railing of an upper deck. Standing between the front seats, Anthony told Billy that the house they were looking for would be just beyond the big sportfisher parked at the next dock.

Slowly the mermaid lamp came into view. She stood as before on her concrete pedestal of waves, blond hair flowing over her shoulders, one hand demurely at her breast, the other holding a white glass globe. If the light was on, it was too weak to be seen in daylight.

The boat nudged up against the bumpers. Billy cut the engines, pushed himself out of the captain's seat, and stepped onto the dock. Anthony scanned the house. There were no lights, no movement at the windows.

"Throw me the lines," Billy said. Martin went around to the bow, and Anthony picked up the line at the stern and handed it to Billy, who knelt awkwardly to turn it around a cleat, protecting his neck from sharp movements.

When the boat was secured Billy rotated toward the lamp at the far end of the dock and stood there staring at it. Only his fingertips were visible at the cuffs of his shiny green jacket, and his legs seemed too thin for his body. Rain dripped off the curled fins of the mermaid's tail. Salt corrosion had eaten into the light fixture, and rust stained her outstretched hand. Patches of paint flaked from her naked torso. Her smile was a curve of pink, and her faded blue eyes gazed vacantly down the canal.

Billy abruptly turned toward the house.

The oversized jacket and the stick legs moved up the slope, then toward a chain-link fence at the edge of the property, then across to the fence on the other side. He made a circle around two of the pilings supporting the house. His sneakers crunched on gravel. He came back, zig-zagging toward the canal. His hood was tilted toward the ground as though to blot out the sight of his lawyer and stepfather watching him. Billy stepped off the seawall onto the dock and stopped with his toes at the edge.

During this series of erratic movements his companions had come closer. They stood on either side of him. Martin asked if he wanted to leave now, but there was no reply. "Billy?"

He staggered away from the edge and sat down on the wall. Anthony bent to see inside the hood. Billy's brown eyes were unfocused and his skin was pale. He was taking shallow breaths.

Anthony asked him if he had heard the dogs.

He swallowed and nodded.

Martin put a hand on his back. "Lean over. Get some blood in your head."

Billy shrugged away from Martin's hand. "This is where Jeremy died. It was here.

The dogs were here. They were in the yard barking. Three of them. Three rottweilers. I remember. Barking and barking."

Crouching beside him Anthony said, "Billy, your brother died behind your parents' house. You were eight years old."

"No, it was here. I'm sure it was here."

The rain was coming harder, splashing on the dock, running down Billy's jacket. Anthony looked at Martin. "Let's take him home."

"Wait. Billy, why do you think Jeremy died here?"

"I remember the mermaid. The light was shining in the water. I could see Jeremy. I could see him. The light — I saw him because of the light."

"He fell off this dock?"

"Yes!" Billy sucked in a long, wheezing gasp of air.

"Take it easy." Martin touched his shoulder.

Anthony said, "If Jeremy was here, where were you? Where was your father?"

"You think I'm crazy. Don't you?"

"Come on, son, let's go." Water coursed off Martin's fishing hat when he bent to help him up. Billy knocked his arm away.

"Stop calling me your son! You want to get rid of me. You want to put me back in the hospital. You've been planning it with Lois, haven't you?"

"No, Billy."

"My father is taking me with him on his boat. I'm going to crew it for him and you won't have me around anymore. Won't *that* be a great day?"

"Billy, for the love of God, I'm not trying to get rid of you. I don't want you to leave. Stay here and let Dr. Vogelhut help you. Don't run away. If you won't do it for yourself, then for Teri. She loves you more than anything in the world."

"I'm gone. You make me sick. You're an old man, and you think your money can get you anything you want. I won't go in a hospital again!"

"Nobody wants you to!"

"You broke up my parents. Yeah, I know about that. They got a divorce because of you."

Martin stared at him. "Is that what Kyle told you?"

"It's the truth. You and her cheated on him. Didn't you?"

"Good God. All right, Billy. Your mother wants to protect you but you need to know what happened. It wasn't me. Your father was abusive to you and your brother —"

"That was in the past. He apologized —"

"Be quiet. He was abusive to your mother as well, even worse than he was to you, so thoroughly that she lost the will to fight him."

"That's a lie!"

"She had you to think about. She believed she had no alternative but to stay. She came to work for me, and yes, we fell in love. I loved her the first moment I saw her. I said that if she left him, I would take care of you."

Billy shoved Martin in the chest. "You're a goddamn bastard, and she's a whore!"

Martin's face darkened with anger. "What did you call her? Teri is *my wife*. What did you say?"

"I hate your fucking guts." Billy turned and ran up the slope.

Anthony shouted, "Billy, stop!"

"Go to hell!"

Anthony went after him and got hold of the back of his rain jacket and slung him to the grass. "Get in the boat or I will put you in it."

"Let me up. Get off, you spic asshole bastard. My neck! Jesus Christ, you're hurting my neck!" He erupted into more curses until Anthony took a fistful of his hair and shook him.

Billy screamed.

Anthony came down close to his ear. "I give you two seconds to shut up, or I will call the paramedics and have you shot full of tranquilizers." He tightened his fist. "You will go straight to a mental ward. Do you understand me, Billy? Do you?"

Billy wept and laughed at the same time. "Ask me about the house. Ask me if I burned it. You never had the guts to ask me straight out if I burned it on purpose."

"Did you?"

"Yes! I poured gasoline on the lawn mower and on the workbench and on the clothes in the hamper, and I lit a match. You believed it was an accident, didn't you? You went for it."

"Why did you do it?"

"Fuck you."

"Why did you do it, Billy? You didn't know the Morgans." Anthony shook him again. *"Why?"*

"I hated them. I hate all of you! I wish the gun had bullets in it. I should've blown my brains out. I should be dead." His words dissolved into great, hacking sobs. He pressed his face to the ground, and his shoulders shook. "Oh, God, I didn't mean to. I didn't. I don't know . . . what to do. I don't —"

Anthony looked back toward the dock.

Martin was waiting. He lifted his hands helplessly, a gesture asking *what now?*

"Billy, you're going to get up and come with us. Nothing is going to happen to you. You go to your room, you take your pills, and you go to sleep for a little while. Can you do that?"

He buried his face in the crook of his elbow. "Don't tell my mother what I said. I didn't mean it. I'm sorry."

"You should apologize to Martin, not to me. Get up." Anthony gently helped him to stand. His eyes were puffy slits, and his nose was running. Bits of wet grass stuck to his cheeks. He leaned on Anthony as they walked across the grass. He felt fragile and small. Martin pulled a handkerchief out of his back pocket and gave it to Anthony, who handed it to Billy. "Here. Wipe your face."

Martin boarded the boat and started the engines. "Anthony, get the lines."

"I'll do it," Billy said.

He was away before Anthony could grab him. He went to the cleats and fumbled to free the ropes, tossing them onto the deck. His movements made it obvious that he was in pain. He gave the boat a shove, got back aboard, and sat in the seat directly behind Martin with his head bowed and his hands pressed between his knees. Anthony supposed this was his form of an apology.

In the narrow canal Martin maneuvered the boat around to go back the way they had come. From the first-mate's seat Anthony kept his eyes on Billy, unable to decide if he wanted to put his arm across his shoulders in sympathy or to backhand him. As soon as they returned to the hotel he would call Sharon Vogelhut. He knew what she would say: that they begin the commitment process immediately.

Billy had deliberately burned down the Morgans' house. He had *known* what he was doing. He had gleefully lied; he had joyously put one over on everyone, even his lawyer. Anthony's state of mind wavered between anger and shame. He had been wrong. Four years ago he should have taken the prosecutor's offer: Send the defendant to a state hospital. But Anthony had wanted to win the case. He had allowed himself to believe, as Teri did, that Billy would be fine, that his therapist could fix him, that $200,000 to the Morgans would make the problem disappear.

Anthony thought of Sandra McCoy lying at the edge of the rock pit, her throat slashed, blood pouring out. A crime that

Billy had confessed to. Perhaps for once he had told the truth, and the possibility made Anthony feel sick.

He looked off the stern. The mermaid stared back at him with her empty eyes and cryptic smile as the rain came steadily down.

23

Kyle Fadden tossed the plastic tarpaulins onto Joan Sinclair's dock. He steadied himself against the up-and-down movement of the water and lifted his toolbox. It was like standing on the back of a horse. The boat shifted. Fadden fell on his backside against the bait well, and his toolbox crashed to the deck.

He let out a long curse, stopping abruptly when he heard the deep roar of engines.

There was a boat about a quarter mile out, coming from the direction of the Whale Harbor Channel. It was bouncing over the chop and kicking up spray, aiming straight at the island. They weren't likely to see him with the dock in the way. Fadden watched as the boat closed the distance. Its trajectory sent it past him toward the Buttonwood harbor. Not a small boat, maybe a thirty-footer, taking the seas fairly well. Before it disappeared behind the trees, Fadden had decided whose it was: Martin Greenwald's. He wondered if Martin Greenwald was out for a pleasure cruise.

Rain dripped off the brim of Fadden's hat. He got a grip on the toolbox and, between lurches of his boat, heaved it onto the dock. He followed that with the canvas bag, which landed with a clanking thud. Breathing hard, Fadden climbed up the ladder to the dock.

A few minutes later everything was on shore, wrapped inside one of the tarps and shoved under some bushes. Fadden got back into his skiff, cranked the engine, and nosed along the mangroves until he found a little cove. He stepped ashore and dragged the boat out of sight. The propeller scraped on sand and turtle grass.

It would be a bitch getting across the water again, running a flats boat on eight-foot seas. Fadden thought he could do it. He felt lucky. He would be long gone before the storm hit.

Gail was able to catch a ride back to Lindeman Key in Martin's boat, as she had hoped to do. Whatever happened when Billy came face-to-face with his mermaid, no one talked about it. Wanting to avoid the salt spray, Gail had joined Billy in the cabin. White-faced and silent, he sat on the forward bunk with his arms wrapped around his knees.

Once back in the cottage, Anthony flung his damp clothes into the bathtub and took a fast shower while Gail poured them both a brandy. She took the glasses into the bedroom. Anthony was getting dressed.

"Are you going to tell me what happened or not?"

He tucked in his shirt. "Besides calling me a spic bastard, Billy said that Jeremy drowned behind that house. Not his parents' house in Marathon. That house. So. If you want a connection between the mermaid and his dead brother, there it is."

"My God. Is it true?"

"Of course it isn't true. He's irrational. He needs psychiatric care. He should have had it four years ago." Anthony stared out the window at the rain. *"¿Cuándo va a parar la jodía lluvia?"* He wanted it to stop. So did Gail. He downed half his brandy in one gulp.

"What will happen now?" she asked him.

"You and I are going to Tavernier." Anthony sat on the end of the chaise to put his shoes and socks on. "We have to hurry.

454

The courthouse might close early. Martin will take us to the marina. From there, you drive my car. I'll use his and come back. Did you pack everything? If not, I'll bring it later."

"Anthony, we don't have to do this. Never mind going to the courthouse. There's no time. Martin can take me to the marina. You stay here with Billy."

"No, no, I have this worked out. It was my idea that we get married in the Keys. It didn't happen, but at least we can apply for our license."

"Oh, sweetie. You don't have to prove you love me. I know you do." She went over to the chaise and sat on Anthony's lap. "I know it."

"What about our marriage license?"

"We can do it later. It's all right. Really."

He looked at her, the whites showing under the intensely dark irises of his eyes. His hair was still damp, combed back in waves off his forehead. He put his arms around her. "I would marry you anytime you want. Tomorrow, next week, a month . . . but not June. I can't wait that long. Do you want to come back here? A sunset wedding. Martin said he would give us the biggest, best party —"

She laughed. "No, thank you. Teri made

the same offer, but I don't think so. Anywhere but Lindeman Key."

Anthony closed his eyes. *"Ay, Dios mío, todo sale mal."*

"Everything is going badly? Is that what you said?"

"I don't mean you, sweetheart." He tried to move Gail off his lap, but she held on. "Gail, please."

"Wait. It's about Billy, isn't it? I want to know what happened. You're not telling me everything."

Seconds ticked by. Anthony let out a breath, then turned his eyes toward her again. "Billy admitted that he set the fire. He wanted the Morgans' house to burn. He poured gasoline on whatever would catch fire, and he lit a match. He lied to me, to everyone, and I fell for it. I bent the rules to save him, and all the while, he was laughing."

"He did it on purpose? But why?"

"Why? For fun. To see the flames. Because they didn't give him a big tip when he mowed their lawn the first time. Because he has a screw loose."

"That doesn't make sense."

"Exactly. He was sick. He needed help, and I refused to see it. But I won the case, no? I earned my fee. And I'll earn a fee defending him on a charge of first-degree murder."

"He didn't do it. Anthony, it isn't your *fault*." She tried to embrace him, but he took her arms away.

"Gail, we have to go."

"I don't want to go. Let me stay here with you. We'll go back on Sunday."

"Are you crazy? Your daughter would kill me."

"We can blame it on the storm."

"No, they expect you. You are going back to Miami, don't argue with me."

"God strike me dead, but I don't care about making sandwiches at a homeless shelter. Karen will just have to understand." Gail put her head on his shoulder. "Don't you want me to stay?"

"*Ay, niñita,* of course I do, but there's nothing more to be done here. I'll make sure that Tom Holtz talks to the police about Doug Lindeman, and then I'll be on my way home, too, as soon as the storm passes. You should go. For me." He kissed her. "I don't want to worry about you. Go now, it's a long drive in the rain."

"I suppose I should. Are you all right?"

"I am already missing you. Come on, let me up."

Gail looked at him and realized why he

didn't want her to stay. Not because of Karen. Not that. "You're afraid of Billy, aren't you? Yes, you are. Anthony, who's being irrational? He didn't kill Sandra McCoy. I don't care what he did four years ago, he wouldn't . . . *do* that. Cut someone's throat like that." Gail made Anthony look at her. "Do you honestly believe he did?"

He thought about it, then said, "There is a difference between what I believe, and what is *possible*. No, I don't think he did it, but . . . but all the same, I think you should go."

Climbing the steps to his apartment, Billy's feet weighed twenty pounds each. His neck hurt. His clothes were dripping. All he wanted was to go back to bed. When he opened the door he saw someone sitting in the lounge chair across the room drinking a beer. His father.

"Hey, Dad."

"You look like a drowned rat. Where've you been?"

"Nowhere. Plantation Key." Billy hung his jacket on a peg behind the door, where it started making a puddle.

His father wore rubber boots and dark gray waterproof pants with suspenders. A jacket had been tossed over the back of a kitchen chair. The apartment was two rooms cut out of a storage area over the cart garage. Most of Billy's stuff was heaped in piles on the floor. His mother used to come in here collecting dirty clothes, but she'd given that up a long time ago.

"You were out in the boat with Martin Greenwald." His father tilted his beer can to his lips.

"He had some stuff to do before the storm hits. I had to go with him."

"Did Martin pay you? Or do you do whatever he says?"

"I don't do anything for that bastard unless I get paid."

His father laughed.

Billy went into the bedroom to change clothes. He found a pair of jeans and a sweatshirt between the bed and the wall, and some dry socks in his hamper. Through the door he could see his father's boots on the extended footrest.

He put on his jeans. "So, Dad, what brings you here?"

"I'm on my way over to Joan Sinclair's place. I went over there last night, but she was home. I didn't want to bother her."

In the bathroom Billy opened his bottle

of Percodan. There were only four pills left, and he thought that Dr. Vogelhut had probably given him so few in case he tried to take them all at once. He slid one into his palm and opened a second bottle for a sleeping pill. He filled a glass. It hurt to tilt his head back, and the water ran down his bare chest. He wiped his mouth and stared into the mirror. He looked sick. He hadn't shaved since he'd come home from the hospital. He touched the dark line of bruises going from under his left ear around his throat. He could see the ghosts of the turns in the rope. His mother, Martin, his lawyer — they were all afraid he would try it again. Sooner or later they would put him back in a psych ward. It was inevitable, especially after what just happened. Stupid, stupid, losing it like that.

They would take him to see the doctor on Tuesday. The police would show up. They would say . . . "Come along, young man, don't cause any trouble," like last time, and they'd take him to the hospital, and his mother would be crying, but she wouldn't stop them.

He turned the light off.

His father said, "You got anything to do right now?"

"Why?" Billy came back into the main room pulling his sweatshirt over his head. He lifted his hair with his fingers. "I'm not helping you with Joan's roof. It's raining."

"Come over here. I want to talk to you," his father said. He pointed to the sofa. "Move some of that junk and sit down."

In no hurry, Billy took a beer out of the fridge. He wasn't supposed to drink with the pills, but so what? When he sat down with it, his father kicked the footrest down and leaned toward him with his elbows on his knees. Lines went across his forehead. His lecture mode. "Billy, you're the only one in the world I trust right now. Do you know that? The only one."

"Okay." Billy opened his beer.

"I'm going to tell you something, so pay attention and don't interrupt. Forget the roof. I never intended to fix it. I wanted to get on her property."

Billy stared at him, beer can poised at his mouth. "What for?"

"Because there's some cash hidden over there."

"What do you mean?"

"Some cash. I don't know how much, but it could be considerable."

"Where? Whose is it?"

"It's nobody's. It's been there a long,

long time. You know, back in the thirties, in Prohibition they called it, alcohol was illegal here, but rumrunners would go back and forth to Cuba bringing it in. They used the Lindeman house as a drop-off point, and one of them hid his cash on the property in a strong box. I don't know how much. Could be millions."

"Millions? Oh, man. Over at Joan's?"

"Yeah. I heard rumors over the years, and I figured, oh, a lot of hot air, but one day I said, hey, why not check it out, so I got to know Doug Lindeman. I thought he'd be able to get onto the property, being Joan's nephew and all, but she hates him, so we had to think of something else. Never mind all that. The point is, the money is there. Not in Joan's house. Not in it, exactly. It's buried on the property. I have a map."

"Where'd they bury it?"

"Somewhere. Don't ask so many questions. No one knows about this except Doug and me and now you."

"It's Joan's money, though. I mean, if it's on her property —"

"Jesus. It belongs to whoever finds it. Billy, she's crazy as a bedbug. I would bet you she has piles of money in the bank. She was a famous movie star. She has money, she's just too crazy to spend it."

"She's not crazy."

His father lowered his head for a second and pressed his beer can to his forehead. "Technically, the money belongs to Martin Greenwald. He bought the island, and Joan Sinclair is living there until she dies, then it's all his. Do you understand that, Billy?"

"I guess."

"Do you think Martin needs more money than he's already got?"

Billy shrugged. "No."

"All right, then. Listen to me. Doug and I were going to go in there together when Joan was out of the house. Then he called me up and said don't do anything yet, we're waiting a couple of weeks. Bullshit. I know what he's planning. He wants to cut me out and take it all for himself. He was talking about Europe, Hawaii, God knows where he'd go. Billy, are you following what I'm saying here?"

"Yeah. I understand, Dad. He's going to screw you out of your share."

"That's why I want to get in and get out. After that, I pick up my new boat. It's mine as soon as I show up with the cash. And then . . . I'm thinking of going to Cabo San Lucas. I want you to go with me. What about it?"

"Cabo San Lucas in Mexico?"

"Near Cozumel. You've never been there. It's a beautiful place. Fish jump right onto the hook, you'll see."

"What about Doug Lindeman? He might be pissed off if you take all the money. He might come after us."

The lines in his father's face deepened when he laughed. "I won't take it all. I'll leave some for him. Here's what I want you to do. First. I put some tools onshore at Joan's dock, and I need you to help me carry them — Billy? Are you listening?"

"Yeah. Are we ever going to come back?"

"We'll be back. We've got to buy that marina, remember? What's the matter? Why am I not hearing, 'Yes, Dad'?"

"My lawyer said not to go anywhere till this stuff with Sandra is cleared up."

"Did you kill her?"

"No, I did not kill her."

"Then tell your lawyer to go screw himself." He clamped his hand on Billy's arm. "I'm doing this whether you're with me or not. You think I *want* to be a bonefish captain the rest of my life, sucking up to the tourists, always in debt? What about you? Martin Greenwald's got you under his control, and so does your mother, but you don't see it. Come with me, Billy. You're good with boats. You could make something of yourself."

Billy said, "My lawyer thinks Doug killed Sandra. He says Sandra knew what Doug was doing at Joan's house, and he killed her."

His father stared at him for a minute. "Sandra knew about it?"

"That's what Mr. Quintana thinks, but he doesn't know about the money."

"Did he mention me?"

"No, not at all."

His father finished his beer and set the can on the floor. "Okay. Now look. I don't believe that Doug will come out here today. He's no boat man, and the seas are getting pretty rough. But he might. He might. I need a weapon. I didn't bring my pistol, and it's too late to go back for it. Can you help me out, Billy?"

"Are you going to shoot him?"

"Jesus, no. It's just insurance."

"Dad, I don't have a gun."

"Get me the one you had the other night."

"I — I think it's locked up in the office."

"Get it for me. Break the lock. I need some protection."

"I guess I could."

"You guess?"

"Okay. I can get the gun for you."

"Good. Next thing. You have to get Joan out of the house for a while. Bring her over here. Make an excuse. You're her friend, she likes you."

"Dad, Dad, she's coming anyway. Mom called her on the phone this morning and asked her. I mean, she left a message and said, like, 'Come over and let's have a hurricane party all weekend.' "

"Great. So you make sure she's on her way, but don't stick around. We need to get going. You never answered my question. Do you want to do some charter fishing?"

Heat flooded into Billy's face, and his muscles wouldn't hold still. He felt the laughter ripple out of his chest. "I want to go with you."

"You sure about that?"

"I definitely want to go."

His father held his hand up for a high-five, and Billy slapped it, then jumped up and danced around the apartment.

"Okay, let's get busy." His father went to put on his coat. "You call if you run into any problems."

"Dad —" Billy's heart was slamming in his chest. "I've been wondering something about Jeremy. Where did he die?"

"What are you talking about?" His father stared at him with one arm in his coat, one out.

"It's so weird because I can't remember. I thought he drowned in the canal behind our house in Marathon, but I'm not sure."

His father put his coat on. "That's right, he did. Our house on Westwood Street. You remember. You saw him and you ran to get me in the garage. I was changing the plugs in my car. I jumped in the water and pulled him out. We tried to save him. The paramedics came, but it was too late." His father hugged his shoulders. "Hey, you're not still thinking about that, are you? Come on. You were only eight years old. It wasn't your fault."

"I know that. It was an accident." Billy listened to the rain battering against the windows. "Okay, so where are we going to hook up?"

"Meet me on Joan's dock as soon as you can. Bring a bag with whatever you absolutely have to take, but keep it light. Do *not* leave a note. You can call your mother later on." He put up the hood of his jacket and opened the door, a black silhouette against gray, slanting rain. "I'll be waiting for you."

467

24

Lois Greenwald had come back to her cottage to make the call, and had lain on her sofa for a long time thinking about it. Dim green light filtered through the leaves, and rain slid down the glass. It was like being underwater; the pressure on her chest made it hard to breathe. Finally she reached for her telephone and hit the button for Doug Lindeman. He answered on the second ring.

"It's me," she said.

"Hey. What's going on? Did Joan come over yet?"

"Who were you with last night?"

She counted off the seconds until he said, "What do you mean, who was I with?"

"I saw your living room light go off at one-twenty-six this morning. At one-twenty-eight a woman came out of the building. Black hair, about thirty. She got into a Lexus with a New Jersey license plate."

"Lois . . . I wasn't with anybody. I remember I got up for a glass of water, but if some woman left the building at the same time, it wasn't out of *my* apartment." He laughed. "Strange women do not go in and out of my apartment in the middle of the night or at any other time. I can't believe you were watching me. What kind of trust is that? What kind of friendship do we have?"

"It was my understanding, Douglas, that we had more than a *friendship*."

"Did you write down that woman's license tag? We can find out her name, and you can call her. Ask her if she knows me."

Lois said nothing. She could feel his lips on her ear where the phone touched her.

"Lois?"

"I'm here," she said.

"Why didn't you come up? I'd have let you in. You could have seen I was alone."

Tears burned her cheeks. She wiped them away. "Don't ever lie to me. I think I'm capable of doing something terrible if you lied to me."

"I'm not lying. Jesus. I can't believe you sat outside my apartment *all night*."

"Not *all* night."

"Poor kid. Next time, would you just knock on my door and *ask* me?"

Lois held the phone so tightly her fingers were cramping. "I'm sorry for doubting you."

"It's okay, cupcake. Do you mind if I call you that?"

"I like it." She laughed. "Nobody ever called me such a silly name before."

"Well, you are silly for worrying. Hey, while we're on the phone, did Aunt Joan come to the hotel this morning?"

"No, not yet." Lois hugged a sofa cushion to her chest. "I spoke to Martin about inviting her for the weekend. Joan won't listen to me, but she likes Martin. He said he'd ask Teri to call because he had to go to Islamorada early with Billy and his lawyer. I don't know why. They got back a little while ago. But Arnel is gone. I sent him to Key West."

"You're super."

"When are you going to Joan's house?"

"Soon as I can. Would you make sure where she is and call me right back?"

"Douglas? You do love me, don't you?"

"Of course I do, cupcake."

Lois ducked under branches and palm fronds so laden with water they drooped across the path. Intending to take a shortcut through the delivery area, she noticed Billy going up the back steps. It was the way he did it that caught her attention. Skulking, slithering around the corner like a snake. She could feel his eyes probing at the bushes that shielded her from view.

What was he *doing?* Lois decided to follow.

In the tiled hallway Billy's footprints shone like neon arrows. She paused at the corner, peered around, and crept to the door of the business office. She had left it open, but now it was closed. There was a folding screen in the lobby, and she went to stand behind it, keeping her eyes on the door. He wouldn't get past her.

The door opened, and through the crack in the panels she watched him come out. There was nothing in his hands. By the time she walked around the screen, Billy was gone, his footsteps fading toward the back door.

What have you stolen this time? The front office appeared undisturbed. She tested the drawer where her assistant kept the petty cash. She went to her own office, saw her desk, and let out a cry. The wood was shattered around the lock. She opened drawers, flung papers aside. There was the envelope with a bank deposit. The cash was still in it.

She slid open the bottom drawer.

The revolver was gone.

Lois ran out of the office and down the hall. What was he going to do with that gun? She stopped short at the back door, breathing hard. She eased it open, willing it not to squeak. She caught a glimpse of Billy's gray sweatshirt vanishing around the corner of the cart garage. Heedless of the rain, Lois ran after him.

He went up the steps to his apartment. The door opened, then closed. Lois stood for a moment in the shelter of the eaves. She imagined Billy raising the gun to his head and pulling the trigger. In horror she looked up at the window expecting to hear the explosion and see blood and bone fragments splatter on the glass.

She turned back toward the hotel. Had to tell Martin. Had to go upstairs and tell him before it was too late. She flung open the back door and ran down the hall and halfway across the lobby. And then her steps slowed.

Something had occurred to her, such an audacious thought that she had to clap her hand over her mouth to keep from saying it aloud. What if she hadn't seen Billy take the gun? What if she simply returned to her cottage and waited? The hotel was so dark and empty. Who would know what she had seen?

Oh, but Martin would know. She wouldn't be able to fake her reactions, and he would know. Anyway, she had to go upstairs; Doug needed to find out where Joan was.

Beyond the patio, over the tops of the palm trees swirling in the wind, Gail could see a wall of black clouds on the horizon. Lightning flickered, silent at this distance.

The Greenwalds' private suite on the upper floor had touches from the South Seas, much mahogany and sisal, with accents of red and gold. An L-shaped sofa faced the windows that looked out over the sea.

Teri Greenwald had made a good effort to hide her swollen eyes under extra makeup, but it was obvious she'd been crying. Her long hair framed a face that suddenly looked its age. She must have found out, Gail thought, what had happened this morning when Billy encountered the mermaid. Her son was more ill than they had realized. But Anthony would be calm and reassuring. He would remind her that Tom Holtz had agreed to tell the police about his law partner's relationship

473

with Sandra McCoy. This was good news. Billy was not likely to be arrested for the crime if they had the dead girl's lover as a suspect.

Gail heard Martin tell Anthony that it looked like all hell would break loose in a few hours, but not to worry.

"Teri and I like to sit right here and watch the show. We've been through a bunch of them. We open a bottle of Dom Perignon and put on some Latin jazz. Great fun. Gail, if you were staying, we'd have a party."

"That is so tempting." Gail came away from the window. "Teri, I was curious about something. When Billy was eight years old, did he know Teddy Lindeman?"

This question, coming out of nowhere, made Teri pause as if to remind herself who he was. "Teddy Lindeman? No." She glanced at Anthony for an explanation.

"Ah. I think Gail is referring to Billy's delusion about his brother's death. He thinks that Jeremy died at Teddy Lindeman's house." Anthony added, "I was going to ask you this myself. Billy was never at that house? Never saw it? Never met Teddy?"

With a small laugh, Teri repeated, "No, we never met Teddy Lindeman."

"Do you think Kyle knew him? Could he have taken Billy to his house?"

Shaking her head, Teri held on to her gold locket, which contained the small photographs of her sons. "Kyle was never involved in anything like that. I never heard the name Teddy Lindeman until . . . when? Until I came here."

The telephone rang from its place on an antique ship-captain's desk. Teri looked in that direction. "I'll get it."

Gail said to Anthony, "Shouldn't I go before the weather gets worse?"

"We'll go now if you like." Martin stood up and took her hands, and his craggy face softened. "Teri and I are sorry you have to leave us so soon."

"So am I. I'll miss you both. And Billy too." This was the truth, and if Gail had not made other promises, she would raise a glass of champagne with the others as the full force of the storm pounded the island. Instead, she would soon be on the road, and tonight she would lie miserably alone in her bed wanting Anthony beside her.

"You won't believe it," Teri announced, coming back across the room. "That was Joan. She just woke up and checked her messages. She wants someone to pick her up. I didn't think she would come, but I'm glad. Martin, should I go?"

"Is she ready right now?"

"She has to get dressed. She said she'd call."

"When she does, tell her I'll pick her up when I get back from the marina. You stay here with Anthony and put some champagne in the ice bucket. Better take out an extra bottle if Joan Sinclair is coming to the party."

Gail groaned. "Please. Another word about what *fun* this storm is going to be, and I might have to stay."

"You're always welcome here." Teri hugged her. "Be careful on the road. Will you call me sometime? I admire you so much."

Before Gail could reply a loud knock came at the door, then again, even louder.

"Who in the world?" As Teri hurried across the room, the door swung open and Lois came in, a gaunt figure in a navy-blue sweatshirt and slacks.

Teri stood squarely in her way. "Can I help you?"

Ignoring her, Lois pushed past. Her wet hair stuck to her forehead, and splotches of red darkened her cheeks. "Martin, I have to talk to you."

Teri grabbed her arm. "You may not

come into our home as if you owned it. You *don't*." Her voice cracked, perhaps from the unaccustomed experience of confronting her sister-in-law.

"Let go of me." Lois spoke through her teeth.

From the windows Martin said, "Lois, what's wrong?"

She pulled her eyes away from her rival and folded her hands at her waist. "I . . . came to . . . to ask whether Joan Sinclair has decided to join us this weekend. If so, I should prepare lunch. And I thought . . . Martin . . . that you could ride over and bring her back, if she's coming."

Teri said, "Martin has to take Gail to the marina. I told you this morning."

"Are you speaking for my brother?"

"Yes, she is." Martin was not pleased. "Joan is coming, and I would appreciate it, Lois, if you would drive over to get her when she's ready."

"She won't get in a cart with *me*."

"We have no one else," Martin said. "Teri is attending to our guest. If Joan gives you a problem, call me on my cell phone, and I'll talk to her."

Lois lifted a hand. "I know. We'll ask Billy to go. Where is he?"

"He's asleep," Teri said. "He's taking a

nap, and I don't want him disturbed."

"Oh, I see. Then let's not disturb him."

Martin said, "Lois, do as I ask." It was an order, curt and final. He could have been speaking to one of the housemaids.

Something flashed between them. It was as though years of interpreting Martin's moods and his wishes had given Lois the power to know his thoughts, and she had read them clearly: Her position with her brother had been radically and forever changed. She lowered her eyes.

"I can't help you with Joan," she said. "I'm leaving."

His heavy brows drew together. "What do you mean, leaving?"

"I'm going to my cottage to pack a few things, and then I shall leave. It's time for me to turn the management of the resort back to you. Naturally I'll be available to smooth out the transition."

"Lois, for heaven's sake."

"The rest of my things can be sent to me later. Don't concern yourself, Martin, with getting me to Islamorada. I have a boat. I can get across before the storm."

"Don't do this. You're being foolish."

"On Monday I'll begin looking for a job. I don't expect any problems finding suitable employment."

"No one has asked you to leave," Martin said.

She made a slight smile. "Are you trying to talk me out of it?"

Wearily he shook his head.

"I have only wanted what was best for you, Martin. That has always been my guiding principle. I am sorry my efforts haven't been appreciated by everyone."

"Wait a moment. Where will you go? How will I find you?"

Her chin rose, and she lifted a shoulder. "I'll probably stay with Douglas. I didn't tell you about Doug, did I? You don't know everything about me, Martin. I have a life apart from The Buttonwood Inn."

He put his fingers to his forehead and closed his eyes. "Oh, Lois."

"We've been in love for quite some time." Her gaze included the other three people in the room, daring them to contradict her. "Doug wants to move to the old Lindeman house and restore it. We'll be together. So I'm not really leaving, am I?"

Anger pushed Martin to shout, "He's using you, can't you see that?" Embarrassed and reluctant to speak openly, he murmured, "Doug Lindeman was sleeping with Sandra McCoy, and there are others. Please. I don't want you to be hurt."

Lois must have heard the truth in his voice, because her face had gone pale as ashes. She turned and walked to the door. It clicked shut behind her.

"Oh, my God." Teri grasped for words. "Martin . . . is Lois really leaving?"

"Apparently so. I'm as surprised as you are." He put an arm around her. "Teri and I had a long talk last night. We'd thought we might move to Palm Beach and let Lois run the resort, but she's made the decision for us. I didn't want to discuss it with her now, with so much else going on, but we'll come to an agreement."

"I feel sorry for her." Teri sounded half-surprised to be making such an admission. "I've hated her for so long, and she has hated me, but now . . . I am sorry for her."

"Teri, you're a saint."

"No, I'm not." She put her head on his chest.

"Indeed you are." He kissed the part in her glossy black hair. "I told Teri about my heart operation, so you see she's being very nice to me."

Teri started to shake him by the shirt front, but looked around when the telephone rang again. "That must be Joan." She hurried to get it. "Hello?" Her smile faded, and the phone nearly slipped from her hand. She took a breath. "Yes. Yes, he is. Hold on."

Martin said, "Who is it?"

Teri's eyes were black and enormous. She put her hand over the mouthpiece. "Detective Baylor. He wants to speak to Anthony."

Frowning, Anthony quickly crossed the room, and Gail drew closer as he spoke.

"This is Anthony Quintana. . . . Courtesy call? Should I say thank you?" His face darkened. "Yes, but he's asleep on the orders of his doctor."

"No!" Teri leaned against her husband as if she might otherwise sink to the floor.

"When can we expect you?" Anthony listened then said, "It is *your* inconvenience, Detective, not ours." He hung up and looked at his companions. "The police have obtained a search warrant."

25

Billy and his father stood on the seawall on Joan's side of the island. It was raining again. Waves crashed into the pilings and spurted up through the broken boards in the dock. Billy had just handed over the gun. "It's loaded. I made sure."

The chambers clicked as they spun around. His father checked the safety, then zipped the gun into his jacket. "Come on, let's get to work."

Billy stepped over a gaping crack in the concrete as he followed him up the slope. He was tired. He wished he hadn't taken a sleeping pill on top of the Percodan, but that was before he found out they were leaving for Mexico in a few hours. He had packed some clothes but couldn't remember if he had brought his passport.

"Help me, will you? Grab the other end of that tarp."

Billy dropped his backpack to the ground,

and they pulled a brown plastic tarp out from under some bushes.

"It's heavy. What've you got in here?"

"An acetylene torch."

"What for?"

"To cut through some metal." His father turned back the tarp, revealing a heavy red toolbox and a canvas bag with leather straps. "I don't need all this stuff. I brought everything I could think of."

"We've got the cart," Billy reminded him.

His father sat on one heel and opened his toolbox. "I spent some bucks on these tools. Nothing that can't be replaced, though. Now, listen. When we get over to Joan's house, you knock on the door. If she's gone, great. If she's still there, I want you to take her over to the hotel, then come right back. But if anyone asks, you're going to your room to take a nap and you don't want to be disturbed."

"I understand."

"See? I knew you'd be a good man to have along."

"Dad, I have to ask you something. You remember the house that burned down? The one the Morgans owned?"

"How could I forget?" He went through the toolbox and took out what he needed. "Hold that bag open for me."

"Did you and Mom and me ever go over there? I mean . . . before the fire."

"To that house? No. I saw it only once, after you burned it."

"There was this mermaid on the dock, and I know I saw her before, when I was a little kid."

"Saw who?"

"The mermaid. Well, it's not a mermaid, it's a lamp made out of concrete —"

"Billy, forget the fucking mermaid and help me. Finish loading that bag and put everything else out of sight. I'm going to check out the weather."

He walked toward the dock.

Billy quickly filled the canvas bag with the tools his father had chosen — a small sledgehammer, a hacksaw, extra blades, screwdrivers and wrenches, crowbar and pliers — then closed it and scrambled to his feet. A wave of dizziness hit him, but he blinked and his head cleared. He shoved the toolbox under the bushes and lay the tarp over it.

On the dock he put up the hood of his rain jacket. The wind changed direction and the mildewed styrofoam floats rolled in a half circle, tethered by ropes tied to the rotting lobster traps. Everything on the dock was black and rotting. It surprised him that the beam had held his weight.

The bill of his father's Mercruiser cap swiveled around. He had a big smile on his face. "It's going to get bad sooner than I thought. I've done some crazy-ass shit on the water, but running a bonefishing skiff in a tropical storm is not one of them."

The water rose and fell in jagged points topped with froth that the wind ripped away and sent flying. "What are we going to do?" Billy asked.

"Can you get me Martin's boat and bring it over here?"

"You're kidding."

"Can you get the boat or can't you? If not, we're screwed."

"Yeah. I can get it."

"Excellent. Get it ready to go and wait till I call you. We'll drop it off at the marina in Marathon with a thank-you note. Do you have your cell phone? Billy? I'm talking to you."

His father's voice faded out. The black dogs were here. They were barking and howling and running up and down the dock. They had huge paws, and their toenails clattered on the wood. Something bumped against a piling, and Billy looked over the edge. It was a little boy with a long green tail like a fish, but the scales

485

were flaking off. The boy rolled over in the water and opened his eyes and laughed.

Billy moaned and slid downward. Then he was on his back on the dock and his father was shaking him by the shoulders and calling his name.

"Billy! Billy, what happened?" A lined face and gray hair came into focus.

"Stop. Dad. My neck —"

"What the hell's the matter with you?"

"Nothing." Billy sat up and leaned over his crossed legs. It felt like a rusty nail about an inch thick was being pounded into the back of his head. He wanted to vomit.

"Nothing? You fainted. Jesus. Don't do this, Billy. Not now."

"I'm okay." Billy tried to stand, and his father helped him up. "I didn't eat anything. Must be light-headed or something."

"You scared the shit out of me." His father turned him around and looked at him. "Are you all right?"

"Yeah."

"Are you sure? What about Martin's boat? Can you get it?"

"Sure, Dad."

They walked back to the tools, and his father put the canvas bag in the cart and tossed Billy's backpack in after it. Billy sat in the passenger seat. He held onto the roof support and watched the bushes come at him and slide out of the way. The tools rattled around, and then he was on the porch at Joan's house knocking and knocking on the door until his father said to get back in the cart.

Billy couldn't remember getting out.

"Okay, Billy, what are you going to do? Let's make sure we have this straight."

The words came out of his mouth so cleanly. "Well, Joan is gone, so I'm going to the harbor and take Martin's boat down off the lift. I'll wait for you to call me."

"All right. Now get going."

A minute later Billy was staring at the open gate in the chain-link fence. He turned around the other way wondering where the cart was, and how he got here. Over his head the tunnel of bushes breathed in and out like he was caught in the throat of a giant animal.

He thought of the razor blades in his kitchen drawer. He'd bought some at a hardware store to see if he could have them around and not want to use them. Five in a little box, edges wrapped in thin strips of cardboard. He had taken one out and pushed the point down on the vein at his wrist. The skin popped back when he lifted the blade. A kid in his ward at the hospital had told him you had to cut up and down, not across.

What have you done? I told you to watch him. I told you!

Billy spun the other way and looked through the gate at the closely mowed grass of the resort. He couldn't remember what he was supposed to be doing. Something important for his father.

The restaurant kitchen was so quiet. The hum of refrigerators. The clock ticking on the wall over the dish racks. From outside came the steady whisper of rain. Such fickle, deceitful weather. It would let go in screams of wind and thunder, then turn its back and withdraw into polite murmurings.

Lois placed the items she needed on the long wooden table in the middle of the kitchen. Bread. Smoked ham. Swiss cheese. Brown mustard. Whipped butter. A ripe tomato. Two crisp leaves of romaine. She had not eaten breakfast. Martin wouldn't begrudge her a simple sandwich. And she wouldn't leave a crumb. She was not like Teri. This morning at seven o'clock Lois had found dirty dishes all over the place. It had taken over an hour to scrub the kitchen and clean the dining room. Teri had dragged herself downstairs for coffee and had the nerve to say, *Lois, I would have done it.* Martin had no idea what a lazy, selfish little bitch he had married.

"He wouldn't listen to me, would he? Men are either *blind,* or they are *liars.*" Lois lined up the ingredients along one of the lengths of wood in the table. Bread, ham, cheese, mustard, butter . . . She reversed the butter and mustard.

A sob burst from her throat, and the kitchen was blurred by her tears. She wiped them away with a dish towel and picked up the spreading knife. Mustard on the bread. Ham on one of the pieces, cheese on the other.

"I might as well be dead. I should be dead." She who had been betrayed by her lover, ruined by the treachery of her brother's wife, then cast out by her brother, to whom she had selflessly given the last fifteen years of her life. Forty-three years old and not a roof, a job, a family, not even a savings account. Lois had never taken a penny for herself. Everything, everything had been for Martin and The Buttonwood Inn.

She took a long serrated knife from the knife block to slice the tomato. What if she lay down in a warm bathtub and used this knife to cut her wrists? She would leave a note for Martin. *Don't grieve for me, my dearest brother. It is you who have been deceived —*

The knife blade gleamed through the red flesh of the tomato as paper-thin slices fell onto the table. Lois decided she could not cut her wrists. Hanging would be less bloody. But it would be long and painful. Drowning at sea would not be painful, but it would be terrible all the same. *Dear Martin. I forgive you.*

She thought of the gun in her desk drawer, and then remembered what had become of it. Billy had taken it to his room to shoot himself. One bullet. Lois didn't think she could open his door, take the gun from his dead hand, and use a second one for herself.

Why? Because it was so *useless.* Her death would be meaningless. It would be better to kill Douglas Lindeman. Or Teresa Flores. "No, it should be Douglas," she decided. "Billy will be dead soon, and Teri will suffer. If I kill her, Martin would suffer."

Tomato slices on the ham. Then the romaine. Lois realized that she had forgotten to butter the bread. She crossed her arms over her face and wept. What use would it be to kill Douglas Lindeman? He deserved it, and she had no fear of killing him, but she would go to jail and then what? It would be useless. Useless.

Her arms slowly dropped away. She had thought of someone else. Joan Sinclair. If Joan died, Martin would finally have Lindeman Key, all of it. At last he could make a garden for his palm trees, a paradise, as they'd always wanted. He would have the dock, and the boats would come. Douglas would never live in the Lindeman house. *Martin, if you ever loved me, tear down that house —*

Lois hurriedly threw away the sandwich, cleared off the table, and folded the towel. The ten-inch carving knife slid out of the knife block and made a slight ringing noise as it touched the handle of the cleaver.

Aware of being on the periphery of this crisis, Gail stood and watched as Anthony explained to Teri Greenwald what would happen when the police arrived. Everyone would have to stay out of the way while they searched whatever areas the warrant allowed.

"Billy's apartment, of course, and the

grounds of the resort, but not here, and not the office, or any of the areas that Billy doesn't have control over. They will ask for keys to all the vehicles that Billy has access to." Anthony took Teri's hand. "I said to expect this, remember? I am only surprised that Tom Holtz hasn't called them. Maybe it's the storm that's making him put it off, but he will tell them what he knows. I'll make sure of that. You mustn't worry."

Teri took a deep breath. "No, no, I'm not worried."

Martin said, "They're insane to come in this weather."

With a slight shrug Anthony replied, "Baylor is frustrated. With a confession, most cases would be tied up in a pretty little package by now. He said they would be here soon. That could mean in one hour or two or six." Anthony checked his watch. "It's eleven-thirty. Billy should get some rest, but I do need to talk to him. Teri, would you call him for me?"

Recovered from her fright, Teri got up and went to the phone.

Martin brought his hands down on his knees. "Well. I propose that we continue with our day as planned."

Teri turned around and smiled at him.

"Would you like strawberries with the champagne?"

"Yummy," said Martin. "She puts strawberries in my glass to reduce the amount of alcohol. She's so clever. Gail? If you're ready, we should go."

"I think I'll stay." Gail came to sit beside Anthony. "Someone needs to pick up Joan Sinclair. You can't let her walk." The men looked at each other. "Lois is on her way to Islamorada, and you and Teri have Billy to look after and the police to entertain. And besides, I want to be here for the party."

Anthony stood up. "Let's go get your suitcase."

"I'm not leaving."

"Yes, you are."

"I am *not*."

"Didn't we agree you'd go back?"

"But it's going to be such fun, all the champagne and the fireworks. Excuse us a minute, Martin." She walked Anthony over to the open door that led to a study furnished in leather and oriental carpets. "Forget what we agreed to. I'm staying here."

"For the party?"

"No, idiot, because I have to get Joan, and . . . and because I can't stand being without you."

Anthony was pleased by this, she could tell, but he maintained his stern expression. "And what are you going to say to your daughter?"

Gail draw a line down his chest with one finger. "I'll tell her the truth. That I love you and you need me here. I hope you do."

"*Siempre*." He put his lips to her temple, and she could feel his warm breath in her hair. "All right. We'll go back tomorrow."

Teri had hung up the phone, and she was waiting to speak to Anthony. Her lovely brows were drawn down with worry, and she was sliding her locket back and forth on its gold chain. "Billy isn't answering. He's such a sound sleeper. Do you want me to get him up?"

"Yes, do that. Gail is staying after all," Anthony announced. "She's going to borrow a cart from you and bring Joan Sinclair to the party."

26

Doug Lindeman slipped getting out of his boat and had just grabbed hold of the ladder on the dock when the damned water dropped the boat out from under him. It came up again and thudded into the piling, scraping across the barnacles, which took a piece out of the fiberglass. He'd barely had time to pull his foot out of the way.

"Jesus H. Christ." Holding the lines in his teeth, he went the rest of the way up the ladder. The wood was soft and slimy with algae. The wind seemed to come from two directions at once, whipping the rain against his waterproof jacket. A few turns of the ropes around the pilings, and the boat was secure. It would get beat to hell on the dock, but it would be there when he got back.

Doug had heard nothing from Lois. Not a damned thing. She wasn't answering her phone. He suspected that she was still

495

testing him, letting him stew. Or it could mean that Joan hadn't left the house yet. Doug had decided it didn't matter if Joan was at home or not. He meant to get in, and if she wouldn't open the door, he'd put a foot through it. If she ran her mouth, throw her in a chair and tell her to shut up. He was sick of waiting, and with Lois Greenwald turning obsessive, he had no choice. He had to get the money now. If he didn't, Kyle Fadden could get to it first and then swear the box was empty, or that Teddy had left only a quarter mil, and here's your share, old buddy. Fadden was not a man you could challenge face-to-face.

With a little jump to relieve the weight, Doug adjusted the shoulder straps of his backpack. He'd brought a steel mallet and a chisel big enough to break an anchor chain, along with a serious hacksaw that would do the job more neatly. He wasn't after neat, he wanted fast. Detach the fucking safe from the chain and drag it out, if he had to.

Head down against the drizzle, he churned up the rocky, weed-tangled slope toward the house. A narrow, sand-packed road led through the heavy undergrowth, and he followed it for another fifty yards or so. He hadn't come this way in years.

"Stop!"

He stopped.

Arnel Goode had come out from behind the old storehouse in Aunt Joan's backyard. A soggy hat drooped over his face, and his gray plastic raincoat hung to the tops of his work boots. "Y-Y-You . . . you're t-t-trespassing. Get out. This isn't your p-property."

Shit.

"Hey, Arnel. I'm Doug Lindeman. Joan's nephew, remember me? Lois Greenwald said you had to run a real important errand, so I said, 'Wow, who's going to keep Aunt Joan company in the storm?' I called her, and she said to come over." Doug would have to tie the little retard up in the storehouse. There would be a rope and something to cram in his mouth to keep him quiet.

With a little nod of comprehension, Arnel said, "You and Lois. She sent me to Key West. You better get out of here."

"Aunt Joan called me, Arnel. She's expecting me."

"You leave. Now."

"I brought her some lunch." Doug swung the backpack off his shoulders. "You can give it to her. Catch." As the bag swung forward Doug gave it an extra push and let go. It hit Arnel in the chest and sent him stumbling backward, colliding with the low wall of a compost pile. He landed in the dead leaves and rotting wood chips. His hat flew off, and thin blond hair fell into his eyes.

Doug sprinted forward to pin him, to flip him over and twist his arm up in its socket, and force him to walk. But in the short interval of time it took for Doug Lindeman to think of this, Arnel had sat up and reached for the pitchfork he had left in the mulch pile.

The knowledge of what was about to happen registered in Doug Lindeman's astonished blue eyes a fraction of a second before he reached the tines of the pitchfork. His weight and his speed were too much. He couldn't turn fast enough. The handle jammed into the mulch, and Doug Lindeman slid forward along the tines, which Arnel Goode had recently sharpened by hand on a whetstone.

The points went through and lifted the back of Lindeman's rain jacket. The handle of the pitchfork remained in place, and Lindeman balanced, then swung sideways and dropped heavily onto the ground.

A whuffing noise came out of his mouth, then blood and a long gurgling moan. He scratched at the tines. Arnel put a foot on his chest and wrenched the pitchfork free as Lindeman's eyes tried to focus.

"I-I *told* you to *leave!*" He raised the pitchfork and brought it down again and again until Lindeman was quiet. Arnel let the pitchfork drop and grabbed one of Doug Lindeman's arms.

A little while ago he had heard the boat coming, and he had watched Lindeman get out of it. He wanted to put him back in the boat and push it out, and let the sea take him, but the man was too heavy, and Arnel could only get him about ten yards before he sank to his knees, breathing hard. He thought of the wheelbarrow in the shed.

Arnel walked over to the mulch pile and picked up his hat. He shook the leaves and dirt off and swung it onto his head.

Then he heard another noise, a rattling sound and a hum. A golf cart appeared on the path from the resort. He stood watching as it came closer, crossed the yard, and stopped in front of the house.

Lois Greenwald got out, but she had her back to him, and she didn't notice him standing there in the trees.

She was carrying something close to her

body. When she put it behind her back, Arnel could see what it was. A knife.

He picked up the pitchfork.

Martin Greenwald sat in his chair, morosely silent, palm supporting his chin, while Anthony folded his cell phone and put it back into his pocket. The tinted windows turned the approaching clouds into a solid mass of grayish-purple granite. A tongue of blue fire lapped at the equally dark ocean. The half-inch thickness of the glass reduced the thrashing of palm fronds to a muted rustle. Anthony looked at his watch.

"She'll be back soon," Martin said, turning on a lamp. "Twenty minutes at most, I should think. I've sat up here watching storms often enough to make a pretty close estimate of when this one will knock on our door. I give it an hour and seven minutes."

Anthony smiled and came away from the window. "So you confessed to Teri about your heart operation."

"It was a mistake. I should have told her after the storm so I could drink. You wouldn't have a cigar on you, would you? God, I'm dying for a cigar. Teri wouldn't have to know."

"I didn't bring any with me," Anthony said.

"What kind of Cuban are you?" Martin slouched further into his chair. "While Teri is gone I want to tell you something about Kyle Fadden. Whatever his faults, he's a damned good fisherman. I know because there isn't a weekend in the Keys without a tournament. Guess who uses Kyle Fadden as a fishing guide."

"I already know the answer. Doug Lindeman."

"You lawyers know everything. All right, try this. You will recall what I told you about Joan's life estate. I bought this island from her brother, Harry Lindeman, but it was Teddy who suggested that she remain in the house."

"I remember." Anthony thought of the $100,000 that Teddy Lindeman had given to Tom Holtz, along with instructions to dole it out to his aunt. "Teddy wanted to be sure that Joan would be here when he got out of prison."

"Teddy was a frequent visitor. I'd see his boat coming and going." Martin's heavy brows rose. "I wonder why. The man wasn't a cinema buff."

"You think he was using the island for his business."

His shoulders duplicated the lift of his brows. Martin said, "After Teddy was arrested, a bunch of DEA agents came around. They wanted to know if I'd given Teddy access to any of my buildings. I said no. They went over to ask Joan the same questions. She told me about it later. I'm not the criminal lawyer here. What were they looking for? Drugs?"

"Either drugs or cash. Anything they could seize, as long as they could tie it to Teddy Lindeman."

"There was some talk around town that the government never could find as much as they thought Teddy had. He lived rather conservatively for a man of his calling. He drove an old Chevy pickup truck. A very low-key fellow." Martin put his chin back in his palm. The gray light through the windows reflected in his glasses. "What does a man like that do with his cash?"

"He might keep it in an offshore account," Anthony said. "About two miles offshore."

"That would explain a great deal," Martin said.

"Martin, you deserve a trophy."

"All speculation," he demurred. "I would prefer a cigar, but you say you don't have any."

"I lied. You can stand downwind."

"You're as bad as my wife."

"You think Teddy told Doug about the money?"

"Probably not. They couldn't stand each other."

"What about Lois? Could Doug have learned about it from her?"

"Not likely. Her relationship with Teddy ended twenty years ago. Lois was into the business in a very minor way. People down here almost considered bringing in bales of pot a local sport, but when cocaine started coming through, Lois got out and cut all ties with Teddy. No, Doug didn't get his information from her."

"Or from Joan either — assuming she knows anything." Anthony got up to look through the window again. "And assuming that what we're talking about even exists." The clouds had spread to cover more of the horizon. He turned his wrist to see his watch.

Gail Connor came out of a tangle of white mangrove and strangler fig to find herself on the south side of the island, looking at the wall of clouds and rain. The inside of one cloud lit up, and Gail counted off seconds. She got to eleven before she heard the thunder. The storm front was about two miles off. She already had her cell phone out, dialing Anthony's number. The battery indicator was blinking: low power.

He answered a split-second after the first ring and asked where the hell she was.

"I'm on my way, calm down. . . . I *said* I'm on my *way*. . . . I took a wrong turn somewhere, and I have to get back on the path. . . . Ask Teri to call Joan and tell her I'm coming. I'll call you when I get there. . . . *I'll call you.*"

The static erased most of his reply, but she gathered that he would come for her if she wasn't back in ten minutes.

"Fat chance of that," she said, putting her phone away. Gail looked once more at the sky. The clouds were swelling, growing, becoming blacker by the moment. A veil of rain softened the edges. There was another silent flash of lightning.

How could Anthony come for her if she herself didn't know where she was?

The thunder came, a long rumble that gradually faded.

Gail soon found herself on a wider road. She was encouraged. It had to lead somewhere. She decided that if Joan Sinclair's house didn't come into sight within sixty seconds, she would turn around and go back.

Anthony closed his cell phone and walked to the windows. Lightning went off in a chain, one pulse after another. The palm trees along the seawall were strangely still, but waves exploded into white froth. Anthony felt the thunder more than heard it, a pitch so low it vibrated the heavy glass. "I shouldn't have let her go."

"Don't worry," Martin said. "We'll take a cart and find her if she isn't here soon, but my guess is, Gail and Joan will walk through that door in fifteen minutes. Come here. I want to tell you something else."

Anthony sat on the arm of the sofa nearest Martin's chair with his feet flat on the floor, unable to relax.

Martin said, "When Teri came to work for me, I took one look and that was it. Within days I was thinking of how to have her, knowing damned well she was married, and she wouldn't be interested in an old man like me, but what do you know? Anyway, my sister, God love her, hired a private investigator without telling me. The fellow dug up an arrest for shoplifting in Key West, for which Teri got ten days, suspended sentence. She was a kid, twenty years old. Big deal. I was also given information about Mr. Fadden. DUIs, resisting arrest, drunk-and-disorderly, spouse abuse — I couldn't have turned back after learning he'd beat her up, could I? There was also a bust at Fantasy Fest in 1991 for possession of cocaine, less than five grams. The co-defendant was Teddy Lindeman. I see your ears pricking up."

"What happened to the case?"

"Dismissed. The police made a mistake in the search, something of that nature, and the judge threw it out."

Anthony processed this information, then said, "It is possible that Teri did know Teddy Lindeman. And that Billy knew him." Realizing that he had just accused this man's wife of lying, Anthony said, "I'm sorry, Martin."

Martin Greenwald dismissed the apology with a wave of his hand. "There are things in everyone's past that he — or she — would rather not revisit. You have my permission to mention it to Billy's psychiatrist — but not to Teri."

"I understand," Anthony said.

The door opened, and Martin called out, "And speaking of my fabulous wife, here she is now. Where is my champagne, woman?"

Teri's face was flushed, and her chest moved quickly with her breathing.

Martin added, "And where is Billy?"

"He refuses to answer me." She gave a light laugh and tossed back her hair. "It must be the sleeping pill. He said he was going to sleep for awhile. I'd go in, but the door is locked, and I don't have a key. He never locks his door. Anthony . . . would you come help me wake him up?"

Perhaps she was trying to be brave for Martin — she was aware now of his bad heart — but her fear was written on her face. Anthony and Martin exchanged a look. Had Billy finally accomplished with pills what he'd failed to do with a rope?

Anthony told Teri to wait with Martin. "I'll go get him."

It had taken some effort, but Kyle Fadden had leaned over the cistern and grabbed the chain and pulled and hauled and grunted until he had raised the box. Water poured off. It was about as big as a footlocker, sealed in heavy plastic, and had to weigh over a hundred pounds. Fadden rested it on the edge of the cistern and waited for his arms to stop trembling from exertion.

He had never seen the thing before, but

507

he had shared enough drinks with Teddy to have picked up some information. More information had come from Doug Lindeman, and the rest had been guesses. Fadden had not been certain, until his fingers felt the chain, that he wouldn't reach into that dead water and come out with a handful of slime.

He gave the box a shove, and the chain clanked over the concrete lip of the cistern. The box thudded to the ground and jerked to a stop. The chain was wrapped around it like a Christmas package, and the other end was hooked to a metal circle about a foot below the water level. Fadden took a towel out of his canvas bag and dried his hands and arms. A butane lantern gave enough light to see by.

There was a noise, like a door closing. Then footsteps. Voices. Fadden turned off the lantern and crept up the narrow wooden steps to listen. The kitchen was just above him, but the voices were coming from farther away, probably the living room. He pressed his ear to the door.

A woman was speaking. "— going to get out of this miserable dump and have a good time. . . . I *adore* Teri and Martin, they're a marvelous couple."

Another person — a male? — mumbled

something that Fadden couldn't catch, but he had recognized the woman. When Billy had banged on the front door, Joan Sinclair hadn't been gone. She must have been up in her room sound asleep, probably with a hangover, though she sounded pretty lively at this point. Fadden couldn't tell who was with her. According to Billy, her handyman had gone to Key West.

Who, then? Doug Lindeman? Fadden thought of the revolver in his jacket, which he had laid across the propane tank at the bottom of the stairs.

Quick footsteps came closer. "Give me the Beefeater. I'm going to fix a drink."

"I-I bought you some soup and cr-crackers like you asked me to, Miss Sinclair, so-so you'd have something to eat if the p-p-p-power goes out. Look what I got you."

The handyman had come back. Kyle Fadden heard the crackle of paper bags, the thud of cans and bottles. Two people upstairs, and Fadden didn't know what he was going to do about it.

"I'm *tired* of soup." There was a crash, and something rolled across the floor. "I'm tired of *you*. Go away, Arnel. I have to get dressed."

"But Miss Sinclair, they . . . they wa-

509

want you to leave so they c-can take your house. It's a plot. If you leave, they'll c-c-come in and st-steal your diamonds and your gold jewelry."

"I said *get out*. Are you deaf?" Wood squeaked, and a door hit the wall. "Out! Go to your cottage and leave me alone. Do not come back until I tell you to. Dear God, I can't *bear* it anymore. Stop crying, Arnel. Don't just stand there, *go!*"

Footsteps shuffled toward the back porch.

Joan Sinclair let out a scream of frustration. "Thank you and good-bye!" The door slammed. She crossed the kitchen one way, then another. Something banged down on a table or counter. Ice cubes rattled. And then her footsteps faded away, and at a greater distance moved up the stairs to the second floor.

Under the kitchen Kyle Fadden listened for a moment longer. Music went on. A jazz band, very loud. He laughed. "Thank you, Miss Sinclair."

27

Billy wasn't there. Anthony had not taken the time to knock on his door. He had kicked it in with one well-placed foot near the door knob, and the wood had shattered. The apartment was empty.

Anthony stood in the chaos of dirty clothes, beer bottles, torn magazines, compact disks, and video boxes, and trembled with relief. Billy was not lying dead or comatose on the floor. But where was he?

"Ay, cara'o, ¿dónde estás?"

And where was Gail?

He ran down the steps and around the building, going back into the hotel through the kitchen, then through a series of hallways to the lobby, up the carpeted stairs that led him to the second floor, then to another hall, at the end of which was an alcove with a set of double doors and a gold plaque marked private.

He opened the door and went in.

Billy Fadden was standing in the middle of the Greenwalds' living room with his head buried in his mother's shoulder, her arms tightly around him. Martin Greenwald stood beside them, hovering but not touching, his brow deeply furrowed.

Anthony placed his hands on his thighs and pulled in several deep breaths.

Martin glanced around. "He just got here."

The boy was mud-spattered, soaked to the skin, and pale as death. Teri murmured something and led him to the sofa. Billy stumbled on legs that seemed only marginally connected to his nervous system.

Anthony came over. "Where have you been?"

Mouth open, Billy blinked and looked up at him. "I didn't kill Sandra."

His mother hugged him. "We know, Billy. We know you didn't."

Still fixed on Anthony, he gently pushed her away. "I called the police because I *thought* I killed her, but it was a movie. It was one of Joan's movies. *Moon of the Vampires*. The vampire carries this girl's body to the cliff overlooking the sea, and he puts her on the rocks and pulls out a knife and cuts her throat and he catches her blood in a goblet. See? I thought I did that to

Sandra, that's why I confessed. I mean . . . I just figured it out."

Anthony exchanged a look with Martin, then said, "Aha. Yes. A movie."

"You want to hear something else? Mom . . . Jeremy didn't die at our house."

"Please don't talk now."

"No, listen. He died at that house with the mermaid."

"Oh, Billy. No." Teri spoke as if staring into the face of hopeless insanity.

"It's true. I remember."

Anthony moved some magazines aside and sat on the coffee table. "What about Jeremy?"

Billy's voice was so flat he could have been reading from a newspaper. "My father told us we were going fishing. It was at night, and I didn't want to go because I was tired. When Mom went to work, he took out his belt and made me do all my chores over again."

Teri bit her lip and put her hand over her mouth.

"I went to bed, but then he woke us up, and he said we were going fishing, so we got in the boat, but then he told us to get in the cabin and go back to sleep. He drove the boat, I don't know where, because we were asleep, then he stopped the boat, and

513

I woke up. He said to stay there and watch Jeremy. 'Don't leave this boat or I'll beat your ass.' Jeremy was asleep. When I woke up again he was gone. I was afraid to leave but I got out of the boat to see if I could find him.

"The mermaid was on the dock. I saw Jeremy in the water, and I tried to get him out, but I couldn't, so I called for my father. I was screaming and everything, and the dogs started barking and barking, and Dad came, and he and some other men pulled Jeremy out, and he hit me and said, 'What have you done, what have you done, I told you not to let him go anywhere. I told you. It's your fault he's dead.' "

Teri wept.

"So then we went home, and he told me that Jeremy fell off our dock by accident, and if I said anything else, the police would put me in jail for the rest of my life. He said he would take care of everything, he would make sure they didn't take me away. So he put Jeremy on the sofa, and he called the police."

The gleam in Martin's eyes was fearsome.

Billy grabbed his mother's hand. "Jeremy died where the mermaid was. I remember the dogs. Mom, I remember everything.

Why did Dad say that? Why did he say I killed Jeremy? It was an accident. I didn't mean to let Jeremy go out of the boat. I fell asleep —"

Teri hugged him. "*Shhhh.* That's enough." She kissed him then looked fiercely over his head. "*Hijo de puta, mató a mi* baby." Sobbing, tears pouring down her face, she rocked her son. "Kyle might as well have thrown Jeremy in the water with his own hands! He's dead, and Kyle will go to hell for what he did. And Billy! Oh, God. Both of my babies!"

Anthony had to get up and pace to the windows and back. He would not have bet on Kyle Fadden's life if he had walked into the room.

Teri closed her eyes. "It's my fault. Oh, God, God."

Martin said, "Teri, you weren't there."

"It is my fault! I should have known. It wasn't the first time! Kyle took me with him before. We needed the money, and he said who would look twice at us, a nice young couple out fishing? Then he wanted to take the boys, and I said no. No, never, and I made him promise to stop. I said I would work double shifts, but don't do this anymore. I should have left him then. Billy, please forgive me. I was too afraid to tell

515

you what I did. I wanted you to think good of me, only good things . . . to make you happy. I love you so much." She began to cry again.

He looked at her, blinking slowly. "It's not your fault, Mom." Then he pulled in a breath and clutched his hair. "Oh, Jeez. Oh —"

"What is it?" Anthony asked.

"I was supposed to get the boat, but I didn't. I forgot!" He leaned over and moaned, then threw himself back against the sofa cushions. "Stupid! I had to pick up my father in Martin's boat. He is going to be so pissed off."

The cart skidded to a stop on the sparse grass in Joan Sinclair's front yard. Tree tops swayed in the wind, and a piece of loose sheet metal banged on the roof. Gail took the steps two at a time and hurried across the porch. She opened the screen and heard music coming from inside. She rapped on the door and waited. There was no response. She knocked louder. Still nothing.

She tried the door knob, and it turned.

"Hello? Joan?" The music was coming from upstairs: the long, plaintive wail of a saxophone, the throb of a bass. She went across the dark living room to the hall and shouted, "Joan!"

The music went off. There were quick taps of heels on a wood floor. Then Joan Sinclair's voice demanded to know who was there.

"Gail Connor."

"As I live and breathe." A raspy chuckle floated down the stairs. "Come on up." The dim light at the top revealed Joan Sinclair in a red robe with feathers at the hem and around the sleeves. Her thick bangs skimmed the lifted wings of her brows, and her hair was a black curtain on the padded shoulders of her gown. Her makeup was dramatically vivid. "Are you alone? Where's that gorgeous Latin lover of yours?"

"Wondering why I'm not back already. Aren't you dressed yet? I've come to take you to the hotel. We're going to have a party."

"More parties. Tom came by last night, now you. Oh, boy, did he leave in a huff. You haven't seen him, have you? We had a fight, and I think he's mad at me."

"Tom went back to Islamorada. Joan, please hurry. If we don't leave *now*, we'll get caught in the storm."

"I'm not sure if I still want to go. How

about a martini?" Joan turned, her robe floating behind her.

"No, thanks." Gail followed, sliding her hand along a wooden balustrade polished by age. The upper hall was lit by a single twenty-five-watt bulb in a screw-in porcelain fixture. Rainwater came through a crack, patting on a runner that moths had eaten to threads. Gail went up the final step. The bathroom door was open, and she saw a bathtub with claw feet. Candles sat in pools of dried wax on the white hexagonal tiles.

Lightning flashed through a window at the other end of the hall. Thunder cracked, grew, then thudded so loudly the balustrade trembled.

The clutter in Joan Sinclair's bedroom was even worse than downstairs. While the living room was crammed with junk, here an attempt had been made at recreating the boudoir of a Hollywood diva. Red embossed wallpaper curled from the walls; velvet swag curtains drooped from cheap metal rods. The same mosquito netting used in the resort's cottages was draped around a four-poster bed. A feather boa hung over the head board, and chenille sofa pillows were piled on a faded blue satin comforter. There were half a dozen movie posters in ornate gold plastic frames. The only illumination came from a flickering bulb in the cut-glass chandelier in the ceiling and the candles on the mirrored vanity.

How desperately sad. What could Sandra McCoy have seen in this dreary room that anyone could possibly have wanted? Nothing. There was nothing here.

Dusty bottles, jars, and atomizers with tasseled squeeze bulbs caught the candle light. Cigarette smoke curled from an ashtray. The diva herself sat on a cushioned stool with her legs crossed, painting her fingernails. A worn-out red satin slipper parted the limp and tattered feathers at the hem of her robe. She raised her hand to blow on her nails. Her image reflected at three different angles in the mirror behind her. Her dark eyes shifted to Gail.

"Are you sure you won't have a drink?"

"Joan, everyone is waiting for you. Teri's going to open a bottle of champagne."

"Ooooh, that could be lethal, after I've started on gin." Careful of her nails, Joan Sinclair picked up her martini glass.

Anthony grabbed Billy's shoulders and held him still. "Where is he? Where is your father?"

"At Joan's house. He's waiting for me." Billy looked over at Martin. "We weren't going to steal your boat, just borrow it to get to Marathon. That's where he left his truck."

Anthony repeated, "Your father is at Joan Sinclair's house right now?"

As if realizing he had said too much, Billy mumbled, "Yeah."

"*Why?*"

"Because . . . there's some money. It was buried on the property by some rumrunners in Prohibition times, but nobody owns it now. It's nobody's, so he wanted to find it and buy a marina. We're going to go into business together, after we get back from Mexico . . . I guess that's off."

"*Ay, Dios,* Gail is on her way to pick up Joan Sinclair."

"Joan isn't there," Billy said, "and my father wouldn't do anything to Gail. He wouldn't! He's afraid Doug Lindeman might show up, so I had to give him the gun. I'm sorry, Martin. It was your gun from the office. He wasn't going to keep it, I don't think. He'd have left it in your boat when we took it to Marathon —"

"To hell with the boat," Anthony said. He forced himself to speak calmly. "Is the

520

gun loaded?" Billy said it was. "And your father and Doug Lindeman are working together."

"I guess so. Sort of."

"Your father has a loaded revolver, and he expects Doug Lindeman to show up at Joan's house."

"*In case* he shows up," said Billy.

Anthony said to Martin, "I'm leaving."

"I'm coming with you."

"No, you're not."

Martin Greenwald took hold of Anthony's arm and pulled him into his study and shut the door. "I have a pistol. I could help."

"Give it to me," Anthony said.

"We're both going," Martin said.

"Your heart isn't strong enough. Give me the gun. Teri needs you here."

Finally agreeing that Anthony was right, Martin unlocked a drawer and handed over a Glock 19. Anthony checked that the magazine was full, then put the gun in his trousers pocket. Fadden's revolver would have only six bullets, unless Billy had brought more.

"Get on the phone to Jack Baylor," Anthony said. "Tell him to hurry up." He laughed. "For once in my life, I'll be glad to see the police."

They hurried down some exit stairs and out a side door. Rain was coming across the open ocean, and Anthony could smell the salt. Leaves raced over the grass. Martin pushed open the door to the cart garage, and Anthony jerked the recharge cord out of the first available cart and got in. Martin told him to go around the north side and when he got to the beach, bear left. That road would lead to the gate.

Anthony paused long enough to say, "Make sure Billy doesn't follow me." He hit the accelerator, and the cart hummed at its top speed of about fifteen miles per hour along the sand path, buffeted by the wind. Waves crashed against the seawall and flooded over the lawn. It wasn't Martin's heart that Anthony had been concerned about, though yes, that was part of it. If Billy's father was going to die, it shouldn't be Martin Greenwald who pulled the trigger.

28

"I don't want to go to the Inn." Joan waved both hands back and forth to dry her nail polish, as scarlet as her robe. "I haven't a thing to wear."

"Joan, please come. I don't want to leave you here alone."

The actress smiled sadly and bowed her head. She spoke with a British accent. "You must go now, Anabelle, and never look back. Your life is just beginning. Be happy, my darling. Just . . . be happy." Long lashes brushed her cheeks. Then she made a slow wink. "Greer Garson. Not bad, eh?"

Lightning flashed at the window. Gail said, "I'll call later to see how you are."

"Yes, would you? How kind." Joan swirled across the room to her stereo cabinet. "I'm in the mood for Sinatra. You know, we met in Vegas in his Rat Pack days. Frank and Dean and Sammy. Talk about wild!"

A draft lifted the heavy curtains. From upstairs came a noise, a rhythmic clanging: the piece of loose metal on the roof. The storm would break at any moment.

Gail hurried out the door and into the hall. Using the finial post for a fulcrum she swung around and went down the stairs so fast she nearly tripped. A few more steps took her through the hall. She pushed through the door and stood on the porch. Trees swayed and moaned, and a crack of thunder split the sky. Water poured off the roof. Running down the steps, shielding her cell phone from the downpour, Gail hit Anthony's number.

"No service? *Damn.*"

The battery was dead. Gail remembered the telephone in the hall, an old black dial model on an oak stand. She ran back up the steps. Unless she got in touch with Anthony, he would be out in this deluge looking for her.

She went back inside and picked up the telephone receiver, which was surprisingly heavy. Upstairs, Frank Sinatra was singing about the cool of the evening. With her finger poised over the circular dial, Gail realized there was no dial tone. She followed the line to see if it was plugged into the wall. The black cord was lying loose on the floor. "Oh, great."

She stood up, turned, and looked into the face of a gray-haired man in a T-shirt and waterproof pants. She staggered backward a step before she recognized him. Kyle Fadden.

"Hello. What — What are you —" She saw the gun pointed at her chest.

Fadden grabbed the front of her shirt and put the gun under her jaw. "Scream and you get a bullet. Understand me? Turn around and walk."

With his hand clamped in her hair and the gun at her back he pushed her to the kitchen. Gail saw a flight of dark, narrow stairs and tried to twist away from him. "No! I'm not going down there."

He shook her by the hair. "I want you where I can see you. Stay quiet and nothing's going to happen. Move." When she struggled, Kyle Fadden put his mouth close to her ear. "I can crack you over the head and push you down those stairs. What'll it be?"

Gail put her hands out like a blind woman. Her legs trembled. She slid her foot over the threshold, feeling for the first step.

The chain-link gate was open wide, and

Anthony aimed the cart straight for it. Within seconds he was on Joan Sinclair's side of the island. The canopy of trees cut the rain but dimmed what weak sunlight leaked through. Anthony slowed to avoid a rock, went around it, and broke out into a clearing familiar from two nights ago. He accelerated the cart until the rain came at him almost horizontally.

The cart suddenly lurched. The tires on the right had dropped into a gully obscured by weeds. As he fell, Anthony instinctively threw himself in the other direction. His hip and shoulder thudded onto rain-soaked earth. He staggered up. The cart's front fender had punctured a tire. *"¡Hijo de puta!"*

He looked around to get his bearings, made sure he still had the pistol, then set out at a limping run.

The house was built eight feet off the ground on pilings. The rear of the house rested on walls of concrete block that formed an above-ground basement. At the bottom of the stairs, Gail could see that Kyle Fadden had taken her down to this room. The harsh white light of a butane lantern shone on rotting sheets of plywood, a twisted bicycle frame, rusted paint cans, a propane tank. An algae-streaked concrete block cistern sat in a corner. Its heavy wooden lid lay beside it.

"Don't put me in there! Please don't —"

"I said be quiet."

Fadden pushed her toward the back of the room. He pulled a knife from a case on his belt. "Get on the ground."

"No!"

"I'm going to tie you to that column, and unless you want a gag in your mouth, shut up." He cut a length of rope, tied her hands behind her, then ran another piece of rope around one of the columns supporting the house. The ground was cold and damp, slick with vegetable rot. He took a hammer and some nails from his canvas bag and went out of sight up the stairs. Gail heard a tapping sound and guessed he was nailing the door shut. Joan wasn't likely to hear it over the music.

The details of her surroundings became clearer. The old cistern, the rusty junk scattered about, boxes, and pieces of wood. On the opposite wall, at ground level, was a ventilation hole. Through it Gail could see weeds, rocks, and the bottom step of a staircase to the back porch. The hole was big enough for a man to crawl through if he removed the wood frame and wire mesh. The frame lay on the ground. Fadden had come in this way, easier than breaking down a door.

Gail pleaded, "I don't care what you're doing in this house, but please don't kill me. I have a daughter. Her name is Karen. She's only twelve years old. She's waiting for me at home. You have a child too — Billy. What would he think if he found out —"

Kyle Fadden came over with the gun. She cowered, but he grabbed her hair and put the barrel under her cheekbone. "Keep talking, see what you get." Gail was silent. He gave her a shove. "That's the last warning."

While Gail tried to regain her ability to breathe, Fadden put the gun on the corner of an old crate and squatted beside a large box on the ground. A chain lay in a pile on the ground beside it. The box was wrapped in heavy white plastic, and Fadden began to saw at it with his knife.

In the semidarkness on the other side of the basement Gail dug her fingernails into the rope binding her to the column, feeling for play in the knots. There was enough length to the rope that she could shift her position. She scooted onto a piece of old plywood to avoid the mud oozing through her slacks. There was another piece of plywood behind her, and when she leaned against it, she was surprised to feel it give. There was a gap in the foundation. A door. Of course. How else could they take things in and out? The steps were too narrow.

Gail pressed harder against the plywood panel, stopping quickly when it began to let go. She thought if she could free her hands, she could break through the panel and run. The fear of dying in this horrible place outweighed the good chance that he might catch up to her in the woods.

She glanced back at Fadden. The plastic had come away from the box, and he ripped it off, exposing a dark metal surface. Fadden put on a welder's mask, tipping it back so he could see, then drew on a pair of heavy gloves. He lowered his mask and picked up a brass torch connected by hoses to two small tanks. He held a loop of wire under the torch, clicked it, and fire shot from the nozzle.

His shadow moved across the wall. He adjusted the flame and put it to one of the hinges on the box. The sharp blue point of the torch ate slowly into the metal.

Gail picked more furiously at the rope.

Anthony slipped, caught himself on the railing, and went up the rest of the way in a low crouch. On the porch he stood against the wall. He could hear the rain on the tin roof and music from inside the house. Holding the pistol he inched closer to the door. He opened the screen, turned the knob, and went inside, gun extended. There was a loud crack behind him. He spun around to see a tree limb crash to the ground.

Anthony looked into the small room off the hall, found no one, then went through the living room, across the TV room with its hundreds of video boxes, then into the kitchen. Dishes and pots were stacked in the cast-iron sink. Pale light came through dust-grimed windows. Anthony noticed a small wooden door, perhaps to a pantry, and turned the glass knob. He pushed. The door didn't give. He went out the way he had come and looked up the stairs.

The treads creaked under his feet as he climbed. He stopped and looked through the balusters into the upstairs hall, then went the rest of the way. The music was louder, a trumpet solo, coming from behind a closed door.

He put his hand on the knob, turned it slowly, then swung the door open.

Joan Sinclair was sitting at a dressing table in a red robe and black wig. Her startled face looked at him in the mirror. She turned around with a tube of lipstick in her hand. "My God. Is this a train station?" She saw the gun. "What are you doing?"

Anthony put the gun away. "I'm looking for Gail. Where is she?"

"She just left. She invited me to the Inn, and I didn't want to go, so she —"

"Is Kyle Fadden here? Billy's father, have you seen him?"

Joan Sinclair pulled a tissue from a box and carefully blotted her lips. "He was supposed to fix my roof, but he never showed up. It's leaking all over the place."

"What about Doug Lindeman?"

"He knows better than to knock on my door. No, I haven't seen him either." Joan took her empty martini glass across the room to the ice bucket on her stereo cabinet. "Would you care for a drink?"

"When did Gail leave?"

"*Somebody's* manners have certainly gone downhill." She lifted a cocktail shaker from the ice bucket and poured. "Five minutes ago? Now please be a good boy and close the door behind you." She turned up the music and smiled at him. "*¿Por favor?*"

Anthony went out. He rounded the stairs just as Billy Fadden appeared at the

531

bottom. His wet hair lay flat on his head.

Anthony shouted at him, "I told you to stay at the hotel!"

"Where's my father?"

"Not here. No one's here but Joan. Come on, let's go." He pushed Billy toward the living room. "Go." Anthony churned with rage and frustration. "You're going to help me look for Gail."

Kyle Fadden had cut through all three hinges of the metal box. He tugged at the lid with a gloved hand. Impatient, he put a crowbar in the crack and tried to lever it up. Failing at this, he relit the torch and pulled the mask over his face.

Gail had no doubt that this man had killed Sandra McCoy with that knife on his belt. She assumed he was working for Douglas Lindeman, and that when he finished opening the box, Kyle Fadden would have to decide what to do next with Gail Connor.

She had freed the line holding her to the support column. The knots at her wrists were impossible. Her hands were still tied behind her back, but that wouldn't stop her from running. Fadden couldn't see her with the mask over his face. Gail shoved on the plywood panel to loosen it. She dug her heels into the ground and pushed.

There was a tickling sensation on her hands that spread quickly to her wrists, her arms. She heard a soft clatter, growing in volume. Something went up her arms, into her sleeve.

She screamed. Palmetto bugs. Giant cockroaches. Dozens of them. Hundreds, scrambling from their nest. Shiny brown bodies, long quivering antennae.

"Shut up!" Fadden lifted his mask. His torch was still burning. "I told you to shut up!" Then he saw, and he stared.

Gail scooted backward, away from them, away, away. They poured from the darkness under the house. They crackled and flew into her face. She rolled on the ground. Her hands were tied, and there was nothing she could do. Except scream.

From somewhere came heavy thuds, then the splintering of wood.

Fadden was looking up the steps. A second later, a man hurtled toward him. "Where is she?" A pistol was extended in his hand.

"Anthony!"

He spun around, and his eyes searched for Gail and found her.

Fadden went for the gun on the packing crate.

Gail yelled, "Look out!"

Anthony crouched and turned. A flash exploded from the barrel of his gun, then another. Kyle Fadden jerked backward. His welding mask fell off, and the torch clanged against the wall and went out. Fadden dropped to his knees.

"Dad!" Billy leaped from the stairs and raced toward him.

Fadden bent over and slowly fell sideways into the crate, held on for a moment, and slid to the ground.

"You shot my father! You killed him!" Billy ran to his father.

Gail was leaning against the wall, sobbing, her hands tied behind her. "Oh, God, Anthony . . . they were all over me. Please get these ropes off my hands. I'm not hurt, I screamed because of the roaches. They were crawling inside my shirt. Do you see any? I can still feel them."

"No, they're gone now." He stamped on something in the dirt.

Gail told him there was a knife on Fadden's belt, and to cut her loose.

Billy sat on the ground beside his father. "Dad, can you talk? We're going to get you to a doctor. Jesus, he's bleeding! Somebody *do* something!"

When her hands were free, Gail ran over

534

to the lantern and held it up as Anthony crouched beside Kyle Fadden. She averted her eyes, then looked quickly. Fadden's right arm was across his body. He held a wound in his side, and blood came through his fingers. Anthony moved his hand aside. The wound went through the flesh at his waist. The second bullet had ripped through Fadden's left forearm. Blood pulsed from an artery.

Gail moved her lips soundlessly. *Oh, my God.*

Anthony rolled his handkerchief and knotted it above the wound. Kyle Fadden grimaced and clamped his teeth together. "Shit, that hurts."

Billy was shrieking. "Don't let him die! Dad!"

Gail set down the lantern. "Billy, he's not going to die. We'll take him to a hospital." She looked at Anthony.

He said to Billy, "Go upstairs and find a bedsheet. We need to cut some strips. Hurry up. Run!"

Gail crouched beside him and whispered, "Is he going to make it?"

"I don't know." She watched as Anthony picked up the revolver and opened the chamber. He emptied the bullets into his hand. Six of them. "I thought he fired."

"You had no choice," Gail said.

He put the bullets into his pocket and threw the revolver into the darkness. "Fadden, wake up. Kyle Fadden!" The man's eyes came open. Anthony leaned over him. "Do you know who I am? I'm your son's lawyer. Billy is suspected of murdering Sandra McCoy. I want to know who did it."

"I didn't —"

"Who killed her? Lindeman?"

"Yeah. Lindeman."

"How do you know this? Fadden, talk to me!"

A woman's frantic voice came from the top of the steps. "What is going on? I heard gunshots. Who's down there? Billy says his father's been shot!"

Gail called up, "Joan, I'm down here with Anthony. Kyle Fadden tried to kill us."

Billy came down the stairs with a yellow striped sheet, ragged at the edges. "He wasn't trying to kill you!"

Anthony told him to shut up and tear the sheet into strips.

Joan was still yelling. "What are you doing in my house? Why is everyone here?"

Gail called back, "Joan, please go upstairs. It's all right."

Anthony pressed a pad to the hole in Fadden's arm. He told Billy to give him a long strip of cloth. The pad was immediately soaked through. Anthony threw it aside and tightened the rope tourniquet.

"Don't let him die!"

"He's not going to die." Anthony went around to lift Fadden's shoulders. "Billy, you take his feet. Gail! Gail, where are you?"

"Joan is freaking out."

"Never mind Joan. Hold the door open and tell her to stay out of the way."

Within a minute they had Fadden on the front porch. The rain was not as heavy, but the wind still whistled through the trees. A rivulet of diluted blood flowed lazily toward the edge of the porch. Anthony said, "We'll put him in a cart and take him to the dock. Billy, can Martin pull his boat up to Joan's dock in this weather?"

"No way, it's too rough," Billy said. "We have to board in the harbor."

Anthony nodded. "All right. You call Martin on the way, tell him we'll need an ambulance to meet us at the marina."

There were two carts at the bottom of the steps. Anthony picked up Fadden under the arms, and with Billy taking one leg, Gail the other, they maneuvered the unconscious man into the back seat of the larger cart with his knees over the arm rest and his boots dangling.

Joan leaned over the porch railing and called, "Billy! I'm praying for your father." She crossed herself and kissed an imaginary rosary. He looked from under the roof of the cart and nodded.

Anthony shouted, "Gail, get in."

She stood in the rain. "Come with us, Joan. Please. You don't want to stay here all alone, do you?"

"Well, I — I'm not *dressed!*" She clutched the robe at her throat, and feathers trembled. "Would you wait for me, Gail? Would you?"

"Yes, but hurry." Gail said to Anthony, "Go on without me. I'll bring Joan in the other cart. We'll be right behind you."

29

Gail watched the golf cart splash through a puddle and disappear around the corner of the house. She went up the steps to the porch and opened the screen.

Joan was just inside. "What should I wear?"

Gail let out a breath. "It doesn't matter. Just hurry. Bring something for tomorrow too, you'll probably stay the night."

"I've never stayed at The Buttonwood Inn. I've been to *dinner*, of course. Tom took me several times, and I enjoyed it tremendously. Their chef is marvelous —"

"Joan, please."

"Of course. I'm so nervous. I want to look nice. Do you think it'd be okay if Tom came to dinner? Would Teri mind? I gotta make it up to him for last night. What was *wrong* with me? Yes, I'll hurry." Joan's footsteps faded away up the stairs. "I'm going to buy some champagne! You and Teri and

539

I can get drunk till the boys come back!"

Gail pivoted and went down the steps. At a front corner of the house where two gutters joined, the weld had broken, and rainwater poured through. She stood directly under the stream until the mud sluiced away from her hair, her clothes, her fingernails. She rinsed out her sandals and pulled open the neckline of her shirt. She was freezing but she didn't care.

On the porch she used her hands to squeegee the water off her pullover and slacks. She went inside and called, "Joan?"

"Coming, coming."

Drawers opened and shut. There were footsteps back and forth over Gail's head. Gail sat huddled on the sofa and pulled a musty afghan around her shoulders. Finally Joan came clomping downstairs in white vinyl knee boots, green tights, and a psychedelic green-and-orange minidress. Green O-shaped earrings swung at her ears, and her blond wig swooped across her cheeks. She carried a brown, hard-sided suitcase with a handle. "How do I look?"

Gail stared, then smiled. "Great."

"The word is groovy." Joan set down her bag and searched through a white purse for cigarettes and lighter. "I haven't been to The Buttonwood Inn since God-knows-when. Yes, I do. Tom took me. Arnel didn't want me going out with Tom. If he was here right now, he'd start whining about it." Her lighter flared.

Gail was shivering. "Joan, do you have a sweater or something I could borrow?"

"Oh! I'm sorry!" She exhaled smoke. "Just grab one out of the hall closet upstairs. Want me to go up and get it for you?"

"No, I can. Thanks."

"I'll be on the porch." Joan pushed open the screen door. "Would you look at that rain? It smells nice, though. You know what? I've been cooped up in the house too much. I used to argue about that with Arnel, and he was wrong, wrong, wrong."

The only hall closet was beside the bathroom, intended for a linen closet but crammed with winter clothes. Gail stuck her hand in and came out with a heavy white sweater with gold buttons and epaulets, size fourteen. With a sigh she put it on. It smelled of mothballs. On her way to the stairs she noticed an umbrella against the wall outside Joan Sinclair's room. She thought they might need it.

The door was open. Gail looked inside. The red feathered robe lay across the bed.

One of the candles was still burning, reflected in the triple mirror whose gold metal frames were pitted with rust. She went to blow it out. Aware that she should not be in here at all, Gail walked carefully across the threadbare faux-oriental rug.

Her appearance in the mirror startled her. Her makeup was gone, and her hair was beyond belief. Combing it quickly with her fingers, she noticed a jewelry box on the vanity. It was green padded vinyl embossed with gold fleur-de-lis, and one of the small drawers was open. A gold medallion dangled over the edge. There was an inscription. Gail lifted it to see what it said. The name "Emily" had been neatly scratched through, and "Joan" incised above it. It wasn't even real gold; the plate was wearing off. It was fantasy, an illusion.

A prickle of fear crept up Gail's spine as she sensed she was being watched. She raised her eyes and looked into the mirror. There was nothing. Behind her, the empty door. The red robe across the bed. And a face on the wall.

It was one of the framed movie posters. Gail recognized the woman from the video box of *Bride of Nosferatu*.

A heart-shaped face both innocent and evil, wide-set eyes, a small chin, and sharp little vampire teeth protruding onto her lower lip. Nosferatu standing behind her. In the distance, bare trees and a ruined castle.

Slowly Gail turned around. She stared into a pair of dark, catlike eyes outlined in heavy black pencil. Joan Sinclair in her twenties, but . . . not Joan Sinclair. The nose was shorter. The face was more . . . delicate. Gail had the sensation of looking at a puzzle-drawing. She thought of the old black-and-white drawing of the young lady at her dressing table fixing her hair. Stare at it long enough, it becomes a drawing of a skull.

As Gail continued to study the face in the poster it gradually began to make sense, even as her mind refused to accept it. Her heart did a dance in her chest, and her limbs felt weak.

"Oh . . . my God." Sandra McCoy must have seen the poster. She had come in here looking around and had seen it. The face of the actress, Joan Sinclair, the same face on the video box that she rushed out to rent and show to Doug Lindeman. That face. Not . . . the face of . . . the woman who lived in this house. But how could that be?

There were quick footsteps up the stairs.

"Yoo-hoo. Did you fall in?"

Gail let go of the medallion and hurried away from the vanity.

Joan Sinclair came into view in her psychedelic dress and white knee boots. She looked quizzically at Gail. "Why are you in my room?"

"I . . . saw a candle still burning." The reason seemed to ring with falsity and contrivance. Gail went to the dresser and blew it out. "We should go." Smoke curled up from the wick.

But Joan's attention was on the jewelry box and its open drawer, from which the medallion was still swinging. "What were you doing?"

"Joan, I was just looking at one of your —"

"You — you were . . . s-stealing my jewelry."

"No, I wasn't. Everything is here. I'll put it back." Gail closed the little drawer. "I wouldn't take anything of yours."

"I saw you. Y-Y-You're stealing her j-j-jewelry."

"No!" The word became a cry of horror as the truth finally crashed through the defenses in Gail's mind and forced her to see the truth. How could she not have known? Behind the mask of makeup and move-

544

ment and voice, it was obvious.

Gail knew as she ran for the door that it would be too late, that someone else was faster, stronger; that she would be dragged to the floor, and that hands would go around her throat.

In the moments before Gail saw nothing else, she noticed the face above her, the lashes glued to the eyelids, the carefully lined and painted lips, and the platinum blond hair swinging on cheeks that had reddened with rage.

And the eyes . . . how strange. They were dark brown with a thin rim of palest blue.

Gail smelled dirt. Leaves. Wet, rotting wood. She could taste dirt, feel the grit between her lips and her teeth. Something tapped steadily on her back, her legs. She felt it on her outstretched hand.

Rain.

She struggled to open her eyes. She focused on . . . logs. Landscaping timbers. A stack of them near where she lay. She saw a wheelbarrow leaning against a tree. Beyond the wheelbarrow, a small concrete block building with a tin roof. Rain washed down the gutters and flowed into the yard.

A strange ringing noise. Something going into earth, coming out again.

Someone breathing. Grunting with effort. Two people. They were talking to each other.

Gail remembered this place. It was the garden compost heap near Joan Sinclair's house. The landscaping logs enclosed it. The voices came from inside the rectangle of logs. There were two people standing in the mulch.

Something sharp went into the pile. A rake, a shovel. She could hear the slight crunch of dead leaves and small bits of wood.

A woman said: "They're going to come looking for her."

Then a man: "Please b-be quiet."

The woman: "Her boyfriend won't like this one little bit."

The man: "He w-w-won't find her."

They went on arguing like this as Gail lay still as the earth itself for a minute more, putting the pieces in place. There weren't two people up there. Only one. Arnel Goode.

Gail tensed her legs, released her muscles, and found nothing broken. She decided to get up slowly and see where he was. It seemed that the voices moved away from her. Gail slowly picked up her head. Joan Sinclair was jamming a pitchfork into the mulch, throwing the mulch to one side. Not Joan Sinclair. Arnel.

Crouching, Gail saw what he had unearthed. The details mounted gradually in terrible impact. An odd curve of yellow plastic, a hand at the opening: a sleeve. Her eyes raced up the arm to find the dirt-encrusted face of a man with white hair. In the next split-second she realized she was looking at the body of Tom Holtz in his yellow raincoat. Not only Tom. Beside him lay a woman with blond, frizzy hair. Arnel picked up her arm in its navy-blue sweatshirt and moved it out of the way. Her face was hidden, but with increasing horror Gail knew it must be Lois Greenwald. Arnel bent to move another leg, and it didn't belong to either of the other bodies. There were three. And Arnel was preparing a place for another.

Arnel must have heard a small noise behind him. He turned around — It was Joan's face, still in full makeup under a blond wig.

Gail was fifty yards down the path before Arnel grabbed her around the waist. Gail tried to knee his groin, to go for his eyes, to bite anything she could get her teeth into. They fell into the bushes.

He hit her in the back of the neck, and

blue flames seared her nerves.

She awoke lying on her back in the mulch pile. Decaying leaves and wood chips were in her face, her eyes. A weight landed on her chest, then another. Gail freed her arms from the weight and frantically brushed the mulch off her face and sucked in a breath. She strained against the weight on her legs. She was pinned.

A woman in a green-and-orange dress was looking down at her.

"Joan! Please don't. I won't tell anyone. I won't —"

Joan went out of sight for a moment and came back with the pitchfork. She spoke, but it was not her voice. It was Arnel Goode's voice, and then it was not.

"You st-stand out of the way, Miss Sinclair, let me take care of it. Put that pitchfork down, Arnel. *I have to do it!*" Five sharp tines were suspended over Gail's chest.

Gail clawed to get out of the mulch.

"Arnel, stop. I mean it! B-But, M-Miss Sinclair — No! You don't give the orders, I do, and I'm telling you to leave her alone!"

He jerked off the wig and threw it. His face was lopsided with one blue eye and one brown.

Gail rose to her elbows. "No! Joan!

Please don't let him kill me. Joan!"

"Let her out of there. No! She — She was t-trying to steal — Don't be ridiculous, Gail was taking me to dinner at the hotel. They all wa-want to steal from you and . . . and send you away! Arnel, don't you think *four* is enough? If you kill her it will be *five*, and that's going too far."

"Please, Joan, tell him not to." Gail screamed, "Please!"

Arnel raised the pitchfork.

Gail twisted away, and the tines sank into the mulch where her head had been. "Joan! Please stop!"

"Put down that goddamn pitchfork, Arnel. Put it down! Now!"

Arnel dropped the pitchfork and started to cry. "But I was only trying to help — When you left for Key West, I thought you'd be gone for *days*, and I was glad! Glad! I'd never been so riotously happy in my life! Then you show up again, dripping on my carpet! I — I'm sorry. Get out of my sight. I never want to see you again, do you hear?" He sat on the logs with his hands over his face. His shoulders shook. "W-W-Where am I g-going to go? I don't give a damn, just get *out*."

Arnel Goode's sobs finally tapered off to a sigh. He was silent for a while. His thin hair was slick with rain. He stood up. The green tights had a hole in one knee. He crouched gracefully to pick up the wig. He put it on and smoothed the blond curls forward along his cheeks.

He looked around at Gail, who lay trembling in the mulch. "Are you ready to go?"

Gail stared up at him.

"To The Buttonwood Inn. For the party, darling." A penciled eyebrow rose. "What's the matter with *you?*"

"Joan?"

"Are we going or aren't we?"

"Going?"

"You said Teri was waiting. She's going to open some champagne."

Gail's voice creaked in her throat. "You go. I'll stay here."

"Why on earth would you want to stay *here?* Where's my phone? I want Tom to join us. Teri won't mind, will she?" Arnel stepped onto the mulch pile and pulled Gail out by her elbows. "Oh, look, the rain is stopping. It's about time."

They walked to the cart. Arnel put Gail in the passenger seat, then went up on the porch and picked up the suitcase and the white purse. He popped up a bright blue umbrella and came down, picking his way carefully in the white knee boots. He put the suitcase in the back, got in, shook the umbrella, and stowed it on the floor.

He withdrew a compact from the purse and looked into it.

"Oh, my *God*." The compact clicked shut. "On second thought, you drive. I have to fix my face. Tom can't see me like *this*."

30

It annoyed Jack Baylor no end that when he and his team got to Lindeman Key in the police boat, after two miles of having his kidneys slammed against the seat and salt water thrown in his face, Billy Fadden wasn't home. His lawyer had taken him in the direction that Jack Baylor had just come from, and Martin Greenwald was gone too. No one was there except for Mrs. Greenwald, who got close to hysterical trying to explain what had happened. She wanted them to wait until the other lawyer arrived from picking up Ms. Sinclair, but Baylor went ahead and served the search warrant.

Mrs. Greenwald showed them where Billy's apartment was, and they got started. Baylor ignored the pirated videos and the marijuana stuffed into a cereal box. Other than that, they found nothing but the junk usually found in a teenager's room.

Billy's mother stood outside the door

telling him that Douglas Lindeman had killed Sandra McCoy, and Lindeman's law partner, Thomas Holtz, was going to tell them about an affair those two were having. To shut her up, Baylor had someone try to reach Holtz, but he wasn't answering his phone.

Then he got a message that Anthony Quintana wanted to talk to him, and he dialed the number. Quintana said that Kyle Fadden had implicated Lindeman in McCoy's death, but Fadden could have been deflecting suspicion from himself. One or the other had murdered Sandra because she had put pressure on Lindeman for a cut of the cash that his cousin Teddy Lindeman had left in the cistern under their aunt's house. Teddy had died in prison before his release date. Whether Joan Lindeman knew about the money was unclear, but Quintana had taken a quick look in the box, estimating at least a million dollars in neatly banded hundreds.

The point is, Quintana concluded, Billy Fadden is innocent. The boy had nothing to do with Sandra's death. His confession had been the product of a severe psychological trauma.

Baylor didn't tell Quintana what they had found. His officers had gone to the marina and searched the vehicles belonging to The Buttonwood Inn. In the back of a panel van they had found long red hairs consistent with those belonging to Sandra McCoy. One of the marina employees had seen Billy Fadden driving that van on many occasions. Unfortunately, the man couldn't swear he'd seen Billy driving it the night of the murder.

When Baylor's partner on the case asked what next, Baylor told him to round up the men and wait in the lobby. Mrs. Greenwald offered to make some coffee. Baylor went out on the porch for a smoke. He was sitting in one of the rocking chairs with his foot on the railing, watching the rain move across the water, when a golf cart came along the road from the north side of the island. It went past the porch and turned in under the portico. There were two women in the cart.

Baylor got up and walked to the end of the porch. He recognized the skinny blond from two days ago, but she looked like she'd crawled ashore after a shipwreck. He assumed the other one was Joan Sinclair. Last time he'd seen her, she'd been a redhead. It was strange she had on sunglasses on a day like this. She was fixing her lipstick.

Connor saw him, then said something to

Sinclair and got out of the cart. Her pants and shirt were filthy, and her hair was hanging in her eyes. She pushed it back and looked over at him.

Baylor took a final drag on his cigarette and flicked it into the bushes. "Ms. Connor. I hear you've had an interesting time of it."

She came up the side steps. "Where is everyone?"

"I'm here. I've got four officers inside. Your law partner is on his way with Martin Greenwald. Mrs. Greenwald is making coffee, and your client is with his father at Mariner's Hospital."

"Kyle is alive, then."

"Barely. He's in the ICU." Baylor said, "Would you mind telling me what's going on? I heard it from Mr. Quintana, but let's have your version."

She turned to glance at the golf cart as if making sure it was still there. "Detective, I think you should go over to Miss Sinclair's house and look in the compost heap in the yard. You'll find three bodies. Tom Holtz, Doug Lindeman, and Lois Greenwald."

Baylor stared at her. "What?"

"Arnel Goode killed them. He also killed Sandra McCoy. It wasn't Billy. It was Arnel. He did it to protect Joan Sinclair. That's why he killed the others too. Give me a few minutes to get cleaned up, all right? Then I want to call Anthony, and I have to tell Teri Greenwald about Lois. After that, I'll explain everything."

"Hold it. Arnel Goode? Where is he?"

"Arnel is . . . in the golf cart."

Baylor wondered if Gail Connor's mind was slipping. "That's Joan Sinclair."

"No, it's Arncl."

"Who was that in my office yesterday?"

"Arnel. But he thinks he's Joan."

Baylor took another look at the woman in the wig, and his mind did a little turn and settled down in the other direction. "Uh-huh. If that's not Joan Sinclair, where is she?"

"I asked Arnel, but the question doesn't make sense to him. Joan Sinclair — Joan Lindeman — probably died two years ago, but I don't know where her body is. I don't know if he killed her too, or she died of natural causes, but she's gone, and he's been impersonating her ever since."

Baylor watched the woman in the cart check her face in the mirror of her compact.

Gail Connor said, "Take Joan inside and find her a place to sit. You should assign an officer — two officers — to stay with her. I don't think she'll be a problem, but I can't guarantee that. And one other thing, Detective Baylor, if you could —"

"Hold it." He walked closer to the cart. The woman — The person in the cart looked back at him through her sunglasses and smiled. She slid a cigarette out of a silver case and leaned toward the railing.

Her voice was a low purr. "Hello again, Detective." She brought the cigarette to her lips. *"S'il vous plait?"*

Baylor took a good look as he slowly reached for his lighter. He held it out and thumbed the wheel. She — He — Whoever it was cupped her hand around his and drew in some smoke. One of her fake fingernails was missing. Her dress was a crazy mix of green and orange, and she was wearing white plastic boots with high heels.

The smoke came out on a smile. "You are too kind."

He walked back to Gail Connor. She waited for him to say something. Baylor said, "We're going to need a psych wagon."

"Do something for me, though, will you, Detective? Tell them to be nice to her. I think you'll get more cooperation that way."

"Be nice?"

"She isn't Arnel Goode. Look at her. She's Joan Sinclair, the movie star."

31

They left late the following afternoon. Most of the clouds had cleared off, leaving a sky that reflected blue in the puddles of rainwater along the highway. The ocean shimmered with hues of turquoise.

Anthony lowered the windows and opened the sunroof. Gail had put on her new white dress with the sea shells embroidered at the neckline. The skirt lifted in the breeze coming through the car, and Anthony's hand went around her bare knee.

They would arrive back in Miami about dark. Anthony had suggested they all go out to dinner, but Gail needed some time alone with Karen. At least Karen had worked herself out of her snit. She had left two messages. Five-thirty-two p.m. yesterday: *Gramma told me everything. Why didn't you call me? This is so totally unfair.* (The phone had slammed down.) Another message at seven-fifteen a.m. *Mom, it's me. Your daughter. I'm on my way with Molly to make sandwiches. I apologize for my attitude. It's okay if you get married. I love you, and I understand. Tell Anthony I said hi.*

The car went over the bridge from Windley Key to Plantation Key. Gail stretched her arms through the sunroof and let the wind race through her fingers. It seemed that everything in the world had been put right again, a naive hope, she knew, but there it was.

She dropped her arms. "What should we do about Kyle Fadden?"

Anthony looked at her through his sunglasses. "We testify. The judge puts him in prison. Why should we cut him any breaks? You could have been killed."

"Don't pretend to be such a tough guy. You saved his life."

"I did it for Billy."

"Sure you did. Is he going to be all right? Billy, I mean."

"Sharon Vogelhut thinks he has a long way to go, but he will probably get there eventually. Like most of us," Anthony added.

"He has Martin on his side," Gail said. "He never believed it before. They're all going to be all right."

"I hope so." The wind lifted Gail's skirt again, and Anthony slid his hand underneath to caress her thigh. "Where is Joan Lindeman? What do you think? Did she meet the lover of her dreams and go away with him?"

"She's dead, Anthony. She has to be. Otherwise, she would have married Tom."

"Did she die of natural causes, do you think? Or did Arnel kill her when she told him to get out of her life? That's a dangerous thing to say to a man. It sets off his animal passions."

Laughing, Gail leaned over and kissed Anthony just below his ear. "I'll watch my step." She sat back in her seat and stared up through the sun roof. "Did Arnel Goode murder Joan Lindeman? No, because to him she was Joan Sinclair, and he was a total fan. She was his idol, his star. He worshipped her."

"He did, but her marriage to Tom would have been the end of him. Adios, Arnel."

"So we'll never know," Gail said.

It was Tom's reappearance that had ignited the war between the two halves of this strange creature. Arnel had won the first battle — he got rid of Tom — but Joan Sinclair had finally triumphed. She had banished Arnel Goode forever.

Anthony said, "There were no other bodies in the mulch pile. Baylor told me they're going to dig under the house."

"That's a depressing idea. Poor Joan."

"She doesn't exist, Gail. She died two years ago."

"God, I keep forgetting."

"I have never seen anything like it," Anthony said. "Arnel was a better actor than Joan Sinclair. *Dios mío*, what an actor. He fooled everyone."

"Not quite everyone," Gail said. "Sandra knew."

"You're guessing, but I agree," Anthony said.

Perhaps Sandra McCoy had not been entirely sure, leaving Joan Sinclair's house that day. Perhaps she had only wondered. She had gone back to the resort, her mind buzzing. She had itched to talk to Doug Lindeman about it. On the shuttle to the marina, she'd had time to get a good look at Arnel Goode, and he must have felt the suspicion pouring off her like heat waves. He had keys to the van in his pocket. He had waited for the right moment.

When the handcuffs went on, Arnel Goode had blinked in confusion. "Where are we going? I don't understand. I don't *want* to go."

561

Teri Greenwald replied, "It's a movie, Joan. You're in a movie."

The officers took him away in the blond wig; they had allowed him that dignity. Last night Baylor called to report that Arnel Goode had made a confession — rather, that Joan Sinclair had explained why Arnel had done it. He had saved her from Sandra, then from Tom Holtz, and finally from Doug Lindeman and Lois Greenwald. And then she — Joan Sinclair — had started explaining to a young female officer how to make it in Hollywood.

At the southern edge of Key Largo Anthony's cell phone rang. He looked at the display. "It's my grandparents' house." Holding it to his ear, he said. "Hello? Ah, *¿Qué tal, abuelita?*" He frowned, glanced over at Gail, then listened. She gathered that his grandmother was on the other end, but could make no sense of the conversation. Anthony appeared mystified, then amused. He told his grandmother goodbye and *besitos, abuela* and hung up.

Gail looked at him but said nothing. He stared through the windshield, and a smile appeared at the corner of his mouth.

"What?" she said.

"My grandmother called to congratulate us on our marriage."

"Excuse me?"

"Your mother called her last night with the news. We were married yesterday afternoon. Digna was not happy that I neglected to tell her, but how could I have, when I myself hadn't heard about it?"

"Wait! Wait a minute." Gail held up her hands. "She thinks we're *married?*"

"Yes, you called your mother and told her that we were getting married on Friday afternoon —"

"I did not!"

"Gail, I am only repeating what Digna just told me."

"I didn't tell my mother anything of the sort. We don't even have a license. I told Mother we were *planning* to get our license yesterday. The phone reception was bad, but she couldn't have misunderstood to that extent."

"Apparently she did, and since she couldn't get back in touch with you, she called Digna to see if she had heard from *me*. No, she hadn't, and this is why Digna is a little put out, you see? Her grandson was married in secret. But she forgives me. She wants to have a little party for us, just the family. Twenty or thirty people, nothing too elaborate. She says you should invite your family too."

"What did you *tell* her?"

"I said . . . *'Gracias, abuela.'* "

"What do you mean? You let her think we're *married?* Are you insane? Everyone in Miami will know. My mother already believes it. And *Karen.* Oh, my God. She must have told all her friends."

Anthony broke into laughter.

"It isn't funny."

"Yes . . . it is. *Ay, Dios mío* . . . you have to laugh. Gail —" He snapped his fingers. "I know what we can do. We tell them we flew to Mexico on the way home and got a fast divorce. *Qué chistoso.*" He wiped his eyes.

"Anthony, we can't do this."

His laughter slowed to a stop. "Why not?"

"Because it's not true!"

"Well . . . technically, but I think it would be wrong of us to cause our families any more confusion. We can take care of the details later."

She looked at him. "You're really serious."

He smiled. "It would be so easy."

She found herself smiling back at him. "So . . . when do we do it for real?"

"Whenever we feel like it . . . *Señora*

564

Quintana." Still watching the road, he took her hand and kissed it.

Gail put her chin on his shoulder. "I'm not sleeping with you without a ceremony. It just wouldn't be right."

"No?"

"No. And I can't go home without a wedding ring."

They made a stop at a jewelry store in Key Largo just as the place was about to close and bought two plain gold bands. From there they went across the street to The Sundowner, an outdoor bar that looked out on the water.

Anthony told the bartender to open a bottle of champagne. Champagne for everybody.

One of the waitresses took the yellow carnations from a vase on the bar and put a napkin around them to make a bouquet. They all went down to the beach barefoot, a ragged group of locals, half-drunk tourists, and people curious about what was going on. The clouds on the horizon had turned pink.

Anthony rolled up his pant legs and Gail lifted the hem of her embroidered white dress. The cool, clear water lapped at their feet.

"I love you, *Señora* Quintana."

"Te quiero." She smiled. "Don't I get a kiss?"

He gave her a long, slow one. Then he swept her into his arms, and she shrieked as he swung her around. Everyone applauded. Anthony put her down and someone poured champagne. Someone else took a photo. They got a copy in the mail a week later.

Gail smiled as she pulled it out of the envelope and showed him.

He laughed. "Look at that, we had a sunset wedding after all."

The flash lit up their grinning faces, the champagne frothing over the rims of the glasses, the white sand, the bouquet of carnations. Behind them the fiery orange ball of the sun slipped into the ocean.

Epilogue

"I would love a cigarette. Do you have one?"

"No, I'm sorry, I don't."

"Who did you say you work for? *Variety*?"

"Well . . . I write articles for journals."

"Now, listen. When you do the article, for God's sake don't say I'm Joan Sinclair, the star of eleven vampire pictures. That's how most of my fans know me, but talk about my Oscar nomination. Carlotta Sands, *The Edge of Midnight*, 1963. I've got to get a new publicist. What *is* this place?"

"What does it seem like to you?"

"One of my movies was on TV the other night. *Rage of the Vampire*. Everyone saw it, and the next day — my God, they wouldn't leave me alone. 'Joan! Joan! You must hear this *all* the time, but I love your movies.' I'm not complaining, I *adore* my fans. It comes with the territory, the price of fame and all that. Could I have one of your cigarettes?"

"I don't smoke. Have you heard from Arnel Goode?"

"Arnel. My absolute, all-time, number-one fan. He traveled *all the way* from Indiana to find me."

"Have you seen him lately?"

"No. I haven't. What newspaper did you say you worked for?"

"I'm freelancing. Do you remember Anthony Quintana? Billy Fadden's lawyer?"

"Quintana . . . Of *course* I do. *Rrowrrr.*"

"Mr. Quintana wanted to know about Sandra McCoy. For a time the police thought that Billy Fadden killed her. They no longer believe this, but Mr. Quintana wants to make sure you had nothing else to add."

"Billy! How is Billy? What's up with that kid?"

"He wants to go to film school. You've inspired him."

"How kind of you to say so. You tell Billy not to take any shit from the directors. He's got the talent, and if he doesn't let anything stand in his way, he'll make it. That's what it takes in Hollywood these days — guts."

"He wants to be a documentary film-maker. He wants to do a project about your career."

"Fabulous! Tell him to contact my agent."

"You told the police that Arnel Goode killed Sandra. Is that correct?"

"I feel very bad about Sandra."

"Do you? Why?"

"I caught her stealing, and I told Arnel about it. I have many, many pieces of very expensive jewelry. I couldn't stand thinking that Arnel could commit *murder*, but I've come around to the conclusion that he did."

"I understand."

"The problem with Arnel, and I am going to sound like *such* a bitch here, but . . . he wouldn't leave me alone. He was always hanging around. I need my rest. I have to study my lines. Is Tom Holtz coming by? He said he would take me out to dinner."

"May I ask a question about Joan Lindeman? Her body was found last week in the Lindeman family cemetery on Plantation Key. Does that surprise you?"

"No. Where else would she be?"

"Do you know how she got there?"

"In a van."

"I see. Did Arnel put her there?"

"I don't know. Should I buy some flowers? Sometimes my dressing room is so full of flowers I hardly have a place to sit down! May I have one of your cigarettes?"

"I'm sorry, I don't have any. I should be going."

A few moments later the nurses came in, two large men with gentle hands. They had seen Sharon Vogelhut signal them through the window. They untied the restraints that held Arnel Goode to the chair.

"She's writing an article about me."

"Hey, that's great, Miss Sinclair. I want to read it."

"I'll autograph it for you." Arnel Goode whispered, "This one is so sweet." As they took him out, he looked over his shoulder. "Do come back, won't you? Lunch at Spago. It's on me."

"Good-bye, Joan."

Gliding along the corridor in her chair, Sharon Vogelhut smiled. *Joan.*

If she had closed her eyes she wouldn't have known a man was speaking. Arnel Goode had seamlessly re-created himself. His delusion was total.

Billy Fadden, in their most recent session, had told her something that Joan Sinclair had said to him years ago, when she was still herself: *People are going to try their damnedest to tear you down, kiddo, and you gotta tell them, This is who I am, and if you don't like it, tough.*

Sharon had made a note of that. It had encouraged her.

Acknowledgments

Islamorada, in the Florida Keys, is a village of five islands situated along U.S. 1, the "overseas highway" from Miami to Key West. I've lived in South Florida most of my life but I was never properly introduced to Islamorada until Brooks and Susan Bateman showed me around. For a look at island living, I am indebted to Jeff and Katie Davis and to Joe and Nancy Hoyt. Many thanks to David Turner for the boat ride and to Grady Patrick for the fishing stories.

Jorge Amaya must take the credit for Anthony Quintana's Spanish, and once again attorney Milton Hirsch gave legal advice. Abigail L. Laurence, psychopharmacologist, wrote the prescriptions for Billy.

Laura Parker made Lindeman Key look real in the frontispiece map. I must admit that The Buttonwood Inn exists only in imagination, but there are many other lovely places to visit in the Florida Keys. Come and see for yourself.